HENRI IV OF FRANCE
Musée National du Château de Pau, Pau, France
Artist unknown

Also by Nelda Hirsh

JULIA DU VAL

A BOHEMIAN LIFE: M. EVELYN MCCORMICK
(1862-1948) AMERICAN IMPRESSIONIST

THE ROYAL HUGUENOT

HENRY OF NAVARRE
1553 - 1610

Nelda Hirsh

Green Rock Books   Boulder, Colorado

PUBLISHED BY GREEN ROCK BOOKS LLC
270 Green Rock Drive
Boulder, CO 80302

Visit our website: www.greenrockbooks.com

Printed in USA
First edition, 2015

ISBN: 978-0-9829650-2-3

Designed by Nick Pirog

Cover portrait: HENRI IV OF FRANCE
Musée National du Château de Pau. Artist unknown.

For my Sons

Daniel and Aaron

CONTENTS

PROEM

Barbara Kingsolver wrote, "Historical fiction may be the literary equivalent of cilantro; consumers tend to love or hate it irrationally, and rare is the artist who can rally a conversion." My goal is not to convert, but, by having done careful research on the man and the period, to reveal the heart of the man, his ideas and motivations.

Historical fiction always presents a conundrum: how much to document as real? how much to footnote from research? how much to reveal as completely fictionalized? Moreover, the farther in time you move away from the original events, the harder it is to document the "truth." Like oral history, the facts often become reshaped as they are retold.

A great deal has been written about Henry IV because of his impact on history and because of his strong character. In addition to the writings of the characters themselves and their contemporaries, I have also consulted the voluminous fictional thread about Henry IV. For instance, Heinrich Mann's *Young Henry of Navarre* (1937), describes Henry the child and young man in a fictionalized account — based on fact but clearly filling in the gaps with imagination.

I believe that considered interpretation of the facts and probing the psychological impetus for an individual's behavior can explain much about the events. My book also raises the age-old question of whether history makes the man or man makes history. In Henry IV's case, he was such a strong personality, it appears that this is a case where he clearly influenced the course of French history.

The Royal Huguenot concentrates on the most important women in Henry IV's life — two wives and three mistresses. In addition to his letters to his mistresses that I found and translated in the Cambridge University Library in Cambridge, England, I have found many other letters: in Marguerite de Valois's diary; in the *Lettres missives de Henri IV*, ed. B. de Xivrey (9 vols., Paris 1843-1876; and others in well researched commentaries and histories about Henry IV.

I have chosen not to footnote my sources in the book, feeling it would interrupt the story. For those who want to pursue the resources, three biographies stand out as exceptionally well researched and documented works: *Royal Cousin, The Life of Henri IV of France*, by Irene Mahoney (1970), Raymond Ritter's *Cette Grande Corisande* (1936), and Vincent J. Pitts', *Henri IV of France: His Reign and Age* (2009). Where Mahoney, for instance, footnotes Henry's letters, I do not, but format them in epistolary style. Also, I have used direct quotes from Mahoney, Pitts, and Ritter when they have printed original material and documented its source. These biographers have added, as I have, their imagination and interpretation to Henry IV's life. My bibliography provides further resources for those interested.

I was drawn to write about Henry IV primarily because of his forward-looking attitude about religious tolerance. He was the man to end the religious civil wars in France between the Huguenots and the Catholics and bring peace to a country torn by religious strife for decades. Like the philosopher Michel de Montaigne, who was his friend, Henry believed that men should respect one another's beliefs and live peacefully together — still a relevant and important message four hundred years later.

Henry was a complex character, driven not only by his ideology, but by a strong sexuality, a brilliant military mind, and a fervent compassion for his fellow men. *The Royal Huguenot* comprehensively explores the role of the most important women in his life, a key element of his story that needed to be told.

Nelda Hirsh
April 2015

THE HOUSE OF BOURBON & GUISE-LORRAINE

François de Bourbon, comte de Vendôme (1470-1495)
m. Marie de Luxembourg (1472-1547)

Charles de Bourbon, duc de Vendôme (1489-1537)
m. Françoise d'Alençon (1490-1550)

Antoinette de Bourbon-Vendôme (1493-1583)
m. Claude, duc de Guise (1496-1550)

Antoine de Bourbon,* duc de Vendôme (1518-1562)
m. Jeanne d'Albret, Jeanne III de Navarre (1528-1572)

Catherine de Bourbon (1559-1604)
m. duc de Bar

Henri IV, King of Navarre & France (1553-1610)

m. Marguerite de Valois (1553-1615)
m. Marie de Médici (1573-1642), daughter of Francesco I, Grand Duke of Tuscany & Joanna, Archduchess of Austria

1. Louis XIII, King of France (1601-1643)
   m. Anne of Austria (1601-1666)
2. Elisabeth (1602-1644)
3. Christina Maria (1606-1663)
4. Nicholas Henri, duc d'Orléans (1607-1611)
5. Gaston, duc d'Orléans (1608-1660)
6. Henrietta Maria (1609-1669)

1. Charles de Guise, Cardinal de Lorraine (1524-1574)
2. Marie de Guise (1515-1560) m. James V of Scotland (1512-1542)
3. François, duc de Guise (1519-1563)
   m. Anne d'Estée (1531-1607)

1. Henri, duc de Guise, dit le Balafré (1550-1588)
   m. Catherine de Clèves (1548-1633)
2. Charles de Lorraine, duc de Mayenne (1554-1611)

*See House of Condé for Bourbon siblings

x

THE HOUSE OF VALOIS

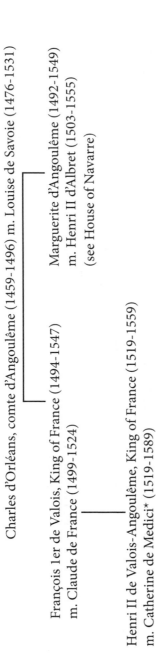

Charles d'Orléans, comte d'Angoulême (1459-1496) m. Louise de Savoie (1476-1531)

Marguerite d'Angoulême (1492-1549)
m. Henri II d'Albret (1503-1555)
(see House of Navarre)

François 1er de Valois, King of France (1494-1547)
m. Claude de France (1499-1524)

Henri II de Valois-Angoulême, King of France (1519-1559)
m. Catherine de Medici★ (1519-1589)

1. François II (1544-1560) m. Mary, Queen of Scots (1542-1587)
2. Elisabeth (1545-1568) m. Philip II of Spain (1527-1598)
3. Claude de Valois (1547-1575) m. Charles, duc de Lorraine (1543-1608)
4. Charles IX, King of France (1550-1574) m. Elisabeth d'Autriche (1554-1592)
5. Henri, duc d'Anjou (Henri III), King of France (1551-1589) m. Louise de Lorraine-Vaudémont (1553-1601)
6. Marguerite de Valois★★ (1553-1615) m. Henri de Navarre, Henri IV de France (1553-1610)
7. Hercule François, duc d'Alençon (1555-1584)

★Born in Italy to Lorenzo II de Medici and
Madeleine de la Tour d'Auvergne
★★divorced, no issue

THE HOUSE OF NAVARRE

Charles de Bourbon, duc de Vendôme (1489-1537)   Henri II d'Albret (1503-1555)
m. Françoise d'Alençon (1490-1550)   m. Marguerite d'Angoulême (1492-1549)

Antoine de Bourbon (1518-1562) m. Jeanne III d'Albret, Queen of Navarre (1528-1572)

1. Henri de Navarre, Henri IV de France (1553-1610)
   m. Marguerite de Valois and Marie de Medici (1573-1642)
2. Catherine de Bourbon (1559-1604) m. Henri II de Lorraine, duc de Bar (1563-1624)

THE HOUSE OF CONDE

Charles de Bourbon, duc de Vendôme (1489-1537) m. Françoise d'Alençon (1490-1550)

1. Antoine de Bourbon m. Jeanne d'Albret, Queen of Navarre (see above for issue)
2. Charles de Bourbon, Charles X (la Ligue) (1523-1590)
3. Louis de Bourbon, prince de Condé (1530-1569)
   m. Françoise de Longueville-Rothelin (1536-1601)

1. Henri, prince de Condé (1552-1588) m. Charlotte-Catherine de la Trémouille (1568-1629)
2. François, prince de Conti (1558-1614)
3. Charles, comte de Soissons (1566-1612)

Note that Henri de Navarre & Henri, prince de Condé & Henri de Guise were Bourbon cousins

PRINCIPAL CHARACTERS

Henry of Navarre
(1553-1610)

King of Navarre as of June 9, 1572 and King of France as of July 30, 1589.

Jeanne d'Albret
(1528-1572)

Mother of Henry of Navarre

Antoine de Bourbon
(1518-1562)

Father of Henry of Navarre

Catherine de Bourbon
(1559-1604)

Sister of Henry of Navarre

Henri de Condé
(1552-1588)

Huguenot cousin and friend of Henry of Navarre

THE VALOIS FAMILY

Henri II
(1519-1559)

King of France. Husband of Catherine de Medici

Charles IX
(1550-1574)

Valois King of France, brother of Marguerite de Valois

Marguerite de Valois
(1553-1615)

Sister of Charles IX. Wife of Henry of Navarre

Catherine de Medici
(1519-1589)

Called the Queen Mother: Mother of Charles IX, Marguerite de Valois, François d'Alençon and Henri d'Anjou (also known as Henri III)

Henri d'Anjou
(1551-1589)

Brother of Charlies IX. Known as the duc d'Anjou and later as King Henri III

François d'Alençon
(1555-1584)

Brother of Charles IX. Known as the duc d'Alençon, later as the duc d'Anjou

THE GUISE FAMILY

Henri, duc de Guise 1550-1588)

Lover of Marguerite de Valois and head of the Roman Catholic League

Charles de Lorraine, duc de Mayenne (1554-1611)

Brother of Henri de Guise and Leader of the Roman Catholic League

HENRY'S WIVES AND MISTRESSES

Marguerite de Valois (1553-1615)

Sister of Charles IX and Henry's first wife

Corisande, Diane d'Andoins, Dame de Gramont and Comtesse de Guiche (1554-1620)

Mistress of Henry of Navarre

Gabrielle d'Estrées (1573-1599)

Mistress of Henry of Navarre

Henriette d'Entragues (1579-1633)

Mistress of Henry of Navarre

Marie de Medici (1573-1642)

Second wife of Henry of Navarre. Queen of France

HENRY'S CONTEMPORARIES

Admiral Gaspard de Coligny (1519-1572)

Huguenot military chief and friend of Henry of Navarre. One of first victims of St. Bartholomew's Massacre

Maximilien de Béthune, Baron de Rosny (1560-1641)	Huguenot minister and friend of Henry of Navarre; later became duc de Sully
Agrippa d'Aubigné (1552-1630)	Huguenot minister, writer, and friend of Henry of Navarre
Michel de Montaigne (1533-1592)	Writer and philosopher; renowned for his essays; friend of Henry of Navarre and Corisande
Marie Touchet (1549-1638)	Huguenot mistress of Charles IX and mother of Henriette d'Entragues

France during the time of Henry IV

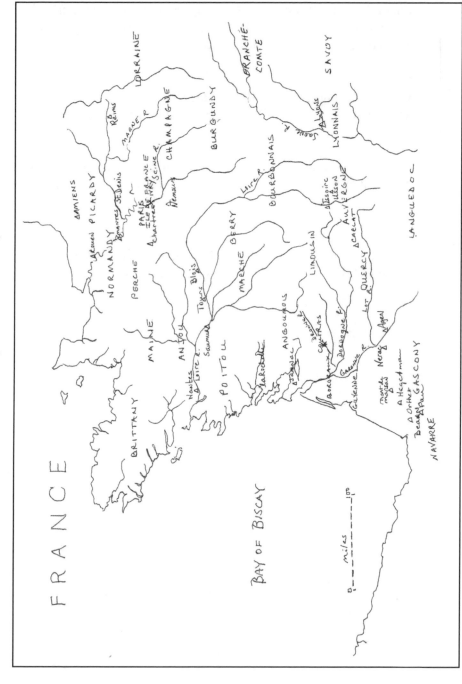

BAY OF BISCAY

BRITTANY

NORMANDY
AMIENS
PICARDY
LORRAINE
Rouen
Caen
Mantes
St-Denis
Reims
MARNE R.
CHAMPAGNE
PARIS
ILE DE
FRANCE
Chartres
SEINE R.
Nemours
BURGUNDY
FRANCHÉ-
COMTÉ
SAVOY
PERCHE
MAINE
ANJOU
Nantes
LOIRE R.
Saumur
Tours
Blois
BERRY
LOIRE R.
BOURBONNAIS
Ambrose
LYONNAIS
SAÔNE R.
POITOU
MARCHE
LIMOUSIN
AUVERGNE
Clermont
Ussoire
Alésson
Marennes
ANGOULÊME
LaRochelle
Jarnac
Brouage
Cognac
Coutras
DORDOGNE R.
GARONNE R.
LOT R.
QUERCY
Agen
Nérac
Montde
Marsan
GUIENNE
Bordeaux
GASCONY
NAVARRE
LANGUEDOC

▲ Huguenot
△ Other
Beaujeu

0 ─────── 100
Miles

Verses from the Oracle of Nostradamus

Nay Souz les umbres et journée nocturne
Sera en regne et bonté Souveraine;
Fera renaistre son Sang de l'antique urne,
Renouvellant Siècle d'or pour l'aerain.

Born in the shadows and during a dark day,
He will be sovereign in realm and goodness;
He will cause his blood to rise again in the ancient urn,
Renewing the age of gold for the treasury.

Au chef du monde le grand Chyren sera,
Plus outre après aymé, craint, redouté;
Son bruit et los les cieux surpassera,
Et du seul titre victeur fort contenté.

Chief of the world Henri le Grand shall be,
More loved in death than life, more honoured he;
His name and praise shall rise above the skies,
And men will call him victor when he dies.

Nostradamus's Oracles have haunted the French populace for centuries. Michel de Nostredame (Nostradamus was the Latinized form of his name, à la mode among scholars of his time) was born December 14, 1503, in the town of Saint Rémy in Provence, France. His family claimed to be of Jewish descent and then converted to Catholicism when Nostradamus reached nine years of age. Nostradamus attended Montpellier, the most famous school of medicine in France at the time, for education in philosophy and the medical arts. His career as a physician became renowned in 1525 when his country was besieged with plague.

BOOK ONE

MARGUERITE DE VALOIS
1553-1615

MARGUERITE DE VALOIS
By Francois Clouet, Court Painter
Oil on panel, 16th c., Musée Condé

Author's Note: Henry's name is Anglicized with a "y" here in order to distinguish him from Henri de Condé, his cousin, and from Henri III, his Valois brother-in-law and cousin.

THE GATES OF PARIS

1572

A BRIGHT YELLOW WAFER SUN in a chalice of blood red sky blazed down upon eight hundred Huguenot lords, escorting Henry III of Navarre to Paris. Hooded by wide heavy lids, Henry's eyes were cast downward instead of curiously darting about in their habitual manner. The long face of the new king looked drawn, and his entourage worried about the uncharacteristic slump of his shoulders. Now that the sparkle of his eyes appeared dimmed, the salient nose gained more prominence.

Henry's army, triumphantly arrayed at their departure from Béarn in July, had deteriorated to a dusty, bedraggled band. After three weeks on the road, by mid-August, once colorful banners drooped and the soldiers' uniforms clung to their bodies with sweat and grime. Henry turned in his saddle to catch the late afternoon sun on his face but found it did little to allay the chill of grief gripping his heart like eagle talons. Since Henry was naturally convivial and lively, this leaden feeling confused and alarmed him.

Henry's mother, Jeanne d'Albret, Queen of Navarre, had departed this earth only a month earlier, bequeathing to her son the small kingdom of Navarre, which she had inherited from her father, Henri II d'Albret, King of Navarre. Henry had spent his childhood there, roaming freely about the peaks and crevices of the Pyrénées. Navarre encompassed many counties, including Béarn, Albret, Guyenne, and Armagnac — lyrical names to one raised in these environs — though the landmass only equaled that of the island of Corsica. Navarre was a child-size kingdom compared to the vastness of the country France, which he and his soldiers had just traversed. Nineteen years of age, bone-tired and saddle-weary, Henry felt hopelessly inadequate to the task that lay before him.

He had made this same trip to visit the royal court in Paris numerous times during his youth, but usually with one or both of his parents, Jeanne d'Albret and Antoine de Bourbon. Wishing he could shake off the protective pall of numbness that enshrouded him and aware of his fellow soldiers glancing frequently at his unusually wooden expression, Henry comforted himself in the knowledge that he had achieved what his royal upbringing had taught him — to press on in a crisis. Having led his retinue up the west coast via Nantes and followed the Loire River for a short piece, he then headed north. Every afternoon about this time, he yearned for a summer shower to soothe him as did the mountain thunderstorms, which left the air smelling sweet and fresh. In Navarre, he thought, you could smell the sunlight as well as the rain.

Only the Bois de Boulogne now lay between him and Paris, and he welcomed its bosky scent and shade after the plains. His bride-to-be would be awaiting him in the city. The impending marriage, he realized with some shame, was almost as appalling to him as the sudden loss of his mother. With this glum thought, he tried to sit straighter upon his white palfrey. Mourning had not paralyzed him, but he felt bewildered. Tired or not, he knew the time had come when he must repel like an enemy these perplexing distractions and focus on the frightening facts.

From his mother, Jeanne, he had inherited the leadership of the French Protestants, called "Huguenots," a minority in a Catholic country. Huguenots were not so strange in the western and southern provinces where he lived. His mother taught him when he was only ten years old that the Catholics outnumbered the Protestants by a hundred to one, but now, about a decade later, the number of Protestants was growing at a rate alarming to the ruling House of Valois, his fiancée's family, ensconced in Paris. The more vocal the dissenters became, the harsher the Catholic crackdown became.

Henry recalled his mother's excitement when she talked about the new religious ideas published by John Calvin* from Geneva. He remembered what she had told him — that Calvin was a great thinker, his book had been printed in 1546, and he had been proselytizing

---

*John Calvin (1509-1564). Influential French theologian and pastor during the Protestant Reformation. Born in Noyon, Picardy, he studied theology at the Sorbonne. His followers in France were termed "Huguenots."

his ideas throughout France since Henry's birth. His teachings were particularly well received in the South of the country and especially among the nobility and educated members of society. The new learning of the Renaissance in Europe had spawned a fresh attitude of questioning traditional thought, including ideas about free will and a declining faith in the papacy. Calvin's new doctrine was considered the reformed faith and its adherents, Jeanne among them, became eager to spread these new beliefs throughout the kingdom. It was an authoritarian and rigid philosophy, emphasizing a strong morality in all areas of life — a perfect fit with her rigid and defiant personality, Henry thought.

François I, Henry's great-uncle and King of France, had tolerated religious dissent at first, but by the time of his death in 1547, he regarded the reform movement as a threat to royal authority. His successor, Henri II d'Angoulême, sided strongly with the French Catholic Church and began sending heretics to their deaths. Henry had grown up learning first-hand, within his immediate family, of the religious schism between Catholics and Protestants in France, and he clearly understood his mother's determination to inculcate a strict Huguenot faith in his soul as well as her horror of the lies, vanity, and corruption of the Parisian court. She had explained to him the Calvinist belief in the total depravity of the human race, softened by the idea that this unrighteousness would not deter God's grace. However, only He could choose who would be saved, and so one must constantly strive to earn His mercy.

Henry wondered whom he could trust in this Catholic ruled country now that his mother was gone. He was well aware that the people of Paris would be particularly hostile to his Protestant delegation. His proud mother had frequently reminded him of the fact that in recent times, due to the decadence of the Catholic Church and the corruption of the Curia, the popularity of Protestantism had grown throughout France.

She also had talked about the importance of the Council of Trent, begun in 1545, when the Catholic Church had begun a program of reform, which unfortunately had backlashed by pitting Catholics and Protestants against one another. This was especially true in towns and cities where ideas were more easily disseminated. The Valois rulers hoped that the wedding now planned between Valois and Bourbon, between Catholic and Protestant, would suppress the Huguenots from spreading their power from the Southwest to the North.

Thinking momentarily of his cousin, Henri de Condé, Henry cheered a bit. Perhaps he could rely on him for support. But on second thought, Condé was probably even more naïve than he was. Henri de Condé, though one year older, had always been the follower when they were children, allowing Henry to make the rules for their games. Condé could be stubborn, however, as his jutting chin and square jaw suggested. Jeanne always referred to the two of them as "my princes," highlighting the fact that only princes of the blood were considered counselors of the king by right of birth and protectors of the kingdom.

The Admiral Gaspard de Coligny, a staunch Protestant and close friend of his mother, surely would be the most reliable and trustworthy ally of all. Henry regarded the Admiral riding beside him, finding comfort in the man's face, worn and cragged like the rugged Pyrénées where he had lived for so many years. Henry had known this man all of his life and always found him a surprising mix of strength and kindness. Yet with an astute perception beyond his years he understood that his mother did not consider Coligny as a leader of Huguenots, but only as a fine military man. Not being of noble birth, he fell short of the necessary rank in her eyes.

"What am I to expect in Paris?" Henry suddenly asked the older man.

Coligny smiled, relieved that the young man had finally spoken. His forlorn silence was getting on everyone's nerves.

"You must constantly be on guard for the devious ways of the Catholics, my boy. I presume you know that already. There are few Huguenots in the city, and I would wager they are all fearful. The Catholics are in complete control, and I doubt if they believe in this wedding any more than we do! But it is your wedding, so try to enjoy yourself and leave the trouble to me. I took care of your mother's battles for years, and I shall take care of yours."

The Admiral's fatherly manner brought tears to Henry's eyes. Since his mother's death he felt so vulnerable, a new and uncommon feeling for him. Jeanne had believed that a future ruler of France needed to know the military arts as well as political science, and so he and Condé had apprenticed to Coligny and the elder Condé* on the battlefield in skirmishes against the Catholics for about three years now. He knew of no one on whom he could rely more.

"Thank you for your sympathy, Sir." Now that he was King of

---

*Louis I, prince de Condé (1530-1569); also known as Louis I de Bourbon.

Navarre, should he still call Coligny "Sir?" The subtleties of kinship and kingship often seemed to escape him.

Henry recalled embracing his mother when she had departed for Paris. She had finally been persuaded that a marriage between her son and Marguerite de Valois, sister of the present French king, Charles IX, would be good for the Protestant cause. Jeanne d'Albret, Queen of Navarre, and Catherine de Medici, Queen Mother of France, had bargained over the terms of the marriage, but Jeanne's letters from Paris indicated she had been rudely treated by the Valois clan.

This was nothing new. As long as Henry could remember, Henry's mother, Jeanne, and Catherine had been playing a game of brinksmanship, bordering on civil war. Jeanne was working constantly to organize the Huguenot movement into a coherent national church, and Catherine believed this to be a threat to the Catholic Church in France and to the monarchy itself. The struggle for religious domination was insidiously interwoven into the fight for hegemony. England and the Lowlands to the northwest and Germany on the eastern flank, being Protestant strongholds, were seen as a particular threat. Yet, Philip II's Catholic Spain on France's southern border, supposedly an ally, deserved a watchful eye as well.

He thought his mother had appeared to be in her typical physical state when she left, and so was shocked when he heard she had fallen desperately ill. He wanted to hurry to her side, but a fever detained him at Pau, the Bourbon family home in Navarre. He would not have arrived in time in any event, for she had died only four days after he received the alarming message. Fumbling in his vest for a handkerchief, his hand touched a crumpled note to a friend. He pulled it out and reread his words written while still lying sick in bed. Too embarrassed by his strong emotions, he had failed to send the letter:

"I have received the saddest news in the world which is the loss of my mother, whom God has called to Himself in these recent days, having died of a lung condition . . . I cannot describe my mourning and anguish which is so extreme that I find it hard to bear. Since I succeed to her position, it is necessary that I take care of everything which was her duty."

Coligny's low voice broke his reverie. "I am sure you have heard the rumors — that your mother did not die of pleurisy and an abscess in the breast as the royal doctors proclaim. I suspect she was poisoned, and I believe the poisoner must have been Signore Bianchi.

He is one of Catherine de Medici's own perfumers whom she brought from Italy. My spies tell me the court gossip maintains he tainted a pair of gloves, which he sold to your mother in Paris."

"Of course I have heard these stories," Henry replied, his voice betraying his fatigue and emotion, "even though everyone tries to keep them from me. But I don't grant them much credence. There is no logic in it, Coligny. You and I both witnessed her becoming weaker from the tuberculosis that plagued her for so long. I was concerned that she might be too weak for this long trip, but as you know, she could be stubborn." He twisted in his saddle to address his listener. "Yet I also know that as soon as she left Pau, I worried when I realized that, in her haste to depart, Mother forgot her bezoar stones.* You know the magic in these stones can remove arsenic from wine and other drinks, but I'm afraid they would not have protected her from poisoned gloves. How cruelly creative of this Bianchi! But as I said before, it doesn't make any sense to me. Why would the Queen Mother want my mother to die, just when she was arranging this wedding?"

"We shall see, my boy. We shall see. But I fear you are very much a novice to the tortuous schemes of these people." Coligny paused but then apparently decided to continue.

"Perhaps it will comfort you to know that according to witnesses of Jeanne's death, she attended only to spiritual matters and appeared relieved to be done with the trials of this world. But you and I must pay very close attention to the here and now, and I believe it would be judicious to insist on guarantees of protection for the Huguenots from the royal family before the marriage."

Feeling even more helpless, Henry confided in Coligny. "It was terrible not to be near Mother at her death, not to be able to comfort her. I hope you do not think I am whining, but I know it would have relieved her to hear my vow to remain a Protestant despite pressures from the Valoises. I sensed she was worried about that. She was always so brave! I realized how alarmed she was in her last letter when she warned me of the duplicity of the court. I even remember the exact words because they were so unlike her. She wrote, 'I am amazed at the way I bear the way they cross me, scratch me, prick me, flatter

---

*Gall or kidney stones. Bezoars were sought because they were believed to have the power of a universal antidote against any poison. It was believed that a drinking glass which contained a bezoar would neutralize any poison poured into it.

me, defy me." It was very unusual for her to complain, and I feel like I am headed straight towards a viper's nest."

"And well you might be!" Coligny exclaimed. "She worried a great deal about the match she had arranged, fearing she was casting your body to unscrupulous enemies and your soul to Papists. I doubt she would have done so if she had known she was to leave you alone."

Henry thought the steady rhythm of the horses' hooves belied the nervous tenor of his little army. He was feeling both eager and apprehensive about their arrival and disliked the fact that his emotions had recently seemed so beyond his control.

"You were an intermediary in arranging this marriage, were you not?" Henry asked.

Coligny smiled somewhat ruefully. "Yes. Many years ago I was banished from court by Catherine de Medici who felt I had betrayed her. She was always suspicious. Then last year she suddenly reversed and decided it would be politically expedient to reinstate me in her good graces. Evidently she decided this marriage would neutralize the Huguenots' rising power in the Southwest more easily than a battle would."

"Yes, now I understand how threatening she views the Huguenots to be."

Coligny interrupted him. "The Queen hoped I would play a role in pacifying the Huguenots, rendering them a bulwark in the South and West against Spanish encroachment. I agree with that strategy, by the way. God knows I want peace, and I concur that the best way to achieve this is to take a strong stand against Catholic Spain. It's not only Huguenots who alarm Catherine de Medici."

Spying the asymmetrical lantern towers of the great Catholic cathedral of Notre Dame rising in the distance, Henry gasped. Sturdier than most Gothic structures, it presented a formidable sight on the horizon. He could not see the palace of the Louvre yet, but these two magnificent buildings represented the royal and theological might against him, the "Huguenot bumpkin" from Navarre.

"Tell me more about Catherine de Medici," Henry urged, sensing his need to know as much as possible before the inevitable introduction. "Did she not have a French mother?"

"Yes, she most certainly did, and so I imagine she grew up hearing more about France than most Italian princesses would. Her father, Lorenzo de Medici, married Madeleine de la Tour d'Auvergne.

But both her parents died when she was young. She was brought up by her cousin, Pope Clement VII, until she came to France at age fourteen for her marriage to Henri II de Valois. I imagine she had an even more rigorous Catholic upbringing than most."

"I know my mother never trusted her," Henry confided. "She once told me that Catherine tried to seduce my father away from her with one of her ladies-in-waiting known as 'la Belle Rouet.'" He changed the subject impulsively. "Do you think it's true that my fiancée had her first lover at twelve?"

Coligny laughed. "I wouldn't know! But from what I have heard, you are not so inexperienced either." Even as he said this, Coligny thought Henry still seemed a boy to him. He would have liked to stroke the dark wavy hair and high forehead to console and comfort the child trying so early to be a man.

Henry grinned for the first time in a long while. He was worldlier than his Calvinist mother would have liked to believe. Nonetheless, he suspected he was not quite ready to fence with the cruel sophistication of the royal court in Paris. As an impressionable young man, he had read Ronsard's poetry, which compared his bride-to-be to Aurora, and he knew those at court called her "Minerva" when they heard her flawless Latin. Yet others likened her to a sorceress, and Henry had heard one contemporary say of Marguerite, "She is made to damn and ruin rather than to save." How was such a young fellow from the provinces to cope with such a girl? She was just his age, but in his mind she had become a shrewd and experienced, even frightening, foe.

Actually he had spent quite a long time at the Valois court, from his eighth until his thirteenth birthday, and so had witnessed the life there firsthand. He had been aware early on of the fights between Jeanne and Catherine over religious tolerance for the Huguenots. But even closer to home, he had experienced the constant friction between Jeanne and his father when they lived in Paris. Antoine frequently called his wife "a woman of a most violent temper" and would send her into more of a rage when he sided with Catherine, most likely seeing that path as more politically expedient. The situation deteriorated until 1562, when Antoine ordered Jeanne to leave Paris with Henry's little sister, Catherine de Bourbon, and he took custody of Henry, who stayed at court. His mother and father would never meet again.

Civil strife had continued throughout the country, with neither Catholics nor Huguenots disarming or disbanding. Sporadic violence rendered a peaceful life impossible, with major towns falling first to one coalition and then to the other. Antoine was killed fighting for the royal forces at a siege of Rouen that same year, when Henry was only nine. Jeanne agreed that her son could stay at court for the time being and enroll at the College de Navarre in Paris. He had studied Greek and Latin and spent much of his free time sparring with his Catholic Valois and Guise cousins, also passing much time at court. Jeanne had made him promise to remain true to her Calvinist faith and never to attend Mass. Remarkably, Catherine de Medici agreed to allow his Protestant tutors to continue as his mentors.

Now, feeling like a hare before a boar's jaws, Henry rode onward toward the gates of Paris. He smiled to himself. Zoology was not his forte, but he wished he had paid more attention to the stories of the cunning foxes in Paris rather than to the wild boars in Navarre. Again he recalled his mother's advice:

> Not for anything on earth would I have you come to live in Paris. Therefore, I wish you to be married and to retire — with your wife — from this corruption. Although I knew it was bad, I find it even worse that I feared. Here women make advances to men rather than the other way around. If you were here, you would never escape without a special intervention from God!

Thoughts of religion were very much on Henry's mind as well. How was a young man to understand a Europe so dangerously divided — with Germany, England, and the Netherlands on the Protestant side and Italy, France and the Holy Roman Empire on the Catholic side, and with rebellious Huguenot and other reform pockets within each country? The Valois family was Catholic, yet despite the Queen Mother's strong entreaties, the Pope still refused to grant a dispensation for this marriage between Henry of Navarre, First Prince of the Blood, and Marguerite de Valois, sister of His Most Christian Majesty, Charles IX. The Pope remained adamant, even when reminded that England was now separated from the Holy See because of his refusal of just such a dispensation. Henry tried to remember when Anne Boleyn had married Henry VIII — about 1532, he thought — so beginning the break with Rome by the Church of England. Naturally

His Holiness saw France likewise slipping away from the Catholic center toward the axis of Protestant powers with this proposed marriage.

However, Catherine de Medici and Jeanne d'Albret had simply decided to ignore the Pope, signing the contract of marriage on April 11, 1572. And Charles IX had carelessly dismissed the Pope as "that old hypocritical bigot." The Valoises appeared to have their own autonomous brand of Catholicism, Henry reflected.

He heard his men behind him joking and bragging. Though apprehensive, they were eager to see the women of the Valois court, about whom they had heard wild erotic tales. The Huguenot entourage drew closer to the St. Jacques gate, and despite his grief, the sight of all the steeples of Paris piercing the rosy evening sky excited him. The number of people on the road increased as they neared the city, and time suddenly seemed to speed up. This was the beginning of a new life and he would make the best of it! A bubble of optimism, more akin to his nature, arose within him, and he welcomed the happy rush with tremendous relief.

Lowering his gaze, Henry recognized the king's brothers, Henri d'Anjou and François d'Alençon, approaching on horses bedecked in royal finery, a shining and shaming contrast to the travel-weary Huguenot band. He also recognized the colors of the duc de Guise, head of a strong Catholic family in Lorraine, in the welcome party. Henry had heard Guise was Marguerite de Valois's present favorite and surmised his former boyhood playmate must be wondering about him, too.

France had been torn by many years of religious strife, even longer than his lifetime, he thought. The fact that the amiral de Coligny, military chief of the Protestants, rode now with the Huguenot party would only increase the suspicions of the Parisian populace. Henry knew the Guises would be particularly angered by Coligny's presence, because they believed he was the murderer of François, the old duc de Guise.* Echoes of years of warfare among the leading families of France, testament to the old feudal system, beat about his ears like black crows' wings.

"Welcome, Cousin. We are honored to receive you and your

* Father of Henri de Guise, Henry's Bourbon cousin. François bore the nickname, le Balafré, because of his scarred face from a wound he received in the Second Siege of Boulogne in 1545. His eldest son, Henri, would also become known as le Balafré because of a wound sustained in the Battle of Dormans in 1575.

company," the duc d'Anjou politely, if stiffly, greeted the travelers as Henry brought his steed to a halt before him. "We have not seen you for quite a while."

"Thank you, Anjou," Henry replied, privately remarking on his Valois cousin's dark eyes and handsome, even pretty features. "*Merci à Dieu*, our journey was without difficulties."

"We offer our condolences for your dear mother," François, prince d'Alençon, said. Henry thought he noticed a snicker in Alençon's tone and searched his face for a sign of mocking. Compared to his beautiful brother, Alençon was strikingly ugly because of an enlarged bulb of a nose dominating his face, a deformation resulting from smallpox.

"Yes, it is strange," Henry observed, "to be too late for her funeral and here for my own wedding."

Anjou coughed. "Well, let us be on our way. The court eagerly awaits your arrival."

The royal party paraded down la grande rue Saint-Jacques lined with the curious citizens of the capital. As they proceeded along the left bank of the Seine, Henry recognized the Latin Quarter with the University of Paris on his right. Espying many young men whom he suspected must be students in the crowd, he envied for a moment these scholars their days of argument, deep thought, and drinking with friends. He had always excelled in his studies but had been easily coaxed outdoors when given a choice of books or sport.

The duc d'Anjou led them through the teeming life on the quais and across the river. He explained to Henry, as though he were an ordinary visitor, that the Seine was the key to the commercial success of the city, its main highway. Henry nodded politely to acknowledge he had heard but chose not to admit his renewed amazement at the number of barges, ferries, and floating timber crowding the waterway or his confusion with the busy banks, muddy with the coming and going of beasts, water carriers, and stevedores. They crossed the Ile de la Cité, dominated by the Cathedral of Notre Dame, before turning left on the right bank of the river Seine. A few people waved as Henry passed, but most regarded him and his soldiers with patent mistrust.

Finally the Palace of the Louvre loomed before them. It had taken seven hundred years to build the royal palace with its balconies, towers, and posterns, and Henry eyed his new home with curiosity. He remembered the Louvre from previous visits and was reminded how he had always found its walls claustrophobic. He must have been about four, he calculated, when he was first brought to Paris by his parents. He smiled, remembering a story (now touched with irony) that his mother had related to him. Henri II, Marguerite's father, had received the family of Navarre and was impressed with the cheerful young prince of Navarre. He had asked Henry if he would like to be his son, but the little prince had answered, "There is my father," pointing to Antoine. Henry II, very taken with the boy's resolute manner, had said, "Then wouldn't you like to be my son-in-law?" whereupon Henry had replied, "Oh, yes!"

Henri II had been mortally wounded by a lance thrust in a tournament, and because his son, Charles IX, was too young to rule, Catherine de Medici became regent until he reached his majority in 1563. Now Charles IX was king, and some believed him to be deranged. Rumors claimed that Catherine, the Queen Mother, directed almost every move behind the throne. Before Henri II had died, she had already lost him to his mistress, the lovely Diane de Poitiers. But Catherine had come from the court of Machiavelli where power, not love, was revered, and she refused to be unhappy for long. Now her reputation suggested she had brought some of the Machiavellian severity and cruelty to her reign in France.

Following his cousins through ancient towers into a courtyard of the Louvre, Henry thought how ornate this Parisian palace of smooth stone was compared to the rough bricks of his castle in Pau. A pair of Switzers, standing guard with sharpened pikes, lowered them at the command of his escort. There would be no more time for speculation; the Queen Mother demanded his presence immediately.

Suddenly lances thrust in the way of Henry's Huguenot guard barred them from accompanying him into the audience chamber. Surprised, he started to object, but quickly decided such a complaint would not be the proper tone with which to begin his visit. He would let this hostile act pass for now, but resolved not to appear so weak in the future. At least Coligny and Condé were allowed beside him. He felt as though he were entering a black widow's web and hoped his demeanor did not reveal his nervously churning stomach. Dutifully he knelt before Catherine, somewhat taken aback by her stodgy unrelenting visage. She appeared heavier than he had remembered.

"Welcome to Paris and the Court of France," she addressed him. He waited for more. When she said nothing, he replied.

"I am most happy to be here and await your pleasure."

Catherine's manner toward the amiral de Coligny appeared

exceptionally cool as she refused to regard him directly. Henry wondered if she felt as strongly about the Admiral as the Guises did. And wasn't it odd, even sinister, that she did not offer her condolences regarding his mother? His thoughts were interrupted as the Queen Mother presented him to Marguerite.

"Margot," as she was called at court, boasted the beauty of the times. Her low cut dress revealed a striking though somewhat abbreviated figure, and her hair, brushed high from her forehead, framed a face with intelligent, dark eyes, round cheeks, and a curved, sensuous mouth, painted in the royal fashion. He knew this had offended his mother.

"I trust this is the beginning of a long and happy relationship, my lady," Henry said. Margot's haughty expression did not change. She simply nodded her head that she had heard him.

LE PALAIS DU LOUVRE
and NOTRE DAME CATHEDRAL

August 1572

NOVEL SENSATIONS ASSAULTED Henry, causing the days filled with preparation for the marriage to pass quickly. What he saw and learned only increased his apprehension but he instinctively played the role of a relaxed bridegroom, his natural charm rising to the challenge. He decided this would be the shrewdest choice of behavior given the rumors about his mother's death. Coligny obviously believed there was reason for uneasiness but had kindly instructed him to enjoy his wedding. Yet how could he if he suspected his bride's family of poisoning his mother? Such an act still made no sense to him. After all, Catherine had demonstrated numerous times over the past years her willingness to negotiate about religious leniency, giving in on occasion to Protestant demands for the right to worship freely in certain locations.

The huge Huguenot visiting party overtaxed the space and staff of the palace kitchens, and despite the summer weather, the ovens blazed all day. The steamy close quarters in the Louvre did nothing to allay the rising tensions which Henry observed with trepidation. Who was siding with whom? He sensed more was at stake than he was aware of — he didn't even know what questions to ask. Believing the sensations were similar, he thought he'd rather be on a narrow, rickety, suspension bridge waving in the wind over a chasm in the Pyrénées than here. Condé wasn't much help, being nervous and excited about his own coming nuptials to Mary, princesse de Clèves.

At the insistence of the Queen Mother, the cousins escorted Henry to the many fine churches of Paris. He could not suppress an exclamation of awe when Anjou led him into the Sainte Chapelle. He had not properly appreciated this gem when he was younger. Stained glass windows, with 1,134 scenes from the Bible, soared to the heavens in splendid brilliant colors, like jewels set in stone. Henry felt he was standing inside an architect's model as he turned to take in the perfect symmetry of the building. The vertical piers were grouped together like a bouquet of lily stems whose fan blossoms spread across the vaulted ceiling overhead.

"This glorious chapel was built by Louis IX in only two years and was finished in 1248," Anjou instructed him. "St. Louis — I don't know if you Huguenots know that is what we have come to call Louis IX — wanted to provide a shelter for the Crown of Thorns and other holy relics which he brought back from the Crusades."

"It is magnificent," Henry admitted. "And that is what 'we Huguenots' call St. Louis also," he couldn't resist adding with a barbed tone. "And remember, Anjou, I attended school in Paris for five years."

Sunlight pierced the tall windows, falling on the marble floor, whose red, blue, black, and white ornate design echoed the intricate patterns of the vertical stained glass above. Despite his nervous preoccupation, Henry was touched by the spirituality of this exquisite tiny chapel. It was easy to believe in heaven and the power of all that is good on earth in a place like this, and he wished he could stand there all day gazing at the serene faces of the apostles standing on small pedestals attached to each pillar. But Anjou, seeming almost as jittery as Henry, guided him immediately out of the coolness of the little Gothic temple to the blinding light, unmuted by the comforting filter of the past arranged in biblical stained glass. How stark and harsh was the present! Henry looked back as they departed and thought the angel on the roof, with a cross held in both hands, was perhaps blessing him. Surely an angel wouldn't penalize him for being Protestant or for trying to end the religious wars by this marriage to a Catholic.

As they passed through the twisting streets, Henry saluted people who stared at his tanned face under his odd Basque cap. His smile drew a few timid reciprocal nods from the curious, but no warm welcome. Finally Henry was guided to the Cathedral of Notre Dame where he would be married in two days. Having swallowed insult after insult since his arrival, he gasped in shock when he saw the standards hanging in the nave. His hosts obviously meant to humiliate him, for suspended here were the captured flags from the defeats of the Huguenots at Jarnac and Moncontour. At Jarnac Catherine de

Medici had waged war on the Protestants, determined to crush the political rise of this ambitious fledgling religion. Here, at only sixteen years of age, Henry had witnessed the mutilation of his uncle, the elder prince de Condé. At the battle of Moncontour, the duc d'Anjou had won his reputation as a fine soldier and leader, and Coligny had been wounded in the jaw. Both had been bitter lessons in the price of war.

Henry ground his teeth to contain his anger over these calculated jabs, but he chose to keep his silence. The Protestants had lost those battles but they had shocked the country with the amount of foreign assistance they had attracted and the destruction they had wrought. If the stories about his mother were untrue, he didn't want to jeopardize the peace his marriage offered. And the more he thought about it, the more preposterous the rumors seemed to him. Seeing the standards of war had also reminded him of the prominence of the Guise family. The young Henri de Guise had proven himself at the Catholic versus Huguenot battle of Poitiers, and Catherine de Medici must surely be worried that the Guises would assert themselves as the primary Catholic power of France.

All of his cousins, Valois and Guise, clearly meant to assert Catholic dominance over the Bourbon Huguenot contingent they were "welcoming into their family through marriage." He could now easily understand why his mother had dragged her feet in agreeing to the union; but she had been right, he thought, to finally put the good of France and peace over her personal demands. "The bastards! May God's plague overtake them," he muttered, clinching his fists until his nails dug into his palms.

The following night Henry gazed down from his palace window at the Seine, its waters still and shimmering beneath the light of the mid-August moon. The Seine was such a still and placid river compared to his mountain streams, with their churning excitement and constant renewal. He wished even now he could be leaping across the slick pebbles of a stream bed in the cool pine-scented air. When the stench of the effluvia rose from the stagnant waters below, his "singing Pyrénées," his land of the troubadours, seemed very far away indeed. The "Béarn," as the region of his home was known, would always be a part of him. His initial excitement had evaporated and in its place resentment and foreboding festered. But he must not let the Valoises' bullying tactics get the better of him. And certainly he would not let them know what he was really thinking.

Somewhat ashamed, he shook off this reflective mood and descended to the hall below where the royal family and lords and ladies of the Valois court were assembled for the betrothal ceremony. Despite his efforts to control his thoughts, the sumptuous gowns with wide floating skirts and silk brocade suits attested to the different world into which he was invited. Such finery always seemed a nuisance to him, and in Béarn he had not been required to dress as a prince. It was all too clear that his days of such relaxed luxury were over. The crowd seemed to know before he did that the betrothal ceremony was imminent. With their ladies on their arms, earls, marquises, and counts were pressing for a place close to a dais which had been erected at one end of the ballroom, decorated with white feathers and every variety of white flower to be found in the city's flower stalls.

Henry felt in his pocket for the ring he was to give his fiancée. It was valued at ten thousand crowns and he would be glad to be relieved of its worrisome weight. His spirit momentarily surged with the strains of festive music. Suddenly Margot stood at his side, and her brother Charles placed her hand in Henry's. Her fingers were cold against the flesh of his palm, this first time that they touched, and neither could totally mask recognition of the impact of this charged moment. He had received only a cool, petulant expression from Princess Margot since his arrival in Paris, but when he slipped the huge diamond on her finger, she granted him a warm smile.

"How beautiful!" she exclaimed with a slight tremor in her voice.

Henry inclined at the waist, his hand at his breast. "I am glad you are pleased, Princess."

If this was the way to gain her support, Henry thought, it would be simple and he would do it. Studying the expressions of his imminent in-laws — Catherine de Medici, Anjou, Charles IX, and Alençon — Henry decided they could be a stone bas relief on one of the cathedrals he had visited: cold, removed, and still an enigma to him. And perhaps a dangerous one if Catherine hoped to weaken the Protestant cause with this marriage. But why should the Valoises be so concerned about him, he mused? François II had died at age sixteen after a reign of only seventeen months, but Charles IX, the reigning king, still had two younger brothers to succeed him in the event of his death. From Henry's perspective, Valois power appeared very secure.

A supper and ball followed. Chandeliers from Italy with golden filigree running through the crystal branches illuminated the ballroom, brightening the gold damask walls and highlighting the whirling taffetas and silks. The color, the music, and a desire to be happy lifted Henry's spirits. Why not make friends with the woman who soon would be his wife? Could she possibly learn to love him? Perhaps this wasn't too outlandish an idea after all. He hoped so. At the least, he needed a friend.

Margot looked dazzling in a gown of flesh-colored French taffeta, heavily draped with gold lace. Flamingo plumes waved in her dark hair and precious stones encircled her neck and wrists. Henry whispered to Condé, who had appeared at his side, "The men are darting around her like hummingbirds with eager, erect beaks around a pink flower."

Condé laughed. "You had better hurry or there will be no sugar left."

Henry bowed before her. "Which shall it be," she challenged, "the Spanish pavanne or the pazzemano of Italy?"

He noticed how delighted she appeared; a party was evidently a domain where she exhibited supreme comfort and contentment. Henry felt more adept on horseback in battle or hunting than he did on a dance floor and was well aware that his thin, short legs made him appear awkward. But he granted her a generous grin.

"I shall do my best to show you off."

Though concerned about his appearance, Henry was confident of the movements which he performed without mistake and with a certain flair. Even Pau had provided a dance master for a young prince, and he was grateful for Marguerite's petite stature.

"You certainly brought a lot of those odd Huguenots with you," Margot pretended to pout.

"Ah, but they are my friends," he explained.

"Your bodyguards, you mean! It seems that you don't trust my family," she accused.

"Should I? Surely you have heard the stories that my mother was poisoned by your stinking royal perfumer." Henry paused for a moment, looking suddenly morose. "Whatever happened, I miss her terribly."

Instantly regretting his frank show of emotion, he was surprised to find he had aroused a sympathetic fiber in Margot.

"But tomorrow you will have a wife," she blurted.

"So, I will," he smiled. Yet how different she was from the stark, angular mother he missed.

Henry's natural optimism rebounded and Margot reciprocated his seemingly jovial mood. Yes, she could be charming when she wished to be, and the crowd, watching them dance, began to relax also. Perhaps this odd wedding would bring peace after all. There were rumors that the Queen still had not yet received the necessary papal dispensation, but events were proceeding as though it didn't matter. In order to assure that the cardinal de Bourbon* would officiate at this marriage of differing religions, Charles IX simply told the cardinal that the papers were en route from the Vatican and might arrive a little late. Evidently Catherine de Medici made her own rules.

Later that night, as directed by court protocol, Margot was escorted by her mother, her brothers, her sister Claude, and the king's wife, Elizabeth of Austria, to the residence of Pierre de Gondi, bishop of Paris. Apparently, custom dictated that royal daughters spend the night before their marriage under that religious roof. Henry instinctively hated the ritual and ceremony of the French court, but at the moment he appreciated all the formalities. They provided the delays and cues he needed. Perhaps he and his mother should have considered the tenders for the hand of a fellow Protestant more seriously, for instance Elizabeth I of England, but they honestly hadn't given it much thought. Marrying the English monarch would have meant sacrificing his prospects to the French throne, meager though they might be, and he had to admit, he now was taken with Margot's beauty. Her smile when they were dancing delighted him, and she had made him feel almost graceful on the dance floor.

On the morning of August 18, 1572, a mob gathered before the Cathedral of Notre Dame long before Henry or Margot awoke. Jostling one another, the rabble sparred to obtain a better vantage point for the procession. Despite the excitement, as the royal wedding party neared Notre Dame, Henry was saddened by the scene before him. The majority of the onlookers were dressed in rags, many were diseased, and most were filthy. The religious civil war had obliterated much of the law and order of the country and left a plethora of

* Charles, cardinal de Bourbon, was the brother of Henry's father Antoine. He later became known as Charles X when supported by the Catholic League.

destitute widows unable to feed and clothe their families. He now understood why the poor of Paris were most hopeful about this "marriage of two religions," for it was they who died in the endless fighting between the Protestants and the Catholics.

A royal coin had been minted for the occasion, bearing the emblem of a lamb and a cross with the significant inscription, *Vobis annuntio pacem*. Despite this "peace," a platform had been erected in front of the cathedral for the wedding because the bishops forbade a heretic such as Henry to walk inside on the holy ground of the chancel beyond the rood screen. But today, everyone chose to ignore all the glaring evidence of strife still at bay; loud cheers greeted the lords of the great French families passing in procession — the Huguenot Chatillons and the Catholic Montmorencys and Guises all walking together.

Henry had chosen a pale yellow satin suit, extravagantly weighted with pearls and topaz. Facing the crowd, he stood poised as the sun brightened the touch of red in his hair peeking beneath the crown of Navarre. Then the clear notes of the trumpets hushed the throng, and the haunting music of the hautboys announced the arrival of the bride, approaching in lavish attire.

Margot's gown of royal purple, embroidered with fleurs de lys, flared at her back to include a mantle fifteen feet long, carefully carried by three princesses. The diamonds, rubies and sapphires of the imperial coronet blazed in the strong light of summer. Her brother the king walked beside her. Henry was shocked at how pale and old Charles IX appeared, though only two years her senior. The unmitigating sunlight, which so flattered his sister, revealed a premature decrepitude that the shadows of the palace interior gracefully hid.

Henry turned his gaze from Charles to openly scrutinize the woman before him. How breathtaking she was! The same sunlight that withered Charles seemed to rejoice with this subject, its brightness accenting the smooth white cheek and glossy black hair. Would Margot be his friend? Or would she be in league with her mother, whom he patently distrusted? Despite her riveting loveliness, the princess's enthusiasm for this occasion was noticeably lacking. It even appeared to Henry that Charles had pushed the crown forward to make her bow her head in acquiescence to the bishop's questions.

The voices of the choir bounced joyfully toward the lofty height of the Gothic cathedral behind them and Henry's spirits lifted with the sound. He echoed the promises of marriage dictated by the bishop with hope high in his heart. He tried to look into Marguerite's eyes as he spoke the words of future faith and loyalty, but her gaze remained locked upon the bishop. Please, Margot, please, he thought, let us at least be allies. The Catholic ritual was not entirely unknown to him, but it did not have the familiar rhythm of the Protestant prayers he loved. Before he expected it, the organ boomed forth the recessional hymn, and he and his new wife were walking away from the cathedral behind an acolyte swaying the censer.

Trestle tables laden with wine and a spread worthy of the gourmand had been set up along the right bank of the river Seine. The crowd rushed and pushed one another across the Pont Notre Dame and the Pont au Change, where the moneychangers had their shops, to have a first chance at the refreshments. Already drunk with the prospect of the wedding festivities, a few merrymakers apparently had fallen in the river and drifted downstream toward the Louvre. Pickpockets, peddlers, and porters stood ready to make the most of the opulent occasion. The people knew they would be allowed to gorge themselves and swill wine for three days until the planned round of entertainments would come to an end.

While greeting those wishing them well, Henry held Marguerite's gloved hand. At first she did not seem to object, but when he began to stroke the top of her hand with his thumb, she immediately withdrew her fingers from his. Most of the people crowding to congratulate the couple were unknown to Henry, and he soon began to feel tired. However, he was determined to remain cheerful and friendly. A joyful bride in place of the begrudging person beside him would certainly help, he thought.

It was not until the early morning hours, after much forced revelry, that Henry found himself alone with Margot in their bridal suite. Henry dropped onto the bed, dog-tired but keen for this moment. His bride remained standing, studying him intently. Neither spoke.

Margot regarded a man with a wiry frame and dark brown hair, cut very close. He was only slightly taller than average, with a long torso and short legs. She had noticed earlier his light step and quick movements, how he could be serious and dignified when necessary, but how he could quickly give way to impulsive emotion. He rolled his r's in the Gascon way, but she had to admit she liked his singsong accent. She found his high forehead assertive, his eyes — a complicated color of gold, green and gray — full of warmth under their heavy lids, his cheeks of good color, but his aquiline nose too prominent. She had to admit that the overall effect was a fine-featured man with an agreeable vivacious countenance. Her taste wished for a less coarse type, but she warmed to his lighthearted manner and good humor.

Henry, on the other hand, was entirely pleased with his wife's appearance, especially her brilliant complexion and graceful neck. Her gown flattened the bosom as decreed by fashion, but her small waist and lips, tinted coral, tempted him. Finally breaking the taut silence, he hoped he sounded reasonably casual and charming.

"When Charles spoke this morning and said, 'In giving my sister Marguerite to Henry of Navarre, I give my sister to all the Protestants of the Kingdom,' I was quite jealous. I don't think I want to share you."

His bantering tone encouraged her but the content increased her nervousness. Did he really expect her to share his bed? But why shouldn't he? Pressing for a delay, she excused herself. "My ladies-in-waiting are expecting to help me dress," she said, and she hurried to the adjacent anteroom.

As soon as she had closed the door to the bedroom behind her, the duc de Guise stepped forward from a dark corner where he evidently had been awaiting her. "As I promised, my love." He reached to take her in his arms, but she pushed him away in agitation. Margot, appearing ready to weep, rapidly composed herself.

"Where are my letters?" she whispered hoarsely.

"That can wait, certainly," the Duke answered.

"No. Give them to me at once, Henri," Margot demanded. Her insistent agitated tone surprised him, and he pulled a packet of letters from his coat. Margot seized them and hurled them into the fire in the hearth.

"He truly means to have me for his wife," she said grimly. "I don't know what to do."

"Surely he jests," the Duke suggested. "I am sure that Mme de Sauve* is awaiting him even now."

"I am not so sure, even though she has been flirting with him. I cannot count on this, and so you and I will not meet again for a few days. I will send a message to you tomorrow. You may leave by this stair."

"But Marguerite . . ."

---

* Charlotte de Beaune de Semblançay, Viscountess of Tours, Baroness of Sauve, Marquise de Noirmoutier (1551 – 1617), was a French noblewoman and widely appreciated courtesan at the Valois court.

"Quiet!" Calmer now, Margot opened a door in the wall paneling. Guise saw in the gloom a narrow staircase leading to the floor above, just one of many hidden escapes throughout the labyrinthian palace. She allowed him a brief kiss, then called her attendants, who earlier must have agreed to Guise's audience with the bride.

Having learned quickly since his arrival the need for suspicion, Henry had been listening at the door. One couldn't remain naïve and survive at the court of the Valoises! He now expected conniving around every corner, but this rendezvous surpassed his wildest surmises. If only he'd been able to hear every word! So, it was true that Guise was his wife's current admirer, even though he had recently been coerced into an arranged marriage himself.

Henry realized he must devise a strategy at once. He tried to recall what he knew about the Guises. They had always been a prominent family and had become more powerful when François, Marguerite's older brother, was crowned at age fifteen under the name of François II and his wife, Mary Stuart, Queen of Scots, became Queen Consort. François was too young to rule, so his mother, Catherine, became Regent along with Mary Stuart's uncles, François de Guise and the Cardinal of Lorraine. Some believed that Henry's father, Antoine de Bourbon, should have been elected Regent since he was the closest male heir to the throne after Marguerite's brothers. François de Guise's arrogance didn't help matters and in March 1560, Protestant rebels headed towards the Castle of Amboise to kidnap the royal family, kill Guise, and place Antoine de Bourbon as head of State. The plot was discovered, though Antoine's implication was never proved. All the rebels were caught, tortured, and executed in front of the Valois family and the entire court. Marguerite had been only seven at the time. Tragedy struck the Valois family again when François II died from an ear infection on December 5, 1560. His Catholic wife, Mary Stuart, had returned to Scotland and was imprisoned for seven years before being beheaded by Elizabeth I, the Protestant queen of England. Margot certainly had witnessed a significant amount of violence at court when she was young, he mused.

Where did Marguerite stand in the fray now, Henry wondered? Most probably with her lover, the Catholic duc de Guise, but Henry already sensed his new wife was a complicated woman. She had a mind of her own, and her emotions would not necessarily dictate her thoughts and actions. It was remarkable news to him that the licentious court expected him to spend his wedding night with the attractive Charlotte de Sauve instead of his new wife. Charlotte was one of the Queen Mother's ladies-in-waiting, and for that reason he felt she could not be trusted. Most likely they were using her to spy on him. Charlotte's beauty had attracted him since his arrival, but he had found her coquettish manner suspicious.

Henry was not a newcomer to sex, only to the intrigue accompanying it at the Valois court. He smiled as he recalled with pleasure his affair with little Fleurette, the gardener's daughter in Nérac, near Pau. In fact, he had been a father at fifteen, and the winsome Fleurette had been proud to bear a prince's child, even out of wedlock. Henry chuckled to himself. His behavior would be unexpected and unpredictable too. He would spend the night with his wife! The man from the provinces was learning fast. Indeed, his nervousness was becoming excitement.

Margot returned, wearing a fuchsia negligée embroidered with white roses. The high color of the robe accented her black eyes and the flush of her cheeks. Henry pretended not to notice her startled expression as he immediately began to pull off his boots.

"I sent my valet away so we could talk. I don't remember you very well from my visits here as a boy," Henry chatted like an old friend. "Where did they hide you?"

"I was with my tutors much of the time," Margot replied. She smiled, albeit stiffly, "I liked to study more than my brothers."

"Yes, I've heard about your erudition and your proficiency in Latin and Greek." Henry couldn't resist jesting. "Perhaps you can write a little *billet doux* to the pope and help me in that quarter."

"Do you take anything seriously?" Margot asked.

"I take you very seriously," Henry responded, his eyes bright with eagerness and perhaps mischief. It was those expressive eyes that diverted one's attention from the too-long nose, and it was those wily eyes that caught Margot off guard. Was there something of the rogue in her husband?

Henry dared to pull her to him and surprisingly, she didn't resist. Perhaps she was even somewhat excited as he slipped his hand under her negligée. The bed sat on a dais, surrounded with heavy brocade curtains — to hide all the illicit love making, Henry thought.

"Your beauty has seduced me," Henry said softly. "It is easy to forget your reputation when your lovely body is so close."

Even though he was still a bit nervous, his natural ease and loquacity seemed to guide him. Apparently his wife never resented a compliment. His desire quickened as he moved his hand over the curve of her hip, and she instinctively pressed her body closer to his. During the evening he sensed that Margot's heart was not involved, but she substituted skill for sincerity quite artfully. As he fell asleep, he felt he had achieved some small victory. Margot lay awake a bit longer, considering the unexpected new respect she had for her Béarnais husband.

PARIS, ILE DE LA CITE

FINDING A TIME AND PLACE to speak privately with Coligny at court proved impossible, for some fawning servant or favor seeker always seemed to be present. So difficult was it to be alone that Henry began to suspect everyone of being a Valois spy. The nagging worry persisted, and the morning after the wedding Henry barged into the admiral's room, insisting that everyone else leave.

"You are the last person I expected to see this morning," Coligny commented.

"I don't doubt it." Henry almost smiled but a strong, and perhaps irrational, sense of urgency made him rush ahead.

"Coligny, I don't understand, but perhaps you will not be surprised to hear what I witnessed last night. Guise visited Margot right under my nose — on our wedding night! Fears about what this might mean made my wedding bed seem quite cold very early this morning."

"Ah, you are right to tell me," Coligny assured him. "I shall have the duke watched very closely."

Henry raised his voice. "I am beginning to see a traitor hiding behind every tapestry and in every suit of armor in the halls. You should leave the court, Gaspard. I have now heard rumors of plots on your life!"

"No, my prince, I cannot," Coligny replied. He looked straight at Henry with a regard of steel reflecting an inflexible will. "It is the safety of France which concerns me. It is better to die a hundred times than to live in perpetual distrust. I am weary of all these alarms at every event, and I have lived long enough. I would rather have my body dragged through the streets of Paris than to engage in a new civil war. And last but not least, I promised your mother I would look after you."

"You are too good," Henry said, but then continued to press his point. "I hear the Queen Mother is afraid that King Charles will follow your advice instead of hers. Her fear of this puts you in special danger."

"And well he should! You are astute regarding the Queen Mother's concerns about Charles's loyalties. He is a decent man, I think, more decent than the rest of his family, but I fear he is unstable."

"What bad luck!" Henry moaned aloud with his plaintive words. Yet he hoped he did not appear to be the child he felt. "There is so much to learn."

"You are right again," Coligny agreed. "And I especially want to discuss the Spanish situation with you. It is imperative that France should wage war against King Philip before he gains any more power. Think hard about that, my boy. The duc de Guise, I believe, has won over the pope and Spain to his camp. If the Valoises are not careful, France will become another Spanish province. But you are not untutored in these matters, Henry."

"No, but I never fully appreciated how complicated my responsibilities would be."

"I have great hopes for you," the older man said. At fifty-three years of age, he was still tall and straight, and after a lifetime of service, he was an inspiration and comfort.

Henry did not press Coligny further. Of course he had known this kind warrior his entire life, but only recently had his affection developed into a profound trust. This was becoming a tough school of realism. He muttered to himself, "It must be better to stay alive to fight for one's cause than to die a noble death." He realized he was already very different from his idealistic mother. She probably would have canceled the wedding if she had seen the flags of defeat from Moncontour and Jarnac hanging like a flamboyant taunt at Notre Dame. He would rather wait and see and try to find a compromise.

The amiral de Coligny had been shot! The news pounded through the palace halls like the beat of the wedding drums that still echoed ominously in Henry's ears. Henry's shock reverberated with each and every story — it was the Guise family seeking revenge; it was the Queen Mother protecting her interests; it was the fanatic Catholics. *Mon Dieu*, what could he do? What should he have done to avoid this? He felt as helpless as a trapped animal. Whatever the motive, it was only five days since the Valois-Bourbon wedding, which was supposed to have brought peace.

Henry chastised himself as he hurried to Coligny's lodging. Why hadn't he realized how imminent the danger was? Why had he let himself be seduced by Margot? But had he not warned Coligny again? He reached the admiral's residence, an elegant townhouse, and noticed that the shutters remained closed. Henri de Condé met him at the door, stumbling through the words of the story with unconcealed emotion. Henry tried to stop his own trembling and hoped he looked more composed than his disheveled and flustered cousin.

"Quickly, Henri! Tell me what happened!"

Condé could not stop wringing his hands and his voice shook. "The old man had just left the King's Council, to which he had been invited, and was walking with a few companions down the rue de Béthisy. There were two quick shots and Coligny fell to the ground. He was obviously hurt, but thank the blessed Lord, not dead. The poor man signaled toward the house where the smoke of an arquebus was still visible."

"Merciful Heaven! Gaspard is still alive!" Henry felt himself begin to breathe more evenly. "Were the villains caught?" he asked.

"I don't think so," Condé answered. He began to stammer in his haste to tell Henry the story. "Th-Th-Three of our Huguenots ra-ra-ran back to force the door and attempted to follow the assassin, who fled, of course, while the others helped poor Coligny home. His left hand and forearm were gravely injured by the shots which missed their true target, the Lord be praised, by the slightest chance. Our dear friend stooped to fix his shoe at the crucial moment!"

Condé was interrupted by a commotion in the foyer as Charles IX, accompanied by his guard, burst in.

"Where is *mon père*? Where is he?" The king rushed into Coligny's chamber, passing Henry and Condé as though he didn't even recognize them. "Ah, *mon père*, I grieve that my friendship did not protect you," Charles IX blubbered as he grabbed Coligny's bandaged hand and kissed it.

Watching Charles, Henry decided that the king's genuine emotion vindicated any involvement on his part in the plot. However, his obvious feelings for the Protestant warrior might have infuriated Catherine enough to prompt her to order the malevolent deed.

"When will the violence end?" Charles asked, more to himself than of his men. "I shall send my surgeon, Ambrose Paré, to you immediately. He is an excellent man. I want you to have the best care."

Too weak to talk, the admiral smiled and thanked Charles, who rushed out of the room as explosively as he had entered. The amount of nervous energy in the king always made him a more imposing presence than his physical stature warranted.

Henry reflected on why Catherine was so concerned about Coligny's presence. She must realize how much Charles needed a father, for Henri II had died when the children were very young. Coligny had served as Charles's tutor at court long ago, when he had been on good terms with the Valois family. The Queen Mother must be frantic with worry that the Huguenot lord whom the king called *mon père* would have more influence than she. However, as far as Henry could deduce from the stories of the witnesses to the crime, the Guises were more clearly implicated than anyone else. Condé interrupted his thoughts as though reading his mind.

"I've just heard that a former page of the House of Lorraine was seen fleeing from the crime. Also, the house in which the smoking arquebus was seen belonged to one of the former teachers of the duc de Guise."

"Of course!" rallied Henry. "Yet those who witnessed the Queen Mother's reaction when she heard of the incident said she certainly had at least known of the plan in advance. Now she will feel even more threatened. I'm afraid her plan to isolate me in Catholic Paris is becoming more and more obvious."

With Coligny seriously handicapped, Henry felt for the first time the full weight of responsibility as head of the Huguenot party. The religious wars were evidently not to end with his marriage. The very short honeymoon was over, and it was sickeningly clear that intolerance and hatred would continue, as rampant as before.

Henry and Condé left the wounded man's residence in the rue de Béthisy to demand justice from the king. Charles, having only just returned to the Louvre himself from Coligny's bedside, appeared still distraught. "This is terrible! Terrible! I assure you we will find these murderous rogues."

Somewhat placated, the two Bourbon princes made their way through the cobbled streets to the admiral's house. Peddlers, scurrying about their errands with carts and barrows, jostled and irritated Henry. He recalled his recent excitement when he first encountered the exuberant energy of the thriving city of Paris, but at this moment he only saw the dingy, seamy side. The Louvre had been erected on the right bank of the Seine and the spires of Notre Dame rose nearby on an island in the river, now called the Ile de la Cité. Originally the site of Roman Lutetia, walls, ramparts, barracks, and dungeons still towered grimly above the city. The Romans had selected this spot because of its natural defenses and to Henry, the royal and religious center still maintained an aura of the citadel. No wonder he had begun to feel like a prisoner.

During the rest of the day and Saturday morning, Henry and his Protestant lords spoke of possible strategies in the rooms of the convalescent although Coligny was in too much pain to offer much advice. The older man had stoically suffered the operation to amputate the arm that had been struck, advised by the king's physician that otherwise he risked death from infection.

Henry whispered to Condé, "I'm afraid this was only the first blow of a mass attack on us all. Yet the king's obvious sorrow and cooperative attitude confuse me. I don't know if Charles is normal or deranged, and I don't know if he is sympathetic to me and the Huguenots or loyal to his mother. When we demanded more protection, he readily sent over fifty men with Jean de Cosseins, a colonel of the guards, as their leader. But Cosseins is openly a Guise man, and so his presence is not that reassuring."

"Exactly," Condé agreed. "And poor Coligny is a helpless prisoner in his bed."

"*Pardieu!* I am more unsure of my position than ever. If this is Guise's work only, perhaps it is a personal revenge for the death of his father and not the beginning of an assault upon all the Huguenots. I wish I could believe that. But since I don't, I think I had better leave five of my own guard behind for Gaspard when I leave."

Henry knew this was a futile gesture in the face of real trouble, but what else could he do? At least it would be a token of his concern to Coligny. Hurrying through the few streets to the Louvre, he despaired over the admiral's condition, which appeared to be worsening with a rising fever. Yet Henry knew he should not allow his worry for his friend to supplant his growing anxiety over the political quagmire.

Margot remained his one hope, his one link with the Valois clan which might, just might, help him discover whether the Catholics planned attacks on the Protestants visiting Paris. If this were the case, he would warn his men to escape, for a fight within the city would be disastrous. They wouldn't have a chance.

Cursing with his fears, he neared his wife's suite. Although they had passed several remarkably passionate nights together, he did not know whether she would be his friend or Catherine's daughter. He realized it would be foolish to expect her allegiance to him and his cause so soon, but she had seemed surprisingly sympathetic toward him. He knocked and a woman of the bedchamber opened the heavily carved door. At the sight of Navarre she looked startled but then motioned him to enter. Henry tried to appear nonchalant as he approached Margot, but her face did nothing to reassure him. She obviously knows something is afoot, he thought. Her first remark surprised him.

"My mother has just sent me from her chambers for the night." She flipped her skirts angrily. "She is up to something, I am sure. She is too excited and was very eager to be rid of me. She said if I remained in my rooms, I would be safe. Safe from what? And my silly sister was crying! I fear for you and your friends, my lord."

"I am pleased to see you care for my welfare, Margot. I, too, am concerned and puzzled."

"If you succeed, Navarre, I will be Queen of France one day. If you die, I am still only a sister to the king. I have nothing to gain by siding with my mother. Although I admit I fear her."

Surprised by her apparent honesty and lucid appraisal of her status, Henry told himself never to underestimate her intelligence. He quickly decided to meet her remarks with equal frankness. "But I am not yet King. At the moment one could put equal money on our cousin, the duc de Guise. He comes from as powerful a family as I."

Margot blushed but replied coolly, "Ah, but I am not his wife."

"At the moment," Henry bantered.

"You are extremely cocky for one who is probably in serious danger. I suggest we go to England where you will be safe. Charles will protect Coligny if I insist."

"You are right, my love." Henry paused, the endearment sticking in his throat, but he knew she thrived on flattery. "We must make our plans. I do not wish to seem melodramatic, but I too am sure danger lies within this palace. However, I doubt I will decide to desert my friends, as you suggest. Please send them to me as they arrive. I have sent word for all to join me here."

He crossed into the adjoining room where he intended to hold a conference and advise immediate action due to Margot's warning. But what action could they take? Attack? No, they were essentially trapped in enemy territory. Could they possibly escape?

Later, when Margot entered their boudoir, she found it full of Huguenots. "What a stench!" she loudly complained.

"I regret we do not share the services of your royal perfumer on these hot days," replied an impertinent soldier.

All of a sudden and with great commotion, a retinue of the king's soldiers also pushed into the room. M. de Nançay, their leader, announced, "The King of France demands an audience with the King of Navarre."

Henry kissed Margot's hand and spoke softly to her, "Do not forget our future." Turning to his followers, he said, "God knows if I will ever see you again. It might be wise for you to leave Paris."

Leaving the room, he felt the heavy-footed soldiers close behind him.

Henry had heard of Charles's madness, but this was the first time he had witnessed one of his rages. A wild, demented fever burned in the king's eyes, giving him the look of the falcons he so avidly hunted, and his mouth grimaced uncontrollably. Henry was the first to speak.

"To what matter of importance do I owe this escort, Sire?" He was proud that his voice did not betray his fear.

At that moment, Condé was also ushered in by the court guards. Henry was struck by how handsome his cousin looked, even in this critical moment. Like Henry, he had dark wavy hair, but the resemblance ended there. Condé was taller and his features more finely sculpted, always creating envy in the rougher hewn Henry. The fact that they shared the same Christian name had been a bond since they were boys, and their many common experiences had cemented their friendship. Yet, throughout childhood Henry had assumed the leadership role, his quick mind always dominating their activities.

"You are both traitors," Charles shouted. "You will see what happens to your kind."

Screams and thuds in nearby rooms suddenly startled the Bourbon princes. When Charles led them to the window, their eyes informed them why. Guards with white armbands, rushing back and forth in the courtyard below, brandished swords and daggers. Several mangled bodies already lay against the walls, and from every window and door Henry saw others trying to escape along pavements slippery with blood. The streets rang with cries of terror all the way from the windmill on the hill of Montmartre. His shocked mind seemed to lag behind what his eyes told him — that the Catholics' fury had been unleashed on the visiting Huguenots. Henry now had no doubt that Catherine's politics must be behind it all. With unbelieving horror, he turned ice cold when he then witnessed the great Petrus Ramus fall at the hand of the king's jester. Henry had been commanded to study this philosopher's writings when he was a boy, and he had thought of him as a life-long family friend. Ramus had converted from Catholicism to become a Huguenot and persuasively explained his change of faith.

As Henry and Condé gazed with blood-chilled fear at the massacre, Charles was busy setting up an arquebus at another window. He laughed excitedly as he took aim at the poor, frantic creatures trapped in the Louvre courtyard. The hysteria of human slaughter seemed to have transformed the king into a demon. After a few minutes of frenzied shooting, he turned to his hostages.

"I have evidence of a Huguenot plot against the crown, Henry, and have ordered the execution of the leaders," he shouted. Then in staccato tones he asked, "And for you, will it be death, the Bastille, or Mass?" His goatee bobbed up and down ridiculously. Henry could not believe this was the same man who had so recently shown such compassion for Coligny. If madness were a changing personality, then surely the king must be mad.

"It would be difficult to make that decision so quickly, Your Majesty," Navarre replied immediately. He didn't want the impetuous Condé to speak. "Would you be so lenient as to give us the night to think it over? Matters of conscience need serious consideration."

Charles hesitated. He squinted his almond-shaped eyes as though he had a headache.

"I won't refuse your request, Henry." For a moment the monster seemed human again. "I like you despite what my mother says. She told me of the Huguenots' betrayal. Besides, you will be in my armory next door. Only I will be able to guarantee your safety tonight."

He led his captives into a paneled room hung with weapons of all kinds. Henry had heard that the king amused himself by torturing and even dismembering domestic animals. One of his hounds lay peacefully by the fire and a book on falconry lay open on the writing table.

"I will visit you in the morning to hear your decision," the King announced, closing the door.

Henry stared as though in a hypnotic trance at the bas-relief carvings in a drapery design upon the door which Charles had closed between them. What evil lay among the folds? *Sacre Dieu.* Perhaps he was becoming hysterical too. He struggled to recover his thoughts and began to talk.

"We must do what they ask or lose our heads. It's a simple choice, Condé. Charles is insane. That is now perfectly clear."

While Henry talked, Condé sat with his head in his hands, quietly weeping. "You can see yourself there is no possibility of reasoning with him. But how could his behavior change so quickly and so radically? First Coligny and now this!" Henry realized he was numb with shock, even though he was trying to speak calmly and persuasively. "It's obvious his mother has triggered this behavior," he added.

"But Henry," his intransigent cousin replied, "If you agree to their terms, you are the worst sort of compromiser, disloyal to yourself and your faith."

"I understand all that, you shit-a-bed," Henry argued in exasperation, allowing the anger he felt toward the Valoises to spill over to Condé. "But if we die, the Huguenot cause dies. You have seen Coligny lying in his bed, barely able to breathe for all the Valois 'well-wishers' surrounding him. And if he recovers, you realize he is not a young man."

"Your mother would not have given in to their murderous tactics. My God, Henry, have you forgotten her already?"

"No, I have not forgotten her and I should punch you for suggesting it. And no, she would not have given in. In fact, she even insisted that Margot become a Protestant if I married her. Of course Margot would not agree to that. Maybe I am not as strong as Mother was, but she was not always realistic. And perhaps her choices were not of the life or death variety — or else she didn't realize it until too late. Just as we were too late in realizing we should leave Paris. Look Condé, so we compromise for the moment. Surely God wouldn't begrudge us a few clever tactics. After all, He gave us our brains."

Condé still was not convinced, and Henry, who would have preferred to use the time contemplating a more detailed strategy, had to spend the night turning his hot-headed cousin to his side. The agonized screams and cries which reached his ears filled him with terror, but no sane man could have imagined the mutilation which was taking place on that St. Bartholomew's Eve.

Condé remained as still as stone, rarely looking at Henry who paced as he spoke. "Evidently Catherine has bullied Charles into submission with stories of treason by those of the Huguenot religion. The king is already unstable as you have witnessed, and it would not be difficult for her to break him down."

Charles's shouts of "kill them, kill them" in the room next door confirmed Henry's reasoning.

"But Henry . . . "

"*Mère de Dieu*, I understand you are not afraid to die for your religion. That is very admirable. But do you not realize that the Protestant cause needs you? You are one of their future leaders. Did you not see Ramus die at their hands? They do not seem to care whom they kill as long as it is a Huguenot. He was one of our country's greatest minds. They will spill any blood supposedly to prove the communion wine is the true blood of Christ, but I believe, more truly, the real reason is to extend their power. And they are committing these executions in the name of religion. If you give your life tonight to these vicious Valoises, you are only diminishing the Huguenots' chances of ultimate success. Please, Henri, see my side, the side of life, not of death!"

"All right, Henry," Condé finally agreed, "but I don't promise how long I can go along with your philosophy."

Margot had just fallen asleep after several restless hours when a loud commotion awoke her. She screamed as a bloody apparition leaped onto her bed. A wild man grabbed her and pulled her down with him, wedging them between the bed and the wall. Her senses finally began to work, and she perceived the poor fellow was wounded and trying to escape the archers who now surrounded her bed.

For the second time in one night, her bed seemed to draw a crowd. The victim was M. de La Môle,* an extremely handsome man she had noticed earlier among Henry's coterie. Despite the hysteria of the moment, she was struck again by his exquisite features. Margot's

---

* Joseph Boniface de La Môle (c.1526-1574)

screams and La Môle's shouting had also roused M. de Nançay, the captain of the guards. When he entered and saw them all in such a state, he couldn't refrain from laughing.

"Have pity, "Margot wailed.

"Away with you," Captain Nançay commanded the grinning archers. "You have shown an appalling lack of courtesy toward the Queen of Navarre."

The guards backed away slowly, obviously reluctant to leave such a curious scene.

"Thank you for your able and ready aid, M. le Capitain," Margot said with as much composure as she could muster. "Please leave me with this man, and I shall be responsible for his wounds."

La Môle was still clinging to her like a child.

"Are you sure?" the captain asked, gazing dubiously at the bloody bed.

"Certainly. Please leave us now."

"Yes, my lady."

La Môle was weak and had lost much blood. Yet for Margot, the pallor of his face accentuated his Grecian features. His relentless gaze made it clear that he admired her also. She summoned her lady-in-waiting and together they cleaned and dressed his arm. It did not seem to bother Marguerite that her own nightdress was now covered with blood. Not one to rue taking advantage of a situation and seeing her patient had gained some strength, she questioned him before leaving to change.

"What has happened tonight, Monsieur?"

"Your husband is safe with the king, my lady," he said. "But alas, I am sure that every other Huguenot lord has perished this fateful night."

So, La Môle assumed she was allied with Henry. "Why has the King of Navarre been spared?" Margot asked.

"Truly, I do not know, for I am sure the Queen Mother wanted him killed." La Môle went on to tell her of his attempt to warn the admiral de Coligny. "Before dawn, Guise swordsmen and M. d'Alençon's Swiss guard broke down Coligny's door. I wanted to alert him, but I was too late and he was too sick to ready himself quickly. The poor man was skewered with a pike and hung out of the window into the street below, where the duc de Guise and his brother kicked the dead man's face."

Margot blanched but La Môle continued his grisly tale. "After further mutilation, the crowd hung the corpse by its heels from a public gibbet while more death and destruction raged on. You cannot imagine, my lady. Neither women nor children were spared in the rampage. It is a veritable cauldron of strangling, rape, murder, and looting." The nerve-racked man began to cry. "I myself somehow miraculously escaped over Coligny's rooftop and found my way to your chamber. It was the only escape I could think of." He paused. "For you have been on my mind from the first moment I saw you," he dared.

"Rest here," she ordered, giving his hand a reassuring squeeze. "I must find Navarre. My lady of the chamber, Eléane, will care for you until I return."

"I knew you would help me," he sighed, sinking back upon her pillows.

Marguerite hurried into the hall to find Nançay again, who confirmed that Henry was locked in the king's chambers. She knew her husband would be devastated when he heard of the gory death of Admiral Coligny. Somewhat surprised, she found she cared how he would feel.

LE PALAIS DU LOUVRE

AT DAYBREAK CHARLES UNLOCKED the door and Henry and Condé walked out. *Mère de Dieu*, what would happen to them now? The king didn't bother to greet them but began babbling to Margot, who stood by his side. She signaled to Navarre and Condé to stay silent and stood next to Charles, listening to him explain the validity of his actions the evening before.

"There was a miracle, Margot, a direct sign from God that He approved of our actions. Toward dawn the Catholic people noticed a hawthorn bush in the churchyard was suddenly abloom. Don't you see? This must be a miracle! Why else would a bush bloom out of season?"

When she failed to answer, he turned to Henry. "I hope God will not be angry with me for sparing you."

"He also teaches us to have mercy," Henry interjected.

"But acceptance of a heretic is a sin, Henry. Your Protestants believe that as well as the Catholics."

"I don't believe it," Henry answered. "I don't doubt that the church teaches us it is merciful to kill heretics so that they might sin no more, but the church is wrong."

Margot interrupted. "Henry, you should know; I must tell you. People are saying at least three thousand Protestants died in Paris last night,* and your friend Coligny is dead. The inflamed populace has used the Seine as a sepulcher, tossing bodies in the water until the whole river flows crimson." Tears began to seep from her eyes, though she seemed too traumatized to be aware of them.

---

* Estimates vary from 2000-4000 deaths in Paris, and the carnage rapidly spread into the countryside.

Henry sat down, forgetting he was standing before the king. Condé put one arm around his cousin's shoulders, but before the two princes had time to absorb the shock, Charles continued, "Now, Navarre and Condé, in exchange for your lives, you must formally recant your heresy before my confessor and then make a public renunciation of your religion." Charles's excitement was suddenly gone, like a child's quick change of temper. He appeared wan and worn as he related the terms for their release.

"As you command, Your Majesty," Henry agreed.

How much did he owe Margot for his life? He felt the king's lenience must be at least partially due to his wife's persuasiveness. When he thought of his fellow Huguenots' disgust and anger at his apparent betrayal, he shuddered, but he and Condé had agreed not to take anyone into their confidence. Their position was too precarious. A deserter! A coward! That's what his men — the few who were left — would call him.

St. Michael's Day, when he was to be initiated into the Order of St. Michael and would receive communion at Mass, came all too soon. He could privately curse his situation, but it would be fatal to reveal his humiliation. It was just as well he could not hear what his men were saying when they saw their leader kneel before the Catholic altar, for it would have made it even harder to carry through this charade. What a tragedy if his mother could see him now. But for the time being, he could see no other way to survive.

As he walked jauntily toward the altar dressed all in white with a golden cape, trimmed in crimson velvet and embroidered with pearls, few would have guessed his inner turmoil. Remembering those who had died on St. Bartholomew's Eve, he found it meager consolation that they were not present to watch him capitulate to all whom his mother had held in abhorrence. She would never have accepted half measures. He heard the Queen Mother laugh aloud. Let her gloat for now. He would have to be satisfied that his face did not reflect his shame. Let her believe he was less proud than Jeanne d'Albret and easier to bend. Hadn't he learned lessons from nature watching the chameleons adapt to their surroundings on the rocks around Pau?

Henry's degradation was not to end with the St. Michael's Day celebration. Charles IX pronounced to Navarre, "Now you must beg the pope's pardon." On October 3, the King of Navarre did so. Charles then commanded, "You must publish an edict which will reestablish Catholicism in Béarn."

"I cannot do that, Charles," Henry replied. "It is part of my own kingdom. Besides, it would be totally ineffectual."

"You have no choice, Henry. Remember, I have given you your life."

Henry recalled how he had been torn as a child between his father's Catholicism and his mother's ardent Protestantism. Now the struggle was the same but the powers pulling him were greater. What they had done to Coligny was a blatant warning. Death, it seemed, would be the prize for any refusal to cooperate.

"Very well, Your Majesty." And may you turn on a spit in Hell for an eternity! That thought soothed his anger, and he tried to relax his jaws, clamped as tight as a lupus on its prey. They will pay for this one day, Henry privately vowed. He drew some satisfaction from the news that the ambassadors of Spain failed to congratulate the Valoises, as Catherine de Medici had expected, after the gory victory of St. Bartholomew's Eve. Even they appeared appalled by the news.

At least he and Condé were allowed to venture out freely, and it helped to confide in his cousin, especially when he was snubbed by other men who had formerly been his friends.

"I don't regret our decision to dissemble," Henry told Condé, "for I still believe it is the only course to safety and ultimate victory. But it is very hard not being able to vindicate ourselves by explaining this to our men, especially La Môle and d'Aubigné. This seems worse to me than death in battle. I can only hope they understand."

"They hate us now," Condé mourned. "Sometimes I think I would rather be dead than this dishonest."

"I feel the same occasionally, Cousin. But remember, there is no glory in death by the hand of the despicable Valoises. And it helps to know that our ally, Elizabeth I, when she heard of the horrific deed, was stunned and refused the French ambassador an audience for eleven days before hearing him out. Other countries in Europe have also sent notes of condemnation to our incompetent rulers."

But this reasoning did not lessen his personal agony. He now knew that the bloody violence of St. Bartholomew's had not ended in Paris but had flowed south like an angry red river until ten thousand

Huguenots lay dead in France.* Every night he asked himself whether he was being so adaptive and pragmatic just to save his own skin or whether it truly was to preserve the future of the Huguenot cause. His loneliness darkened his perspective, and he began to feel like a nocturnal animal even during the light of day.

"I miss Coligny terribly," he added. "His velvet toque was always a reassuring sight." His eyes watered, and he wished he were not so quick to weep.

"You'll manage, Henry," Condé replied. Henry looked up in surprise. Well, if someone had confidence in him, it helped. But where was his life going? He longed to be back in Navarre, ruling his small kingdom. But even if he were allowed to return, he doubted if Margot would share his enthusiasm, or even agree to accompany him. And now his life was inextricably tied to hers. She was more attached to her family than she admitted even to herself, he thought. She spent little time with him, and the single moment of honesty between them before the horror of St. Bartholomew's Eve seemed to have evaporated along with any naïveté he still harbored. He suspected she might be almost as mystified as he as to what their future might bring.

On especially idle days Henry let himself dream of leading all of France. Even with his feelings of inadequacy due to his captivity, it was not difficult to see himself as more capable of ruling than any of the Valois brothers. They all seemed more interested in the intrigues at court than in the business of managing the country. He didn't know if he was more shocked by their disinterest or their ineptitude. He began to spend a great deal of time writing to heads of state across Europe carefully explaining his position and hoping they would understand his need to dissemble.

No one suspected Henry's treasonous daydreams since he filled his days with the activities expected of a courtier: gambling, sporting, and sexual dalliance. As the months rolled by, his capacity for enjoyment seemed boundless and he was amiable with everyone. He was pleased to see Catherine de Medici gradually begin to relax, and he purposefully confused her more by cultivating the friendship of

*Death toll varies from reference to reference.

the duc de Guise. These cousins by blood but not of religion played boules together daily, and it appeared that Henry was ignorant of the Guises' role in Coligny's death. Henry seemed neither to remember his past nor to be planning for the future, amusing the young with his banter and charming the old by his respect for their wisdom and experiences. He made friends easily and seemed to hold no grudges. The King of Navarre was becoming the most popular man at the Court of France as he played the role of a nonchalant nineteen year old. He resembled his father physically more than his mother, and he knew this played to his advantage in this game. By the time a year had passed, everyone assumed the son favored the father's opportunistic ways as well as his physiognomy.

Henry yearned at times for a real friend. Such hypocrisy was hard work. If he and Condé were together too often it aroused suspicion, and it would be unacceptable for him to fraternize with the few remaining Huguenots in the city. In fact, few dared to call themselves Huguenots outright.

Margot often occupied herself elsewhere, which bothered him more than he cared to admit, and he found his sexual appetite no less demanding than before his arrival in Paris. Having noticed a kitchen wench who pleased him, he set out to capture her attention. She had large dark eyes, rimmed with heavy black lashes, and a most inviting swing to her hips. She had smiled at him just this morning as he'd purposefully passed through the pantry. Needing no other invitation, he wandered down to the kitchens for the second time that day. There sat his prize perched on a stool, hastily cramming a tart into her mouth.

"May I have a bite?" he asked. She grinned and held out what was left. He took it from her clasp with his lips, licking her sticky fingers one by one.

"Delicious," he murmured. He offered her his hand and they walked outside with all the bakers', chefs', and servers' eyes upon them. Henry knew of a tack room in the stable that didn't get much traffic at this time of day. They wouldn't be long anyway. He pushed her in front of him so he could watch her undulating gait. She looked back over her shoulder at him and giggled.

"What's your name?" he asked.

"Nanette . . . "

"I am Henry of Navarre."

She giggled again. Of course she knew who he was. He directed her through the stalls, and she paused to pat the nose of a restless bay mare. Henry put his arms around her waist and pressed his body to hers, lifting her hair to kiss her bare neck. Pressing back toward him, she swayed her body gently. She must be only seventeen, he thought, but she certainly knew how to tease a man.

"Come, Nanette." He led her to the tack room and pulled her down with him onto the earthen floor that had been freshly swept and sprinkled with hay.

"You are an enticing little piece," he whispered. "It must get hot in that kitchen all day. You need to cool off, I'm sure," he said, beginning to undress her.

"*Oui*, monsieur." Her eyes laughed with him. She gazed steadily into his eyes as he ran his hands over her breasts and down to her thighs. She unfastened his breeches, and he lunged upon her, his lust demanding to be spent. As he stood over her, re-buckling his sword, he remembered a broken doll that had belonged to his sister, Catherine. He'd found it, thrown away, its limbs askew, under the hedge at home. He pushed the unwelcome vision aside.

"*Merci*, Nanette." He strode away, his mind quickly returning to other matters.

Henry and the king occasionally rode together on hunting expeditions in pursuit of hart, roebuck, bear, fallow deer, wild boar, hare, pheasant, partridge, and bustard, the choice of victim being so extensive as to often become a source of contention. Charles, more depressed than usual since St. Bartholomew's Eve, sought Henry's company and Henry responded tentatively to these gestures of friendship.

"I realize St. Bartholomew's Eve has changed nothing," Charles grumbled. "In fact, instead of the peace my mother promised me, I see the Huguenots assembling behind walled cities and into battle phalanxes. For every murdered Protestant, there is a younger brother to take his place."

"Yes, and I am sure you must understand they are angrier and more determined than the previous group, Charles," Henry replied. "The Huguenots were essentially Royalists before the slaughter, asking only for freedom of worship. I think that has changed now."

"Yes, I can understand that," Charles replied. "I have heard some Catholics are joining the Protestants out of disgust — you could even call it contempt — for a government that could have condoned such an evil deed as St. Bartholomew's 'massacre,' as the events of that gory evening are now called. I must admit I can understand their reaction. I've also been told this group is even questioning the concept of monarchy itself."

"Exactly," Henry echoed. And no wonder, he thought. It was clear to him that the St. Bartholomew Massacre was more of a political than a religious attack. But what should he say to Charles? "I've seen some of their literature," Henry continued. "It suggests the people have the right to take arms against a king when that king has proved himself to be an irresponsible tyrant. I've heard the word 'tyrannicide' bandied about by those who believe the monarchy overstepped its authority with the massacre." He realized these could be dangerous words to a man as unstable as Charles, but Charles evidently did not take it as a personal attack. For the moment, he seemed to trust Henry again.

"These people call themselves the Politiques, I'm told, and frighten me more than the heretics do," the king admitted. "I know the civil war in general has become more political than religious. I'm afraid, Navarre, that time has run out; I can no longer evade the problem of a rebellion in La Rochelle. They refuse to accept our choice of governor. This town, I believe you know it well, is particularly separatist, being both a Huguenot and a Politique stronghold. The Politiques have found Catholic leaders, Montmorency-Damville among them, who have agreed to ally themselves with the Huguenots. I shall have to secure La Rochelle or sustain an important strategic loss."

Henry didn't answer. He knew he would have to go; to refuse would be a tacit admission of treason.

LA ROCHELLE

1574

ON JANUARY 12 THE DUC D'ANJOU departed for the West with his army. Among his captains were the King of Navarre and the duc de Condé, who had been forced to fight on the Catholic side. For all practical and visible purposes, the Bourbon cousins had been sucked wholly into the Valois camp as a snake swallows its meal. Henry and Condé rode side by side as the French cavalry headed toward the coast, south of Brittany. Intolerable self-repugnance accompanied the months of hypocritical obsequious behavior, and for Henry the royal standards were a scarlet stain against the gray sky of mid-winter. The soldiers followed the Loire River, retracing the steps Henry's band had made on its way to Paris sixteen months earlier, with foreboding but hope.

"This act of disloyalty is hard to bear," Henry confessed to Condé. "I visited La Rochelle with my mother when I was a child. The people cheered us, and I remember how elated and warm-hearted I felt. I recall a lively and boisterous city and now, taking up arms against them, I feel like I am cheating my brothers and helping my enemies. I don't know if I can continue with this charade."

"You got us into this, Henry," Condé grumbled. "I must admit I am glad to escape the court, but I worry about leaving my wife behind. There are such undue familiarities between the gentlemen courtiers and the queen's ladies, and a license to joke and devise lewd things, that other nations cannot believe it. If some pimp or bawd arrives, if some ruffian or scamp capable of devising mischief presents himself, he is warmly received and in less than no time becomes a favorite. And what's more, ever since the Queen Mother has ruled over the kingdom, such a swarm of Italians has entered the court that many now call it the 'colony and sewer of Italy.' "

"Right you are, Henri. It is hardly a healthy atmosphere." But Henry really thought his cousin too much of a prude, more like his own sister, Catherine, or his mother. Condé was becoming a less sympathetic listener and he desperately needed someone to talk to.

As the king's retinue approached the city of La Rochelle, Henry saw in the distance the familiar blue and white harbor framed by its two massive lantern towers. An enormous chain connected the towers, and the people boasted — foolishly, Henry thought — that this chain could keep France safe from any intruder. On his earlier visit to the town, the Rochellaises had greeted him and Jeanne d'Albret with smiles and garlands of flowers. Now Henry would have preferred numbness to the desolation that gripped him. He suspected his soul must look like the dirty, crusty snow on the barren ground.

The Royalist troops set up tents about one kilometer from the city walls, a hostile guard against any friend or foe entering or leaving. Their goal was to free the city of the dominant Huguenots and their political allies, the Politiques, and to impose royal and Catholic authority on its citizens. The soldiers' fires, which burned day and night, became beacons of despair to the town folks' eyes. Ironically, the city did not have a chain on the side that faced France. Nevertheless, the Rochellaises bravely resisted the Royalists' assaults until spring, holding out with the hope of aid from Queen Elizabeth I of England, the strongest Protestant power in Europe. Finding an unusually large number of shellfish in their estuary that year encouraged the people's belief that they were receiving direct aid from God.

Henry drowned his sorrows as he usually did — with women. The guards at the gates always looked the other way when young women slipped in and out of the besieged city to the soldiers, making it easy for one particularly pretty little bourgeoise to come to him. Suzanne de Moulins was married to a professor of Latin and Greek. This poor cuckold was too busy in his study to notice the frequent absences of his flirtatious wife, who apparently preferred the tents of the battlefield. One day she had simply presented herself at Henry's tent flap, and it was quickly understood that Henry's virile advances were more exciting to her than her cozy cottage in the town. The soldiers whistled as they watched her cross the muddy fields toward Henry's tent. Having heard the signal, he came out to greet her and hurried her within.

"I was hoping you would come," he admitted, eyeing her greedily. She put her arms around his neck and kissed him. "That old fusty house was getting on my nerves." She licked his ear and he could barely restrain himself. He felt her breasts swell against his chest. She seemed as eager and aroused as he but he savored the moment, knowing how long and tedious were the hours of waiting for a military confrontation. He unlaced her bodice and she wriggled free of her clothes.

"And I would go crazy here if it weren't for you, my pretty," he replied. "Are you ready for my great pleasure rod?"

She responded by helping him remove his codpiece, and Henry pushed to the back of his mind Condé's recent nagging: "You shouldn't carry on so blatantly, Henry. You will lose the respect of your men."

"Henri, you are blind. I gain their respect for every filly I bed. Besides, pleasure is so cheap here."

"Still, Henry, our wives . . ."

"Ah, don't worry about Margot; I don't," Henry interrupted.

These irritating thoughts finally ceased and his lust took over. Suzanne lay beneath him, smiling, asking him, he believed, to dominate her. Here he was still all-powerful.

As Suzanne was leaving, Jean de Léry, a captured Huguenot clergyman who had requested an interview, was ushered into Navarre's tent. Henry thought Léry regarded Suzanne with a mixture of contempt and envy.

"Prince Henry, conditions in the town are worse than you can imagine," he began. The man's eyes were bright in a drawn and pinched face. He wore a dirty and torn cassock, albeit with remarkable dignity. "We cannot believe that you wish to destroy our city. You must try to end the siege. You are our only hope. There is hunger and disease and the dreaded plague has begun. The people are eating the hides of oxen and cows; the skins of sheep and other animals are substitutes for meat as well. The best way of preparing all kinds of skins is not to strip and scale them but to nail and stretch them out on a plank so as to scorch and scrape off the hair more easily. After this is done, they are soaked a day or two, changing the water frequently, and then prepared and cooked as desired."

"*Mon Dieu*, Monsieur, hush! You can spare me the details, my good man!"

De Léry babbled on as though he had lost his mind. "No, Sire, if you know the horrors, perhaps you will do something. People who are hungry will try anything, and the supply of hides and skins has begun to diminish. The more subtle and ingenious persons have begun to experiment with the use of parchment. This being a success, the rush is so great that not only are they eating blank parchment skins, but also letters, titles, printed and handwritten books, no difficulty being found in eating the oldest and most ancient, from 100 to 120 years old."

"You have made your point, M. de Léry," Henry replied. "I promise you I shall do what I can."

When the clergyman departed, Henry paced up and down in his tent. Most likely he had made an empty promise. He certainly empathized with M. de Léry's pain, but not having his own army made him as much a prisoner as the people of La Rochelle. *Ventre-St.-Gris!* What could he do? Pray? It seemed as though the litany of "God help me" was a constant background refrain in his mind. Tears of frustration clouded his vision. All the men who had counted on him now believed him the worst blackguard in the country. To deceive his friends seemed less serious than deceiving his God — but God knew he had no choice; his friends did not.

A rumor circulated that a young girl had slipped out of the town, along the coast and over to England to petition Elizabeth I for aid. But she was too late. By the time England sent help to the Rochellaises, Anjou had mustered the French navy into action. The French ships turned the English away from their shores, and La Rochelle was forced to capitulate or starve. For Henry it was similar to watching a friend slowly die. The French army was not in much better shape than the besieged city after the prolonged effort, with at least half the men dead or dying from dysentery, but this was no solace for Henry. A peace that both sides found unsatisfactory was finally signed in July. The Rochellaises were granted freedom of worship. However, they were the only people in France who had won this liberty. The treaty allowed only freedom of conscience to all other Huguenots in France, which was insufficient for the Protestants but enough to aggravate the Catholics. It could have been worse, Henry thought.

PARIS

1574

TIRED AND DISILLUSIONED AFTER many muddy months camped outside La Rochelle, Henry returned to the Valois court, swearing every day that his life was unbearable. He had survived but that was about all he could say for himself. He wanted to lead, not to follow; he wanted to proclaim his ideas, not pretend; yet month after month, he continued the shameful pretense he believed necessary to remain alive. Feeling isolated and desperate for a friend, he still mourned his old friend and advisor Coligny. But he dared not speak to anyone about his true feelings of disgust and disloyalty. Nor could he think of anything to do to change his situation.

Charles surprised Henry one evening by extending to him an invitation to the place the king loved most, his mistress's house. Their carriage headed toward the quarter known as le Marais. The streets were dark and crooked and lined with tiny houses tightly fitted within the city's ramparts. Their upper stories cantilevered outward over the street and gargoyles, carved on wooden beams that upheld gables, warned evil spirits away. Here and there, abbeys, churches, or important residences, built of stone and decorated with sculptured relief, crowded the clusters of little houses.

"There has been little attempt here at designing the entire city in the manner that is going on in Rome," Charles commented.

"I know this area used to be a swamp," Henry replied. "I've learned it was then converted into arable land sometime in the thirteenth century. How exciting the architectural development of Paris as a capital would be! Are there funds in your treasury for such a project?"

"I doubt it. Our coffers always seem low. But here we are." Charles indicated they had arrived and led them to a narrow, half-timbered house at 30 rue François-Miron in an inauspicious neighborhood. Charles introduced Marie Touchet, the Huguenot daughter of a minor court official. How strange, Henry thought, that the Catholic king would have a Huguenot mistress. Perhaps because of his love for this woman with dark hair and large brown eyes, Charles tolerated his cousin's Protestant beliefs more easily than the rest of his family. More likely, Henry surmised, since she was a woman of common birth, her religion and her politics were unimportant, an attitude Henry generally shared. Marie cradled in her arms her illegitimate son by the king, the future duc d'Angoulême.

"I am as close to happiness here as I ever shall be," Charles said, putting his arm around Marie in a cozy, husbandly manner. "I would prefer a simpler life without the responsibilities of wealth or royalty. It is your country simplicity, I think, that draws me to you."

Henry laughed. "I hoped I no longer seemed the country bumpkin."

"No," Charles said quickly, "I don't mean that. Perhaps it's your honesty which I admire."

Marie projected warmth and generosity, happily serving them a meal she had prepared and appearing proud to please her lover. She poured second cups of coffee during a contented comfortable silence. This gentle and domestic scene gave Henry more feeling of intimacy than he had experienced since his arrival in Paris.

"Henry, would you be willing to give your protection to Marie and our child when I die?" Charles asked. "I care for them and their welfare above all else."

"Of course. I am honored that you would ask me." He thought of adding "And trust me," but the words stuck in his throat.

The arrival of a royal retinue from Poland at court proved to be a welcome distraction that helped mask Henry's constant dissatisfaction. Their exotic presence owed its purpose to serve as an escort for their new king, the duc d'Anjou, back to Poland. Because of Anjou's military success at La Rochelle, Catherine de Medici had successfully manipulated her second son onto a European throne.

The entry of the Polish ambassadors into Paris offered a magnificent tableau. Fifty carriages, each drawn by four horses, with Monluc, chief ambassador, accompanied the Bishop of Posen, leader of the Poles, in the first coach. The entire populace of the capital hurried to gape at the novel and imposing panorama. Spectators hung out of windows along the route, and some feared that these houses, so laden with people, would collapse beneath the weight. The Parisians first gazed with admiration at the stature of the Polish magnates, their majestic carriage, their long beards, and their caps sparkling with rare gems. However, their scimitars, their bows and quivers full of arrows, their wide boots studded with spikes of iron, and their shaven crowns looked frightening. Indeed the Polish delegates appeared coarse, almost barbarous to the French lords and ladies. Of course, it had been Anjou's ability as a soldier at La Rochelle and not his urban sophistication that had convinced Poland the French prince could be their king. Catherine had assumed her son would do as she commanded, but persuading the Poles to accept him proved less difficult than coaxing Anjou to go.

Margot related to Henry how Catherine had received Anjou in her apartments. Henry could imagine the scene, with the paintings of all her children by Clouet, court painter to the Valoises, hanging on the high walls and the stink of the river's waters wafting through the open windows. He had noticed that the Queen Mother usually refused to sit down, as though aware that she had more persuasive powers standing. She was short but her bulk was a domineering spectacle. She would have been standing for her attack, he assumed.

Margot paced and mimicked her mother's low voice. "'Poland is the largest and most powerful of the Slavonic states,' she instructed her stubborn son, attempting in vain to garner enthusiasm. She pleaded with him, and said, 'After Poland only Spain is a more considerable Catholic power in Europe.'"

Margot laughed at her mother's discomfort. "But he only defied her. 'By the twenty-four balls of the glorious apostles, I won't go,' the Prince screamed."

"I can hear him now," Henry replied, amazed at Margot's acting.

" 'Your reluctance is tiresome and childish,' Mother chided. 'I refuse to listen to any more of your raving.' After an hour of argument, Anjou finally capitulated."

"It seems none of Catherine's male children ever really manage to counter her will," Henry observed.

Margot simply shrugged. It was all right for her to make fun of her mother, but she wasn't so comfortable with Henry's insinuating remarks.

Catherine arranged a number of ostentatious diversions for her guests. The grandest was a ballet spectacle, which welcomed them the first evening. The ballet, born in northern Italy, had become a theatrical form under Catherine's tutelage. Primarily employing Italian talent she had brought with her when she came to France as the bride of the future Henri II, her preparations were rewarded as the Poles marveled at the formal choreography. They declared the dancing of France could not be equaled by that of any king on earth. There being no such thing as a raised stage, the dancers performed on the ballroom floor with everyone crowded around to view, and at the finale the guests were invited to join in amid much posturing and laughter. With fascination Henry observed Margot as she impressed the visitors with her beauty and wit. Having welcomed them upon arrival, she appeared before them now, stunning in a gown of crimson Spanish velvet with a high organza ruff of neck wheels and a bodice spectacularly embroidered with gold bugle beads. The extravagant dress was further adorned with a gold and ruby necklace and her headdress of sweeping plumes and precious stones enhanced her dramatic style. His wife had rarely seemed to notice him since his return from La Rochelle. Moreover, her behavior with Alençon, supposedly her favorite brother, seemed markedly cool as well. Henry wondered if she were not just jealous over all the attention Anjou was receiving now and hurt that he too was ignoring her.

During the performance, Henry noticed Charlotte de Sauve, who flirted with him daily. Upon his arrival at court, he had been amused at how forward she was. Then he had learned that she was a member of the Queen Mother's notorious group of beautiful female spies and informants recruited to seduce important men at Court, and thereby extract information to pass on to Catherine de Medici. Now her voluptuous and appealing figure awakened his thwarted desire. A cone-shaped bodice pushed her heavy breasts up and largely out of the confining material, a very blatant advertisement, he suspected. Making his way to her side as soon as the program ended, he spoke to her softly, "The sight of you makes me cheerful for the first time in a long while."

Charlotte looked into his smiling face, where she discerned a hint of mockery in his eyes, making her uncomfortable. But as usual, she found his magnetic charm compelling. It was difficult to decide whether the long nose or light, heavy-lidded eyes dominated the face, but the eyes drew her in. His mouth held a quizzical amused look as if to say, "So, this is what life is all about, eh?" Charlotte obviously had flirtation down to a science and readily accepting his attentions, led him through the crowded confusion of the Louvre to her apartment.

LE PALAIS DU LOUVRE

THE NEXT MORNING DAWNED clear and cool. Henry's stomach felt like churned butter, as he knew that in only a few minutes he and François d'Alençon would bolt for freedom. Only with François's accompaniment could Henry pass the stable guard, and it would be easy to give Alençon the slip once they were far enough away. François seemed eager to do whatever would irritate his family, but Henry was somewhat surprised he was willing to incur the wrath of his mother. His fickle nature was a definite risk.

Henry held his breath as they took off, then laughed at himself. He used to hold his breath when he would play hide and seek with his friends in the Pyrénées, hold his breath until they found him, then shout with glee when he was discovered. They gave their horses their heads as they left Paris behind, the sylvan surroundings north of the city already a haven.

"*Pardieu*! Look ahead, Alençon. May the devil piss on the man who has betrayed us!

A number of the king's men stood abreast in the path before them.

"How did anyone know?" Alençon cried.

"I suspect you were not as clever as you should have been," Henry growled.

"That's not true!"

"Then I don't understand either."

The runaways were easily apprehended and immediately brought before Charles, who appeared slight and pale this morning in a black velvet jacket embroidered with gold and studded with pearls. He wore the necklace of the Order of St. Michael, which hung heavily on his concave chest. François fell upon his knees.

"I beg your forgiveness, Sire. If I tell you the truth, I am sure you will be merciful. You should know that the Huguenots are about to rise again. Navarre and I were on a mission to flush out any information we could to safeguard your throne."

Alençon was lying and Henry perceived that Charles knew it. Henry thought Alençon's pale thin lips and enlarged nose, as well as the perfumes he wore, revolted the king as much as they did him. Disgusted by this display of cowardice, Henry decided to stand his ground. No more pretense.

"I know nothing of such an uprising, Sire. I simply yearn to return to Navarre because I prefer the mountains to palace life."

Henry bowed his head under Charles's look of affection mixed with disappointment. Charles would know the latter statement was no lie. But he must be wondering how the man whom he had trusted with his closest thoughts so recently could stand before him now accused of treachery. He wants to doubt my guilt, Henry realized. The bond between them established in his mistress's home remained even now.

"You shall both be confined to the palace, but I shall not imprison you at present," Charles proclaimed. He waved them away as though weary with the matter.

Henry avoided looking Charles in the eye and was glad they had been brought to Charles rather than Catherine. *Mère de Dieu!* Was he becoming such a coward as to fear a woman?

Margot lay in the arms of her beautiful Boniface de La Môle. She felt the muscles under his skin with her fingertips, then blew lightly into his ear. Ever since she had learned his name was Boniface, she couldn't say it enough. "Boniface, Boniface, Boniface," she whispered.

"Eh, my nymph, what are you up to?"

"I am only showing you how delighted I am with every bit of you."

"Tell me something else, my Queen of Navarre, should I be afraid of your husband? Is he jealous? Or angry?"

"He doesn't care. He has his Charlotte and others, I imagine.

Ever since the king confined him to the castle, his dalliances are the court's favorite subject."

"He may have his Charlotte but still not like your being with me."

"Don't worry, Boniface. I doubt he gives me a second thought. And besides, he doesn't know the details."

"And it's the details I like," he said, cupping her breast with his hand.

"I also."

But Margot wasn't completely convinced Henry didn't care. He treated her very well at times and then suddenly with stunning disregard, which irritated her more than she liked to admit. For instance, the night of the Polish reception, he had not even asked her for a dance. His indifference was insulting! But then hadn't she set a free tone with him at the beginning? Catherine constantly badgered her about Henry: What was he doing? What was he thinking? But Margot honestly didn't know.

Vacuous days of courtly pleasure rolled by with nothing to differentiate one from another — until Alençon burst into Margot's salon one morning, when she was sitting for a portrait by François Clouet.

"At last! You can be separated from your despicable husband," he proclaimed gleefully in front of the artist. The subtleties of deceit seemed beyond his understanding, she worried.

"What do you mean? What has he done now?" Marguerite asked. She nodded to Clouet, indicating the session was over for the moment. She was dressed lavishly for the portrait in a pale lavender satin dress stitched with silver and trimmed with amethysts and pearls. The inverted triangle bodice nipped her waist and the skirt ballooned about eight inches from her hips before falling straight to the floor. It appeared that the designers were purposefully trying to mask the true shape of a woman's body.

"What has he done?" her brother exclaimed. "He insults you every night with Mme de Sauve. You are brave to pretend not to care, my sweet sister." He took her hand. "Mother has devised a clever scheme to trap the swine."

Oh, dear, now her family wanted to frame him. Realizing he could be in real danger, she quickly contrived a plan to help him and was a little surprised with her ready desire to rally to his aid. She liked his forthright ways and quirky wit, she thought. A young boy's devilment gleamed in his eyes sometimes, and she would feel herself disarmed. She had witnessed fury and fun from the expressive light beneath his heavy lids, but she knew never to expect cruelty, a behavior too often exhibited by members of her own family. And one day he might be the door to a powerful future for her.

"It is too wicked of him," she wailed to her adoring brother, almost managing tears. "How lucky I am that my family always helps protect my honor." François embraced her consolingly, stroking the back of her neck.

"I'll inform you as soon as I discover Mother's plan," he promised. Watching him leave, Margot reflected on her brother's behavior. She thought he sought her approval and favor because he always felt Charles and his mother were disappointed in him. She could use that need to protect her husband.

Hastily writing a note to Mme de Sauve, she hoped this lady's affection for Henry would make her a ready ally. But wasn't she Catherine's ally? Obviously Catherine planned to apprehend Henry in Charlotte's bed and to trumpet his behavior as treasonous. But perhaps they could outwit her, if only Charlotte would cooperate.

When Charlotte opened the note, she read the contents with growing surprise. What could Marguerite possibly have to say to her? Ah, Margot had cleverly deduced she didn't want to endanger Henry or herself. Without hesitation, Charlotte sent off a missive to Henry commanding him to come to her at once.

A page found the recipient outdoors on the lawn and interrupted a lackadaisical game of boules with a note on a silver salver, while everyone tried to see from whom it might be. Henry shielded the paper from inquisitive eyes, only increasing the curiosity when he excused himself from play. He hurried to Charlotte, remembering with pleasure how her chestnut hair had glistened in the firelight last night as he ran his fingers through the thick tresses. How convenient and troublesome was this palace living, he thought, having everybody under one roof where all could keep an eye on everyone else and notes could be sent within the hour.

"What's the trouble, my dearest?" Henry inquired, noticing her agitated manner.

"The Queen Mother plans to trap you here, possibly tonight. Margot has sent word that you must go to her apartment this evening."

"The serpent wants to crush me again, eh? Why won't she leave me alone? She is more perverse than her children and they relinquish their power to her. May she be afflicted with bleeding diarrhea!"

"Why do you call her 'the serpent'?" Charlotte asked.

"Whether she is referred to as 'the Florentine Woman' or 'the Serpent', you must have noticed that few indicate affection when speaking of Catherine de Medici."

"Well, now that you mention it . . . " she trailed off.

Henry noticed that Charlotte seemed genuinely upset, but he knew his political thoughts meant little to her. She was not particularly bright, with pleasure and lovemaking occupying her mind completely. She pouted like a child who has lost her best playmate. He must give her credit this time for recognizing the possible danger for both of them, but as she was part of Catherine's group of spies, he doubted if he could truly trust her.

"Do not fret, my love," Henry encouraged in a calmer voice. "This will blow over quickly, and I have you to thank for saving me from prison or probably worse. We will make up for this little 'inconvenience' later." He gave her a kiss, held her for a brief moment and departed.

Margot welcomed Henry warmly, knowing there was no need to elucidate a plan with him. Reclining on the bed in Margot's apartment, they talked little, each wondering what would happen. A painted frieze of vines and cupids encircled the room like a jeweled necklace — a choker, Henry thought. The windows, shut tight for the night to guard against dangerous nighttime vapors, faced the banks of the Seine. No sound seeped through the louvered shutters and as usual, Henry found the room stuffy and oppressive. They didn't have to wait long. About midnight they heard a key in the lock. The Queen Mother insisted on having a key to all her children's rooms, and she looked in upon a happy, conjugal scene.

"What is it, Mother? And at this late hour?" Margot asked in a natural voice. She has inherited her mother's art of deception, Henry observed, ashamed to have an ungenerous thought about his wife at the very moment she was helping him.

"I've decided I should discuss an excursion to the Huguenot graves with you," Catherine dissembled. "It is fine weather, and I think we should remind ourselves of the scourge that still persists in our country. Don't you agree, Henry?"

The woman is truly morbid and cruel, Henry decided, as her hard, blue eyes set in broad cheeks struck a note of terror in him. As always, her dumpy figure was cast in a black dress, her neck held straight in a white ruff.

"An outing with my beautiful wife is always a pleasure," he replied, looping his arm around Margot.

"Then we shall go on the morrow. At noon," Catherine announced.

When she left, Henry pulled Margot closer. "She has been tricked but has no way to prove it. I imagine this event will place me under even more suspicion now. Not only does your mother hate me and fear my potential power, but even more, I think she resents being outwitted. I wonder what she said to Charlotte when she didn't find me there."

"I don't even care," Margot declared. "And what's more, I think we should be lovers for several weeks."

"We might even enjoy it," Henry opined with a smile, easily adapting to the new situation. "I hear people are calling our marriage 'the scarlet nuptials,' Margot. It is true there was more blood upon our bed than even a virgin such as you might yield!"

"I do not find all your jests amusing," she chided.

"Joking aside, Margot, I now believe your mother had my mother murdered. To put it mildly, I never know whether I can trust you either." He had rarely spoken so bluntly, and thought her expression, after fleeting surprise, almost welcomed his honesty.

Drawing away from his encircling arm, Margot regarded him. She enjoyed being with Henry, but she wished his features weren't so like the craggy mountains where he grew up. Even his new beard resembled the rough mountain growth. "You know, La Môle wants to help you escape. He thinks that is your plan."

"Ah, he is a good man," Henry observed.

"I know," Margot smiled. "But I think I'd rather he not become involved with you. You are too risky."

"*Touché, chérie.* But probably not risky for you to help me, and you, I believe, could be good for me."

"Now it is my turn to thank you," she replied, pulling him a little closer.

Henry was afraid with every bite of food he took and vaguely ir-ritated that he must do without Charlotte for the moment. He knew the situation was also a strain on Margot, for though she didn't admit it, he believed she preferred La Môle's intimate company. Damn her soul! Why couldn't she be satisfied with him?

Sport quenched some of Henry's nervous energy, and at every chance, when allowed, he joined Charles and his men for a boar hunt. The forests near Paris were full of these vicious animals, as well as buck, badger, and other game. As diverting as he found the hunt, he still longed for the crisper air of the mountains, their vistas of high crenellated towers and the slate roofs of hamlets perched on steep escarpments.

One foggy morning the hunters surrounded a wild pig, drawing dangerously close. The angry beast made threatening rushes in every direction, the curved tusks brushing the horses' legs. The snorting of the boar and the whinnying of the horses mixed, becoming a dreadful cacophony of fear. Henry saw François take aim with his arquebus. Beyond the boar, the king was in the line of fire.

"Don't shoot," Henry shouted. With lightening reflexes he lunged from his saddle, pushing Charles to the side and causing them both to crash to the ground. Charles screamed with pain. Everyone rushed to him, forgetting the prey which darted into the brush. The king's pallor was alarming, but to everyone's relief he spoke almost imme-diately.

"Thanks to you, Navarre, I have only a surface scrape on my leg," Charles muttered between his teeth.

"Perhaps we should make a litter for you."

"No, I shall be able to ride. You 'missed' the boar, did you Fran-çois?"

"I didn't realize you were so close," his brother replied in a sulky and hostile tone.

The company fell silent on the return trip to Paris, the energy of the chase replaced by hostile tension. As they rode through the mercantile district of the city on the right bank of the Seine, Henry's stomach turned at the stench of rotting food in the gutters. The smell of smoke met his nostrils as he fought for a breath of fresh air. In the jammed shopping streets vendors hawked their wares and customers bargained over every price. The horsemen had a difficult time push-ing their way through the passages, narrowed by stalls added onto houses already shoulder to shoulder. Permanent eaves attached to the fronts of houses provided weather protection for the merchants who entreated the royal party to buy meats, spices, and roasted chestnuts as they rode by.

During the next few days Henry passed much of his time with the wounded king. François skulked around like a dog that had been reprimanded, seeking only the company of his sister. Henry and Charles spoke mostly of hunting and falconry, which interested the king greatly, and occasionally they would touch upon more intimate matters.

"Navarre, you know I care about you, and it grieves me you are so unhappy here."

"I am happy to be with you, Sire."

"Yes, yes. But you are made of stronger stuff than the Valoises, and I would like to see you follow me on the throne. My mother realizes this too, of course."

"*Sang du Christ*! Do not talk of such a thing, Sire, for these thoughts are dangerous for me. I do not consider such matters, for surely your reign will be a long and good one."

"No, Navarre. The Valois taint is in me. These coughing and bleeding attacks I suffer cannot bode well, and my strength is not what it should be for a man of my age. My mother is powerful, but she cannot stop us from dying."

"These are gloomy thoughts," Henry said. "Your accident has depressed you. But look. Here is something to cheer us both which I found on my night table. I have never seen such a beautiful book on falconry."

The two men eagerly scanned the book. When the pages stuck together, Charles licked his fingers to make them turn more easily.

"I will leave you with it for awhile," Henry said. "I want to look over some new horses in the stables."

Later that evening Henry again was called to the king's rooms by a distraught servant. Charles IX was vomiting uncontrollably and his muscles tightened in violent spasms. The doctors, obviously baffled at this sudden illness, conferred in hushed tones in a far corner of the room. Henry held Charles's hand and tried to calm him. With affection, he straightened the king's nightcap and rearranged his pillows. The book he had brought him earlier lay on the floor by the bed. A horrifying thought flashed through his mind. He didn't know from whence the book had come. Had it been placed in his own room to tempt him, not to falconry but to death? He had been overly suspicious lately, but he was still alive. Rushing from the room, he promised the king he would return within the hour.

Flickering flames from the wall sconces barely afforded enough light to see one's way, but Navarre fled through the shadowed passages like a frightened marmot in a tunnel. Coming to a halt outside Cosimo Ruggieri's door, he banged rudely for entry. When the dapper perfumer himself opened the door, Henry barged into the room.

"You murderer! You have poisoned the book!" Henry accused.

"I don't know what you are talking about," the Italian said, feigning surprise.

"Do not deny it," Henry seethed. Continuing in a harsh authoritative tone, he said, "The king is very ill and I know somehow it must be from reading the falconry book I so mysteriously found in my room and lent to him. From what I have learned about you and your friend Bianchi, it stinks of you both!"

Ruggieri paled considerably at this news but remained silent.

"If you give me the antidote, I will shield you," Navarre pursued relentlessly. "You cannot allow the king to die."

"You are talking like a wild man," the perfumer charged.

"Ruggieri, I will reveal what you have done if you allow Charles to die. And finally I would have revenge for the murder of my mother — whether it was you or Bianchi!"

"The Queen Mother will protect me from your foolish accusations!"

"Yes, she would try, but I do not believe Alençon, Margot, or the king's ministers would accept this. They would tear out your evil tongue and hand you up for the vultures to eat."

Ruggieri winced. After a prolonged silence, he finally spoke. "I imagine you know of Nostradamus's Oracle."

"Certainly," Henry replied. "But I do not understand it. Nor do I put any faith in fortune telling. *Ventre-St.-Gris!* One must make one's own future."

"Ah, but I understand it," Ruggieri said confidently, "and now I am sure that one day you shall be King of France." In a haunting tone, he began to chant,

> *Au chef du monde le grand Chyren sera,*
> *Plus outre après aymé, craint, redouté;*
> *Son bruit et los les cieux surpassera,*
> *Et du seul titre victeur fort contenté.*

"You are the '*grand Chyren*,' for now I see it is an anagram for Henry. Your deeds will astound the heavens and you will not be satisfied until you have earned the title of conqueror. Yes, I am certain you will be able to protect me."

Henry stood rooted to the floor. Momentarily he felt wildly excited, but his reason quickly gained control. "Stop talking nonsense! Whatever the future may be, we must save the king. What was your poison?"

"Amygdalin. It comes from the pit of the almond. When I combine prunase, which I obtain from prunes, with almonds a reaction occurs which releases cyanide. The cyanide dissolves in boiling water and is neutral to the taste. I made it into a clear paste and put it on the corners of the book. That is why the pages stuck together slightly and it was necessary to lick one's fingers to turn them. Very clever, *n'est-ce pas*? It was meant for you, of course."

The Italian's eyes glowed with pride and delight.

"Of course," Henry replied sardonically. His mouth felt dry and his tongue stuck to his lips. "But I don't need an alchemy* lesson. What is the antidote? Tell me, can you make it quickly?"

"Yes. I have some of the necessary mixtures already made. I only need to combine them."

"Well, do so as quickly as possible!"

When Henry returned to Charles's chamber with the medicine, the poor man appeared exhausted. More people were crowded around him in consternation and lamentation.

"Drink this, my lord. I have obtained it from an old servant who knows folk medicine, and I have much faith in her potions. She has cured me many a time," he fibbed in order to cover the source of the potion.

Charles asked no questions of this weak tale and drained the cup. "It seems it is your turn to save my life again," he whispered.

Henry picked up the lethal book and took it to his rooms. Burning it, he watched the flames consume a fate that could have been his. As he reflected on his situation, the sweet smell of the burning poison lingered in the room, making his heart beat more quickly. Since Ruggieri was Catherine's tool, she must have been the instigator of this treacherous plot. She had almost been the murderer of her own son!

---

* Chemistry was not differentiated from Alchemy until Robert Boyle in 1661.

Sacrebleu! How intent she now had revealed herself to be for his demise. She surely would not release him from her lair if she interpreted the oracle of Nostradamus as Ruggieri did.

In fact, Nostradamus had correctly predicted the death of Catherine's husband, Henri II. From that point, the Queen Mother had befriended the famous astrologer, even enticing him to come to the Louvre to observe all the "Princes of the Blood"* when Henry lived as a youngster at court. Henry also knew that the Queen Mother had recently made Ruggieri and Bianchi sacrifice a lamb to examine its liver. When Margot learned of this experiment from Alençon, who had accompanied his mother, she had shared the secret with Henry. All three sections of the liver were found diseased, which, according to Nostradamus, prophesied doom for the three brothers of the Valois family. Henry truly did not believe in these mysteries, but the Valoises did. And now he feared for his life more than ever. He must flee from the walls of this veritable palace of terror. He must!

---

* The young men in line for the throne because of the rules of primogeniture, the system of inheritance or succession by the firstborn.

CHATEAU DE VINCENNES

1574

HENRY BEGAN TO CONCENTRATE on a second escape. Ever since the tragedy of La Rochelle, the time marched by like the slow beat of a funeral drum. He and Alençon might get away during a hunt — that still seemed the best way — aided by La Môle and a few other loyal souls. He did not dare reveal his true thinking to many, but continued to maintain an outward appearance of fealty to the Valoises. But once more they were betrayed, and once more, François broke down in a cowardly weeping heap. I cannot bear this pile of putrefaction any longer, Henry despaired. The very sight of anyone but Charles or Margot made him want to wretch. His stomach knotted as though to confirm his thoughts, and he longed for a clove of garlic to chew. In Pau he used to wear a garland of garlic around his neck as many of the peasants did, believing the root to be the best medicament for good digestion.

He was not to get off as easily as before, with only a reprimand from Charles. Again, it was Charles who negotiated that his life be spared, but this time the king ordered him to stand trial before the commissioners from the Parliament of Paris. Aware of Margot's writing finesse, Henry requested that she prepare a declaration of his innocence. He never could predict the workings of the minds of this strange Valois tribe, and her ideas might be a useful revelation. Only recently she had told him that Machiavelli's *The Prince* was her mother's favorite book, and Catherine had insisted that Margot study it well. Perhaps they could defeat Catherine with some of her own tricks.

"You must include how I came to Paris for our marriage, prepared to love and serve the royal family," Henry instructed his wife.

"Then describe the perfidy of the St. Bartholomew Massacre that followed, and ask them to remember with what loyalty I served by the side of Anjou at La Rochelle. Heaven knows how difficult that was for me!"

"I sympathize, Henry. But if you were truly loyal, you wouldn't want to leave."

"Loyal to what? Valois perfidy? Is it loyal to threaten my life?"

"No. I will try to help you."

Henry thought she seemed pleased to have been asked.

On the day of the trial, Henry spoke with feeling and conviction. In conclusion, he explained his recent efforts to escape:

"Seeing that my enemies had such influence with His Majesty as to make my efforts powerless to dispel the distrust that he mistakenly had of me (despite the fact that I have twice probably saved his life), I believed as true the rumors that had been circulated that there was an intention to harm me. Because of this fear, Monsieur le Prince d'Alençon who heard them as well as I, told me of the plots that were framed against him, and I told him of those against me. Aware that His Majesty's suspicions grew day by day, and having received fresh news of the harm that was intended to us, M. d'Alençon determined to escape from this danger and to flee in order to safeguard his life. I promised to accompany him and from thence to go into my own lands for my own safety, as well as to reestablish order in Navarre, where, during my absence, I have not been obeyed. When we were on the point of departure, word reached us that His Majesty was aware of our plans and thus we were called into his cabinet where we told him all we knew. There he assured us of our lives and told us that he would take things in hand so that we would have no cause of complaint in the future.

"Since then, while we were in the faubourg St. Honoré, we heard the same alarms as before and were told that we were going to be taken prisoner to the Bois de Vincennes . . . Upon hearing this, I resolved to accompany him and to withdraw into my own lands for the same reasons that I have indicated before. This is all that I know, and I beg you to judge whether I have not had just and manifest reasons for my departure."

Henry had reversed the roles very cleverly, sounding more like the accuser than the accused. But all this brilliant reasoning did him no good. Charles was unable to withstand his mother's pressure this time, and Henry and Alençon were sentenced to incarceration in the

Château de Vincennes on the eastern outskirts of Paris. Built in the thirteenth century by Louis IX, the massive manor occupied the site of Louis VII's original hunting lodge. Its heavy looming towers filled Henry with dread, but at least he understood that fear of a Huguenot uprising had staid the Valois family from ordering a sentence of death for the time being. Somehow Condé had escaped notice for now, and he tried to figure out a way that Condé, still free, might help him.

Henry never had allowed himself to think about being locked up because the idea was so terrifying to him. To be without light or fresh air would surely drive him insane. However, at Vincennes, evidently because of who they were or because Margot was able to intercede somewhat on their behalf, the two renegades were treated fairly well. Their food was fresh and they inhabited a small room with a window. Henry did not dare complain about the rats that kept them company for fear his lot would become worse rather than improve. He was probably better off if he didn't remind Catherine de Medici of his existence.

Jailed but alive, Henry heard the fate of his accomplices, who were not so lucky. Boniface de La Môle was beheaded perfunctorily at dawn the next day. It was discomforting to think that his wife's lover had been killed for his sake, just as she had feared. He was glad he had not been there to witness her grief. What odd relationships could transpire at this court! A rumor traveled quickly to Vincennes: Margot, sick with sorrow, had done her lover's bidding and obtained his head from the executioner, vowing to keep it with her always. Henry was sick with shock upon hearing she had decorated the eyes with jewels before putting the gory trophy away. Where would she keep it? he wondered.

Margot astonished him with a visit the next day. When the guards ushered her into his cell, she began wailing, "Oh, Henry, this is more than I can bear." She sank into a chair supplied by the guard.

"Please accept my condolences, Margot. You were right that I was too great a risk, *ma chère*, and I know you will miss him. It is horrible but not surprising, I am afraid." He noticed that her eyes were still red-rimmed but couldn't help thinking it would not take his wife long to find another lover. "Black does not become you as do the brighter colors, my love. I hope you will not remain in mourning too long."

"I miss you, Henry, and pray we can get you out of here soon."

"Believe me, I hope so too! This is even too simple for my taste," he quipped. He regarded the bare stone walls, his cot, and the pissoir ruefully. "I am happy to find you so affectionate. But tell me, Margot, is it true what I hear? That you have preserved La Môle's head?"

"Yes, of course. I have preserved his beauty."

"*Ventre-St.-Gris*, you needn't do that for me!" Henry laughed, but his chuckle sounded macabre even to his own ears.

"I don't usually do for you what I do for my other lovers!"

"We shall have to change that, don't you think, *ma chère*?" He smiled at her but the thought of her recent ghoulish behavior jarred him.

"Perhaps," she responded.

During his days in prison Henry had more time to meditate than was his wont. He began to feel sorry for himself, but then remembered St. Bartholomew's Eve. Hadn't everything looked hopeless then? Now he had cut himself off from his fellow Huguenots by his deceitful charade. What in God's name could he do? His thoughts continually returned to his wife, and he shivered, thinking that if she were to bear him an heir, her family might want to kill him. They would no longer have use for him.

When he requested it, Margot had written the apologia for him and at every crisis she had agreed to help him. Her beauty both soothed and excited him, and the nights they had spent together had not been without their pleasures. However, as a matter of choice, they did not seek one another's company. Only when the situation demanded it did they spend time together. Why? She was a Catholic, but surely this was not what stood between them. Obviously she was willing to forward his interests, for she identified his future with her own. He was grateful to her, but this did not constitute feelings of love. Perhaps too many basic temperamental differences intruded. For instance, he was repulsed when he witnessed the perverse relationship between Marguerite and her brother Alençon. Also, at times, she seemed so complicated and eccentric that he became irritated with her. It didn't really matter though, he thought, since she allowed him his freedom, but he did wish she would not openly indulge in so many affairs. If she did conceive, how could he know the child was his? The licentious behavior condoned by the Valois court certainly could have striking political and practical implications. In any case, she was his only hope, and if the past three years had taught him anything, it was how to be a shrewd tactician and a calculating politician.

Henry also occupied himself with worry over the king's health. He heard rumors that Charles was in bed again, hemorrhaging subcutaneously. Although he was only twenty-three years old, at the trial Henry had noticed that the king stood stooped like a buzzard, his neck thin, his head bald. Yet he drove himself maniacally. When hunting, he remained in the saddle twelve to fourteen hours at a stretch. Chasing a stag for two or three days in succession, he would pause only to snatch a brief rest or a bite to eat. He blew the hunting horn continuously, hardly a wise occupation for one with a pulmonary condition, which the doctors proclaimed was his primary problem.

If the king died, Henry would be without an ally (weak as that ally had been) except for Margot. Catherine had made the error of identifying Henry with his vacillating father rather than his iron-willed mother, but he doubted she would make that mistake twice. His two attempts at escape within weeks of each other had put her on her guard.

The dreaded news arrived. Charles was dying, actually lying abed in the Château de Vincennes, where he had come for a hunt. On May 30 Navarre, imprisoned at Vincennes, was told the king requested his company. When brought before the king, Henry found him too weak to speak. The court's vultures crowded around the carved bed, so heavily hung with velvet and tassels and piled high with quilts it was difficult to find the king's wasting figure within. Knowing that the dying man wished to remind him of his promise to care for his beloved mistress and their son, Henry leaned close to him. Charles smiled.

"Cousin, you are losing a good friend. Had I believed all that I was told, you would not be alive. But I always loved you. I trust you alone to look after my mistress and our son. Pray to God for me. Farewell."

He must want Marie Touchet with him now, Henry realized, but understood it was better for the boy's safety that she not be here and that the child not be legitimized. The Valoises would destroy such weak prey all too easily. Henry clasped the king's hand, and whispered his assurance. Bowing his head, he wondered who could protect him now?

Two hours before noon the king died. Henry's sadness turned to desolation when he read the typical Valois hypocrisy the king had written the day before his death:

I have begged the Queen my mother, because of my illness to assume greater care than ever for my affairs and those of my kingdom . . . until my brother the King of Poland, who is my legitimate successor, should return. I have made my will known to my brother, the duc d'Alençon, and the King of Navarre, who have promised to follow and obey Madame, my mother, according to the love and devotion they bear her.

Alençon and Navarre were moved from Vincennes to the Louvre, where Catherine could keep a vigilant eye on them. She had even ordered bars be put on the windows of their apartments. Henry dreaded an audience with her but bowed to its inevitability. Since black was her color, these new days of mourning changed her dour appearance not a whit. When the call came, he knelt before her, awaiting whatever strange command she might levy on him.

"Rise, Navarre. You seem intent on leaving us these days."

"Yes, Madame, I am."

He thought she almost laughed. "But you know that is out of the question."

"I would think you would be as glad to be as free of me as I would be to be free of you." There was a gasp from those nearby who heard his daring remark.

"You are foolhardy, Navarre, and have a vile tongue in your head."

Henry felt only exhilaration that their argument was out in the open and continued in the same dangerous vein. "I swear to you that unless you free me, I will burn down the palace."

Suddenly he could no longer bear his past self-imposed hypocrisy. He risked throwing years of strategic tactics to the winds for the freedom of saying, at least for the moment, what he felt. He was somewhat puzzled and even disappointed when Catherine didn't rise to the challenge of his impetuous behavior. She only granted him a sardonic smile.

"Navarre, we cannot take your threats seriously. You, as we all, must wait patiently for the arrival of our new king from Poland. If you were not so hot headed, you would realize it is to our mutual advantage to work together for France."

"Do not expect me to work with you, Madame," he said and left without awaiting her dismissal. He was sorry about the king's death, but at least it had freed him from the close walls of Vincennes.

PARIS and REIMS

1575

"WHAT HAS CATHERINE HEARD from Anjou, now our own King Henri III?" Henry asked Margot.

"Mother received news of his departure from Krakôw in mid-July, but recent word is that he is still in Italy. She wishes to retire to Chenonceaux, which you know is her favorite residence, but she doesn't dare leave Paris until his arrival."

"*Mère de Dieu*, I wish she could leave too," Henry growled. Margot started to reprimand him but decided not to argue for the moment. Her tone instead was placating.

"Anjou is not the only one who is worrying her now. Alençon is making her increasingly nervous, for he is openly associating with the Politiques. He is doing it just to spite her, I believe."

"It appears her younger son has broken the umbilical cord at last," Henry observed. "He has a mean and treacherous spirit, that one! I believe his thirst for power is now greater than his need for security."

"Perhaps you are right," Margot admitted. "But you should not talk about him that way, Henry. Anyway, he ignores her authority, and she won't leave him alone."

"Well, she still manages to make my life hopelessly miserable. I pray she will be stricken with inflammation of the rectum!"

"Your bad mood is evident to everyone," his wife admonished. "Mother really does trust you more than Guise, you know. It would help your case if you were not so nasty to her."

"Ha! Margot, you must have forgotten recent history. It is impossible for your Mother and me to trust one another."

"I suppose so, but I find you both exceedingly tiresome," she fretted, her patience worn thin.

Finally, when the poplar leaves began to drop into the summer dust, Henri III arrived, his entry into the city of his birth more strange than triumphant. The people gaped at his foreign dress. His close associates appeared even more bizarre. Did the men in Poland or Italy wear earrings? Navarre greeted the new king with apathy, too disgusted to bother with him. He watched as Henri's effeminate behavior became more extreme and more overt daily. Henri's dandy friends, dubbed *les mignons* at court, competed with one another in outlandish dress, and the people began to complain more loudly about the royal extravagance. The treasury stood virtually empty, for it had taken forty days at a cost of one hundred fifty thousand crowns to place Charles IX in his tomb.

Because of international uncertainty, neither Venetian nor Florentine bankers, who usually lent Catherine money at 10 percent interest, were able to lend her the 700,000 crowns she requested. The merchant bankers of Lyon, frightened by the failure of the three chief houses of the city, would not even lend 300,000 crowns at 15 percent. So Catherine, not to be daunted, pawned many of her own jewels and withheld the pay of the army. Still, the king and his friends continued to spend a fortune on silks and laces, some actually dressing as women, which seemed to amuse Henri III.

The men wore short, baggy trunk hose or narrow close-fitting ones, gathered and reaching to the knee. The doublet was fitted in front with a "paunch," a hump stuffed with horsehair and wool and imported from Poland. It tilted the waist and belt forward in a ridiculous manner but at least had the practical use in the army of stopping bullets. Collars were high pleated ruffs starched with a concoction containing rice flour. The men tottered around on Grecian style shoes, which had a heel at both ends or a single heel in the center. The new king made it clear he did not intend to grant concessions on more substantive issues regarding the Huguenots, nor reduce taxation, nor summon the Estates, as the representative body of clergy, nobility, and bourgeoisie was called.

In November the court traveled en masse to Avignon, where Henry and Alençon took part in a ceremony swearing their allegiance to the new king. While visiting the Papal Palace there, Henri

III joined a *confrérie*, a religious society whose members engaged in processions designed to be public expressions of penitence, marching through the streets flagellating themselves.

Upon their return to the Louvre, Henry regarded the court scene with a mixture of disbelief and relief. Surely such a decadent family could not continue to rule one of the great countries in Europe. But this moping wasn't getting him anywhere. Hadn't he just been released from Vincennes? With this thought, his will to survive abruptly conquered his self-pity, and his bad humor disappeared. Just as the mud of March becomes the new smooth spring lawn, once again Henry became the cheerful, witty, affable person who pleased most everyone except the Queen Mother. But why was Margot so distant? It worried him, for he doubted she was still mourning La Môle.

The monotony of the days at court broke in January 1575, when the royal assemblage made the trip to Reims for the coronation and marriage of Henri III. Catherine had been telling everyone that her son's odd behavior would soon cease, but Henry doubted Henri III would suddenly grasp the responsibility of power after he was crowned.

Reims was an exhilarating sight even in mid-winter. The Gothic spires of the cathedral rose quickly to the heavens, meeting the falling snow. The sculptured figures which stood free of the architecture wore snowy hoods like monks' cowls, accepting the eternal change of seasons. In the earlier Gothic cathedrals such as Chartres, the sculpture was chiseled in deep relief but still clung to the stone from which it emerged. Here at Reims, the stone took on a life of its own, restless in its movement and vitality.

The beauty of the environment heightened the expectations of the crowd as all eagerly awaited the ceremony. They stomped their feet to counter the cold for almost the entire day as Henri III arranged and rearranged his robes and jewels to his satisfaction. At last, late in the day, the Bishop of Reims anointed Catherine's second son King of France and placed the jeweled crown on his head. It slipped and the priest tried to right it. Again it slipped and as he adjusted it, Henri murmured petulantly that it hurt him. All of a sudden the feeling of pageantry and hope fled, as when a child cries at his own birthday party. In the late afternoon light the sculpture outside the cathedral looked eerie instead of festive, and the crowd hurried home to avoid the evening frost.

The court remained at Reims the next day for the marriage of their newly crowned King to Louise de Lorraine-Vaudémont, a cousin to the Guises. Henry understood that this was yet another attempt by the Queen Mother to unite dissident factions and families, just as she had done when she arranged his marriage to Marguerite. Navarre and Valois, Guise and Valois. She believed she could control them all through marriage. But she had failed to factor in the weakness within her own family, Henry mused, as he watched Henri III arrange Louise's dress for the ceremony, taking more interest in her then than he probably ever would again.

Soon after the court's return to Paris, the Queen Mother had more to worry about than the king's idiosyncrasies. Margot broke the news to Henry.

"Alençon has fled!"

"*Merde*! How?" Henry asked with a mixture of fury and envy.

"He advertised he was to pay a visit to a 'certain lady.' Of course this is always a pastime permitted to a gentleman. After visiting the address given, he evidently rode far from Paris." Margot appeared extremely agitated and her color flamed higher than usual. "I hope he is all right."

"*Au Diable les yeux*!" Henry cursed. "Now Catherine will be frantic and France will be split by tensions with the royal family as well as by forces outside."

"You are just jealous," Margot accused. "Everyone is saying he was acclaimed by the Politiques, who eagerly joined him along the way. His supporters call themselves the 'Army of Monsieur.' "

"Of course I am jealous," Henry replied, "but even more, I am concerned for France."

Alençon paid no attention to Catherine's pleas to return, nor to the commands of his brother the king. Henry watched with some pleasure as Catherine, in desperation, began to chase about the countryside, trying to persuade the renegade to grant her at least an interview. Alençon drove them wild with worry, actually accomplishing little in the way of victory; but he was always buzzing around as a potential threat. Still, Alençon's freedom piqued him. How had that idiot succeeded where he had failed? In January 1576 he wrote a letter to a d'Albret cousin in Navarre:

The court is the strangest you have ever seen. We are always ready to cut each other's throats. We carry daggers, wear coats of mail and very often a breastplate beneath our capes. This King is as badly threatened as I am; he is more friendly with me than ever. Monsieur de Guise and Monsieur de Mayenne never move except with me. You have never seen me so strong. In this court of friends, I defy everyone. For the third time they have forbidden my mistress to speak to me, and they have reined her in so short that she dares not even look at me. I am waiting for the moment when I can give battle, for they say they will kill me, and I wish to strike the first blow.

Finally, Henry decided not to wait any longer. He would take advantage of Alençon's diversionary tactics. Whom could he possibly trust? Théodore Agrippa d'Aubigné, his first gentleman of the bedchamber and a survivor of St Bartholomew's Eve, had been one of his closest boyhood friends in Navarre. He liked to write poetry and entertained him endlessly. Aubigné certainly could be depended on. In fact, now that he'd decided, he couldn't wait to tell his friend that he was not the traitor he'd led everyone to believe.

As soon as he found Aubigné alone in his room, he revealed his plan to escape. "I am ready to join our Huguenots again," he declared with jubilation barely hidden in his voice.

Aubigné's dark eyes held Henry's gaze for a long moment. Then he suddenly embraced the man he'd always considered his king. "That is not hard to believe and wonderful news. Your men are still awaiting your return."

"It is true, Aubigné! It is true!" Henry strode about the room with renewed exhilaration. "We shall return to Navarre. But who else will be trustworthy?"

"De Roquelaure*, certainly."

"Ah, my master of the wardrobe. Tell him to be ready to go. I certainly must have his filthy mouth along. I would sorely miss his scatological tales."

"And you will want Condé."

"Of course."

---

*Antoine de Roquelaure, Baron, fellow Gascon, and friend of Henri IV.

Yet, for eight days in a row after this conversation, Henry went hunting as usual. On February 6 he again formed a hunting party to go to Senlis, asking the duc de Guise to join him. Guise sent his regrets at the last moment, and Catherine was still away chasing Alençon. At last, Henry had his chance. There must have been a traitor somewhere, who at least suspected Henry's plan, for the king was warned. Aubigné, who had remained at court as a decoy, heard the alarm. He rode at once for Senlis and did not bother to dismount before telling Navarre, "The king has discovered your plot."

With Aubigné, Condé, Roquelaure, and two more trusted friends, Henry turned his horse's head westward. "*Allons-y!*" he shouted. They rode without speaking or looking back for hours. Henry knew he would lose his head if he were caught this time. Henri III was not the friend Charles had been, and Catherine could not be expected to excuse him again. At last, as he crossed the Loire into his own Kingdom of Navarre, Henry said to his companions, "God be praised who has delivered me. I'll never return unless I'm dragged."

For the moment he had forgotten he still had a wife in Paris.

NAVARRE

1575

LIBERTY AT LAST! THE FRESH clean smell of the country-side intoxicated him like the Jurançon wine with its aroma of peaches and apples that he so loved from this area. A life of duplicity and suspicion lay behind him and in its place, the exuberance of freedom invaded his senses. He wanted to throw his arms wide and run like a wild stag. The forests near Paris were not so dense as here in Navarre, but still, he had felt stifled in the Bois de Boulogne. He began to hear and identify birds again — black-capped warblers, chaffinches, and blackbirds — and realized the city's songs had not touched him.

As word of his escape spread ahead of him, men and horses wait-ed for him along the road, men and horses who pledged their loyalty to him. Henry had not expected that men would flock to him so soon, and he was touched to the point of tears. As he headed south-west toward Saumur, the first Protestant stronghold along his route, he felt proud and light-headed with excitement. Looking over his fellow Huguenots, he saw they weren't a ragged bunch at all but neat and alert. Ready at a moment's notice, they had left their homes to join him. But how would those in Béarn receive him, those whom he had patently betrayed? And what were his plans?

Clarifying sunlight matched his optimism. But he must not be fooled again. First and most obviously, he must be constantly alert. Although he had escaped, most likely his life would still be in danger. If he managed to survive, he would work toward solidifying his rule in Navarre and on a grander scale, ending the civil war in France. Yes, he could even think of that. When his little band stopped for a rest, he tried to assure all who rode with him.

"I weep at this evidence of your faith. What I did at court was not with the consent of my conscience. I was trapped, but constantly waiting and watching for this moment to join you."

As the months passed, men cheered and waved their banners. How many times in captivity he had dreamed of such moments! He found it difficult to hide his emotions, and welcomed a chance to speak in private with Aubigné.

"This reception has been beyond all my hopes. At times I did not even dare to dream. Yet I know I will need all my persuasive powers in the coming months to convince my people I am genuine, for I have just spent the last four years at the Louvre presenting an opposite view of myself."

Aubigné, though even shorter than Henry, was a strongly built man whose presence demanded confidence. Henry was impressed by his intelligence and often laughed at Aubigné's biting humor, which destroyed those he disliked. Yet even this man could be set down by Henry's quelling look of anger or a command. His loyalty to Henry seemed total.

"I will help convince them," his friend answered. "It is the answer to my prayers that you are free to lead us again. A letter to the lords of the South is a necessary and important first act, I believe."

Henry sat down to write to these men immediately:

> My foremost desire is for the peace and tranquility of this realm, and particularly for those of the Religion. I beg you and your friends to muster horses and arms and to join me, for the times are too urgent to remain at home. I assure you that my word is trustworthy.

As Henry proceeded southward from Bordeaux, he followed the river Garonne's verdant valley. The river was hidden from view by a curtain of poplar trees, and the fruity aroma of the apple and peach orchards intoxicated him as much as the wines his retinue purchased along the way. For weeks there were no more serious problems than bee stings, almost lulling Henry into a state of euphoria. He would stay here a while and stabilize his kingdom. There were many towns to visit and many souls to secure.

NERAC

1576

KEEPING IN TOUCH WITH THE news of the royal family, he slowly made his way to Nérac, his family's château in Guyenne. While there, he learned that King Henri III had agreed to negotiate peace with him. In fact, the king had little choice since Alençon, Condé, and himself, with their growing armies, all posed a possible threat to the monarchy. Henry knew that Henri III had compounded his tenuous position by spending money on his frivolous bodyguard of forty-five *mignons* instead of the army, and the army needed munitions, not the fashionable uniforms which appealed to the king.

In May 1576, Henry received by messenger the terms of the Treaty of Beaulieu, also called the Treaty of Monsieur in honor of François d'Alençon. It was a weak olive branch but worth serious consideration. Henri III disavowed the Massacre of St. Bartholomew, which he said had been carried out "much to his annoyance." It pleased Henry that the property of the victims which had been confiscated at that time was returned to their heirs, and the Protestants were recognized as an important political and administrative minority. But even better, the Huguenots were also granted freedom of worship, except in Paris. The people of the forty-five towns allotted to be regarded as Protestant strongholds would be jubilant, Henry surmised, but most of the Catholics living in those areas would now feel compelled to leave. What a relief it would be for the Huguenots not to have to hide during their worship services. However, the Queen Mother still would not allow Margot to leave the court for Nérac.

Henry compared his feelings now to the moment when he had been forced to bow his head in the St. Michael's Day celebration. Force had done nothing to change his own heart, and he vowed to himself never to compel another man to change his religion. His own experience told him this was impossible, and perhaps there was some natural facet of his personality which tended toward tolerance. He must think more about that when time warranted.

Henry found himself turning to Agrippa d'Aubigné as he had once turned to Coligny. That wasn't so long ago, but it seemed like a decade.

"You have seen this treaty, Agrippa?"

"Aye."

"I am worried, for it seriously weakens the monarchy as an institution. But I believe we should support it because it is a victory for the Huguenots."

"Of course! Of course! We should back anything favoring the Huguenots! The Catholics' reaction to the agreement has been explosive. Picardy refuses to become a Protestant state, and the Romanists have formed a 'League' whose theoretical purpose is to maintain the rights and privileges of the Catholic Church. They have the gall to ban all the Protestant sects and they denounce all Protestants as traitors."

"I would wager that the League now must be under the leadership of the duc de Guise and his brother, Charles, duc de Mayenne," Henry replied. "Those two are as ambitious and unscrupulous as Satan himself. And of course Guise is still angry he did not win Margot. But hark, the League will be as dangerous for Henri III as for ourselves, and it would never have been necessary if the monarchy had remained strong. The degeneracy of our king and the ambition of Guise have split the Catholic cause."

"The Guises receive secret subsidies from Spain and are openly encouraged by the Vatican, I hear," Aubigné added. "They will try to expand their territory at every chance."

"What perils await us?" Henry wondered aloud. His initial jubilation at being free was eroding quickly with the threat of war. However, he signed the Treaty of Beaulieu on May 6, 1576, and forwarded it by messenger back to Paris.

Henry's joy upon returning to his land was palpable to his men. The Kingdom of Navarre was primarily the home of simple, frugal, and industrious folk, who either harvested the fish along the shore of the Bay of Biscay or farmed the sunny slopes of the mountains. Many lived near the streams meandering through rich green valleys, fed their flocks, harvested their grain, and pressed hearty wine from the grapes of their vineyards. The rugged style of life here suited Henry perfectly. He liked the château at Nérac and felt almost as much at home here as he did at the family castle in Pau.

Built on the left bank of the river Baïse, Nérac displayed a graceful charm. The land, cleared immediately around the house, sloped gently down to woodlands below. These woods, with soft shadows and filtered light, where Henry could indulge in his favorite sport of hunting, were full of game. It was tempting to fall into a life of leisure, but he knew he must direct his attention to the pressing matters of leadership. In mid-June he decided it was time to address his Huguenot supporters directly once again. Calling all his lords together in a small ceremony at his château, he formally abjured the Catholic faith and acknowledged his return to the Protestant church. Speaking to them honestly, he tried to express his true feelings:

"Religion is implanted into the hearts of men by the force of doctrine and persuasion and not by the sword. Being all of us Frenchmen, we should be able to live in Christian amity. Those who follow their consciences sincerely are of my religion, and I am of the same religion as those who are good and brave."

He went on to ask his people to observe the terms of the Edict of Beaulieu and to remain loyal and obedient to their lawful King, Henri III. In return, he pledged to protect them against those who wished to destroy them. He spoke:

> Let us then take a firm and needful resolution, Messieurs, to work for our own general conservation against the schemes and artifices of the enemies of our peace; and I swear before God, who is our Judge and who sees the depths of our hearts, that under the authority of my lord the King, I will uphold all those who are under my protection. I will, with the help of your counsel and that of the chief lords, as well as of all lovers of peace and tranquility, oppose all violence, mobs, and oppressors, and in so doing I shall spare neither my life nor the means God has given me.

A deafening cheer greeted his words, and Aubigné could barely hear Condé standing next to him. "It seems our Henry has a way with men, a talent he has kept well hidden these past four years."

"Now I invite everyone to join me in the dining room," Henry bellowed.

Henry enjoyed the life of the country gentleman in every respect, finding special pleasure in entertaining the seigneurs of the neighborhood at his table. An eight-foot-wide stone fireplace with roasting meats over a roaring fire, even though it was summer, backlit Henry. He took the carved high-backed armchair at the head of the table and pounded the back of the man on the nearest bench.

"Eat up, my Gascon friends! There is enough here for five times more of you."

Looking down the trestle tables crowded with 50 men and laden with 180 pounds of beef, 74 pounds of veal, 295 pounds of mutton, 13 kid, 9 turkeys, 200 capons, 11 rabbits, 10 quail, 18 partridges and 24 teal, he was happy. The amount of wine necessary to wash all this down was equally generous, and the pewter goblets from Holland were filled and refilled by roving stewards.

Henry leaned close to Aubigné to confide in him. Aubigné was becoming accustomed to such mercurial changes in his leader, and so registered no surprise at his now serious tone.

"Having been brought up a Protestant, I feel more at home with this religion, but the peace of the country seems of first importance."

"Yes," Agrippa agreed, "but the primary thing is that your men are more at ease with you now. You have done a good job of convincing them." Indeed, Aubigné constantly marveled at Henry's ability to speak of the ideal to inspire his men, while remaining grounded in the harsh realities facing them.

"I hope so," Henry rejoined. "I want Catholics and Protestants to live and eat together. I am determined to make this work here, for only with religious peace will I be able to concentrate on the administrative tasks this province needs. And my sister's presence here will help me convince the Huguenots of my loyalty."

Roving around the country in the coming weeks, Henry witnessed extreme poverty due to the ravages of war and a political situation unstable to the point of chaos. He began making speeches, addressed particularly to the common people, and soon he had their support. He understood them well and they sensed that his blunt, honest, and racy tongue was no façade. He was truly a man of the

Pyrénées, a Gascon. He loved, as much as they did, the inns with dark smoky beams, from which hung hams, chitterlings, garlic, onions, and pimentos, where one shared spicy stories and raunchy songs. His humane moderate policies appealed to the people of the South and soon, with this strategy, he restored Guyenne to a state of order and stability.

Henry preferred to stay virtually free of amorous ties for now. Fleurette had welcomed him back and proudly displayed their bastard daughter, now five years old. Henry often rode down to their cottage to visit them. It was easy to send little Jeanne outside, then dally with the mother as he wished. Fleurette made no demands, for she was only the gardener's daughter. But she was still young, desirable, and proud to be known as Navarre's mistress.

Without any depressing Valois family around, he found life gayer and lighter. In an exchange of letters with his wife, he heard how unhappy she was at court. Her mother kept her there, a prisoner as he had been; he suspected Catherine hoped Margot would eventually be the bait to pull him back within her serpentine grasp. No chance of that, he chuckled to himself. He sensed that the Queen Mother was as eager for peace as he but that she was sadly unable to control her weak son on the throne or the second son seeking a powerful place of his own.

Henry began to pursue efforts by the written word to ensure peace, employing Philippe Duplessis-Mornay* to write and disseminate his ideas. He argued that the wars of religion had virtually destroyed the country, bringing in their wake misery, poverty, and disorder. The so-called "heretic Huguenots" worshiped the same God as the Catholics and belonged to the same fatherland.

"As men, let us love one another; as Christians, let us teach one another; as Frenchmen, let us stand with one another." Henry had finally articulated his message.

---

*Philippe Duplessis-Mornay (1549-1623), French Huguenot and writer, who gradually was recognized as Henry's right-hand man.

THE NETHERLANDS

1577

MARGUERITE DE VALOIS WAS bored. The usual courtly pastimes seemed tedious and her friends dull and witless. Her husband had been only one among many lovers, but life at court had become strangely bland without him. He couldn't have taken her with him; she would not have gone. Yet he should have asked her, at least confided in her. François d'Alençon, temporarily back at court, discovered her, chin in hands, gazing out at the river. He patted her back and let his hand rest on her shoulder.

"Margot, I have a plan."

"You look feverish," she answered.

"No, I am serious. Listen to me." He drew his shoulders back and raised his chin in what could have been a mock regal gesture. "The Netherlands could be our kingdom."

Margot raised her eyebrows but allowed him to continue.

"Listen! The people of the Lowland territory have begged France for protection against the encroaching power of Spain for many years. You know our brothers have not been willing to become involved because it is a Protestant country, and England considers the Netherlands her sphere of influence."

"As far as I know, François, none of those things have changed. Any meddling on France's part would lead to a direct confrontation with either Spain or England, with either the Catholics or the Protestants — or perhaps even both!"

"You are always so practical. And that is why I need you. I have returned to Paris only to put this plan into operation. I think you could travel — be my emissary to the Netherlands and try to detect the people's attitude and our chance of success there."

"Which are very low, I suspect," she argued.

"I'm not so sure. More and more, rumors of discontent are drifting from their direction. We might propose replacing Spain's power there with that of Henri III."

Ridiculous as his plot sounded, she felt a stirring of interest as well as a desire to spite her mother. She would be only too glad of an excuse to leave the court and obey only her own orders. After all, her latest affair with Louis de Clermont, Squire de Bussy d'Amboise, had just cooled. Perhaps her brother's imperial dreams of personal glory were not impossible. And it would be more exciting than nursing a dying love affair.

"Very well, François. I will ask the king for permission to visit the spa at Liège today. That should be a perfect excuse."

When her brother put his arms around her, she allowed him to hold her in an extended embrace.

The king granted her request, but she was very careful to omit any news of her planned exploit in her letters to Henry. In a style befitting a princess, she began her journey into Flanders on the sixth of July 1577. Followed by ten maids of honor on horseback and six coaches carrying her trunks and other attendants, she rode through Picardy in a litter constructed of pillars, hung with ruby velvet, and embroidered with opal and gold. It was hardly an entourage designed to avoid detection.

She saw everything a tourist should see — the curious clocks at Valenciennes with their moving figures and melodies and the exotic topiary in the gardens. And she was careful not to forget her reason for being here. She adeptly turned the conversation with the leaders who received her to the Flemish reaction to Spanish rule, to Don Juan, the Governor of Spain, and more important, to their desire for independence. Surreptitiously she let them know her brother might be able to help them remove the yoke from Spain, and she believed her news was received with enthusiasm. Marguerite began to feel like a heroine, even envisioning herself as the liberator of the Netherlands.

When Don Juan of Spain finally welcomed her at Namur, she was her most charming, most deceptive self. Indeed, he could not have wished for a more tantalizing partner through four days of royal festivities. So smitten seemed Don Juan that Queen Marguerite would never have guessed he suspected her of a thing. And would have never called herself naïve.

"I have always loved your Spanish dances," she flirted. She had to look up to him for he was six feet tall or more. "They speak of restrained passion, do they not?"

"Indeed they do, Your Highness, but it is a passion which loses its restraint when a woman is very beautiful."

Smiling, she posed herself, ready for the music to begin again.

After Namur she left for six weeks of limitless pleasure seeking at Liège, where her visit came to a sudden and unceremonious halt when she received a letter, secretly delivered, from Alençon:

> My dearest sister, I am grieved to tell you that I have learned from my spies that the Spanish are suspicious of your presence and are already laying plots for your capture. You must flee the country at once. Your loving, Alençon

Everywhere, Margot found the people suddenly in arms. She told herself not to panic and laughed aloud when she discovered herself enjoying the critical turn of events; the edge of danger could be a stimulating place to be. At Huy, a tiny town on the Meuse, halfway between Namur and Liège, she lay all night in the public inn, listening to the shouted threats of the drunken villagers who had surrounded the building. Surely they wouldn't harm the Queen of Navarre. But at Dinant she learned that the gallant Don Juan, who had charmed and flattered her and whom she had flattered and charmed, now had plans for her capture.

With furious and desperate haste, she abruptly abandoned her trunks and litter and took to horseback. Near the château at Cambrésis, her party, reduced to a few armed guards, barely eluded pursuit by a group of Huguenots, now also alerted to the plot. Riding all night, she reached Le Catelet and safety early in the morning. Weary and shaken but triumphantly back on French soil, she declared herself more determined than ever to give her support to Alençon.

It took several more days to reach Paris, but the stimulation of the past weeks seemed to have revived her spirits. Life apparently held previously unsuspected melodrama for a willing participant. She looked for Alençon immediately upon arriving at the Louvre.

"You mean you aren't angry with me?" her brother asked. "The situation appeared disastrous. I was afraid you would be killed!"

"Well, I wasn't. And of course I'm not angry with you. We fooled them all for a while, François. We really fooled them — Huguenots, Spanish, Dutch — and our brother, the king! I loved it. How exhilarating it was being chased!" she laughed.

"Then you mean you would help me again?"

"I'm ready for any other diversion you have in mind." Alençon shook his head in adoring wonderment.

PARIS

1578

MARGOT HELD THE ROPE FROM a window in her room while Alençon, who still wished to avoid a direct audience with his mother, descended to safety and freedom. Now what to do with the rope? When she tried to burn the incriminating evidence, it only produced a black cloud of smoke which she feared would eventually seep under the door of her room. Finally she buried the charred remains under her mattress.

Alençon's flight was discovered within the hour, and the Queen Mother immediately arrived at her daughter's door. "Where is your brother?" she demanded.

"I haven't seen him today," Margot casually replied.

"Do not lie to me, you little vixen." Catherine slapped Margot soundly across the face. "Your room will be searched. Your behavior is extremely disappointing to me."

Margot prayed under her breath but the rope was easily discovered.

"I did not put it there," Margot sulked. "Someone obviously wanted to implicate me."

"I don't believe you. You will not leave the palace anymore without an escort by my guards. Perhaps you should be with your husband instead of left here to play dangerous games with your brother. Indeed, I am surprised you did not present us with a baby before Henry so rudely departed."

The nonsequitur jarred her but she quickly rallied to the charge. "Do not criticize so fast, Mother. You only need remember that you 'waited' a long while before giving France an heir."

"Guard your tongue, Marguerite, or you will find your freedom even more hampered."

Margot now longed to leave the capital and join Henry. Hearing of his successes in Béarn made her wonder if she should not have followed him earlier. Writing in her journal alleviated her ennui somewhat:

> At the court there is nothing but talk of war; in order to render Alençon more irreconcilable with the Huguenots, the King appointed him leader of one of his armies. Genissac* came to tell me of his rude dismissal by the King, and I went straight to my mother's antechamber, where the King was present, to complain of the way in which he had abused me up to that time, he having always prevented me from going to join the King, my husband . . .
>
> I told him I had not married for pleasure nor of my own free will; that it had been the will of King Charles, my brother, of the Queen, my mother, and his own. Since he had given me to Navarre he could not prevent me from sharing his fortunes; that I wanted to go to him, and if he would not permit it, I would escape in whatever way I could and at the risk of my life.
>
> The King answered, "It is not the time, sister, to importune me about this permission to leave. I admit what you say. I have purposely delayed granting it, because since the King of Navarre has become a Huguenot, I have never thought it well for you to go.
>
> What we are doing, the Queen and myself, is for your own good. I intend to make war on the Huguenots and to exterminate this miserable religion which has done us so much harm. For you, who are a Catholic and my sister, to become a hostage in their hands would create a most impossible situation. And, who knows, but so as to inflict an irreparable indignity on me they might take your life in revenge for some injury they may suffer at my hands. No, you shall not go.

But as Margot suspected, the king was only beating the war drum for her ears. Navarre was in much too strong a position for

---

* A Huguenot emissary from Henry of Navarre to the Valois court, whose commission was to press the Valoises to release Marguerite to her husband.

the weakened monarchy to attack. She would finally have her chance to join her husband in September. The Queen Mother, realizing that any lasting peace depended on the goodwill of Navarre at this point, decided a trip to the South was necessary in order to speak with him. And Margot, understanding that total acquiescence was her only hope of accompanying her mother, agreed to try to mend the rift between Navarre and the court of France. She wrote in her usual stagy style in her journal:

> I am determined to do everything in my power for him (Henri III) in whatever will not be prejudicial to the greatness and maintenance of my husband . . . in order to persuade him (Navarre) always toward peace and to bring him to conform himself to the will of the King . . . in whatever will be for the peace and tranquility of the state. I will do this for there is nothing dearer to me than this; for I would prefer death to war.

NERAC

1578

IT HAD BEEN ALMOST TWO years since Margot had seen her husband, and she was a bit nervous about the proposed meeting. Clearly his influence had grown in the interim, for her mother found it necessary to bring along several of her court beauties to entice and mollify Henry. Insulting! Margot thought. Obviously her mother believed she had lost some of her bargaining power. Henry's old flame, Charlotte de Sauve, was part of the company, but there were younger temptations too, in particular a Cypriot lady-in-waiting called Dayolle.

The royal enfilade heading south consisted of three hundred persons. Traveling with the queens were Michel de Castelnau,* ambassador to the court of Elizabeth I, Claude Pinart, Catherine's secretary of state, and Guy de Pibrac,** the president of the Parliament of Paris. Only her trusted advisor, Bellièvre,*** remained at court to guard the government. This time Catherine was determined to spare no effort to bring Henry into her sphere of influence.

Besides these important personages, there were grooms, coachmen and hostlers, and of course the Queen of Navarre needed her personal lackeys. Numerous minor nobles, always stuck like leeches

---

* Michel de Castelnau, Sieur de la Mauvissière (c. 1520–1592), French soldier and diplomat, ambassador to Queen Elizabeth I.
** Guy du Faur de Pibrac (1529-1584); also see footnote, page 135.
*** Pomponne de Bellièvre (1529-1607), a French statesman who served on many diplomatic missions for Henri III and the Catholic cause, and later as chancellor of France for Henri IV.

to the court, accompanied the royal caravan, as well as muleteers to care for the litters and wagon men to lead the unwieldy wagons loaded with tableware and kitchen utensils. The women could not imagine traveling without head cooks and second cooks, fishmongers, salad chefs, bakers, carpenters, goldsmiths, haberdashers, leather workers, spur makers, tailors, hairdressers and barbers. The pace of their city on wheels proceeded very slowly toward Guyenne.

Margot exhilarated in the feeling of having an important destination. The peasants, gaping at her from the roadside, reinstilled her belief in her beauty and influence, which she had feared forever lost before the Spanish escapade. Yes, the future did hold promise. Catherine, however, ground her teeth with discomfort as her obese body rocked with the carriage. Finally, after two months of travel, in mid-October, at la Réole, the two queens dismounted before Henry, now twenty-six years old. He greeted them graciously, but Margot felt a distinct lack of warmth in his embrace. In fact, he exhibited more enthusiasm as he ran along the courtly train greeting friends with slaps on the back. She thought his forward easy manner lacking in politeness and certainly kingship. Noticing with distaste his usual disarray, she saw he had not even bothered to button his boot tops.

The Queen Mother presented Henry with a watch, the first ones having been recently produced at Nuremberg. Despite her gifts and pleas, Henry avoided negotiations, allowing only the brief encounter. Catherine decided to lighten her pressure momentarily and arranged a detour to the southern cities to disburse a little royal patronage. Therefore, it was not until December 15 that Marguerite de Valois and Catherine de Medici made their formal entrance into Nérac to meet Henry and Catherine de Bourbon. Margot remembered Henry's mother from his family's visits to court when they were both children and more recently, from her visit before the wedding. As an adult, Catherine de Bourbon reminded her of Jeanne d'Albret — the same angular frame, bony face and stern expression. She was not without friendliness, however, and Margot hoped they might get along well. At court, during her and Henry's essential house arrest, she had simply made it a point to avoid Catherine. Again, Henry appeared polite but formal. This was his home ground and this time she was the visitor. What would her life be like here?

Every room was warmed by a fire, stoked frequently by a rustic but hovering staff, although it was not as chilly here as in Paris. Henry had arranged a sumptuous feast for the welcome party. Braces of quail and pheasant by the dozen had hung until they were "on the turn." The nearby mountain streams supplied quantities of various fishes and the forest yielded delicate tasting thrush to tempt their gourmet palates. The Huguenots at Nérac became more and more shocked at the dissipation and extravagance in the days that followed, as the Valois visitors arranged nightly celebrations for their own entertainment. To Margot, the endless merriment suggested she might make a tiny Louvre of this southern château.

The small palace crowned a flat hill by the river Baïse. On the second floor a graceful Italian style loggia with thin, spiraled columns faced northwest, and Margot enjoyed strolling its airy length several times a day. Charming narrow columns with ornamented capitals and linking arches appealed to her sense of proportion, and she found it a pleasant and easy place to daydream. Planning for the spring, she spoke with the gardener about new fountains, orangeries, and groves of laurel to stretch down the slope to the ivy-covered riverbank. She had a stone bench placed just far enough from the water so that she wouldn't be splashed by barges passing down the narrow waterway.

The sight of the queen with her parasol reading by the river in the winter sun aroused great curiosity and wonder at first. Soon, however, the locals became used to her and some dared to wave, though Marguerite apparently felt it beneath her to return their greeting. The garden was joined to the right bank of the river by a little wooden bridge. Orange trees and laurel shaded the rustic bridge spanning tranquil gray-green water, and for a while she was pleased with redesigning the gardens. But she was not content to stop there and set diligently to work to refurbish the court at Nérac.

The château, though small for a queen, had style, Margot thought. The creamy stone, typical of the region, glowed in the afternoon sun, and the conical roof atop its single tower appeared simple but harmonious. She could dignify this place with her decorative flair, and this project occupied her for a good while. Henry humored her, doing all he could to embellish it according to her wishes.

"You will have tapestries from Pau to ornament the walls, and I shall order Venetian glassware ornately decorated with mother-of-pearl and gold," he promised.

Excited with her plans and decorations, Margot cheerfully chose exquisite mirrors with ebony frames and intricately carved chests to be ordered from Spain. Henry agreed with his queen when she decided she needed a silver urinal. He even allowed Margot to hire musicians — six violinists, two lute players — and didn't say no to a music master to train her chapel singers. Happy with his generosity, she also discovered Nicolas Léon, a well-known actor, who could entertain her husband with the broad farces he liked. When native talent grew thin, she brought troops of Italian players to add a cosmopolitan note to the court of the Béarnais.

No longer was Henry allowed to wear his hunting clothes in which he felt so comfortable. He succumbed to Margot's pressure and donned satin doublets, linen shirts she ordered from Holland, yellow satin breeches (she knew he always liked yellow), silk stockings, and velvet hats decked with feathers. His cloak was scarlet with gold and silver embroidery. He even moderated his language around her, but when she pressed scent upon him, he drew the line.

"I will not stink like one of your brother's *mignons*," he bellowed.

Directly down the hill from the castle, Henry built a platform at the water's edge where he bathed no matter what the temperature. Margot complained so much about his smell that he found this arrangement convenient and easier to bear than her barbs. When it was warm, like today, he liked to dawdle there and draw battle formations in the mud with a twig from a nearby oak tree. When he placed a lilac sprig behind his ear, its tiny lavender bells seemed to make his eyes shine even more. Whether shrewd, laughing, or dark with anger, the light eyes with wide drooping lids always dominated his face and caught his companion in their mood. His was a personality to be reckoned with, but he had not yet learned its power.

While the aristocracy was involved with balls, hunting, and court games, always veiling mutual suspicion with politesse, the populace was forever on the brink of civil war. Constant skirmishes between Protestants and Catholics arose, and small towns were captured and recaptured by one side or the other. The populace could not settle down to their lives as the leadership whipsawed back and forth between Huguenots and Papists. It wasn't only religious tenets that separated the groups. Huguenots living in nearby villages continued to be scandalized at the behavior of the visiting Parisians and vocally condemned their boisterous high spirits. The schism dividing the country was revealed daily to the leaders attempting to share the castle of Nérac.

One day, strolling back to the château, Henry unexpectedly met Catherine de Medici in the flagstone courtyard. She seemed determined to corner him.

"Henry, while my daughter has been busy improving Nérac, I have tried, so far unsuccessfully, to speak to you about cooperation. But all you seem to want to do is to evade me."

"Ah, yes, we both want peace," he offered, "but when confronted with the details, our little differences still remain, do they not?"

Catherine came as close to pleading as she ever had. "Yes, I'll admit this is painfully true. But Spain and England threaten France from without and Guise threatens from within. Even though we are of different creeds, we would present a stronger force if we were allies."

Henry appeared to contemplate what she proposed. In truth he was thinking about something she had said more than once: "I use every man as he can serve me."

"You should know, Madame, that I have only recently learned that M. Philibert de Gramont, Seigneur de Béarn and Navarre, whom I believe switches his loyalty between you and me like a dancer changes partners, has been in communication with Philippe II. I believe you and I should at the very least present a united front to Spain, don't you?"

The Queen Mother appeared surprised, even speechless for once.

"But," he added, "I am afraid, Catherine, that you and I will never be allies."

"I have come a long way for nothing," grumbled the aging woman. "And my sciatica will soon prevent any more peace missions."

"Madame, I believe you grow strong on this trouble! If you had peace, you would not know how to live."

"I have never appreciated your humor, Henry," Catherine replied.

The Queen Mother returned to Paris in May 1579 without learning or gaining much from her son-in-law. He had allowed his wife to wheedle affirmatives from him pertaining to interior decorating but had agreed to nothing weightier. Charlotte and Dayolle, who had temporarily amused Henry, returned to Paris with Catherine. Henry was sorry to see them go, but like all his women, they had not touched him deeply. Women were a pleasure to be sought and enjoyed, not unlike the pleasures of hunting. Marguerite, who had decided to stay and secured agreement for this plan from her mother, breathed a sigh of relief.

PAU

1581

MARGOT HAD RARELY SEEN HENRY so excited. They were on their way to Pau, his birthplace and often mentioned "home." Bringing his mount up short, Henry gazed at the castle towering above them, the heavy ragged clouds and eternal grandeur of the mountains forming a dramatic backdrop. He told Margot, just as his mother had recounted to him, "The castle was erected by Viscount Gaston III of Béarn as part of a defense plan. Military strategy was a subject which appealed to me and my head was always teeming with imaginary battles." As they crossed the drawbridge, the people recognized him and began shouting *Bibe lou Rey.**

"I suppose that means 'Long Live the King,' " Margot said. "What an odd sounding dialect!"

"It's not a dialect, Margot. It's Basque," he rejoined.

As they passed the huge, dark-red brick tower at the entry to the courtyard, Henry continued, "Brick was a relatively new technique of construction in the fourteenth century." This tower obviously interested him much more than the lower staircase which they presently entered. Margot looked up at the ceiling, rather prettily decorated with the letters H & M, representing Henry's grandfather, King Henry

---

* Béarnese is a dialect of Gascon spoken in Béarn (in the French department of the Pyrénées Atlantiques, in southwestern France). As a written language, it benefited from the fact that Béarn was an independent state from the mid-14th century up to 1620. Béarnese was used in legal and administrative documents long after most other Gascon provinces were incorporated into France. The French language definitively replaced Béarnese language for legal documents in 1789, after the French Revolution.

II d'Albret, and his grandmother, Marguerite d'Angoulême. Henry gathered steam with his monologue:

"Marguerite d'Angoulême found the castle at Orthez much too chilly and uncomfortable for a lady who read classical meter and was nurtured with every luxury. So she altered the castle of Pau, enlarging it with pretty rooms, terraces, and huge windows, all in the elegant style you now see. The work took six years and by 1535, this austere fortress was transformed into the present-day royal palace. It's quite magnificent, don't you think?" Not receiving an immediate reply, he pressed on. "Despite this, the queen was not fond of it and rarely stayed here, preferring the company of her brother François I to that of her husband, whose tastes and habits were too crude for her liking. However, her alterations had the effect of increasing the importance of Pau, and Henri II made it his capital."

As they wandered through the palace, Margot was inclined to agree with the former Marguerite. Pau was not a palace in her eyes; rather its narrow windows and dark high towers seemed like a fortress. For the moment, however, she kept quiet.

Henry was so clearly enjoying himself, and as much as she hated to admit it, she understood her fate was more dependent on him than ever.

Settling in at Pau, Margot winced as Henry slipped from his refined Nérac ways to his more natural, shoddy style. Since Pau was a Huguenot stronghold, Catholicism was outlawed, and Margot was forced to practice her religion in clandestine conditions. She complained to Henry frequently,

"I must hear Mass in a cold, small chapel only three or four feet in length and so narrow, it can scarcely hold seven or eight persons. It is cruel that you raise the drawbridge during the time of the service to prevent the townspeople from attending."

Henry listened but did nothing. On Pentecost Margot became especially angry when Navarre's secretary, the fanatical le Pin discovered her plot: feeling sorry for some local Catholics, she had managed to sneak them into the Whitsunday service. Le Pin arrested them all and Margot ran to Henry.

"I cannot bear this forbidding place another day," she wailed. "How can you treat me so unfairly?"

"That is the law here, Margot," he said. "I am trying to be patient with you, and you know I am making an exception in allowing you to conduct Mass at all."

"I wish I were in Paris!"

"Well, that is idiotic because thousands upon thousands are dying of whooping cough and plague in your beloved city this winter."

"Next you will say I am lucky to be here."

"I think you are. And not so long ago you were glad to leave Paris."

Margot tossed her head in anger and turned away. Suddenly she swirled her skirts back toward him. "It is as austere here as when your mother ruled with her Calvinist ways. I feel her control and reforming presence in every room. There is no light. Please, Henry, let us leave this 'little Geneva' tomorrow!"

"I have too many things to do here," Henry responded. Turning on his heel, he departed. With some surprise, Margot perceived he was more hurt than angry. Well, it was too bad she hated a place he loved so much, but she refused to remain any longer!

The next day Henry burst out of the kitchen door into the inner courtyard, leaving the heat of the cooks' fires behind him. He knew he made them nervous, hovering over the evening meal preparations, but he liked the hustle and bustle and the feeling of satisfaction that comes with finishing something, even if it was as simple as preparing a meal. After tasting, he always advised they add more garlic and pepper. He claimed he would feel better if his food were spicier, not milder. Did it not make sense he would have more punch if his food did? He refused to serve any of that Parisian mousse at his table, despite Marguerite's complaints that the food was unrefined. She could order those milky, weak dishes when she took her meals with her ladies.

The courtyard was empty except for a cart loaded with logs drawn up to the kitchen door. He had no mission in mind except to get outside, never wanting to stay indoors for long. He turned right outside the château's entrance of three white marble arches, with a low balustrade above, connecting the two wings of the castle. The oldest tower rose on his right, and he ran his hand over the rough bronze colored brick as he walked by. Its few small windows were witness to its original purpose of fortification, and though linked to the late Renaissance wing by a graceful entryway, it still stood as a sentinel to the past. Henry looked up to its crenellated roof, recalling his games as a boy, aiming his arrows from above at the tiny figures below — animal and human fantasy enemies. Now his enemies were real and much more difficult to target.

Rounding the corner, he headed to the herb garden behind the castle. He would gather a few peppers for the timid cooks. The new wing of dove gray stone was attached to the thirteenth century tower but was much lower, rising only five stories, each level marked with a different exterior decoration. The windows framed in white stone looked down from the hill of the castle's site to the small stone and timber houses of the town. At the back, the view included the Gave de Pau, a small muddy river, which wound its way down to the château from the higher reaches of the Pyrénées. Oak trees lined the river, blocking the view, except from the higher windows of the castle.

Three square plots comprised the herb garden, and he could see Margot had been at work, instructing the gardeners to plant roses and lavender in place of garlic and onions. What a nuisance she could be, claiming she needed the lavender for sachets to protect her nose from his "barnyard" odor. It was just easier all around to avoid her.

Henry decided against harvesting the vegetables immediately and dug his boot heels into the mud to slow his precipitate course down to the river. Thick vines of vinca major slowed his progress more as he neared the water, and he heard voices to his right above the river's gurgle. A lady's voice surprised him as the softer sex usually preferred to head toward the shops of the town, simple though they were in Pau, rather than the rough terrain behind the château. He immediately recognized the low timbre of his wife's speech, a tone he had always found seductive. And the laughter which answered her was male. How dare that slut betray him in his own home! Her free ways might be accepted in Paris, he thought, but not here with his mother's portrait looking down on them. He didn't even care whom she was with; he simply was repelled by her licentious behavior in this place that seemed almost sacred to him. And he had no doubt she was guilty. The fact that he had behaved in a similar manner in this very spot never entered his mind.

Tearing through the brambles, he terrified the couple in a tight embrace with his sudden appearance. Marguerite screamed and the younger man, jumping back behind a thick walnut tree, paled at the sight of his king. Henry was not surprised to see the handsome soldier Margot had chosen. Tall and tan, slim and strong, with a black beard and blue eyes, he would have attracted the avid desire Henry's wife failed to share with him. Banishing regrets, he barked to the frightened young man, "Get out of my sight. You are excused from your commission and I never want to see your conceited mug again." The soldier darted off, not looking back to see what would happen to his flirtatious partner.

"But you are the true guilty one, my Queen, not your pitiful young victim. Oh, how you disgust me! What is wrong with you and your family? Your perversions are beyond my comprehension."

Marguerite began to cry, tears of fright mixing with anger and humiliation. "You are not fair," she wailed. "You avoid me and I have nothing to do here, no friends, no entertainment. Nothing! It is a backwash I hope never to see again."

"Then how do you expect to give me an heir?" Henry flung at her.

"You have lovers too," she complained, gaining her courage at this taunt. "You are more guilty than I."

"Perhaps. Not more, but also," he admitted, already a bit seduced by her rumpled attire and beauty. "I never have understood why we cannot get along. You are not my enemy, you know. You are my wife. Hah! That changes the meaning of the word." His eyes changed in a flash from conciliatory to hot anger again.

"Oh, Henry, you make me tired. What do you expect me to do here?"

"I don't know. Whatever women usually do. How should I know?"

"That's just it. No one understands me here. You can't expect me to be friends with your sister — I don't think she even likes me — and there is nobody else I can imagine talking to for miles around."

"No, actually I don't see at all why you and Catherine cannot be friends. You are both well-read, educated women of royal lineage. And, are you telling me that you and your male friends have no need to talk?"

"I don't find you amusing, Henry. I can see we shall never understand one another," Margot sighed, whereupon she turned her back on him and began to walk away.

Henry grabbed her by the arm. "Just a minute! You will return to the château with your husband, Marguerite. And hereafter, appearances, at least, had better matter more to you. I will not be shamed by my wife in my own kingdom! I will be more than happy to return you to Nérac soon.

Henry kept his word and they left in two days. He had more serious matters to worry about than Margot, however. Even though he had refused to be controlled by Catherine, he had essentially agreed to try to maintain peace in the South. Now his more zealous Huguenot cousin, Condé, was meddling and muddying his options. He and Condé could never really get along, he thought. Now Condé refused to accept the articles of peace that Henry had agreed to and continued to stir up enmity between Catholics and Huguenots. Henry also felt the need to write to Elizabeth in England to warn her of atrocities committed in the South in the name of religion.

Adding to the complexity was a recent offer from Philip II of Spain to marry his sister, Catherine, to reestablish an independent kingdom of Navarre, and to affirm an alliance with Catholic Spain. As angry as he was with Condé and Catherine, he trusted them more than he did Philip. As he and Margot neared Nérac, he saw her face brighten.

Marguerite immediately understood why she preferred the smaller village to Pau. Not only was the château more to her taste, but the countryside suited her better as well. Manicured vineyards and gentle hills soothed rather than assaulted her senses as did the craggy, crowding peaks of the Pyrénées hovering tightly nearby. Even the peasants seemed less rough here and the wood smoke less acrid and dense. But the locals' way of speaking was still unintelligible, and she saw no reason why she should try to decipher their patois. What on earth could they possibly have to say to one another? And how irritating it was when these dirty simpletons couldn't understand her orders. Henry apparently spoke all their dialects and knew everyone's name and their children's nicknames.

"But why do you bother?" she asked him.

"It's no bother," he answered with surprise. "I have known them and they have known me as long as I can remember."

Margot sensed she had lost much of Henry's affection and struggled to regain his good graces. She had her chance in March when, soon after returning to Nérac, he fell ill. She nursed him solicitously, seeing to his every need and comfort. The infection was severe, and it took weeks for him to regain his strength. She stayed by his bed during most of his waking hours, and during his convalescence, she called in a charming young member of the court to read to the patient. The girl's name was Françoise de Montmorency-Fosseuse, though she was simply called "la Fosseuse." At first Margot was relieved someone could distract Henry, so irritable and impatient had he become with the slow pace of the sick room.

One afternoon she startled the fifteen year-old blond beauty with particularly brilliant eyes sitting on her husband's knee as they chatted together. Henry didn't even bother to remove his hand from the girl's waist for his wife's benefit. She watched him with a sickening and growing fear as his finger moved upward and gently stroked the side of the girl's breast. She heard him call her "my little girl" and watched him shower her with gifts over the next few weeks. La Fosseuse particularly craved the beautiful Italian marzipan he imported just for her. In June the extent of Henry's infatuation and success became inevitable court knowledge — La Fosseuse was pregnant.

This was not the only thing bothering Margot. She felt her inadequacy more and more because of her inability to have a child. She had taken advantage recently of the baths nearby at Bagnères in the Hautes Pyrénées, taking the waters there without admitting her reason. But so far they had proven useless.

A chill silence settled between Henry and his wife, each studiously avoiding the other. Though Henry had recovered fully from his illness, her bed curtains remained closed. He no longer wanted her. In July Margot could wait no longer and accosted Henry.

She wanted to say, but restrained herself, "How can you bear the simpering smile and pouting large mouth of this silly girl?" Instead she spoke forcefully, "You have overstepped yourself this time, Henry. Your mistress brags that you promised her that if she has a son, you will marry her and she will be queen."

He did not deny the accusation and only replied coldly, "You have been infertile so far, Margot."

"I should kill you," she screamed. Yet her mother also had been late to bear children. Perhaps she would be like Catherine de Medici.

Knowing her husband's ways, she didn't blame the girl and surprised Henry with her next remark.

"You must be concerned for your young beauty, Henry. Why don't I take her away from the gossip and snickers to Mas d'Agenais? There she would be able to bear her child more discreetly."

"You cannot expect her to trust you, Margot. Besides, I have not yet told you she is pregnant."

"Do not be ridiculous!"

The humiliating months dragged on until one icy, December dawn, Margot heard commotion in Henry's apartment next door. She hurried out to the corridor in time to listen to the messenger tell Henry that La Fosseuse's pains had begun. Then she heard Henry's door slam.

Shivering, she pulled the coverlet closer around her. In a short time she was startled to see her bed curtains part. Henry leaned close to her and spoke so formally she wanted to laugh. But she must not become hysterical.

"My friend, I have concealed something from you that I must now admit. I beg of you to excuse me and to forget all that I have said to you on this subject. Please, get up immediately and go to help Fosseuse, who is very sick. I am sure that on seeing her in this state you would not bear a grudge or resent what has happened. You know how much I love you and love her; I beg of you to oblige me in this matter."

Margot remained quiet for a moment, then answered in equally official tones. "I honor you too much to take offense at your issue. I will go and will act as though she were my daughter. I insist, however, that you must go away and take everyone with you in order that no one hear of any of this."

He kissed her. "I promise you, my love. You are an angel."

Margot dressed quickly. She ordered that Fosseuse be moved from the room she shared with the other ladies and put in a boudoir near her own with her own doctor. Later in the day, La Fosseuse was delivered of a girl, stillborn. Margot nursed La Fosseuse through the day with stiff politeness and finally instructed she be moved back to her own quarters. When she returned to bed herself, she wept with relief and nervous fatigue. Had she really thought of killing the child if it were a boy? NO. She couldn't have.

When Henry returned late that night and heard the news, he came to her again. "Please, Marguerite, go to her again as you do whenever one of your ladies is ill. Then the talk will be hushed."

"I did so, Henry, when she really needed me. Now it is no longer my affair. Everyone will point their finger at me now as the duped wife."

"Don't make me angry, Margot," Henry growled.

"You selfish lout!" she yelled. "How can you expect me, a Valois princess, to degrade myself so?"

"I haven't degraded you, Marguerite. You have done it yourself with your numerous affairs and your behavior at court even before our marriage."

Margot raised her hand to slap his face, and he caught her wrist. She dropped to the bed, weeping as he left their chamber. How had she sunk so low? Her mother had demonstrated that gender didn't matter; you could wield power whether male or female. As a royal, Margot expected respect and a gracious life. But she was finding it dangerous to be an infertile queen.

PARIS

1582

IN PARIS CATHERINE DE MEDICI grew restive with Henry so far away from her influence. She heard he had successfully consolidated his power in the provinces of Guyenne and Béarn; moreover, she knew the people of France were becoming more and more discontent with Henri III's orgies at court. The Queen Mother sent Margot fifteen thousand *écus* for a trip home, strongly urging her to bring Henry with her. Henry refused, but Margot jumped at the chance to escape the scene of her recent bitter humiliation. To the surprise of everyone, La Fosseuse accompanied her, perhaps lured by Catherine in the hope that she would be future bait for Henry.

On March 28, at St.-Maixent, Catherine met the entourage. Henry, who had traveled to this point with his wife, refused Catherine's last entreaties to join them in Paris and returned to the South, eager to resume his bachelor's existence. He didn't wait long before letters from Margot began arriving from Court. First she wanted to assure him that the Guises were no longer a threat:

> You no longer have anything to fear from the Guise faction. The duc de Guise has become thin and older than his years and his brother, the duc de Mayenne, has become almost too fat to move.

She went on to point out reasons he should come to court:

> You would be a person on whom others depended. You would have gifts from the King himself; you could

take care of all your affairs and could do far more for
those of your party, being here at court and near the
king, than all those in your service would ever know
how to do by their solicitations.

She knew these were the matters that interested Navarre, but she
was more in her element here with the clothes and the entertainments
at the Valois court. The banquets and balls suited her taste better than
the Huguenot restraint of Nérac and Pau. She could show off her
beautiful gowns and twirl around the dance floor until dawn. And
to make it perfect, she had recently met the most beautiful man in
France, Jacques de Harlay, Marquis de Champvallon, who was master
of the horse for her brother Alençon. It did not seem to bother either
of them that he was married.

Margot was nearly thirty years old. When the Marquis seduced
her — first in the woodland glades of the Castle of Cadillac — her
self-confidence re-flowered with his words of love. They continued to
see each other secretly in Paris, and she happily forgot Henry's cold-
ness toward her and his preference for La Fosseuse. Now Champvallon wanted her and her alone. Losing all restraint and eagerly devot-
ing both her mind and body to this intelligent man with a body like a
Greek statue, she felt exceptionally pleased with herself and her new
life. She dashed off an ironic note to her husband, saying, "I have
dismissed Fosseuse because of danger to my reputation." She was offended when she received his galling reply:

In order to silence the Queen Mother, Henri III, and
the chaste Louise de Lorraine, you need only tell them
that your husband loved Fosseuse and consequently,
you yourself cherished her.

Having recovered her dignity, the Queen of Navarre wrote in
bitter response:

Your answer would be fitting if you were speaking
of one of your servants, but of your wife! If I had been
born of a state unworthy of the honor of being your
wife, this response would not offend me; but being
such as I am, it would seem to me to be very improper.

Catherine, also highly incensed and apparently alerted to the correspondence, wrote to her son-in-law:

> You are not the first young husband to be unwise in such matters; but I find you certainly the first and the only one after such an occurrence, to use such language to his wife . . . This is not the manner in which to treat women of noble birth, to insult them with the appetite of a public harlot . . . which I am not able to believe comes from you; because you are too well born . . . But also, it is necessary that you do what you should, to love and esteem her for what she is and is to you, and to be happy that she removes from her presence anyone who would be able to alter the friendship that you ought to hold for her; and I have counseled her to this, and I have made this unchaste, beautiful beast leave.

As time passed Margot and Henry grew further and further apart. He was angry with her for her treatment of La Fosseuse, but apparently he didn't care enough for this mistress to plead her case more extensively. Margot was irritated with his treatment of her and in love with Champvallon. Their letters became less and less frequent and more and more bitter, until in mid-June, Renieri, the Italian ambassador, wrote in his dispatch to Florence:

> The Queen of Navarre has declared that she no longer wishes to live with her husband, who is a liar and a Huguenot.

BOOK TWO

CORISANDE, DIANE D'ANDOINS
COMTESSE DE GUICHE
1554-1620

DIANE D'ANDOINS, COMTESSE DE GUICHE,
and HER DAUGHTER
Attributed to Sofonisba Angouissola
Musée National du Château de Pau

Catherine de Bourbon, Duchesse de Bar,
Sister of Henri de Navarre
Portrait en crayon, 16th c. de la Cour de France

PAU

1582-1583

THE SCENT OF LIME TREES just budding penetrated Henry's memory as the pungent aroma from a fragrant orange astounds the senses. Urging his steed on toward Pau, he remembered the month of May was his mother's favorite time of year. It was hard to believe eleven years had already passed since her death. She would be proud of all he had accomplished in Navarre since his return from Paris. Perhaps because of her sudden death, he always felt so much was unfinished between them. Strange that he thought more often of his mother than of his wife, whom he had not laid eyes on for many months. Here it was, already spring, and his bizarre matrimonial state continued without change.

Still convalescing after a serious illness contracted during a recent trip to La Rochelle, he knew he was too weak to stay in the saddle much longer. He cursed his physical handicap because he greatly enjoyed these tours of his Protestant strongholds, proudly reminding his people they had a leader they could count on. He would probably pay for his personal neglect and for pushing himself by spending weeks in bed, his urinary tract burning like the stubble he passed in the fields. Another reason for visiting La Rochelle this time had been to see his cousin, Henri, duc de Condé, hoping to improve their relations. Condé was too narrow minded, he thought, certainly without any political instincts. Yet they needed to suppress their differences in order to better guide the Huguenots.

The Kingdom of Navarre remained dominantly Huguenot, but Catholic pockets existed within its borders. Even in towns where Protestants were the clear majority, lingering suspicions and veiled animosities would surface and sporadic riots would erupt. The Catholics in Paris still feared that the religious domination of the Huguenots in the Southwest would expand geographically and politically, and even worse, that Henry would threaten the French throne.

As usual he pressed his mount harder, impatient to catch the first glimpse of the castle where he had spent his youth. As he hurried toward the familiar sight, he let his thoughts wander to the stories his mother had told him, her voice still sounding clearly in his mind. Without the presence of his antagonistic wife, he noticed his thoughts flowed more freely.

"I was the Princess of Navarre and called the favorite of kings, but our Calvinist teaching warned me against pride. My father and my uncle, King François I, were distrustful of one another and wanted to use me as a pawn in the politics of France. The Emperor of Spain, Charles V, played into their hands with his wish that I marry his son, Philip II, proposing this as a means to pacify their differences touching the Kingdom of Navarre. But King François I refused to introduce such a powerful and potential enemy into France and insisted instead on my engagement to the duc de Clèves. I was so loudly negative and so stubbornly disagreed about the contract that François I decided he had no choice but to allow me to marry the prince with whom I was in love, Antoine de Bourbon."

Henry remembered the smile that softened her angular face as she recounted her tale. "My wedding took place at Moulins in the year 1547, the same year François I died. The celebrated poet Ronsard was present to compose exquisite verses for the occasion. I considered that a great honor. I learned much about political conniving from these experiences, and I want to teach you all I know. Too soon I learned the meaning of sorrow. Your father and I had two sons in the first three years of our marriage, both of whom died in infancy by extraordinary accidents. A cold-natured governess kept the first child so hot that he was stifled by the heat, and the second also died from the carelessness of the nurse. While dancing with a gentleman, they tossed the child back and forth and let him fall to the ground. My love for Antoine sustained me, and I eagerly and hopefully awaited your birth."

It must have been her personal courage which helped as well, Henry thought, as he guided his horse home. What a life his mother had led! He listened to his memories echoing in her voice.

"I wondered if it would be unwise to leave my husband when my father, King Henri II d'Albret of Navarre, called me to come to him. Antoine and I had been living a roving life, moving from camp to camp in Picardy, where he was governor. I longed to be with him when our child was born, but I knew too much was at stake. I had heard that Henri d'Albret had made his will to my disadvantage in favor of a lady he then loved. Evidently he was quite the rogue, leaving my poor mother, Marguerite d'Angoulême, while he chased numerous beauties.

"When Antoine was called from La Flèche to command an army against Charles V, I decided to obey my father's wishes. Sad and anxious, I kissed my husband goodbye at Compiègne in mid-November. I was in my ninth month of pregnancy but made my way across France to the family kingdom in the Pyrénées. Fortunately, the winter was not yet severe, nor the roads too muddy. Arriving at Pau, where my father awaited me on December 5, I embraced him fondly. I was eager to see the will but dared not speak about it immediately.

"I was not a stranger at my father's court for I had known so many of his men, ladies, and servants as a child. When I passed into the great dining hall, the Béarnais people bowed and wished me well. Henri II had thoughtfully ordered many of my favorite dishes for my first evening at his castle. Since I bore his heir, he was more interested in me than he had ever been before. We had not been long at table before he said, 'I imagine you desire to see my will, my dear.' I'm sure I blushed but replied with honesty, 'I must think of our future, especially now that I am with child.' "

"He answered, 'You shall have it in your hands when the child is born, but only on the condition that you sing a song to the end of your labor, for then you will not bring a weak and weeping infant into the world.' "

" 'I am practiced in not weeping,' I answered." Henry was always amazed at her saying that. How strong his mother must have been.

"On December 13, 1553, a little after one in the morning, I kept my word. You, my curious boy, came into the world without crying, contrary to the common order of nature. There is a Béarnais legend, which holds that this is a sign the child will be strong and enjoy life. As soon as you were born, Henri II came into my bedchamber. He handed the important document to me and picked you up, his first grandchild, telling me, 'My daughter, see there what is for you, but this is for me.' "

Then Henry recalled the colorful story of how Henri d'Albret had held him in the skirt of his robe; his mother had watched while the King rubbed his little lips with a clove of garlic, then regarded as an effective antidote to the plague, and made him suck a draught of wine out of a golden cup so he might render his temperament more masculine and vigorous. Henry smiled at this story of his pagan baptism, for some now surely would say he had partaken too much of that wine. He then remembered his mother's words, which were his favorite part of the story.

"Henri d'Albret lifted you high and showed you to the crowd outside the château, saying, 'Behold, my ewe has given birth to a lion.' Your grandfather saw in you a chance to regain the lands of Navarre which had been lost to Spain, and his will made me and you his heirs. Your great-grandmother, Catherine I, was the last sovereign of an independent Navarre. In 1512 the southern half of her kingdom was annexed by the all-conquering monarchs Ferdinand and Isabella of Castille and Aragon. Catherine then transferred her capital to French Navarre. The remaining minute border state still retained the considerable influence of our family, and the Albrets were rich and powerful in the counties of Béarn, Grailly, Albret, Foix, Armagnac, and Bigorre. Your grandfather called himself Henri II, King of Navarre and Senior Sovereign of Béarn. He is counting on you to restore his parents' land, for his will stipulated that his body be transferred to Pamplona when that capital is once again the territory of the Albrets."

His mother also had recounted to him the story of his formal baptism, which had occurred the following year on Twelfth Day, January 6, 1554. "For the immersion, richly gilded fonts of silver were made for the chapel of the castle of Pau, and you were carried to the holy waters in a giant tortoise shell. You were blessed with the name of your godfathers, Henri II, King of France, and Henri II d'Albret, King of Navarre. Your godmother was Madame Claudia of France, afterward the duchesse de Lorraine."

Henry had been too young to remember the death of his grandfather, but he felt that Henri d'Albret had managed to pass on to him his love of the somber outline of the mountains, the steep wooded slopes and the black, chasmal depths of the ravines. King Henri d'Albret had died at Hagetmau in Béarn in 1555 at 52 years of age. Jeanne and Antoine were at the court of France when the news reached them that they were to succeed him. The royal couple experienced great difficulty in obtaining leave to retire to Béarn, because King Henri II of

France wished to deprive them of Lower Navarre, which the Albrets still claimed. Henri II maintained that all the land below the Pyrénées was the property of France. When Antoine threatened to seek the aid of the Spanish, King Henri II backed down. The parties reached a settlement whereby Jeanne and Antoine retained the government of Guyenne but gave up Languedoc. It seemed to Henry that his ancestors traded parcels of land like game pieces.

His mother and grandfather certainly had left him a full legacy, he thought — a legacy of memories to cherish and obligations to fulfill. So deep was he in his reminiscences, he didn't notice a storm coming up, a storm which would leave the mountains smelling fresh and pure. Scents of wild marjoram and thyme, crushed under his horse's hooves, wafted up to him, causing him to notice horsemint, sicklewort, and agrimony also along the rocky path. Oh, to be a barefoot boy again, roaming the rough hills, snagging birds to roast on a stick for a snack! The chant of the western wind excited him as he pressed his steed homeward. The small band accompanying him were glad to pick up the pace, and following the Gave de Pau, they arrived at the château within the hour.

Henry carried little baggage, never wanting to be encumbered by dragging things about the country with him. Although he always was accompanied by several of his men, he toted only one valise of yellow velvet banded with orange velvet and a second of yellow suede with black and white velvet bands. Feeling tired after the long journey, he chose to rest awhile. The nostalgia persisted and he sought out his mother's room, where he reclined on her bed — an act he knew she would probably regard as weak and overly sentimental. But he had a sudden desire to see the intricately carved bed which had so inspired his imagination as a boy. When he was sick, she would allow him to lie there and throw his chicken bones under the bed where a wooden skirt hid such expected debris tossed from above.

It was some time before he joined his sister and her guests in the great hall. Genuinely pleased to see Catherine, he embraced her warmly. As usual, she looked too thin and very much like their sharp-faced mother. He was uncomfortably reminded of the many gaunt faces of civil war he met in his travels around the country. Over his sister's shoulder he caught sight of a woman with shining dark hair and a gentle face and asked Catherine to present him at once.

"This is the comtesse de Guiche, Brother. You met her when you were a boy, when mother took us to her engagement party. She was then Diane d'Andouins, and she married Philibert de Gramont. You probably remember — he was Lieutenant General and governed Béarn during our mother's absences. The Count was killed in battle in the summer of 1580, and the Countess has preferred to occupy her château at Hagetmau since his death."

"What an oaf I must have been not to have noticed your beauty then, Comtesse."

"I was only fourteen when I married, and you must have been fifteen. Your head was full of military stratagems, if I remember correctly. You were busy becoming a man," she smiled.

"Corisande, as she is called by her friends, is indeed a good friend of mine and often visits me for a few weeks at a time," his sister enjoined.

Immediately charmed by this lady, Henry replied, "One is not a man until he recognizes beauty." The Countess's face was not perfectly proportioned, for her nose was a trifle short and her forehead too high, but the whole presented an air of intelligence and soft friendliness.

"You must call me 'Corisande' also," she said, "for I am sure we will become friends. Corisande was the heroine in *Amadis de Gaule*, one of my favorite books, and I have taken the liberty of adopting her name."

Henry heard no hypocrisy in her tone, only quiet warmth and dignity. He felt a gentleness sweep over him as he gazed into dark brown eyes. Suddenly he laughed.

"Excuse me, Corisande. I am not laughing at you. It must be out of relief. For it is such a pleasure to have an honest exchange, be it only of the social graces. Such a thing was impossible with the perverse Valois clan with whom I was coerced to spend so much time. The court was a place only for mutual jealousy and hatred — and no, that is not too strong a word."

He remembered with disgust how he had embraced people who were repulsive to him. His reverie was broken when Catherine suggested they dine. Hurrying to take Corisande's arm, he escorted her to the large formal dining room, where he found his close associates already at table. They stood when their leader entered. Among them were Agrippa d'Aubigné and M. de Rosny. Whereas Aubigné was his first advisor on military matters, Rosny was becoming increasingly invaluable to him as a political and financial counselor. A close associate of Henry's since his escape from Paris, Rosny had escaped on the night of the St. Bartholomew massacre by disguising himself in a Catholic priest's garb. Rosny moralized too much for Henry's taste, but he had to acknowledge the man's financial wisdom.

Henry immediately raised his glass to his retinue. "Thank you, thank you, my friends. Let us drink a toast together to success in the days ahead."

His eyes met Corisande's again, and he wondered if he would be in such a hurry now to return to the battlefield. Her enchanting presence transformed his mood of action to one of peace. Tall and slender, her refined noble carriage suggested a proud attitude, which he expected could pose an interesting challenge. She wore a black dress of regal style with puffed sleeves adorned with slashes showing a sateen underlying material. He wondered if it were in his honor. Even Margot would be impressed with this attire, he thought.

Sitting with her in the great hall long after the company had retired, Henry found himself telling her of his past, especially about his mother and father, whom she had known. The old castle had instilled a sentimental mood, and the presence of this understanding woman was the catalyst.

"My father, I think, was a vain and ambitious man. Unfortunately, Antoine was not clever enough to realize he was surrounded by people as hypocritical as he. He believed them when they flattered him, always a dangerous temptation for those in power."

"Yet I remember him as being quite charming," Corisande commented.

"Yes, he was. And his energetic schemes could be appealing too. But all his energy was wasted on court intrigue rather than in really getting something done, in achieving any goal. He was as ineffectual and vacillating as mother was honest and intransigent."

"You loved her very much, I think," the lady observed.

"Yes, and I respected her too. Many thought her narrow face unattractive, but her eyes were warm. She had me beaten regularly and sent me out on challenging errands. She would explain that she was helping me to grow up hardy and strong. I understood this treatment pained her though she believed in it, and I have no doubt that her methods developed my resourcefulness and adaptability."

"And your courage and self-reliance," Corisande echoed.

"Often she told me how difficult I was to bring up and how she despaired when the sixth and seventh nurses gave up the task. I suspect I was lonely and needed more friends my own age. She finally appointed my aunt, Suzanne de Bourbon, to be my governess, and she became primarily responsible for my education. I spent several peaceful years in the Castle of Coarraze in Béarn, in the valley of the Gave de Pau. The castle was as rugged as the granite upon which its foundations were laid. Evergreens clung to the hillsides and darkened the view from the slit windows in the heavy walls, giving a frowning, gloomy aspect to the place — at least that is how my wife describes it. Gales and storms often swept through and eagles wheeled around the towers. But I found these wild regions exciting rather than depressing and learned much about the natural wonders of life, both animal and human. The remote site and coarse surroundings still appeal to me."

"Your mother probably believed she had to be mother and father to you."

"Exactly," Henry agreed. "I believe she was overly concerned about me, having lost her first two babes. Also, she resented being less strong physically than a man. She and my father fought continuously when they were together, about religion, people, everything. But she depended on him in a way, and was very hurt when he converted to Catholicism and affiliated himself with the Guise contingent. When he was offered the lieutenant generalship if he returned to orthodoxy, he converted immediately. She knew he was an opportunist, I'm sure, but I don't know if that was the worst blow for her. He was unfaithful constantly after that. I was only nine when he was killed, and it always bothered me that people laughed about the way he died. Evidently, at the siege of Rouen in 1562, while relieving himself against the ramparts of the city, supposedly in a gesture of contempt, he was hit by a musket shot."

Corisande listened intently and noticed that Henry laughed when he told the story, but the sound seemed hollow. "I can understand why that has been difficult for you," she replied. "My father was killed in the same battle, only he died nobly. But I was essentially orphaned early. I never knew my mother and I was very young when my father died, and then I was affianced to Philibert de Gramont when I was only twelve, when I reached my majority. My parents were Catholic, but I believe I was greatly influenced by Philibert's father, M. de Gramont. He ruled over numerous seigneuries in Béarn and hoped to unite Navarre and Bearn. He preferred amiability to violence and took a much more relaxed attitude to religion than your mother. He was always looking for a compromise between your mother in Navarre and Catherine de Medici in Paris. His spirit of cooperation impressed me greatly, and so my father-in-law became more important to me than my father. I was very sad when he died in 1576. "

"Yes, I remember M. de Gramont well. I'm afraid I maligned him recently, claiming he switched loyalties between me and Catherine de Medici. But perhaps it can be seen as an attempt to bridge the two. He was present in Paris for my marriage to Marguerite. Since he was from Béarn, it is extraordinary that he escaped death during the massacre of so many Huguenots on St. Bartholomew's Eve!"

"Perhaps his long allegiance to both the Catholics and the Protestants earned him protection from Catherine de Medici. It is remarkable that he was able to keep a foot in both camps," she mused. "Fortunately, I didn't travel to Paris for the festivities because I had recently given birth to our first child, Antonin."

"You are so lovely," Henry said with some wonder, soaking in her agreeable amenable countenance.

She smiled. "Do you know that I have two children?" It was as though there was a mutual understanding to reveal as much of one another as possible very quickly.

"Evidently that blessing only increases your attractiveness."

He drew her to him and the fire his kiss inspired surprised them both.

"Yes, I think we are going to be friends," he said, smiling.

He accompanied her to her rooms, happier than he could ever remember, before retiring to his own apartment.

Henry awoke late the next morning. I am free, he thought, truly free. His escape from the Valois court had happened years ago, but only now did he at last feel unconstrained. Of course, he felt more relaxed in his old house, among his own Gascon people, but he had been here before with Margot. He suspected the woman he had met last night had a great deal to do with this sudden, soaring feeling. She had removed a lurking depression, a mental paralysis.

Corisande appeared again at lunch. Unusually warm weather had prompted the staff to set up a few tables in the courtyard. Patterned Basque quilts dressed the tables and the silverware sparkled in the sunlight. The heady aroma of hyacinths wafted on a cool breeze and narcissus cut from the garden crowned earthenware jugs upon the tabletops. Gazing appreciatively at Corisande's pale rose gown of watered silk and a single strand of pearls against her creamy skin, Henry longed to touch the softness beneath the smooth pearls.

Though aware of much animated conversation between Rosny and Aubigné, Henry chose not to join in. His eyes sought only those of Corisande. For several moments their united regard separated them from the rest, and when Henry returned to his surroundings, he felt he had shared a communion as strong as when making love. They had been one for a brief moment and it had left him shaken. She too seemed flustered and glad when he helped her from the table. He suggested they take a walk in the garden nearby. Noticing Rosny's critical eyes on him, Henry simply glared at his counselor as he took Corisande's arm.

The sight of the Pyrénées rising in the distance always filled him with exhilaration, their enduring strength and stability encouraging him. This afternoon was no exception. "Do you like our landscape?" he asked his companion.

"It is rugged and quiet," she responded. "The people are good; it is a fine place for my son too."

"I doubt if you are as rigorous a mother as mine was, but these mountains will make him hardy. I should like to meet him."

"He is a joy," she said. "My husband was good to me, and I believe we cared for one another. We were married when I was so very young, but I only realized what real love was when our son Antonin was born. When Philibert died, I chose to make our home here, and he bequeathed all the land and administration of it to me and our children. It is a big responsibility, but I am proud to oversee our estate."

"Corisande," Henry began, "I have known many women. Many have amused me, some have charmed me, most have eventually irritated me. I have never felt compelled to tell any one of them I loved them. But now, hardly knowing you, I want to speak of love to you."

She looked straight at him, studying the seemingly permanent ironic fold of his lips. It was difficult to read his expression, but she answered honestly. "I feel the same. The past few years have been lonely ones. Oh, Henry, I hope . . ." He was only faintly aware that she had abandoned all propriety and called her king by his Christian name as a kiss that was gentle kindled a passion that shook them both. He had thrown stable girls on the ground, royal ladies on divans, taken them all without hesitation. But he didn't want to abuse this woman in any way.

"Shall we take a ride?" he suggested, holding her at arms length, Corisande accepted with alacrity, requesting only that he give her time to change into a riding habit. Soon they were trotting through the picturesque countryside surrounding Pau. Hamlets with yellow walled houses and red roofs clung miraculously to the crags. Below meandered the Gave de Pau and beyond it were rambling hills, yellow-green with early growth of grain and forests. Behind the first hills rose others, fold on fold; and beyond them all jutted a great jagged gray and purple wall of mountains, over sixty miles long, high against the azure of the horizon. To the east they identified the Pic d'Arneille; to the west the Pic d'Anie and beyond these the distinct cone of the Pic du Midi de Bigorre; and to the southeast and southwest, the majestic display of the sharp twin Pics du Midi d'Ossau.

"It is overwhelming," whispered Corisande. She turned to Henry. "And what are your plans for our beautiful kingdom?"

"I must continue to restore order in my own lands. If Henri III pushes me to a fight, then of course I will fight. But my foremost goal now is peace. Progress has been slower than I expected and at times it seems like I am only running in place."

"But how can there be peace with religious feelings running so high?"

"I believe Catholics and Protestants should be able to live side by side. Do you know that in 1564 the Catholics outnumbered the Protestants by 100 to 1? Now almost one-sixth of the population in France is Protestant. They are going to have to learn to tolerate one another or complete anarchy will come. We are almost to that point now."

"I am a Catholic," she said proudly but not defiantly or defensively.

"You are also the most desirable woman I have ever met!"

Corisande laughed. "Are you always such a logical conversationalist?"

"Only when my listener is so beautiful."

Corisande regarded Henry riding beside her. His face was tan and his body exuded energy. His nose was overly long, but the light in his eyes, which could register quick and easy hurt or a flash of humor, moved her. He can be kind, she thought, and he is so full of vitality. She doubted if he would stay with her for long, but she would enjoy every moment in the present. The loss of her husband had taught her that it is useless to worry about the future. It is only the present that counts. She gave her horse full rein, and they galloped home, both feeling exhilarated.

As they strolled together from the stables, Corisande recalled with a smile, "You know, my marriage to Philibert de Gramont took place in the reformed church and I remember your presence with your sister at the ceremony."

Henry laughed. "I remembered that too, but I didn't want to remind you of that awkward gawky fellow at your wedding. Now it simply seems like I have known you for a very long time."

After dinner that evening, Henry accompanied Corisande to her apartments. He knew Margot labeled him coarse and rough; in fact she often accused him of being malodorous, but Corisande did not raise any such objections. She seemed to accept his love as natural, as something they both wanted. His body was hard but his manner was gentle. When he made love to her, for the first time in his life he completely lost himself, forgetting time and place.

"I am happier than I have ever been before," he whispered to her. He recalled Margot's beauty, like an iris bloom, obvious, even garish. Whereas Corisande's appeal was more subtle, a pale peach rose in a perfect pattern. Henry was sensitive to this hidden power within her and repelled at the memory of the extravagance of his wife.

Corisande kissed him, offering herself to him again. She was a trifle taller than the other women he had seduced but her curves were graceful and appealing. Her body was soft like her face and her sweetness poignant to one who had been schooled in malicious sex.

Aware of a pleasure far beyond satisfied lust, he said, "I believe I have found something that will be very precious to me."

"When you have time," she suggested. Henry didn't hear her for the blood was thundering in his ears.

⚜

So enchanted was Henry that the next few weeks with Corisande — riding horseback, playing lawn tennis and making love — seemed like time out of time. One day when the weather was particularly fine, they strolled along the dramatic Gave de Pau. Near the water, moss and lichen covered the rocks like velvet, and as they entered the chestnut forest, ferns and mushrooms crowded their path. Taking Corisande's hand, he guided her through the dense growth.

"I am almost afraid to leave this place again," he admitted. "I guess I am really afraid to leave you, for I have never experienced delirious happiness like this. I understand now what Charles IX meant when he told me he would like to escape the responsibilities of royalty. But I must say, with the responsibility comes control, and I would not want to give up what little power I have gained."

"You don't really want to escape the responsibility either," Corisande replied. "You would explode if you didn't have an outlet for your energy. What we have now is all the more intense because we know you must leave soon. You are giving me at this moment all that you can give. I cannot ask for anything more."

"You don't ask, my angel. But I shall love you forever."

Henry held her so tightly that they swooned to the ground as one. The branches of the ash trees above climbed dizzily to the heavens, entwining above the lovers. Corisande whispered to Henry, "This moment is timeless for me. There is nothing more permanent than this brief moment of ecstasy."

"Do not be so tragic, my love, I shall always be yours."

"It is not tragic, dearest. There is no need to seek the future because the present is infinite for us."

Henry departed the next morning for a brief skirmish with a roving band of Catholic soldiers, and Corisande felt less brave and secure than she had when she had lain in his arms in that "timeless moment."

The King of Navarre was away periodically for several weeks. Catherine and Corisande preferred outdoor activities, but in the evenings or on rainy days, they found indoor diversions. Often, gentlemen from all the Béarn came to Pau, and the palace provided a grand setting for their evening entertainments. The paneled ceilings gleamed with gold, and tapestries covered the walls. On a background of red velvet, embroidered with bargello patterns, were scenes of the life of St. John the Baptist and Charlemagne and the Wonders of Hercules — the mysteries of religion, power and mythology all represented.

Tapestries depicting allegorical subjects with Latin inscriptions decorated several rooms revealing more of the religious tendencies of Marguerite d'Angoulême and Jeanne d'Albret: *Ubi spiritus Domini, ibi Libertas** — or under a group which reunited near the Lord, a monk and a monkey — *Littera Occidit; Spiritus Vivicat.*** Having been woven in Belgium, they were of the finest quality.

Corisande reflected how times had changed since these walls were decorated. During the period of her favorite medieval novel, people's preoccupation had been with eternal salvation, all of the art from that period being inspired by the ideals of humility, suffering, and resignation. Now everyone seemed concerned only with immediate happiness. Man had become the ideal, sufficient unto himself, able to fight his own battles and rise by force of his own power. She wasn't sure but that she felt more comfortable with the medieval philosophy, yet she knew Henry was the prime example of the "new man." But it was only a passing thought during the entertainment.

At the sound of the violins, she hurried to dance. Young women and girls, in white ruffs and tight blouses with ample skirts of silk or brocade balanced on a farthingale turned around their men. The farthingale, consisting of a large piece of linen stretched out on wide wooden or iron hoops to which the skirt was sewn, made dancing a tricky business. A gentleman needed to step quickly to avoid being struck in the shins by a twirling iron band.

Corisande noticed the only frown was on the face of Mme de Tigonville, the former governess of Her Highness (as Catherine de Bourbon was called in Navarre). Mme de Tigonville was a severe Huguenot who had kept the traditions of the court of Jeanne d'Albret. Distrusting worldly amusements, she called them "traps of luxury and impiety." Corisande knew Madame had been a constant bane to Margot during her short stay in Pau, and she could well understand it. Indeed, she knew many wondered how she and Catherine could be such close friends, she a Catholic, and Catherine a staunch Calvinist. But the two women found they could gladly and easily overlook religious differences for the pleasure of reciprocal delights — literature, music, and a high regard for morality.

We are having a pleasant evening. I am scratching the paper with a hasty pen because in the neigh-

*Where the spirit of the Lord is, there is freedom.
**The letter kills; the spirit gives life.

boring room, chords are beginning to sound from the violinists' bows. The only thing missing is you for the pleasure to be perfect.

Henry and his soldiers were engaged in a less delicate operation. The King of Navarre hated to resort to force, but certain villages refused to succumb to his rule in any other way. The people did not understand yet that his rule meant freedom to worship as they chose, but neither did all agree that this policy was correct. His men were loyal and clever fighters, but their bestial tactics often displeased him.

Full of visions of Corisande, Henry had no taste for the villainous debauchery which followed the seizure of a town in which his men raped six local girls, filled them up with gun powder and set light to it. He knew such brutal tactics were not unusual in these turbulent times, but he would not excuse them. He dismissed these men from his fighting force but expected few would remember such explicit discipline the next time they were intoxicated with the victory of battle. He remained baffled at how a difference in religion could make men behave toward the "enemy" as though they were inhuman.

While Henry was busy cementing his power in the South, Henri III was at work in the Low Countries attempting to knit Calvinist and Catholic around the common cause of independence from the Spanish crown. Henri III found Philip II on his southern flank a constant worry and was appalled to learn in the summer of 1583 that the Spanish king had suggested he would marry Henry's sister, Catherine de Bourbon, and Henry should marry an infanta, so forming a Navarraise-Spanish alliance. These possibilities terrified Henri III and gave more leverage to Henry's position. Provoked by Henry's negotiations, in Paris, Margot and Catherine attempted to lure Henry back to court, even endeavoring to persuade him to reconvert to Catholicism.

HAGETMAU

1583

UPON HIS RETURN TO PAU, Henry discovered Corisande had already left for her château at Hagetmau. The gathering night's shadows would not deter him for he refused to wait one more day. With difficulty the grooms calmed and readied two fresh impatient steeds in the courtyard while Henry exchanged his gentleman's great-coat trimmed with braid for a warm, white woolen cape the Béarnais shepherds wore in the penetrating fogs and icy nights of the mountains. He knew he wouldn't draw the curious attention of the locals in this familiar ghostly garb.

Henry and Antoine de Buade, his favorite squire, energetically jumped into their saddles. The archers on guard at the gates saluted them as they crossed the château's arched portal, carved with eagle talons, and headed across the eight leagues through Gascony to Hagetmau. First they passed Lescar, on a plateau with its high gabled tower rising above a belt of crenellated walls, and the imposing cathedral, where the kings and queens of Navarre, now free of the responsibility of rule, reposed. Henry reflected on a story he had heard about one of his ancestors two hundred years earlier. The handsome Bernard d'Albret had led an English princess across this same territory to help her escape from the plague, which had left thousands dead behind them. He had brought Isabelle safely home to her father, King Edward II, but during their five days alone, the young couple had fallen in love. Bernard chose the church to escape from his powerful feelings for a princess whose rank would prevent their union. The rules that governed the lives of kings caused so much tragedy, Henry mused. Most princes and princesses had to leave the protection of their mothers before they were ready to fulfill duties beyond their age and capacity.

The moon rose at the horizon, radiantly projecting on the ground the silhouettes of horse and rider. With pleasure, Henry watched low clouds playing among the mountain summits, vague wraiths appearing and dissolving and disappearing in the black and silver mystery of the southern moonlight. Riding past cream-colored limestone cottages where the peasants slept, the occasional call of a nightingale echoed through the night air. They passed chokecherry bushes and blackberry brambles, piled high by the peasants' pitchforks for burning in the country ovens, which baked huge loaves of dark, dense bread. The thought made Henry's stomach grumble a bit. A little later, on their left, appeared a clock tower and the dungeon of the château of Orthez, a little village where Corisande was seigneuresse.

Suddenly the fields were filled with peasants, as though they had just sprouted there, some on foot, some on horseback, running in every direction, making a hellish noise. It resembled a midnight orgy.

"*Ventre-St.-Gris*! What could these earnest people of Orthez be doing at this unholy hour? They are peaceful farmers, usually early to bed in this season when they must be up at the first cock's crow."

De Buade reminded Henry of the superstition of the area. "All these rustics, brandishing iron rods, are pursuing witches. You will recall that the Béarn is infested with them at this time of year."

Henry burst out laughing, both at the situation and at de Buade's serious tone. Indeed, the melancholy land between Lescar and Orthez, where dark oaks stood knee-deep in muddy swamps, seemed the place demons would choose for secret meetings. To the eyes of the superstitious townsfolk, these two horsemen appeared to be evil envoys with white mantles floating in the wind like ethereal wings. "To the chase," cried the village mob as they threw themselves upon the heels of the king and his squire. Alerted by the furious din, the parish priest began to sound the tocsin. Never really fearing capture and laughing at their pursuers, Henry and de Buade spurred their mounts onward.

Corisande, awakened by the sound of an approaching gallop, leaned from the windows of her château and was alarmed at the increasing racket. Her romantic imagination believed it was the king, and suddenly the troop of spirit hunters broke into her garden trailing behind His Majesty. Her vassals stopped short, as surprised to see her looking down upon them as she was to witness their sudden arrival. Her smiling assurances immediately put an end to the chaotic uproar, and she sent the rabble of Orthez on the road to their homes, complaining they had been cheated of their demons.

"I see that, impervious to fatigue, without worry in these dangerous times of brigands, pitted roads or dense woods, my knight errant is coming to bestow a kiss on his lady," she playfully expressed her fantasy. "And tonight he had to fight off the goblins to see me!" she laughed.

"On the contrary. They thought I was a goblin." Henry also delighted in the charm of this unusual liaison. The difficulty, the unexpected, and the thrill of risk made his meetings with Corisande even more exciting, and his daring spirit welcomed the risk with gusto. When the lovers wandered dreamily in the park of the château and its perfumed silence heightened their senses, Henry was able to forget the constraints of power and the demands of war.

"I wish I could be with you more often," Henry admitted. "The obscure battles I have been fighting are not worth the time away from you."

"Perhaps it would help if we knew our relationship was permanent," his mistress hinted.

"Of course it's permanent, my silly dove. Why shouldn't it be?"

"Your wars and your wife, to mention only two."

"Ah, but they are temporary problems. You are mine forever."

"I hope so, Pétiot," she murmured, using her new pet name for her soldier.

Again, Henry was obliged to leave Corisande after three idyllic days. Traveling to le Bazadais, he put an end to several disorders and then travelled to Langon to meet the Maréchal de Matignon.* Henry suspected the duc de Guise of stirring up the Catholics again, and so he called upon all the nobility loyal to him in the area to join their battalions and prepare for battle. The nobility were essentially a warrior class, their money allowing them to be free anytime for the call to arms. Suspecting spies behind every tree as he had at the Valois court so many years ago, he activated more rigorous training.

His absence lasted two months, and the memory of his mistress haunted him — her originality, her independence, and her fantasy. He flushed at the thought of her soft curves. Now he understood why she had chosen a name from a novel of chivalry — as a promise to

* Jacques II de Goyon de Matignon (1525-1598), maréchal de France. He fought for the Valois and Catholic cause for much of his life, but eventually switched sides to serve Henri IV.

others and to herself to carve out a romantic destiny. Her husband had been far from the knight in armor she desired. Though she spoke well of him, Gramont had been a compromiser, which Henry knew his mistress detested. For example, he was aware that the count, when he was governor of Navarre, had tried to borrow ten thousand *écus* from Philippe II of Spain in exchange for the government of Bayonne, then part of Navarre. How repugnant that must have been to his idealistic wife. At the end of August, when Henry returned to Pau, he wrote to Matignon:

> I have come here to have the pleasure of seeing my sister, hoping that this sight and the walks at Pau will give me back my health. I plan to be back at Nérac in 10 or 12 days.

But he was lying. On the pretext of visiting Catherine, he had returned to Béarn to see Corisande, who was installed at Pau. How much more suitable and desirable she would be for a wife than the Valois bitch, he thought. When he thought about Corisande now, he realized she reminded him in some ways of his mother — both were tall and thin, with high foreheads and refined, elegant carriage. He saw in both women, whom he loved so much, a natural tendency to dignity, fidelity, and valor. His mother had insisted on a chaste education, denying him profane music and the company of provocative women. She would have approved of this upright lady, he smiled, to whom his voluptuous temperament was now so passionately drawn.

PAU

1583

AT PAU A LETTER FROM MARGOT awaited Henry. Pleading loneliness, she recounted for him the splendors of all the entertainment he had missed. Swearing her brother was loyal, she said no harm would come to Henry in Paris. Henry hooted with disbelief. How could she expect him to feel safe in that vipers' nest? How could she forget that the extravagant nightlife of the Valois court would not entice him? He suspected that Marguerite wasn't lonely for him, only afraid her position as queen might be in jeopardy.

The same day would bring a veritable shower of news regarding his wife. In the evening, another courier from court arrived with two letters, one from the king, one from Margot. Labored and polite, the letter from Henri III baffled him. The gist of it, from what Henry could decipher, was that on August 7 Henri III had taken the liberty of expelling two women from Margot's retinue because of their "bad influence." The king inferred that the not-so-virtuous Queen of Navarre was being further corrupted by several serving maids, Mme de Bethune* (ironically, a relative of Corisande's) and Marguerite de Gramont, Dame de Duras. Therefore, Henri III would soon be packing Margot off to Navarre for safekeeping. Henry thought this story must be fabricated, knowing the upstanding character of Mme de Bethune.

The letter from Margot was another matter altogether. Tears blurred the ink in numerous places, probably from her ranting and raving. Melodrama was her style, Henry recalled.

> My cruel brother mercilessly shamed me in front
> of the entire court of France! I was presiding at a ball
> in place of my mother and Queen Louise, who was

---

* Marguerite de Rohan (1617 – 9 April 1684) was a French noblewoman and suo jure Duchess of Rohan. She was the only child of Henri de Rohan, Duke of Rohan and Marguerite de Béthune, a daughter of Maximilien de Béthune.

indisposed, and seated on the royal dais with Henri III. Suddenly and without provocation, my hateful brother turned on me and charged me before the assembled dancers with every kind of profligacy. I am in disgrace!

Henri named my lovers loudly until the whirling dancers before us stopped. How shall I ever hold my head up again? Then he shouted that I had even borne a child to my latest paramour, M. de Champvallon.

Henry remembered this man because of his remarkable physical beauty. Just Margot's type, Henry grinned. Then, recalling the gory head of La Môle, he shivered and read on:

I beg of you to realize how unfair such an accusation is! For am I not already grieved that I have been unable to bear you a child?

Henry did sympathize with Margot on this point, recalling with some shame how she had tended La Fosseuse for him during her labor pains. Then he shook his head. How like his wife to seize on the one charge which was unfounded, then feel herself maligned and wrongly slandered in general. She simply conveniently overlooked the fact that the other accusations were probably true.

What right has the Queen Mother to ask me to apologize to the King? I will not do it! Indeed, I have refused to temporize in any way, and so was given no choice but to leave Court. Do not worry, Henry, for I shall leave like a Queen; my behavior will belie any dishonor, and I will come to you immediately.

Henry asked the courier to wait while he disappeared into the Great Hall to reflect on what action he could take. He found Corisande and his sister there, busy with needlework, carrying on a desultory conversation. He rarely sat down, but his pacing finally drew a comment from his sister.

"Is something bothering you, Henry? You are bouncing about like the poplar leaves in a storm."

"*Ventre-St.-Gris*! This damn wife of mine wants to return to Navarre. It seems she has been such a blemish on the Valois court that

Henri III has thrown her out like some common courtesan. The little vixen thinks she can return to my protective arms."

Recounting for the women the story of the scene at the ball and of Henri's veiled letter, he suddenly stopped in mid-sentence, "Ah-ha! That foolish woman and her stupid brother have played right into my hands. It is so simple. Why didn't I think of it right away? I shall refuse to receive her unless the king will grant the Huguenots more security. I am sure Henri cannot afford to have his sister rebuffed by her own husband as well as by her family."

Henry dashed out of the room to give the courier the message that Marguerite was not to appear until terms had been negotiated. He would send his minister to present his case to the court in Paris shortly.

Enjoying his meal immensely that night, Henry talked boister-ously with his friends. Even M. de Rosny, who was usually so serious, was louder than usual. He had noticed a lady in Catherine's company who apparently charmed him. Perhaps now he will be less hard on me, thought Henry. He did not notice that Corisande was unusually quiet, so pleased was he with his inventive strategy.

Not until August 17 did Henry of Navarre send his Huguenot minister M. Duplessis-Mornay from Nérac to Paris to deal with the "Margot situation." He had decided to play the role of the aggrieved husband and insulted monarch and to bear this message, he chose the perfect emissary in Duplessis-Mornay. Mornay was a rigorous Protestant who regretted the passing of the Calvinist strictures of Jeanne d'Albret. Moral indignation was no pose for him, and his stiff neck encircled with a white ruff and black formal suit looked the part. He and the prudish Mme de Tigonville, a close friend of his sister's, found solace in condemning the wild behavior they witnessed among the contemporary generation. He constantly warned Henry of the "dread disease" and seemed to take pleasure in saying he would take the pox in exchange for freedom for the Huguenots. All his self-righteousness aggravated Henry, but he rightfully intuited it made Mornay the exact missionary he needed.

Henry's pointed note had obviously frightened Henri III, who had scurried from Paris to Lyon for safer refuge. When Mornay finally found him in this southeastern city, he beheld a man with gaunt cheeks, shifty eyes, and a mouth sucked in like an empty wine skin. Mornay informed the King of France that Henry's own reputation would be jeopardized if he received to his court and his bed a wife of dubious morality.

Totally at a loss as to what to do, Henri III did what he often did and relegated the affair to his mother. He found it so much simpler to play with his tame apes, monkeys, and little performing dogs than to cope with Henry. Dupléssis-Mornay's sense of duty prompted him to try again, and he managed another audience with the king. He had heard rumors of Henri III's recurring bouts of religious mania, during which the King would flog himself, but Mornay had discounted the tales as calumny. Now this time Henri appeared before him in monk's clothes, his head wrapped in a cowl and a rosary of small ivory skulls at his waist.

"I have no time to give you, Monsieur, for I am leaving on a pilgrimage to Chartres. I will go barefoot and pray for our country."

Shocked, disgusted, and wondering what would happen to France, Mornay left the whining sovereign to report to Henry of Navarre.

Henry followed up Duplessis-Mornay's message with another through Pibrac,* Margot's Chancellor. Pibrac went to court to demand reparation for the ill treatment accorded Margot. He also strongly hinted that if the King of France should remove his troops from several towns in the South, Navarre would be more flexible in the negotiations. Henry found out how intolerable inaction was to Margot when she wrote to him after six weeks of waiting and moving from place to place:

> I cannot rest until I am liberated from this purgatory, for I can find no better name for it, since I do not know whether I am to be consigned to Heaven or to Hell.

Henry realized he was now using poor Margot as a pawn just as her brother Charles had. But it is her own doing, he rationalized.

---

* Guy du Faur de Pibrac (1529-1584). Having studied law in Paris, he wrote a Catholic Apology for Saint Bartholomew's Massacre. Thereby, he was able to merit entry to the Valois court as a Huguenot emissary from Henry of Navarre to press the Valoises to release Marguerite to her husband.

HAGETMAU

HENRY WAS AWAY AGAIN. Corisande waited. Anxious. Yet she knew her lover would come.

On November 15 Henry returned to Hagetmau for a day and a night. Upon arriving, he found Corisande in her bath, a large tub raised on a dais. Reclined on the steps, he watched his mistress perform her ablutions noticing her skin looked as luminous as the white marble in which she bathed. Her first lady-in-waiting was bathing with her, as was the custom. Henry's excitement grew as he saw her breasts grow taut and rise with arousal. She stepped over the cold marble sides of the bath and came to him.

Henry understood that this relationship went far beyond an attraction governed by his sensual nature. He also realized that until now the only woman in his life who could be compared to the comtesse de Guiche was Marguerite. She possessed similar qualities, being refined, cultivated, and artistic. He had wanted to possess her and hoped for her admiration, but knew he had not loved her. With Corisande he was discovering satisfactions previously unknown and in her he found the confidante and advisor he needed. The comtesse was able to bring him inspiration when he was discouraged, not with empty words of encouragement, but with reason and understanding. He kept no secrets from her and openly discussed politics as though she were one of his military mates. For the first time, Henry's words of affection were not just formal gallantry but reflected deep respect.

Henry suspected Corsande was dazzled, knowing herself loved by her King, and that he fit her romantic ideas of a knight in armor. But he also recognized that her noble character would not allow her to use him selfishly or take him away from his duties to his kingdom.

She wanted more to assist him. There was something maternal in her love as she leaned over his shoulder, murmuring, "Pétiot."

"My heart, my soul, my love . . . " she heard him reply.

Waves of passion pounded over them and then the tide of love receded. The sounds of war too soon returned as skirmishes between Catholics and Protestants suddenly increased. Near Pau, Catholic troop movements had begun. Henry wondered whether the trouble was due more to Guise or to the Queen Mother, who perhaps was the one in charge of Catholic France now that Henri III was busy praying in Lyon and Chartres. Across the Chalosse and the Marsan the cannons rolled, and the chariots groaned under the weight of munitions.

Corisande awakened to the sound of Henry buckling his sword on November 17 as dawn spread white light upon the hills. She knew he didn't want to awaken her and so lay quietly, wishing the morning had not come so quickly. An instant later she heard the clatter of hooves as the King of Navarre exited the courtyard and took the road to Nérac where the prince de Condé would be waiting. She tried to assure herself that he was headed to a victory, but his cruel absence was all she truly felt.

Uncertainty dominated her days while she vainly attempted to replace it with hope. Corisande wandered among the dried hollyhock stalks and withered damask roses, constantly and impatiently watching for the couriers. On November 21 the messenger brought her news of Henry's victory, when, in the early morning he had surprised the people of Mont-de-Marsan before their breakfast. His soldiers essentially only had to show themselves, and the merchants agreed to open their shops under their new Protestant ruler.

The capture of Mont-de-Marsan was a dexterous coup that impressed all of France. However, this process of containment and separation of the Protestants and Catholics bothered Henry for several reasons. First, it was too slow and usually with short-lived success. Suspicion and fear would brew and fester until hostilities exploded again. But more important, he believed experience bore out that harmony would be possible only if both sides agreed to live together in mutual respect. As long as domination or fear of domination existed, peace would forever be out of reach for France. He knew of no other way to effect this outcome than to become the ruler of the country.

Numerous important affairs in the conquered town retained Henry, but as soon as he was able, he again took the road to Hagetmau, which lay midway between Orthez and Mont-de-Marsan. Rustic wagons represented the only traffic on the road. Loaded with wood and drawn by white oxen, these carts were the only vehicles capable of climbing the stony escarpments of the mountains. A peasant marched behind, invariably dressed in a woolen vest and brown breeches. Sometimes garlands of garlic and red pimentos, the jewelry of sustenance, encircled his neck.

Henry turned his horse toward the moss and heather from which white rocks peeped out like white bones. Everything here was so clean and simple. Corisande surely appreciated these mountains as much as he did, and her spirit seemed as pure and lofty as the thin mountain air, unsullied by the pollution of Parisian duplicity. He did not give a thought to Margot's frustration while she waited at Plessis-lez-Tours.

The Comtesse saw him on the afternoon of Saturday, December 3, but the next day Henry had to return to Mont-de-Marsan. At his plea, Corisande accepted his invitation to join him there for several weeks.

"Only if Catherine de Bourbon will be invited to come as well."

"But why is that necessary, Corisande?"

"Surely you must understand that it will make my presence appear natural. From feelings of what I owe to my birth, my rank, my children, I refuse to pass as the vulgar favorite that a sovereign carries in his baggage."

"But you came to Pau to see me," Henry argued.

"At Pau I sojourned before being loved by you, and I was always received by Madame."

"And at Hagetmau?" he inquired.

"At Hagetmau it is my duty to welcome Your Majesty. But I will never go to Nérac as your mistress. Nor will I be seen in the camps of Gascogne or D'Aunis."

Though frustrated by her inflexibility, Henry marveled at her idea of the honor of a woman and how her dignity imposed on her a rule by which she disciplined her passions. "You wish to remain a *dame de chevalerie*," he teased. "But whatever you may call yourself, you are mine!" he said, crushing her to him as tightly as he could.

NERAC

1584

HENRY ALLOWED MONTHS TO pass before determining Margot's fate. The back of her coach had meant good riddance to him and now he dreaded her return. He especially worried about jeopardizing his present life with Corisande, and he could not help but notice her anxiety whenever the subject of Margot came up. It had been almost a year since he and Margot had been together. Mentioning this to Corisande on a ride through the sun dappled woods near Pau brought a welcome smile to her face.

"I am in no hurry to have my wife back," he added, "and I have no compunctions about using her as a bargaining point."

"You must not trust her brother the king, either," she concluded.

"You are right, my love. Through his envoy, Bellièvre, Henri III has tried to persuade me to receive Margot. The king says that if I do so, then we might talk about removing the royal garrisons from Huguenot areas, which he insists are 'not at all dangerous.' "

"I think he knows you have him trapped."

"Exactly. I shall send a letter explaining that as soon as I learn his garrisons are withdrawn; then and only then will I leave for Nérac to receive Marguerite."

Corisande could not help flinching inwardly every time she heard her name or the words "my wife" but tried to restrain herself from complaining about Margot's return. At the very least, Marguerite was a political reality which could not be ignored.

During this blissful time, Henry was filled with indefatigable energy, sleeping only four hours a night, hunting deer and wild boar or playing tennis during the day, eating his favorite foods of anchovies, olives, paté, and melons, imbibing liters of Jurançon, and enjoying the caresses of his mistress at night. But at the back of his mind there was the nagging thought that he was not furthering his goal of bringing peace to France.

By March Henri III understood he had no choice; his back was against the wall. Subsequently Henry heard that the king's troops had been removed from the towns he had specified. Rejoicing at the success of his coup, he agreed to meet Margot, but still stalled on setting a firm date. He dreaded her vindictive tongue, sensing that ever since the Fosseuse affair, she no longer was his trusted ally. He wrote her an ambiguous letter:

> It is necessary for both of us that when they see us reunited it will be with our full consent . . . I want it to appear to everyone that I do nothing by coercion and that I believe none of all these calumnies. This, my love, is all I can say for the present.

Finally, in early April Navarre advised Bellièvre he would come to Nérac, where Margot would be awaiting him. Henry explained he could not come during Holy Week because, "It is the time of devotions, but I would like to be reunited with my wife immediately after Easter." He was not about to deprive himself of spending Holy Week at Pau where Corisande would be the guest of his sister. But the moment for departure did arrive.

"I will miss you," Corisande said.

"It will not be for long. Only long enough for appearance's sake, and then I shall return to Pau and you. I regard her only as a nuisance which is keeping me from you."

"Will Margot be angry when she learns about me?" his mistress asked.

"She has always allowed me my affairs and I have cared nothing about hers. Our relationship has been one of convenience and ambition, I believe. However, she is very bothered right now about not being able to bear a child, and this might make her fearful of my alliances where she was not before. Also, I expect her to be spiteful because I made her wait for our meeting, but she won't dare make me too angry."

"You are probably right, *chéri*. One catches more flies with a spoonful of honey than with two liters of vinegar."

Her kiss was so forceful as to be painful. It was as though she wanted a bruise to remember him by when he was with his wife.

The reunion of the King and Queen of Navarre took place on Easter Friday, April 13. They rode the final approach to Nérac together. Muddy roads and skies gray with the threat of a spring shower added to the pall over the party. The people gathered to watch the royal train did not shout welcomes as they had when Navarre had introduced his queen to Nérac. Now the talk was muted, the atmosphere awkward and strained.

"You are looking lovely, Margot," Henry conjoined the conversation.

"You were certainly in no hurry to see me," she reprimanded.

"Diplomacy is always slow. You know that. I suggested you join me at Nérac since I know you prefer it to Pau, where I have been residing with my sister, whom you do not seem to enjoy."

"You are quite thoughtful," she replied in a sarcastic tone. Then she abruptly changed the mood. "The leaves are just budding; spring is beautiful everywhere."

"Indeed," he said, wondering if this was the limit of recrimination she would cast in his direction. Although she was still a young woman, he observed a marked change in her. It seemed as if her mouth remained in a permanent downward position, and he found her more subdued than he expected. Perhaps this indicated she would be more dangerous as well. His fears were compounded when she became tearful at dinner that evening. Would she become hysterical and hard to manage? Had she expected a warmer welcome from him? Was she truly mourning her loss of honor due to the scandal? He guessed she was resentful her court would be at Nérac for the moment rather than the gayer Louvre, and she certainly had been having a difficult time lately. Whatever, she was not a happy queen and Henry could not afford an enemy. He determined to remain at Nérac with her for longer than planned and to check on the garrisons in the area while here. Corisande would understand.

François d'Alençon lay dying. The news reached Margot and Henry at Nérac. For months it had been evident that he was declining rapidly. A fever, which his physicians diagnosed as tertiary ague, continued to plague him intermittently, and in April he arrived at Château Thierry, sicker than before.

Margot moped around Nérac day after day. "My poor brother," she wailed. "Ever since he returned from Flanders in defeat, he has been morose over his failure to gain that throne, and equally dejected by Elizabeth I's rejection of him as a husband."

"Indeed, she did keep him dangling for a long time," Henry laughed. "Calling him her 'little frog.' *Ventre-St.-Gris*! I cannot believe he really thought one day he could be king of England. And his wild folly in 1583 to take the Netherlands again was completely beyond my understanding."

In the back of his mind, Henry had rather liked the idea of Alençon marrying Elizabeth. It would have removed him from the succession to the French throne and cemented the alliance of France and England. Yet his death would accomplish the first goal at least, and Henry had been able to depend on the English monarch's support in the past without a nuptial liaison.

Margot glared at him, and he guiltily wondered if she had read his mind. "You sound absolutely heartless. Poor mother! At another son's bedside. She must be almost as desperate as he. She already has buried a young husband and seven children. Three died when they were only babies and now Alençon is her youngest — only 29 years old — and he is feeble, exhausted, and childless."

"Margot, you have always been eloquent, and I am sorry about Alençon. However, it is very difficult for me ever to feel sorry for your mother! Or for your dissolute brother, who has taxed the poor of this country to pay for his frivolity and excesses!"

His wife ignored his plaints. "Do you remember, Henry, how she tried to learn about magic when her womb seemed to be infertile? You know that finally, after years of potions and rhymes she miraculously brought forth an heir to the throne. More children followed, and she naturally came to believe her seed would people the thrones of Europe. Now it is becoming all too clear that this has been a false hope, a cruel illusion."

She bit her lip. And what illusions she had held about her own life! Henry perceived it was no accident that she was reminding him of her mother's lateness in bearing heirs. She continued, "I'm afraid she has little reassurance now to give her youngest. I am told she watches the blood of the house of Valois trickle from his nose and mouth."

Nérac remained a busy place for while Catherine de Medici was caring for François, Henri III sent his emissary, Epernon,* to suggest that the First Prince of the Blood come to Paris to consider conversion to Catholicism. The King of France was astute enough — or at least his mother was — to realize that the succession must be established immediately, and if Henri III should die also, the King of Navarre would be the presumptive heir to the crown of France. Salic Law, which was the original body of Frankish law governing the country, awarded the succession in order of primogeniture to the nearest prince in the male line of descent to the previous king. To most of France, it appeared that Henry of Navarre had forfeited his right to the throne by his stubborn adherence to a heretical sect. Since the king of France had always been Catholic and the king's coronation oath demanded that not only must he be the chief protector of the Roman faith but that he must solemnly promise to extirpate heresy from his kingdom, the people believed only a Catholic could be king. Henry and his followers argued that the Salic Law of succession alone trumped this Catholic rule and the two should not be entangled. Moreover, Henry worried that his conversion would be interpreted by his Huguenot supporters as a betrayal, and so his domestic support would be lost and his foreign Protestant alliance compromised.

He tried to discuss the issue with Margot, but just when he was beginning to feel compassion for his wife, her melodramatic style would repel him.

"I don't like Epernon," Margot pouted. "Why should I receive him?"

"Because the Queen Mother is desirous of settling the perilous question of the royal succession and has begged you to stop your caprice," he responded. But in a way Marguerite's reluctance served as a buffer for him.

"I don't see why it is so important," she lied.

"I would expect you to be eager to help insure the throne for me and yourself," Henry said. He suspected she might be pretending to be on his side, but he could never trust her.

"It is difficult to be practical in the midst of my grief," she sobbed. Henry granted this could well be true, but he was so accustomed to her hypocrisy, he often failed to note true emotion.

---

* Jean Louis de Nogaret de la Valette, duc d'Epernon (1554-1642) supported Henri III and the Catholic cause and was one of Henri III's *mignons*.

François d'Alençon died on June 10, 1584, and Margot at last surrendered to her mother's wishes to receive Epernon. She told Henry, "I believe the Queen Mother to be so grieved by the loss we have sustained that the fear I have of irritating her and of losing her has made me do violence to myself in a way I thought was beyond my power."

Henry answered only by rolling his eyes to the ceiling. How he wished for the constant Corisande beside him rather than Margot, whose dramas irritated him more and more. Excusing himself to take care of some letters, he immediately sat down to write to his mistress:

> I know the Huguenots of the South, despite the eight years I have spent among them, still do not entirely trust me. I know not to trust the Valoises, yet because of the turmoil which would overtake France should the line of royal succession remain unestablished . . . I believe it best at this time to receive Epernon with cordiality but to refuse the King's offer.

Even though Henry knew François d'Alençon and Henri III had been more inimical than brotherly, he also wrote to the king:

> The news of Alençon's passing has brought me great sadness for I recognize my inestimable loss; but of course how much greater is this for Your Majesty, and yet I am sure that since you have so often overcome so many adversities, you will be able to surmount this one, seeing in it the will of God.

He couldn't resist a sarcastic touch, even in the face of death. He confided more sincerely to Corisande by letter about the aspect of succession, which was uppermost in his mind — conversion. To her, he wrote, "I do not wish in changing my religion to lose friends of whom I am sure, in order to acquire others about whom I am doubtful."

Henry knew he was taking a big chance by evading the issue. If he converted now, the throne was not necessarily his. There was always the possibility that Henri III would divorce Louise and try to have a child by a second marriage. He doubted this would happen, however, because of the king's fear of being proven the sterile partner. Also, ever since Duplessis-Mornay's report of the king's bizarre appearance at Lyon, he felt sure the king didn't have the energy necessary to fight the pope over the divorce question.

Henry was well aware that the Catholics, threatened by his growing strength, had begun to centralize their opposition. He knew that Henri, duc de Guise, who claimed descent from Charlemagne, had been waiting for the chance to seize power ever since Henri III had taken the League from him. Henry decided the best antidote to the Guise threat must still be a wait-and-see policy. Also, groups of Catholic extremists opposed to any sort of acceptance of Protestants gathered into "leagues" that were operating in all sixteen districts of Paris. They called themselves the *Seizes*. Henry enjoyed doing much of his political planning in his letters to Corisande, and so he wrote:

> I rely heavily on my close and cordial relations with England and her proud monarch, Elizabeth I. For further backing I think I should take steps to establish firm friendships with other Protestant nations. I shall keep in friendly contact with the Duke of Saxony, the Duke of Sweden, and Frederick of Denmark.

It was always best, he thought, to preserve friendships and avoid any unpleasantness. He stretched his legs in front of him and rang for Roquelaure to bring him a snack of goat cheese and Jurançon wine. When Margot entered in his valet's stead with the tray, he felt he could bear her company no longer. He yearned for Corisande. His wife's manner and her feelings of pride and passion became more and more exasperating, and her chatter jangled his nerves. Corisande's letters could relieve for an instant his poignant desire to be with her, but all too soon, the pining and loneliness, like the soughing of the wind in the forest, would return. He knew Margot had heard of his liaison with Corisande, but she had not mentioned it yet to Henry.

"Ah, thank you, my dear," he dissimulated, pouring some wine for both of them. "You know we had news this morning that my sister, Catherine, is ill. I am worried about her and believe I had better make a brief sojourn to Pau to check on her."

Margot took a sip of the wine, regarding him over the rim of her glass. "Is it only Catherine you are going to see, Henry?"

Ah, he mused, we are about to have one of our few honest exchanges.

"Perhaps not," he answered, still unsure of what he should conceal or reveal.

"Is this more serious than your previous affairs?" she asked, her voice becoming unsteady.

"By all means," he answered.

"And what does that signify?"

"It means I am going away to enjoy myself! — And check on my sister."

"You are a hard, ungrateful egotist," Margot screamed. "How can your silly mistress care for such a secretive, boastful lout?"

He should not have antagonized her, he thought, but she irritated him so.

"Margot, I think we have too much in common. I would feel perfectly in my right calling you those same names. No, perhaps I would substitute 'vain' for 'boastful.'"

"Get out of here, you filthy swine."

"With pleasure, my Queen."

HAGETMAU

1584

CORISANDE RECEIVED HENRY, who was still dressed in mourning garments in honor of François d'Alençon. All of his servants wore black as well, and even the horses were clad in black. Corisande had properly prepared the King's room at Hagetmau, draping the walls with funereal colors, putting black curtains on the bed, black rugs on the floor and a black slipcover on the King's chair.

Promptly escaping the macabre interior for the garden, the lovers recalled it had been spring when they had first met. Everything had been as it was now: the softness in the air, the excitement of expected growth, nature in her most luxurious and welcoming attire. Around the large château, the long hills of Chalosse sloped toward the horizon, dramatically changing where the snowy peaks of Béarn and Navarre pierced delicate silky clouds. The raw green of young sprouts in the vineyards reached toward the liberal light of an early Gascon spring. Cherry and plum blossoms scented the air and the songs of goldfinches supplanted the dirges of the preceding month. Henry thought how easily one was inclined to an effortless optimism here, springing from the fertile land, surplus wine, and a forgiving climate.

Wearing a dress with a high lace collar framing her face, with her silky hair swept high off her forehead, Corisande appeared radiantly beautiful to Henry. But more important, he realized, he was happy to see her because she was his closest companion. Oddly she had supplanted all of his male advisors on whom he had formerly depended. He believed they could speak intimately without constraint or self-consciousness, relying on an intuitive understanding of each other.

But they had been separated for many weeks, he with his wife and she alone. An awkwardness, which he hadn't foreseen, prevailed, and he felt a little like a guilty child with a parent. Noticing that she hadn't touched him, he experienced a new shyness at touching her. His nervousness made him chatter at first but finally, simply the vision of her began to calm him.

"You are more necessary to me, Corisande, than my ministers, my first gentleman of the bed chamber, and my first gentleman of the stables — all together," he remarked.

"But they are all men," Corisande laughed, breaking the ice a bit.

"You are male and female to me," Henry replied seriously, stroking her cheek with his finger. "Everyone else could leave and I would not care; but you, I want you with me forever."

"And I shall be. I love you more than I believed it possible to love another person."

Continuing to converse, they meandered through the park of the château, which was essentially a great wood on a hill, lying cozily among meadows and cultivated fields. Colonnades of grand oaks lined long solitary alleys arched over them, while to the left, the lofty trunks of ash trees mounted the back of the hill. Only three hundred paces away, the Gave de Pau tumbled between steep banks. They climbed hand in hand, Corisande holding her skirt above the ground, and looked over the meadows, where the warm sun of the Pyrénées made the vigorous verdure shine more richly. Henry found a mound of grass to sit upon near a group of live oaks, where they saw the feet of the trees were bathed in water, the continuation of the pellucid stream bordering the road.

"You know," Henry began, "in March when I learned of the terms of the secret pact between Spain and Guise, it frightened me. I learned the parties met in the old feudal castle of the Guises at Joinville. I understand the Spaniards agreed to help defend the Roman faith in France, and extirpate heresy, and affirmed the right of my uncle, the cardinal de Bourbon, to the throne of France with Spanish money and Spanish troops. In return, Guise promised to fight the Flemish rebels and to return to Spain the disputed territory of Cambrai."

"Yes, I heard this also. I presume this treasonous treaty is no longer a secret at all for I know that Guise is already in arms," she said. "In fact, we are nervous here for he has already taken Chalons-sur-Marne and his brother the duc de Mayenne has captured the beautiful city of Dijon."

"*Sacrebleu*! The purpose of the new League is now clear — to keep the crown away from me!" Henry remonstrated. "I have offered to help the king, but Henri III has the sense to know he would lose all credibility if he accepts aid from his heretical Huguenot cousin. He has already lost the people by his policy of appeasement to us, and Guise's militancy appeals to the majority. The king cannot afford to alienate the Papacy too. The best outcome for Henri III would be for me to convert and thereby become a legitimate heir. For Guise and his faction, the best thing is for me to remain loyal to the reformed religion."

"So what do you plan to do now?" his mistress asked.

"I fear these are rather poetic wars I have been fighting. I have only needed a small company to capture the hostile castles in the neighborhood. We intercept their body of arquebusiers, scale the fortress, threaten the owners at gunpoint, extricate ourselves from their midst with pistol in hand, and then I am free to return to you. I believe it is going to become much rougher soon. In fact, I have been fooling myself in thinking I could get anywhere with these skirmishes. These religious civil wars must be stopped, once and for all. I don't wish to cause more suffering by stirring up matters, but the Catholics, feeling threatened here in the West, keep launching small and potentially dangerous incidents. Now the League, led by Guise, is building up its forces too under the battle cry, *Un roi, une foi, une loi*,* and I certainly will not get far by only conquering the small Catholic outposts in the Pyrénées."

"I expect your absences, Pétiot. It is enough for me that you will return, that I am yours and you are mine. At times, though, it is difficult for me to understand why you don't accept Catholicism, not only for your own interest, but for the peace of the kingdom which is so important to you."

Henry pondered and answered slowly. "Having been nourished and raised in the religion I now profess, it does not have roots so weak they can be easily removed; and as this matter is the only one we are accountable to before God, perhaps I should await clear and certain inspiration from Him. Moreover, such a rapid change on my part would imply hypocrisy, inconstancy, and infidelity, all qualities which would certainly make me unworthy of being king. Although I haven't publicly admitted it, I'm sure you know I very much want to become King of France."

---

* One king, one faith, one law.

"I remember when — it must have been when you were under house arrest in Paris before your escape — le comte de Montgomery and his men ravaged Béarn, destroying Huguenot churches, looting their valuables and leaving cadavers behind. So I have witnessed personally the horrors both sides can inflict in this horrific civil war. Indeed, how foolish the country is not to accept you as a Protestant!" she sympathized.

"Instead they joke that I have more nose than kingdom and more to say than money," he laughed in a healthy self-deprecating tone.

"The latter is certainly true!" She laughed with him.

They returned to the château, glad to be together. But Henry sensed something was bothering Corisande.

"What is troubling you, my love?" he asked as they entered her suite.

"It is Agrippa d'Aubigné, your ambitious master of the horse," she admitted. "I believe he is jealous of my closeness to you. I cannot tolerate his ignoble insults! He calls me your resident strumpet. I feel everyone is talking behind my back now. He has composed a verse about us, and I spent the day indoors yesterday, too ashamed to show my face. I am beginning to hate his beady black eyes and sneering smile."

"Tell me his rhyme," Henry commanded.

Tu as choisi la comtesse,
Pour te mener à la Messe,
Cela n'est rien de nouveau
Et pourquoi? Et vraiment parce
Que c'est le fait d'une garce,
De mener l'autre au bordeau.

You have chosen the Countess
To take you to Mass
But that is nothing new
Why because 'tis true
'tis the duty of a trollopy lass
To lead you to the whore's palace.

Henry roared. "Rather clever of that bastard. Don't let it worry you, *chérie*. He is just a nervous, visionary type, who is outraged that you have more influence with me than he does. He is extremely loyal to me and worried lest anything threaten me or my chances of success. But you may rest assured that his bitter irony cannot harm us."

"I am not so sure, Henry. He has even accused me of being a sorceress who has bewitched you. I heard he went to consult a Doctor Hotteman to find out if he could provide some philters which would disenchant you."

"But that is ridiculous! Will these dolts never learn to leave magic alone? I will speak to Agrippa tomorrow."

"And Henry, the folks in the villages are beginning to gossip about us. They say the reformed church of France should not permit you to hold the title of protector as long as you lead such a dissolute life."

Henry shook his head in despair. "If only they understood how wonderful you are. Damn these Huguenots! They are blinded by religious passion as much as the Catholics and are incapable of understanding the spirit of tolerance which is so natural to you. What the Huguenot leaders really fear is that my beautiful Catholic mistress will draw me into a dangerous trap. M. de Rosny, that stiff buzzard, passed on to me that one of them recently said, 'The pleasures of the comtesse de Guiche will retain the King of Navarre longer than the welfare of the general good requires.' "

"I have been thinking for a long while of cutting some of the wood in my forest so I can give you some money for your cause. Perhaps that will quiet some of their malicious tongues," she suggested. "You know I am willing to sacrifice anything but my faith for my loved one and to my king — who happen to be one and the same."

"You are an angel and I would gratefully accept. But these Philistines would only say your magnanimous act was a clever diversion to catch me off guard. Moreover, I'm sure my wife is encouraging their doubts about your loyalty. She is proving to be a viper as lethal as her mother."

Corisande didn't answer immediately. "Sometimes I wish Margot didn't exist," she finally blurted to her lover.

Henry looked surprised. "But my dear, I spend more time with you than with my wife; you know I love you and not my wife."

But Margot was his wife and he had not spoken again of changing this status. During his absences this fact bothered Corisande more than she confessed, he realized. "She doesn't exist for me. *Pardieu*! You know that."

"Yes, but you do have certain duties toward her you must fulfill."

"This is not like you, *chérie*, to worry so. Someday you will be my wife and you know I am always faithful to you," he whispered.

Tears filled her eyes at this evidence of his love. She wiped them quickly away, never wanting to be a burden to him.

But Henry had seen her hurried movement. He hated to see anyone around him unhappy and would try with a joke or a gift to lighten the atmosphere or bring a smile. But just as he wanted his friends to have their desires gratified, he was equally — if not more — demanding and impatient that his own be granted. Not believing self-sacrifice necessary or desirable for obtaining results, he preferred persuasion, action, and open-mindedness as the better means to bring satisfaction to the greatest number.

Later in the day Henry extended himself at his mistress's feet, watching her busy hands embroider pearls in a trefoil design onto green velvet. How he adored her sweet tempered face and kind eyes! A blue satin counterpane and drapery fringed with gold and silver adorned the bed. On the floors were rugs from Turkey, and rich cushions of blue velvet softened the caskets and benches.

"Perhaps you really have cast a spell over me," he teased. "Otherwise, how could Henry, the warrior, be so quiet for so long?"

She correctly saw this as a subtle introduction to his need to depart.

"I don't want to keep you from your duty or jeopardize your position," she replied. "I love you too much to hold you here."

Seized with his usual energy, Henry jumped up and paced the room, explaining his plan for increasing his forces and for besieging key cities held by the Catholics. He was more worried about the recent advances of the League and the encroachments of the duc de Mayenne than he liked to admit. And of course Guise was behind Mayenne. They were capitalizing on the self-evident truth that it was intolerable to most Frenchmen to accept a Huguenot monarch.

"In the country," he began, "I came across hordes of haggard, emaciated children — children who begged and threatened any passerby who refused them charity. Freezing wind whistled through their wretched hovels; the poor souls didn't even have enough wood for a fire. And this is not the coldest time of the year! Civil war has obliterated the order necessary for an ordinary life and death dogs the footsteps of the poor, the old, and the sick. I cannot stand for it to continue like this."

"Then you must leave soon. If I write and ask you to return to Pau, do not listen. It is only a moment of weakness when my love and worry for you have dominated reason."

"There is no other woman like you, my Corisande."

She embraced him so he wouldn't see her tears, and this time she had more success in hiding them.

Michel Eyquem, seigneur de Montaigne, the celebrated philosopher and essayist, was expected for dinner this evening at Corisande's château. Presently mayor of Bordeaux, he had been a member of Henry's bedchamber earlier in his career. Montaigne remained a Catholic, which bothered Henry even more than Corisande's loyalty to Romanism.

The comtesse's maître d'hôtel, Pierre de Ruveray, opened the door to M. de Montaigne and escorted him to the grand salon where Corisande and Henry awaited his arrival. Henry sprang up and rushed across the room to greet his friend, glad to see his bald pate and rough goatee. If someone whom he liked came for a formal audience, Henry never could resist hurrying to them rather than awaiting their obeisant bow. The men embraced, thumping each other on the back.

"You'll need to come near the fire to keep your head warm," Henry said, pulling Montaigne into the room. "If anyone should wear a wig, it is you! It might improve that sour puss of yours!"

"Please remind me, Sire, what is it about you that the people find to like?" Montaigne asked, smiling.

"Well, we know it is not my beauty," the king responded.

Turning to Corisande, Montaigne presented her with a book of his own verses but which also included twenty-nine sonnets of the great poet La Boétie. The book was dedicated to the comtesse de Guiche. Corisande read aloud so Henry could share her pleasure in this magnificent gift:

> Madame, I do not offer you anything that is mine both because it is already yours and because I cannot find anything worthy of you. But I wished that these verses, in whatever place they are seen, carry your

name at their head, for the honor it will be for them to have as a guide the great Corisande d'Andouins. This present seemed to me appropriate for you, in as much as there are few women in France who judge or serve poetry better.

Henry could see she was extremely touched. "I cannot think of a more beautiful gift," she said as she embraced her friend, "except of course any and all of your own work."

They were served one of the rich wines of Jurançon, but Henry took only mineral water.

"Since when do you prefer water to wine, Sire?" Montaigne inquired. "I cannot believe that is the choice of a fellow Gascon."

"I have another damned attack of the gout and Corisande's doctor insists I keep a strict diet for several days. The idiot prescribes no wine, no venison pâté or jugged hare. I hardly think his cure can be worth the sacrifice."

"He is as difficult to counsel as a donkey," Corisande chuckled. "But let us go into dinner and perhaps the partridge with garlic and the melons and plums from Agen will soothe your spirits, Pétiot."

Montaigne followed the couple into the dining room. He didn't believe in the fatality or all-powerfulness of love, but like Henry, he was impressed with Corisande's extraordinary personality. He had worried when he observed her driving a permanent wedge between Henry and Margot. Now he hoped she might help direct Henry and his kingdom along a reasonable path. He knew it was her ardent passion for poetry which particularly charmed him, but he recognized a singular intelligence and quiet nobility which might complement Henry's vitality and passion.

Never being one to evade what was bothering him, Henry spoke to his guest, "Why don't you join our Huguenots, Michel? You know that many of the Catholics of Bordeaux would follow your example if you advocated our cause. Your essays have a wide audience. You are for me and yet you are against me."

"Ah, Henry, as much as I respect you, I have remained a Catholic because I see Protestantism as more dangerous to the Republic than it is profitable to Christianity."

"The danger to the Republic is the ambitious malevolent Guise and his Catholic ally, Philip."

"You are right, Henry, but the Huguenots now are equally as divisive a force. We agree in basic philosophy, you and I. We both condemn fanaticism and cruelty, the horrors of civil and religious war, and support the restoration of order and peace. But my conversion to Protestantism will not guide us in that direction."

"Perhaps you are right, my friend," Henry answered. "But it bothers me that you are not entirely with us."

"You will find that I am with you in the important ways. I see in you a sense of humanity and tolerance that is the essence of my essays. If you prevail, I believe all France will benefit, and anyone who reads my works will understand that."

"I hope so," Henry grumbled. "At first the Catholics and Protestants could not agree upon specific ideas. Theirs was an intellectual disagreement. At some unknown point in time, the rational argument disappeared and the split became an emotional one as well which is much more dangerous. Now they have returned to intellectualizing as a rationale for their gut responses of hatred for one another. As though the endless debates at the university could excuse the countless lives being lost!"

"Many ask why you do not want to destroy the Catholics as they want to destroy you. And I suspect your reasons are similar to mine." Montaigne smiled at Henry with these words, but then his tone became severe. "Nothing is more alien to religion than religious wars; religious wars are not born of faith nor do they make men pious. For some they are the pretext of ambition, for others the opportunity of enrichment. They weaken a nation, which becomes prey to foreign aggression."

"How right you are, my philosopher king, how right you are!" Henry boomed. "Destroying one another is certainly not the answer. I believe in tolerance for reasons of humanity, and personal experience has taught me no other way will work, which I guess you could call simple pragmatism. Ah, give me the society of a Gascon! Everyone else is too serious." Henry paused to crush the head of a delicate ortolan between his teeth, then spat out a mouthful of needle-like bones. "I cannot be served by a melancholy man, for how can a man who is bad for himself be good for others? Can one hope for contentment from a man who isn't able to content himself?"

"I doubt it," Montaigne agreed. "But the scatological humor of the Gascon would not be everyone's idea of contentment."

"Then they are the losers. The Béarnaises are to other people what gold is to silver."

"Do not let the Parisians hear you say that!" Montaigne reminded him.

"*Mère de Dieu.* It is difficult for me to remember to be diplomatic. My sweet lady here tells me I would have been hung as a thief if I had not been born a king." He chuckled and Montaigne and Corisande laughed with him.

"She is probably right," Montaigne concurred again. "I do not know another king who wears muddy boots, has a shaggy beard, and such strong breath in such a filthy mouth."

Yet he can speak with elegance, and he has the gift of quick perception, Montaigne thought, having witnessed Henry read others' eyes and hearts before they knew their inner thoughts themselves.

After dinner the talk again revolved around politics, and Corisande chose to listen rather than join in. When Montaigne visited during Henry's absences, they always talked of poetry. In 1578, when Pierre de Ronsard had published his collective works, she had read them with deep appreciation. Montaigne loved this poetry as she did and delighted in her ability to speak of literature with ardor and taste. But he heartily disagreed with her about l'*Amadis*. This novel of chivalry from which she had borrowed her name satisfied her instinct for the romantic and her propensity for dreams and fairy tales. Montaigne had told her that for him, it was useless and trite. They had argued these points during happy hours of sharing a common interest, as kindred literary spirits. Corisande ceased her daydreaming and listened carefully to Henry's assessment of the League and its growing danger.

"I received alarming news from my spies in the Guise territory of Lorraine," he revealed. "Evidently the duc de Guise has strengthened the Holy League, creating a union of militant Catholics for whom the conservation of the Catholic faith is the primary goal. Its clearly defined objective is to prevent the crown of France from falling into the hands of a heretic. Its political philosophy is that religious unity is the social foundation of any state, and Guise has rallied the old cry, 'One king, one faith, one law'. The king they determine to restore to the throne is Henry IV's uncle, the Cardinal de Bourbon, now old and uninspired."

"You are right, Henry," Montaigne responded, "and I fear the League. But more than that, I fear the Guise alliance with Spain. The king finally has been aroused from his lethargy by this news and on November 11, he issued a declaration against the League . . . 'against all persons making leagues, associations, intrigues, and practices against the estate of this realm.' "

"Yes, yes, I know," Henry replied impatiently. "But we also know that since Henri III is now powerless, his declaration is likewise impotent. It is time for me to respond with all the military might I can muster before the Guises, their League, and puppet king, the Cardinal de Bourbon, fill the vacuum the Valois incompetence has created. The Guises are using the pretext of religion to unseat the rightful monarch and to wage war on me. Their true goal is power."

Watching the two men talk — one such a quiet intellectual, the other such a vigorous intellectual and soldier, Corisande was surprised she preferred the soldier to the writer. She let her eyes caress his dark beard and expressive eyes. Tonight would be even more pleasant after their guest left.

Henry felt her sensuous mood and took her hand. Her tender manner always made him love her anew.

The next day dawned despite Corisande's prayers that the night last forever.

"You are my courage and my heart, *chérie*," Henry whispered before he mounted his horse. Then suddenly her solicitous tenderness seemed suffocating, and he was eager to be away. He always looked more imposing on horseback than off because of his thin short legs. His chest was robust and his fan-shaped beard striking. As he rode off, Corisande felt her resolution momentarily wilt, and she wished he were less a man of action. She probably loved the vitality that propelled him to dynamic behavior, but her affair was more with the man within, the man who wanted so much to be loved. She had understood this about him for a long time. Now, she feared her love would not be enough for this ebullient and mercurial man who cried as easily as he laughed and who campaigned with such ferocious energy.

Her romantic ideas from her novels of chivalry helped replace her misgivings as Henry's letters began to arrive. Despite the hazards of sending messages through occupied territory, the lovers' clever and inventive couriers delivered letters, hiding notes in the linings of their caps, the heels of their shoes, or the scabbards of their swords.

Responding to Corisande's interest, Henry wrote chaste messages of fact, full of events. She was happy to hear his news of a battle, of a town taken, a comrade wounded, the plague rampant, for she knew she was really part of him when he talked to her of these things. She was then sure that he wanted to share with her everything he did and thought. Precious to her also were the words with which he always ended, "Live assured of my fidelity; if possible it is stronger than ever."

War became a way of life for the king of Navarre. But Corisande knew she was never long out of his mind, and on June 17, she received a letter from Marans, not far from La Rochelle:

> I have never seen a place so suitable for you. With this in mind I intend to make some exchange for it. It is an island enclosed by woodland marshes, where every hundred steps there are canals so that you can explore the woods by boat. The water is clear and rather fast running. The canals are wide and the boats all very splendid. In this woodland there are a thousand gardens which can be visited only by boat . . . One can be tranquil here in time of peace and secure in time of war. One can rejoice in the presence of someone you love or lament in his absence . . . My soul, keep me in your grace and believe my fidelity is pure and spotless; there has never been its equal . . . Your slave who adores you madly.

The proximity of the fighting soon imperiled Catherine and Corisande as well, forcing them to leave Pau for safety elsewhere. Together, they decided to retire to the town of Navarrenx, where, early in the century, the princes of Béarn, wishing for a strategic fortress at the foot of the Pyrénées, had built a bastion. Henry found them there late in June and managed to stay for one week. The Huguenot chiefs met him there to talk about joining Henri III, who now needed their help desperately to combat the League. A Catholic League, controlled by the pope and Spain, suddenly seemed a greater threat to the Huguenots than domination by their weak French king, be he Catholic or not.

Corisande was able to return to Hagetmau, and on the fourth day of the month Henry decided to join her there. He knew the road and tracks between Hagetmau and Pau as well as the expressions on his mistress's face, he thought. The separation had been long, but he still very much wanted to see her. She could soften his spirit as no one else could. How long this road to kingship was! Even the three or four hours the trip took seemed longer and harder than it used to.

With the mountains at his back and the setting sun before him, he used his time in the saddle for planning his next battle strategy. He would need to take Fontenay-Le-Comte soon and it should not be a difficult battle. Crossing the tranquil waters of the Lux de Béarn, he saw he had the advantage of his knowledge of this terrain. He knew where the thick stands of long-needled pines with tall bare trunks were, where the streams crossed the land, and when and where the fog usually would appear. Thin milky wisps of cloud were beginning now to slide between the trees, causing him to shiver from the dampness. He must be tired. The soft creamy air reminded him of Corisande's skin, and he spurred his horse to hurry. Surprising a covey of quail that scattered before him, he laughed at the sudden flurry of wings.

Corisande was shocked when she saw her soldier. His mustache had turned white and his face appeared more furrowed. Stroking the creases of his tanned skin, she tried to imagine what he had endured.

"Do you like this way of life as much as you seem to?" she wanted to know.

"I become intoxicated in battle," he tried to explain, waving his arms. "I enjoy soldiering in much the same way I do hunting. I love the drama and excitement, the rolling kettledrums and shrilling fifes, the jangles of harness and clatter of weapons."

"It's so hard to understand." She wanted to weep. Together they sojourned to Navarrenx to visit his sister and obtain cannons. Corisande took Catherine a brooch crafted by the Portuguese Jewish jewelers of Bordeaux.

"How glad it makes me," said Henry, "to see the friendship between the woman I love and my gentle sister." Since Catherine was often unwell, Corisande remained in refuge with her at Navarrenx. But this did not stop her from responding to Henry's call whenever they could spend several moments together at Hagetmau. In spite of the plague which was ravaging le Bordelais, les Landes, and even la Chalosse, in spite of the enemy in the neighborhood, Corisande would rush to him. For Henry the risk was even greater, because the enemy knew him to be invincibly drawn toward his mistress and so watched the roads to Hagetmau. The thrill of their love at this moment reflected the constant need to maintain platonic proper rules of conduct around his military colleagues, but even more electrifying was the ever-present threat of death.

NERAC AND AGEN

1585

BROODING, MARGOT SAT IN HER apartments, a book open upon her lap. The rain struck the leaded windows with insistent rhythm, irritating her frayed nerves as did the background chatter of her few ladies-in-waiting. Rising, she wandered to the window for the fourth time in half an hour. Shrouded with low-lying clouds and dense fog, the river and garden were obscured from view. She knew she should not allow the metallic clouds to burden her spirits in this way, but her feelings of helplessness were becoming overwhelming.

Mère de Dieu. Why didn't Henry come to her at Nérac? How could he expect her to live alone here? With him away, there was no excuse to hold a dance. Because of the League's evil intentions against Henri III and Navarre, the nightly entertainments they did manage were dull and constrained. What a waste of her wit and beauty on these country dolts! If only she could see her beautiful Champvallon; flirting with what Nérac had to offer severely starved her ego. Remembering La Môle, she quivered with ecstasy. Even her husband would be a welcome partner, she smiled grimly to herself. How dare that simpering widow take him from her! Her anger kindled as she reflected upon how she was being mistreated. She, a sister of the king – and a Valois!

The boredom of her daily life upset her as much as the damage to her reputation. And how Henry's mistresses galled her! She never used to worry, but now she was mortified, wondering if she appeared ridiculous or pitiful. How dare he do nothing to maintain appearances! She had been the star of the beauties of the court; now no one seemed to know or care. She had to admit to herself she was frightened by her easy dissolution into what seemed to be a conspiracy of disregard. Despite having become a little plumper since her marriage, she knew she was still a beautiful woman, though she failed to notice her stubborn chin and the lines of anger and unhappiness etched more deeply around her mouth. However, at night she worked olive oil on her face before the mirror, believing it was age rather than ill humor that was damaging her smooth voluptuous skin.

She would give Henry one more chance, but if he didn't come this time, he would pay for it. Sitting down at her writing table, with revenge uppermost in her heart, she raged, he has no right to treat me like a worn-out discard. She wanted revenge against the Huguenots, against her brother, and against her husband. The Huguenots had never accepted her, her brother had embarrassed her at court, and her husband had caused her overwhelming humiliation by refusing to take her back. She wished equal indignities upon them! Margot remembered finding herself alone on January 6, the Day of the Three Kings. This had always been a day of feasting and revelry, and she had been stranded with the servants in this country retreat while Henry was occupied with love and war. The only sounds here, she lamented, were the munching of the sheep and the lowing of the cattle. Loneliness caused her anger to grow and she wrote:

> If I thought that news from Nérac would be important enough for you to bother reading, Monsieur, I would tell you about our Feast of the Kings which we have solemnized in the usual way . . . The feast would have been very lovely if it had been graced by your presence; for without that, nothing seems very pleasant to me.

Despite these recriminations, Henry stayed away until late February. He will pay for this, Margot muttered over and over to herself as the days of waiting slowly passed. One day she was delighted to receive a letter from her former lover, the duc de Guise, if only because it recognized her existence. He wrote:

> Marguerite dearest, You have always been the first lady in my heart and in my mind, the first lady of France. With all great humility I seek your help in returning our great land to its former glory. The League would welcome your aid, especially in Agen.

She chose not to answer for the time being, but began to think more often of Guise. What a handsome and wonderful lover he had been. Reminiscing more about him, she decided he was probably the man she had really loved, probably the man she should have married. But of course, her mother had planned her marriage to Henry and she'd had no real choice. Now, she told herself she should have refused and wedded her true love.

When Henry finally arrived, Margot carefully remained calm and dry-eyed. Wishing to conceal her jealousy over Corisande, she feared the absence of accusations might equally arouse his suspicions. The next day when a woman in her service died, supposedly from consuming a soup prepared for her, Margot was unable to suppress her fury any longer.

"Corisande told you to poison me," she screamed. "I know it. You both wish me dead."

"Margot, shut up! Corisande could never wish anyone dead. She is a loving and generous person. You have simply lost your head," Henry replied in a deadly and measured tone.

Margot became genuinely alarmed. She had understood Henry's previous affairs because they had seemed only a part of the game of power or passing flirtations to amuse him. With Corisande, it appeared he was no longer playing.

"I insist you cease this ridiculous affair with the comtesse de Guiche. 'Corisande!' Who does she think she is, giving herself names from novels?"

"You don't understand her, Margot, and that is why you hate her. You are very intelligent and have helped me in many ways. But she is intelligent without being selfish or complicated."

He should have known better than to compare them. So, he had given himself without duplicity. His guard was down, and it was rumored that Corisande returned his honest love with the gift of herself. Their mutual feelings obviously passed beyond gallantry or passion, and Margot panicked, unable to fathom the depth of their love.

"I don't want to hear any more about her." Margot was strangely silent for a moment. "I simply want permission to spend the weeks of Lenten devotion in the Catholic community of Agen."

So relieved was Henry at the prospect of being rid of her that he agreed without hesitation or questions. She was disappointed when he offered no complaints against her proposed absence.

"That's fine, my love, and pray for me too," was all he said.

"You don't even care if I leave," she accused.

Henry shrugged his shoulders. "It is you who are angry."

Margot resolved to go ahead with her plan to help Guise, which had been slowly simmering during her lonely siege. "If you were more attractive, I might have loved you," she suddenly said. "You were certainly my most intelligent lover."

"As usual, I don't know whether to thank you or damn you. Have a pleasant journey, my dear."

The Queen of Navarre jounced toward Agen in her royal carriage, her desolate anger prompting her to call out to the drivers to quicken their pace. She tried to avoid feeding on her resentment toward Corisande, but her hatred continued to bubble toward the surface. In a less emotional state, she realized that so gentle a soul as Corisande could not contrive such a horrible plan as poisoning her, but reason escaped her now. She conjured up only a woman envious of the king's wife and eager for the throne.

Her thoughts returned to a second pain which consumed her. If only I could bear a child, if only I could bear a child, if only I could bear a child. The rhythm of the horses caught the rhythm of her words and she could not break their monotonous power.

Despite her agitation, Margot began to grow excited as she neared Agen. Rage had driven her here, but once on her way, she was surprised she had not come before. It was only a half-day's journey from Nérac and more important, the folk who lived there were sympathetic to her religion. The terrain appeared welcoming as well, with gentle hills and wide fields. Small seigneuries perched atop hillocks so that each lord could spy on his neighbor's honey-colored stone fortress upon the adjacent grassy summit.

The town itself occupied one side of the wide Garonne river, which the Queen's party followed along the west bank before crossing a wooden bridge into the city's center. Marguerite's bodyguards asked the curious townsmen of Agen to direct her to the convent of the Jacobins, for she hoped these austere monks would prove friends and temporarily take her in. She knew of their mendicant order because they had originally inhabited the rue St. Jacques in Paris and had taken their name from this original home. The Place des Jacobins was situated not far from the river but the parade of onlookers, who had never seen royalty before, quickly swelled and filled the streets around her train. The commotion brought out several of the brothers, who were astounded to find the Queen of Navarre descending from her carriage before them.

"You honor us with your request, Your Highness," welcomed the Brother Superior. "If you find our lodgings adequate, we would be more than happy to serve you."

"I wish to observe Easter among fellow believers," she explained, and they had no reason to doubt her.

"Of course," they murmured. What a wonderful and beautiful queen! And that she would choose to worship with them was glorious in the extreme. They would add special prayers to the service in her honor.

Entering the church dedicated to St. Dominique, Margot was struck by its simplicity. Unlike the Gothic cathedrals that had nourished her upbringing and which were all built in the shape of the Latin cross, this church was a single rectangle with one bell tower. The monks explained to their illustrious guest that this shape was conducive to teaching, for this was a studious and pedagogical order. Also, to avoid ostentation, sculpture was proscribed, and only wall paintings from the thirteenth century decorated the pale brick walls. But the paintings were serene, and Margot found the stained glass windows tucked into the early Gothic arches uplifting.

"The beauty of your church is inspirational," the clever queen commented. "I am most grateful for your hospitality." She smiled at the brothers in their identical plain robes, her own dress shot with gold thread glowing like the lighted windows behind her.

After several days however, Margot began to weary of the ascetic life, finding the bed too hard and the food too simple. Her hosts were impressed with her knowledge of Aristotle, whose philosophy they admired, but despite her intellect, the number of royal visitors taxed their scant supply house and the saintliest of natures. So, after Easter services, both parties parted amicably but with relief, and Margot moved to the château of a local squire, who could see future recompense in a royal liaison.

To the people of Agen it seemed normal that this good Catholic queen would wish to spend these days of penance and prayer apart from her heretical husband. Wasn't she pious, and generous? If they had any doubts, her charm won them over. After a short while Margot asked to meet with the principal men of the city and confided to them, "I am in great danger from my husband and urge you to fortify Agen for your sake as well as mine." Enjoying their surprised faces, she explained, "I have been forced to flee from the King of Navarre because of the evil designs of the comtesse de Guiche."

Her eloquence and rank won their favor as did her revealing bodice. She wisely took great care that the men of Agen did not realize she was in close contact with Spain through the agency of the duc de Guise. The League issued the Declaration of Peronne on March 31, proclaiming Henry's paternal uncle the Cardinal de Bourbon the heir to the French throne and criticizing Henri III's toleration of heresy. Knowing this to be the League's first step toward conquering the entire country, Margot began to act less like a guest and more like the mistress of the city. How stimulating this all was! Now Henry would realize he should have considered her more often! When she brought twelve hundred men into the town and placed her soldiers under the leadership of Duras, a Guise supporter and friend, it became evident she was an ally of the duc de Guise. She wrote to the Duke:

> My Hercules, I assure you I do not desire you to spare the King of Navarre and the French King. I shall trust and follow only you, my Alexander.

Margot began to feel as euphoric as she had in the Netherlands. Then, throughout the summer the days began to pass more slowly; where was Guise?

Margot heard that on July 7, 1585, Catherine de Medici had signed the Treaty of Nemours with the League. Clearly she had finally persuaded her son to make war on the Huguenots. All edicts of leniency were revoked and freedom of worship by the Reformed religion was forbidden everywhere. Huguenots had six months to convert or leave the country. Huguenots were declared ineligible for public office, thereby barring Henry or Condé from the throne. She knew that she need not hope for any help hereafter from Henry.

In August, Margot sent Duras to Spain to secure increased subsidies from Philip, but Duras returned without a peseta. She began to seriously worry about her role in all these affairs and wrote again to her "Hercules":

> I am forced to increase taxation. I have already
> lost the favor of the citizens by billeting our soldiers
> in private households where they demand the small
> quantities of food available as well as the wives and
> daughters of the householders. I doubt if they will
> tolerate this situation much longer.

She was right. Her callous behavior toward the citizens became an outrage. In late summer, when the plague made its appearance in Agen and she refused permission for the citizens to leave the city, riots erupted. Their fury made Margot realize she must flee immediately, and she didn't even dare to take the time to gather her possessions. Guise had failed her, and this time she couldn't write to Henry to take her back.

The renegade queen finally found refuge in September at the fortress of Carlat, not far from Aurillac. She spent the winter of 1585 in the castle high on a bleak rock of black basalt. Here she found security from her enemies but no protection from the strong winds blowing from the Auvergne. She felt constantly cold and became ill, unable to stop shivering as the chill crept through the broken windows. Remembering her cozy room at Nérac, she wept. Sister of one king, wife to another, she now feared capture. There was no doubt in her mind, or in theirs she suspected, that she was guilty of treason.

Hoping to find more comfortable refuge, she left for a château belonging to her mother near la Colline Ibois. Afraid to take the roads, and with only a few loyal attendants, the Valois princess stumbled up and down steep mountain paths, waded through icy streams and slid down the stony scree of the hills. When she finally arrived at Ibois, it was nighttime and neither protector nor provisions awaited her — only some walnuts, bean pods and lard. Slumping down on a bench in the courtyard, illuminated only by the light of the moon, she alllowed the tears to fall which she had courageously held back during her frightful flight. She leaned her head against the wall of the château, too exhausted to travel any farther. But where else could she go?

So often the stimulation of a dimly perceived goal or even just the idea of a trip had propelled her into action. The security of her position would always protect her somehow, she had thought. So how had she gotten herself into this agonizing situation? The sound of her sobbing was suddenly broken by a pounding upon the gates. Who had finally tracked her to find her in such squalid shame? Opening

the gates, she saw a group of horsemen under the Marquis de Canail-
lac.

"I have come to take you into custody on your brother's orders,"
he proclaimed.

Margot knew she could not resist and found herself even too
weak to care. She saw pity in the face of the Marquis as he explained,
"Scandal upon scandal has frayed the royal patience, and there are
some who say your brother would have you killed were it not for the
restraining hand of the Queen Mother."

"Bless Mother," she whispered.

Dragged from one crumbling castle to another in Auvergne, the
Queen of Navarre was finally placed under guard in the high château
of Usson. Clinging to a volcanic peak with a view of the Puy mountain chain, this château, where Louis XI had incarcerated his prisoners, was so impregnable that Margot wrote in her journal, "Only the
sun can force an entrance here."

HAGETMAU and ILE DE MARANS

1585-1587

HENRY SWELLED WITH outrage when he heard of Margot's treachery. By receiving Spanish subsidies she had betrayed France as well as himself. "Damn her," he muttered to himself. But he always felt some inkling of blame for not being able to control Margot's wilder impulses. When Henri III promulgated the infamous Treaty of Nemours, Henry, still licking his wounds, wiped away angry tears as he told Corisande, "Every Protestant minister is commanded to leave the kingdom within one month, and unless we abjure our religion and accept the Catholic faith or depart from France within six months, the penalty for disobedience will be death and the confiscation of property. It was also signed by Catherine de Medici and the duc de Guise."

"But why would the Queen Mother agree to this if she wants peace? Corisande asked.

"Who knows? I never seem to learn that I can never trust her!" Henry was suddenly flooded by memories of the St. Bartholomew's Massacre. He paced around the room as he tried to explain his growing despair to his mistress. "I am reminded of a verse from *Exodus* — I think it reads . . . *thou shalt not oppress a stranger; for Ye know the heart of a stranger, Seeing ye were strangers in the land of Egypt.* [*Exodus 23:9*] It expresses how I felt when I first came to Paris and foolishly believed the Valois might accept me. I had no idea how to deal with them then and I still don't."

"I think she must know the Huguenots will not accept such terms."

"I agree. But she has lost all of her bargaining points," Henry speculated. "Henri III has weakened the monarchy irremediably, and the duc de Guise has dictated his terms. She knows she is beaten, but she continues to try and stuff such abominations down our throats."

Corisande sank into a chair. "I am afraid to say the words," she murmured, "that surely this means you must rouse the Protestants to arms again."

"I'm afraid it does, my love. With this document they have wiped out all the progress I believed we had been making. This is a travesty and a threat, which I must answer. But one day we will have time together, I promise you."

Henry quickly wrote a letter to Henri III:

> I understand a peace has been concluded without me, and indeed, against me. You have joined your enemies to ruin your servants, your most faithful subjects and those who have the honor of being your nearest relatives. Even more, you have divided your forces, your authority, your resources, to make them the strongest who are armed against you. I find this very difficult and almost unendurable.

Henry's troubles multiplied quickly, because the League immediately intensified its efforts to enthrone the elderly Cardinal de Bourbon. Their purpose, he knew, was, to essentially place Guise as the ultimate power behind the throne. Wanting to clarify that his primary loyalty was to France, Henry wrote a declaration of his position to various princes: What was done at Nemours must be condemned for it was:

> . . . a peace made with strangers at the expense of the Princes of the Blood; with the House of Lorraine at the expense of the House of France; with rebels at the expense of obedient subjects; with agitators at the expense of those who have brought peace by every means in their power . . . I intend to oppose it with all my heart; and to this end to rally around me, according to my position in the kingdom, all true Frenchmen without regard to religion, since at this time it is a question of the defense of the state against the usurpation of foreigners.

When the hostilities resumed, Henry learned Corisande had joined Catherine at Pau. Despite the boredom, she waited for those rare occasions when he could successfully evade enemy troops with only a few soldiers and would knock upon the gates of the château to spend the night with her. She even sent her son to his service and cut down her forests, selling the timber to support his troops. She no longer gave any thought to her Catholicism and his Protestantism, for she firmly believed his ideas of tolerance and freedom of religion were the only answer for their country. He took for granted her fidelity, which never wavered from his cause, and wrote to her daily.

> How much pleasure you give me by going to Pau! Ah, my dear mistress, what I would give to be there! But such contentment is out of the question. I am enclosing copies of letters that the Queen of England wrote to the King and Queen Mother about the League and peace. You will find the language elegant and the style pleasant.

In October he found his way to her again but his peace was shattered by an urgent message delivered to him soon after his arrival. He sat down before Corisande, the shock usurping his manners.

"The Pope has promulgated a bull excommunicating me and the prince de Condé, declaring us unworthy and incapable of acceding to the throne of France and dispossessing me of my states in Navarre. This is surely the work of Spain at the Vatican. Margot's treachery has afforded Spain more leverage, I fear. I feel assaulted on so many fronts I do not know where to strike."

Corisande blanched. "But what right does the Pope have to excommunicate you? You are not a Catholic. Or how can he take away Navarre? You must be correct that he is speaking for Spain and adding his power to theirs."

"May I speak, Sire?" the messenger dared. So upset had Henry been, he had forgotten the boy's presence.

"Certainly, young man," the king replied.

"If you please, Sire, I overheard the lords in Paris. They said the Parliament should respond by saying that French princes have never submitted to the justice of the Pope and that the bull should be thrown into the fire in front of all the Roman Church."

Henry chuckled. Nevertheless, with the Edict of Nemours and a papal bull ranked against him, he felt his buoyant Gascon optimism falling away. For one of the few times in his life, he remained seated.

"I am a king without a kingdom, a husband without a wife, and a general without money," he mourned.

The messenger departed and Corisande put her arms around him. "But you have a most loving mistress," she said.

"Indeed I do." But he spoke as though his mind were elsewhere.

"The support of Elizabeth I of England has become even more critical. Without it, I shall surely fail." Recalling the story of the girl who had sought the English monarch's aid for La Rochelle but the help had come too late, he anxiously continued, "I have appealed to her, but so far there is no aid forthcoming."

"Perhaps you should impress upon her that you are her only bulwark against Spanish power in France," Corisande advised.

Henry jumped up and began his thoughtful pacing. "Since I am dealing with a powerful woman, perhaps I should heed the advice of another powerful lady," he replied, acknowledging his mistress's astute mind. "Elizabeth must see that her days of peace are numbered if she loses this opportunity to send men or money to me."

"Have you heard, Henry," Corisande inquired, "that this war is now called the 'War of the Three Henrys,' — Henri III, Henri, duc de Guise, and of course, Henry of Navarre."

Henry winced. "Which Henri did Nostradamus refer to in his famous oracle?" he couldn't help but wonder out loud. He always seemed to be struggling against fate. He would seem to have matters under control, then he would lose control. But he didn't have time to feel sorry for himself; he must continue to struggle toward the goal that was so important to him — to end these religious wars and bring peace to the country he loved.

The war dragged on and on. The League was superior in numbers, but they were continually circumvented in all their plans by the energy and valor of the Protestants. Fortunately, the approach of Henri III and the Queen Mother was to mediate rather than to fight. The argument of the Spanish threat must have swayed Elizabeth, for at last she consented to secret subsidies to supply foreign mercenaries in the field against the League. The Huguenots then found themselves supported by German and Swiss troops paid in English pounds. Moreover, the papal bull, instead of reducing Navarre's power, seemed to have increased his popularity enormously. France as a whole disliked Roman interference in French affairs and the Counts Montmorency and Damville, who for years had vacillated between the cause of the Politiques and the loyalty to the crown, now in a surprise move, declared for the Huguenots. Other Catholic leaders also determined to oppose the foreign influence the League was introducing into France.

The French would answer to neither Spain nor the Vatican, they declared.

Again, Henry and Corisande parted. On December 7, 1585, he wrote to her from Saint-Sever:

> There is nothing truer than the fact that they (the enemy) are brewing all they can. They thought I had left Grenade to see you; at the Montgaillard mill there were fifty arquebusiers who captured my lackey and kept him until they knew I had left to come here. Fear nothing, my soul. When the army which is at Nogaro shows me its intent, I will come to see you and I will fly on the wings of love, out of sight of these miserable earthlings, provided that, with God's help, this old fox (Joyeuse) does not execute his plan.

In January he sent her a copy of his letter to the clergy:

> I believe in one God, we recognize one Jesus Christ, we accept the same Gospel. I believe the war you prosecute so keenly is unworthy of Christians, unworthy between Christians, above all of those who claim to be teachers of the Gospel. If war pleases you so much, if a battle pleases you more than a disputation, a bloodthirsty plot more than a Council, I wash my hands. The blood which flows will be on your hands.

That he should want to share his thoughts with her made Corisande giddy with relief. No shadow shaded her happiness in loving and her glowing certitude of being loved when he included her in this way. Yet she experienced small moments of fear. Hadn't he seemed less tender lately — more the aggressor and the conqueror? In February he again came to her at Hagetmau, staying for three glorious and passionate days. Corisande could not resist commenting, "It seems that the lighter joys under the trees of Pau are relegated only to memory and that we only may meet for rare and feverish hours where the possibility of death hovers constantly."

"That is one of the hazards of war, my love. I cannot gain a throne by remaining by your warm side and picking blackberries."

"I know, Henry. But please keep in mind Montaigne's advice, that taking up arms should always be the last recourse. I am afraid that you all will only succeed in annihilating one another and France will not be at peace." But then she broke down and said what was really in her heart, "I do not mean to complain but letters do not have arms that can hold me. And sometimes I need to be held." Her voice broke. "It must be difficult for you also."

But she did not really think so. He seemed too busy to feel any pain, his political life ample compensation for love.

After their too brief, three nights of passion, Corisande wrote to Henry, showing she had managed to regain her composure.

> If they (the enemy) are unchained, you must enclose them. Fortune will be more favorable to you than M. le duc de Bourbon desires . . . I am extremely anxious because of the uncertain situation in which I see you, not knowing who is your enemy and who is your friend. When you know, tell me and what you have resolved to do. Until then, I shall only suffer. Adieu, Madame kisses your hands. It is the fifteenth of the month.

Henry smiled when he read her virile words and concise authority. He was not astonished, nor did the lack of words of love bother him. She was speaking to the man of action she adored. In August, after a lonely summer, she wrote:

> I am very glad to know that you are beginning to take care of yourself. Certainly you have more reason to do so than you think. Do not forget anything which could serve toward your conservation and to your grandeur, and if you are forced to experience an unfortunate fate, make your followers and your enemies see a constant and assured visage in the midst of disasters. You are worth a great deal to me, more than for anyone else in the world. Show yourself still more worthy of the friendship of the one who has esteemed nothing more than you.

Tears ran down Henry's face. In this critical moment of his life, her sense of duty and honor were the code and inspiration she wanted to share. Perhaps she belonged more on a pedestal than in his arms.

Finding himself at the Ile de Marans, near La Rochelle and between two battles, he felt happy and appeased. The wind from the nearby sea and the perfume of the fields stirred his senses. Relaxed by this contact with liberty and nature, he chatted with the fishermen, examined the wheat, and bargained with the merchants. He wrote letters to Corisande, full of easy sentimentality. Already away from her for six months, he knew he would not be able to visit her for a long time. Her warmth, her shape, her face, had dimmed in his mind. It was easier to remember her noble ideas, her confidence in him, and her admiration for his cause than to recall their mutual ardor.

But serenity was not a mood to last long with Henry. Recalling his earlier conquest of a pretty bourgeoise Rochellaise, Suzanne des Moulins, he smiled. He remembered her cuckold of a husband, the stuffy professor who had latinized his name from Martines to Martinius. Suzanne must be over 30 by now. He would not bother to seek her out again. But his heroic Corisande was far away, and his insatiable lust demanded more real and immediate satisfactions than her courageous letters could bring. He wanted his pleasures pure and simple, without an ache at the center.

At a dinner given by a Seigneur de Boyslambert, lawyer at La Rochelle and baliff of the grand fief of Aunis, he noticed the eldest daughter of the host. Esther was twenty-one years old with black hair curled beguilingly around her face. Henry found her way of running her tongue over her bottom lip more than he could bear. If he appreciated a young woman, and this time it was Esther, he wanted her immediately. He was easily aggravated by long preludes and refused to put up with any delay. As King of Navarre, he assumed he would succeed by either strong demands or money.

Henry stared at his prey all evening, obviously unnerving the girl. Sauntering over to her, he clasped her waist tightly with his left arm and pulled her to him. "Where can I meet you?" he whispered hoarsely in her ear.

"I beg your pardon, Your Majesty?" Esther tried to pull away.

"Do not pretend you do not understand me, *ma petite*. I must be alone with you immediately."

Henry's imperious manner and compelling arm were difficult to contradict, and Esther thought she could deal with him more effectively in private than in front of everyone. "In the library then. In half an hour."

When Esther entered the library, she found Henry standing, legs apart, in front of the fireplace, one hand upon his sword at his side.

"Come here, *ma chère*. You are a delight to look at."

The girl hung back and took up a safe position behind the divan. "I hardly know you, Your Majesty."

"Do not prevaricate with me, *ma belle*. You know you want me to kiss you."

Esther didn't move as he came toward her. "And I shall do so right now."

He crushed his mouth to hers and was further excited when she whimpered. He forced his tongue between her lips and suddenly she returned his kiss. "Where, *ma petite*, where?"

"I cannot," she demurred.

"Of course you can. I will meet you after midnight and you must tell me where."

"The third staircase in the upstairs hall. The second door on your right."

Henry could barely hear her low voice but he had secured what he wanted. He was like a male bird who flutters his brilliant plumage and continues his dance until his female choice finally accepts his dominance. Easily and without shame, he had returned to his style of love before Corisande, where his sensuality governed.

The next day, M. de Boyslambert entered the library unexpectedly and surprised his daughter in the arms of the monarch. He pulled her free from the king and slapped her face.

"I must recall you to a sense of propriety in my house," he commanded Henry, sending poor Esther fleeing from the room.

Somewhat abashed and piqued, it was, nevertheless, a sharp lesson for Henry. He would at least abide by the forms of decency hereafter. He could not afford to lose the support of the townsmen. His relations with Esther became more staid in public, but evidently not in private. In November Esther revealed she was pregnant. As usual, his quarry had bowed in acquiescence to his gaiety and forceful charm.

He continued to write Corisande, and the tone of his letters was that of a man in love. He was in love — but not with Corisande exclusively. The protestations of his fidelities should have warned her, for his light delicate touches were those of a man as love is just budding.

❧

Corisande's suffering increased. Her lover's absence had stretched to over a year. He continued to write, but she realized that the earlier fire was missing. Still, she enjoyed the way he included her in his political thinking. He wrote on February 18, 1587:

> Mary, Queen of Scots, has been beheaded. Henri III must have been an accomplice because Elizabeth I could not have done it without the assurance that the French king would not protect Mary.

Corisande thought she might disagree with him. After all, Henry II of France had been Mary's father-in-law, and it had been a Protestant queen who had beheaded a Catholic queen.

The rest of his letters were unemotional. She had known his strengths — his confounding determination, his audacious courage, a quick intellect, and his marvelous activity. But by her closeness to him, she had also perceived his weaknesses — his mobile humor, his Gascon bragging, and his insatiable sensuality. Once she asked if she were passionate enough for his taste, and he had answered she was all he could ever want. Now jealousy tore at her heart, ripping it apart like a tiger tears at its meat. She heard of the scandal at La Rochelle and her horseman, Pierre de Licerasse, a Basque of complete loyalty and devotion, to whom she trusted her secret and perilous missions of communication with Henry, confirmed the report. She ceased to write, but upon receiving his letter of March 12, 1587, she finally spoke to Catherine.

"Your brother is pretending to be offended by my silence. Listen to what he has the effrontery to say":

> The more I put myself out, the more it seems that you try to make me feel how little I am in your good graces, but still in your memory. By this lackey, you have written to your son but not to me. If I am not worthy of it, I have done all that I could . . .

Catherine smiled wryly. "He always takes the offensive, even when he is in the wrong. He has done it since childhood."

"I'm afraid I love him too much not to pardon him."

"I understand, Corisande, for I let him get away with unfair behavior too."

"I hear Esther bore him a son in August. She called the child by the pompous name of Gédéon. Licerasse found out. Sometimes it hurts more than I think I can bear, but I hope I lost him just for a moment and not for a lifetime. I don't think he is with her now any more than he is with me."

"I think your generous nature might always lead you to sacrifice everything in the cause of the king," Catherine said.

"I have already sent him every available penny to contribute for the recruitment of mercenaries, as he tells me events are becoming precipitous. Henri III has just placed the duc de Joyeuse* at the head of his army on the Loire, and he is an excellent general. But Henry said I must not underestimate their striking power."

"Try not to worry too much, dear friend. I have every confidence in my brother's military skill, and he will come back to you when his battles are over."

"I hope you are right," Corisande breathed.

*Anne de Batarnay de Joyeuse, Baron d'Arques, Vicomte then Duke of Joyeuse (1560 - 1587) was one of Henri III's *mignons* and an active participant in the French Wars of Religion.

BOOK THREE

ATHENA-IN-ARMOR

MATTEI ATHENA, GODDESS OF JUST WARFARE
The Louvre
Roman copy from a Greek original, ca. 1st century B.C.

FRANCE DURING THE HUGUENOT/CATHOLIC WARS

(Map by author)

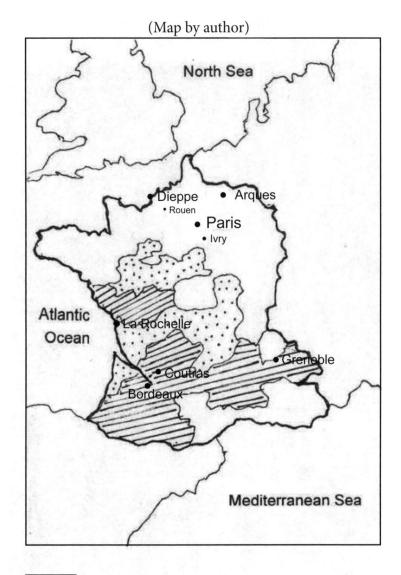

☐ Mostly Roman Catholic

▨ Mostly Huguenot

▨ Disputed Areas

COUTRAS

1587

THE KING OF NAVARRE AND his army were trapped. Henry feared the Huguenot troops could not possibly escape the great Catholic army abruptly assembling before them. With customary boldness Navarre began by leading a handpicked force, the flower of the Huguenot military, right across the enemy's front, away from the shores of Biscay where the Catholics hoped to pin him.

The majority of Henry's force, including his Bourbon cousins, Condé and Soissons, and numerous other Huguenot captains, slept the night of October 19 in the little village of Coutras, between the Dronne and Isle rivers, on the road that ran from Tours in the north through Poiters to Bordeaux. In this picturesque country town, the fate of a nation and dynasty would be decided the next day.

The Huguenot army awakened from shallow restless sleep in the dreary dawn of October 20 to the sound of distant popping of small arms in the woods north of the village. Apparently, the powerful royal army they were trying to evade, under the leadership of the duc de Joyeuse, had stolen a night's march on them and was already in contact with their pickets. In an hour, perhaps less, Joyeuse would have them forked between the Dronne, which they had crossed yesterday afternoon, and the Isle, which they expected to cross this morning.

Duc Anne de Joyeuse was married to Henri III's sister-in-law, Marguerite, daughter of Nicholas, Duke of Mercœur, but probably had been helped most in his rapid rise by Henri III's weakness for handsome young men. Others among the *mignons*, who minced around the king, were equally handsome, but Joyeuse was distinguished by his passion for command, a reckless effrontery, and sublime self-confidence. Henry, being a shrewd tactician, never meant to fight Joyeuse but to elude him. He had succeeded with this plan all summer, even pushing the Catholic army toward disintegration by constant harassment and guerrilla tactics.

Loving military strategy, Henry understood that all his years of learning and experience had culminated in this moment where he must gamble on his own survival. Had not Athena, the goddess of just warfare, not always been by his side? The amiral de Coligny, who had been the first to tutor him in the arts of war, had been his best teacher. But Henry felt, as in many endeavors, that not everything could be taught. Much depended on native talent and intuition. He would be master of his own fate. Now he must make a decision in a split second or all would be lost. If he hurried, he, Condé and his captains, with most of the cavalry, could still get away. The infantry would have to be left behind, to buy with their lives enough time for the cavalry's escape. The leaders at least would be saved. By the same reasoning, he and Condé had saved themselves on St. Bartholomew's Eve. On the other hand, if they remained to fight and were beaten, few of any rank were likely to survive. The rivers that flowed together behind them were too deep to ford and too swift to swim, and the one bridge at the end of the village street was too narrow for more than one file to pass at a time. If these leaders died, the Protestant power in France would be broken, and the future would belong to the house of Guise-Lorraine, to the radical fanatics of the Holy League and the paymaster of both, the king of Spain.

In a rapid study of the lay of the land and a quick calculation of the odds, Henry formed his plan. More truly, he intuited his plan in a flash. Not for a moment did he seriously entertain the idea of escape. He was ready for the fight of his life. He gave his captains the impression this was just the place he would have chosen for battle. He would choose the better position and dispose his troops the more skillfully. It would be his only chance. A constantly changing situation seemed to be his favorite situation, and he grew excited with the challenge.

Just before the battle, Duplessis-Mornay came to Navarre. "Sire, it is known you have sinned against God and injured a respectable citizen of La Rochelle by the seduction of his daughter. We cannot hope that God will bless our arms in this approaching battle while such a sin remains unrepented and unrepaired."

Henry was horrified. He must not lose this important moment to Calvinist prudery. His impulsiveness would always get him in trouble, it seemed, but his improvisational shrewdness would turn this threat into a victory. He dismounted, knelt, and in the presence of his men, avowed, "I am sincerely grieved for what I have done. You are all my witnesses that I implore the forgiveness of God and the family I have injured. I pledge before you now I will do everything in my power to repay this wrong."

Then placing a plume of white feathers on his helmet so he would be distinguished in the midst of battle, he remounted his charger. Across a few hundred yards of open battleground, the opposing horsemen had time to eye one another. The Huguenots appeared plain and battle-worn, in stained greasy leather and dull gray steel. Their armor consisted only of cuirass and morion, their arms primarily just broadsword and pistol. The Huguenot gun makers had developed an elegantly shaped, wheel-lock pistol with a light-weight and easy-to-use mechanism, giving their firearms a distinctive appearance and advantage. However, some only carried a mace to club their enemies to death.

Opposite these weary ranks, the battle line of Royalists rippled and shimmered. It billowed out here, shrank back there, as its components jostled each other and jockeyed for position like racers, curvetting their horses and now and then breaking rank to exchange a greeting with a friend. Their lances sported pennons, gay bannerets and knots of colored ribbon, which honored noble ladies. A great display of armor, cuisses, gauntlets, gorgets and visored casques, with every conspicuous surface densely chased in the French fashion, filled the horizon. The most popular designs decorating the heavy metal were delicate foliate scrolls inhabited by allegorical figures.

"Never have I seen an army in France so bespangled and covered with gold leaf!" Aubigné said to the man next to him.

"Perhaps their finery will weigh them down," his mate replied, but with little conviction in his voice.

Dangerously close to the enemy, Henry began a general advance to the open meadows at the north end of the village and there began to redeploy his army. He understood the risks he was taking, but the danger only heightened his senses. The smell of battle honed his intellect to a shining edge like the sharp sword he wore at his side. As the sun was just rising, the Duke's light horse emerged from the forest upon the spectacle of their foes. Two hours later Navarre's artillery, later on the field than the Duke's but earlier in position, opened fire.

The enemy's cavalry was still adjusting its alignment like minuet lines at a ball when Navarre's three guns, ensconced on a hillock, opened fire. The round shot, fired at an almost enfilading angle, tore holes in the Catholic ranks. Served by veterans and commanded by first-rate artillerymen, the Huguenot guns fired eighteen deadly rounds while Joyeuse's battery managed six harmless ones. But then the Duke's trumpets signaled the attack and soon the Huguenot ranks were surprised to hear Catholic cries of "Victory" in the village behind them.

Instead of being intimidated by the Catholic audacity, the Huguenot band of infantry on the left appeared to become angry by this challenge, as well as inspired by their leader's daring and courage. Thinking they might as well die attacking as attacked, they flung themselves in a headlong rush, pell-mell, across the brook. Before the Royalist regiments grasped what was happening, the infantry was dragging them aside with their hands and closing in with sword and dagger. The startled enemy broke ranks and the whole of that side of the field dissolved into confused hand-to-hand mélée. Yet it was in the center that the battle was decided.

The Huguenot veterans galloped to meet the enemy, singing Psalm 118, "This is the day which the Lord hath made; we will rejoice and be glad in it."

The arquebusiers fired their volley, and the massed column of Huguenot horses, led by Henry, quickened their gait and crashed straight into the galloping line. Henry knew this blow brought him victory. Under the impact of solid columns, the Catholic front in all its finery broke into pieces, and the Huguenots began rolling up the fragments by the flank. There followed a short time of desperate, scrambled fighting. The King of Navarre, having pistoled one adversary and taken a sharp rap on the hand with a lance butt from another, recognized the Seigneur de Châteaurenard, the standard bearer of the enemy troop he had smashed. Seizing his old companion around the waist, he crowed, "Yield thyself, Philistine."

Henry was careful and adroit in protecting himself with his shield of embossed steel, which depicted scenes of the abduction of Helen, the struggle of Achilles and Hector before Priam, and the entrance of the wooden horse through the gates of Troy. The shield, a gift from Corisande, surely had saved his life on countless encounters, and he always thought of her before heading into battle.

In another part of the field, the duc de Joyeuse found himself cut off by a clump of horsemen as he tried to escape. Flinging down his sword, he called out, "My ransom is a thousand crowns." One of his captors swiftly put a bullet through his head. For the commander, who had ordered that the wounded Huguenots be killed on the field, who had hung prisoners by the hundreds and butchered garrisons, and who had surrendered relying on the traditions of war, there was no chance of quarter.

Indeed, until Henry furiously intervened, little mercy was given to any of the royal army. Three thousand common soldiers were slaughtered, more than four hundred knights and gentlemen, an impressive roll of dukes, marquises, counts, and barons; more, Aubigné thought, than had fallen in any three battles of the century. The Catholic horde was utterly destroyed, with little left of its glittering army.

"At least," Henry of Navarre commented at the day's end, "nobody will be able to say after this that we Huguenots never win a battle." He perched his casque with the white plume upon a pike stuck in the mud outside his tent. That night, as it magically waved in the moonlight, the white plume became a good luck symbol as well as a sign of the audacious determination of their leader, and his men came by to touch it.

Henry proved magnanimous in the hour of victory. The heady excitement of the battle over, when asked what terms he should now demand of his foes after so great a loss, he replied, "The same as before the battle. I deplore war and drew arms only in self-defense." He would not deal harshly with his enemy as the Catholics had done at Jarnac.

Henry had not seen Corisande for a year and a half. Yet he thought of her now, in this moment of incredible victory. He remembered her devotion, her wisdom, and her strength. On impulse he decided to deliver the standards of victory to her and lay them at her feet. What a grand woman! She surely deserved recognition for the part she had played in the achievements of this glorious day. He had temporarily abandoned Corisande, when Athena, the goddess of just warfare, led him through the travail and horror of war. Now he would properly thank his earthly mistress.

These presents would mean a lot to his heroic lover, but Henry realized with some shame, they were all he could honestly offer her. He recalled how his passion had driven him across Gascony in hazardous heady rides, seamed with ambushes and pitfalls. Now she scarcely occupied his heart and aroused his desires even less. Although guilty of many inconstancies of the flesh, he had always kept a singular fidelity of the spirit to this woman, so marvelously gifted, who had communicated to him a flame equal to his own fire. Though she no longer exercised her physical charm on him, he had continued to correspond with her dutifully. In the difficult days — those of 1585 as those before Coutras — she had never ceased to represent the living figure of victory in his eyes. He sensed he could always rely on her love of country and sense of duty to override her personal emotions.

He sent a messenger ahead to alert Corisande of his coming and went to inform his captains of his plan. They were astounded. Duplessis-Mornay spoke frankly, "Sire, it would be a tragedy not to follow up our advantage. You have crushed the army that threatened us, and now they know our strength. You cannot leave for Béarn now."

Aubigné spoke up too. "You must realize, Navarre, the presence of your Catholic cousins has affirmed the national and dynastic character of the struggle. You must launch another attack. Immediately! Against the king. Now! This is the moment to press for a total victory. This is our chance for the Huguenots to rule France!"

"We shall win the struggle," Henry jauntily replied. "I shall return in a few days."

So incredulous was Aubigné that he dared speak out. "Your men may love you for your impetuous spirit, Henry, but if you are not careful, it may be your downfall."

Henry waved his captain's remark aside and turned to ride for Béarn. Aubigné threw down his helmet in despair. Coutras would be a success without a tomorrow.

At Navarrenx Corisande and Catherine awaited the arrival of the king with equal impatience. A messenger had told them Henry was not coming alone; he would be accompanied by his first cousin, Charles de Bourbon, Comte de Soissons. Charles de Bourbon was 13 years younger than Henry and was also a French prince of the blood as he was the son of the Huguenot leader Louis I de Bourbon, the elder prince de Condé. As recompense for being his partisan, the King had promised Charles the hand of his sister in marriage. Henry clearly understood that he must stabilize his throne by marriage as well as on the battlefield. So far he had been more successful on the battlefield, and it seemed he was always fighting on several fronts at once.

Soissons was the brother of the young prince de Condé, and Catherine had known him when they were children, when they were both still unaware of the demands of royalty. Overwrought with excitement, Catherine, now twenty-eight years old, paced her room. At last she was to be married, married to a 22-year-old prince, one who was directly and legitimately descended from a king of France in the male line, and a handsome hero from Coutras. Henry had teased her imagination with other betrothals and she had worried she would never wed. Of unstable health but possessing a courageous optimism similar to her brother's, she constantly maintained a cheerful demeanor and remained surprisingly loyal to her brother despite his continual trifling with her emotions.

Corisande viewed Henry's coming as the apotheosis of all her lonely dreams. In this exalted mood, her lover and her king, under the wings of victory, seemed to her ennobled with a new grandeur. Her future with him was surely limitless.

On the afternoon of November 9, Charles and Henry stepped through the portals of Navarrenx. Corisande and Catherine stepped forward to greet their chevaliers. Henry did not embrace Corisande immediately but knelt at her feet, strewing before her the variegated silks, embroidered and fringed with gold, torn by bullets, spattered with blood. The banners of Coutras represented homage and sacrifice. If life corresponded to the novels she so loved, if destiny and death were benevolent, joy would have lifted her heavenward at this moment and these standards would have become her shroud.

Princes usually offered these trophies to God alone, and Corisande, for a brief moment, forgot the fleeting love affairs of her knight errant — even forgot Esther and her bastard child. Nothing had changed in her love, and she believed the lord who knelt before her in homage would be hers always.

Catherine, also, was immediately blinded by the ecstasy of the occasion and was easily seduced by the handsome strength of her soldier. A tall, proud man with a noble bearing, Charles de Bourbon wore a moustache and a small neat beard while his friendly blue eyes belied a generally stern expression.

Five days later the two pairs of lovers sojourned together in Pau. Happiness had rejuvenated Catherine, visibly reviving her wilted youthfulness.

"Love becomes you," Corisande said, observing a touch of peach in Catherine's usually pale cheeks.

"I should not have doubted Henry would do well for me," Catherine rejoiced. "Charles is more than I could have ever hoped for. He is so very intelligent and thoughtful."

"I am pleased and happy for you," Corisande replied, hugging her friend. "It never seemed fair that I should have so much happiness and you so little."

"But you appear a bit worried today," Catherine ventured, always sensitive to the feelings of her friend. "Or are you feeling unwell?"

"No, Catherine. I am just surprised and a bit disappointed, I admit, to see Henry come and go so relentlessly. We have had so little time together, it seems he would want to spend more time with me now."

"You must not worry. You know his need for exercise. He always hunts with a frenzy when he is here, and his level of activity always appears incredibly intense to us more sedentary types."

"Yes, perhaps you are right. But we have been separated so long. And he seems . . . well, distracted when he is with me. But I shouldn't spoil this glorious day with silly moping. Let us take a walk to the park to see if the hunters have returned."

Corisande decided she should not worry her friend needlessly, especially when Catherine appeared to be in such an exalted state. Yet she intuited, with a lover's insight, that just when she believed her happiness assured forever, the most unjust fatality was ready to overwhelm her. Stirred by instinct, she sought to attract Henry to the solitude of Hagetmau, where they had lived so many ardent hours. Pushing away the dread crowding into her heart, she determined to enjoy what happy moments she could. Henry arrived again on November 18, but after making what seemed to her pitiful excuses, left again the next day for Pau.

Why must I be so lofty and heroic? Corisande asked herself. What reason was there to remain so composed, so concerned with her duty? She would tell him her fears when he returned, her fear that he no longer loved her. If this were so, they would agree to remain friends. But he says he loves me, she reassured herself.

Henry reappeared on November 27 and remained for three days. Why didn't he caress her as he used to? But whenever the chance arose, she found she was too afraid to raise the subject most important to her. She told herself he would only make light of her doubts if she said anything. Her heart ached until she wanted to tear it from her chest. Finally, one last time, Corisande received him on December 2. His baggage was already on its way to Mont-de-Marsan. A new separation was about to begin, but Henry, never stingy with beautiful promises, assured her, "I have no intention of straying far from Gascony. Do not fret, my love. I will be able to return easily to Pau or Hagetmau."

She brightened and started toward him. Her movement was interrupted by the arrival of a messenger with an anonymous letter. "What is it, Pétiot?" she asked as she saw his face contort with anger.

"It contains the worst implications against Charles de Bourbon, Comte de Soissons. It maintains that if this prince marries Catherine, he would then abandon me and my cause."

"But Henry, who wrote you such lies? You cannot take this miserable calumny as gospel, nor should you even be suspicious. Who could you ever trust more than Soissons? It makes no sense."

"That shit-a-bed deserter will certainly not marry Catherine now!" he raged, as though he had not heard a thing she said.

Corisande anxiously tried to calm him. "Surely you cannot believe an anonymous letter, Henry. You know your cousin has been faithful to you for years. *Mon Dieu*, Henry, have you forgotten he is Condé's younger brother? And why would he turn against you, especially when you do him another favor and give him your sister, whom he loves? You cannot take him from her now. She is happier than I have ever seen her."

"She will get over it. I cannot afford to have traitors close to me."

"*Mon Dieu*, think more about it before you do such an unreasonable and ruthless thing. Please, Henry. Please!" she begged.

Giving Corisande one last distracted kiss, he jumped gracefully into the saddle. Far away now, the staccato beat of the horses' hooves rapidly died away and disappeared in the grand silence of the countryside, sleepy under the winter sky.

He wrote to her from Mont-de-Marsan:

Hold me in your good graces as the one who will be your faithful slave until death. I have two baby boars and two bitch fawns. Let me know if you want them.

Twenty-four hours later, he wrote to her of a skirmish and ended:

I am writing dispatches tonight. Tomorrow at noon they will leave and I also to kiss your hands. Bonjour, My worthy sovereign. Please love Pétiot.

But the League prevented the king from realizing this promise. When he left Mont-de-Marsan on December 14, it was away from Hagetmau and toward Casteljaloux and Nérac that his horse carried him. Carried him away from the only one who truly listened and obeyed when he whispered, "Love me."

NAVARRENX AND PARIS

1588

AFTER HENRY'S DEPARTURE, Corisande's agitation increased. In a letter in February he told her the Comte de Soissons was leaving for Navarrenx, where he would pay court to Catherine, and invited Corisande to oversee the meetings of the lovers due to his new concerns. How wrong he is to count on me to destroy his sister's dream, she thought. She would not interfere with that affair nor do anything to mar her friend's happiness. How can he be so heartless, she wondered, or doubt Soissons's loyalty? Perhaps, she surmised, all the years of suspicion at the Valois court had eradicated his faith in men.

The days dragged by at the pace of a boring sermon. Noticing the discrepancy between the loving tone of his letters and the lack of zeal he revealed by not coming to her, she understood its significance. Like his early morning escapes from her bed, she lamented. When she ceased writing to him, however, Henry countered with an offensive. He affected indignation at her silence and seemed disposed to let the quarrel become worse, writing:

> You do not find the roads at all dangerous to give the least pleasure to your friends; but if you should write me to give some contentment, the roads are suddenly too dangerous. This is the indication I have of your good grace . . . I must certainly wind up believing you do not wish me well at all. It is in your power to give whatever impression pleases you.

Corisande's response was both tender and jealous, and she received a forgiving missive sent from Nérac on March 1:

> I have received your letter, my mistress, in which you tell me you wish me no harm but that you cannot feel any assurance in anyone so changeable as I. It was a great pleasure to learn the first, and as for the other, you are very much mistaken to remain in such doubt. What action of mine has seemed changeable to you? You begin to interpret your suspicions and they fall upon me. I am faithful in my love and my service is beyond all quarrels.

The next letter Corisande received contained a shock. The prince de Condé had been poisoned. She liked Condé, probably more than Henry did, for she found his naiveté and occasional bumbling incompetence appealing. Also, she had sympathized with him recently upon hearing stories of his wife's deceit — with one of her pages, no less! She read Henry's account:

> As I was finishing dressing, one of the most extreme misfortunes I could imagine happened — which is the sudden death of M. le Prince. I pity him for what he claimed to be, not for what he was to me.

Corisande knew the cousins were not always in perfect agreement; in fact, Condé often irritated Henry by continuing to express regrets over his publicly abjuring his faith in Paris so long ago. For Henry that was over and done with, and he still believed there had been no other realistic choice at the time. She read on:

> I am at this moment the sole target at which all the perfidies of the masses are aiming. They have poisoned him, the traitors! . . . this poor prince (not in heart) on Thursday, having eaten his supper was feeling well. At midnight a violent vomiting came upon him which lasted until morning. All Friday he remained in bed . . . On Saturday morning . . . he got up and began to walk around his room. All of a sudden, he said "Give me a chair. I feel very weak." He was scarcely seated before he lost his speech and soon af-

ter he died. Still seated. The signs of poison suddenly
came out . . . Pray to God for me. If I escape, it will
necessarily be He who has watched over me. Until
death (to which I am nearer perhaps than I think) I
will remain your faithful love slave. Good night, my
soul. I kiss your hands a million times.

In his next letter, she read:

The Roman preachers preach loudly in the villages
around here canonizing this beautiful act (the poisoning of Condé) and the person who did it; they ad-
monish all good Catholics to follow the example of so
Christian an enterprise. And you are of this religion!
. . . Do not wait another moment to cast your religion
on the dung hill!

Corisande was wounded, but not wanting anger to obscure her
reason, she replied:

If all the Catholics wished you so much good will as
I, they would not try to displease you as most of them
do . . . Keep the promise you made to me to trust few
people and to speak less than you have done; your
business will go better for it.

Without Henry's visits to cheer her solitude, the winter seemed
interminable. Snow lay upon the black branches like an ermine coat,
and still, feathery flakes drifted earthward. Weekly, Corisande heard
more stories of his unfaithfulness, yet she remembered with hope that
he had brought to her the mangled banners of Coutras after a separation of one and a half years. She had not heard of any lasting liaison,
and a soldier on the road could not be expected to be pure. Surely
Henry would send for her when he needed her, when his last battle
was won. After all, hadn't he once promised she would be his wife?
At least it seemed he still needed her because the political situation in
Paris worsened daily. Picking up his last missive from her escritoire,
she reread his woeful story:

The devil is unchained . . . The violent trials my
brain must endure! This year will be my touchstone.

All the Gehennas a mind can receive are exercised
on mine without respite. I will remember your receipt to keep silent. Believe that nothing except a lack
of friendship could make me change the resolution
I have to be eternally yours; My all, love me. From
Nérac, March 18, at midnight, 1588.

Looking up, Corisande saw the snow still fell, and the black
shadows of the trees lined the snow like wrinkles in a white face. In
her lonely isolation, she was sure these protestations of love were only
to soften her and to draw attention from a departure which was, in
truth, a flight. He had never really wanted her — France was the only
mistress he truly sought.

Toward the end of winter, since Béarn no longer seemed to be
menaced by an invasion from Royalist troops, Catherine and Corisande resettled in Pau. Sitting together in rooms with portraits of
Henry's ancestors looking benevolently down on them, Corisande
tried to hide her misery and to comfort Catherine. Soissons had informed her that Henry did not wish to hear anymore about her marriage to him at present. The Count continued to fight at the side of
the Béarnais, but he no longer hid his discontent at being played with.
One could see that at any moment he would break from the king. The
two women, tormented with a similar anguish, with nothing to distract them from their bitter preoccupations, simultaneously wished
for and doubted the arrival of the royal couriers.

Corisande knew it would be a mistake to reveal her anguish and
jealousy to Henry. She had won him partially by being above moping
and tears of self-pity, but the loneliness and frustration of the long
winter months had eroded her courage. She grimaced, remembering
her words to Henry long ago about the present being all that mattered. Moreover, she had to face the fact of encroaching middle age.
She saw herself in the maturity of her 33 years, too soon married,
plumper, paler. Finally, her love conquered reason, and she let loose
a torrent of accusations, knowing full well they were the epitaph to
their love.

At the same time she heard that the news for Henry from Paris was becoming worse. A junta of fanatic Catholic bourgeoises, which zealously obeyed Guise, had taken control of the city. Duc Henri de Guise entered Paris on May 9, 1588, to the welcoming cries from the mob of "Hosanna to the Son of David and Long live the pillar of the Church." To the Parisians, Guise, so handsome in white satin, looked far more a king than Henri III, whom some called "their painted, mincing sodomite." Corisande's friends in Paris informed her that the Hotel de Guise now seemed more important than the Louvre.

She mused on Henry's chances for success. Several years had passed since the death of Alençon, the last Valois heir, and many were impressed by the genealogy of the House of Lorraine, which showed descent from Charlemagne. So perhaps the duc de Guise had a better right to the French crown than any descendant of Hugues Capet. This would not have been a possibility except for the fact that the direct heir to the French crown was considered a heretic and also proudly accepted the title of chieftain of the Huguenot party.

The Guises understood, as did Corisande, that the best way to cement their political power would be to capitalize on the religious divisions. The people primarily objected to Henry, not because of his lack of a royal claim to the throne, but because they feared Protestant domination. Whipped up by their preachers, Parisians seemed more willing to revolt than to accept a Protestant king. The capital was roiling with the bitterest ingredients for a war since the aftermath of St. Bartholomew. Though she received bulletins daily from Paris, one day Corisande gladly welcomed Montaigne, who had more immediate news and opinions to impart.

She was shocked at his appearance, for now at age fifty-five he appeared to be more a pale and wrinkled gnome than the strong man he once had been. On his side, Montaigne found his friend's lassitude unusual and attempted to stir her interest with his stories.

"Henri III certainly understands that both his throne and his life are in danger. He dares not trust Guise, while any alliance with Navarre would set the League against him. He ordered Guise not to come to Paris, but then discovered he had no choice but to receive him."

"Oh, dear," Corisande sighed. "I must admit Guise alarms me far more than Henri III, who is too incompetent to rule, and more and more people understand that every day."

"I am told that the Sorbonne professors are arguing whether it is lawful to remove government from princes who are unfit to rule, just as one takes away the stewardship of any other untrustworthy guardian," Montaigne responded. "Paris grows visibly more tense as clerical demagogues rant with frenzy, waxing against their sovereign, and an excited rabble roams the streets, hunting down heretics."

When his listener made no comment, Montaigne continued, "I have tried to facilitate negotiations between Navarre and Henri III, but to no avail. They must understand that they have a common enemy and so should band together. Now I fear it is too late. On May 12 the king's army attempted to establish control of the city's strong points and failed. The mob then set up barricades and humiliated the royal troops by crying *Vive Guise*. Fearing destruction of his city and yet too afraid to make a decision, Henri III refused to give the Swiss Guard the order to fire. With no other choice, they retreated to the Louvre in confusion. Then Guise strode into the streets, quelled the uproar, and demanded concessions, which would leave Henri III a mere figurehead. The terrified weak Valois king fled his capital and the agitated rabble hailed the confident and aggressive Henri, duc de Guise, whom they now call *le beau roi de Paris*. It's being called the 'Day of the Barricades.'"

"*Mon Dieu*, Michel, it is clearer than ever! Guise will certainly be a more difficult foe for Henry, yet at the same time, he can never know what to expect from the untrustworthy Henri III. He is besieged on every front."

But when Montaigne took his leave, the chaos of Paris seemed very far away to her. Corisande felt a stirring of desire as she moved languorously on her day bed. As the passion mounted, she daydreamed of Henry's presence. No, he isn't coming. He isn't coming today, tomorrow, nor the day after. Melancholy quickly replaced her fantasy, like black ink spilled on her white letter paper, and she fought back the tears of loneliness that came so quickly to her eyes.

After six years she knew Henry all too well, and these last months had enlightened her all the more. Knowing Navarre's taste for very young women and his constant need for female company, she recognized that the pitiless passing of time would condemn her. He would be incapable of turning away from any woman who offered her body to his incurable sensuality. He didn't see himself as dishonest for having loved before. Feeling each moment was unique and fresh, he believed himself sincere in his protestations of constancy and ephemeral oaths. But she knew this fickleness would destroy her, even as she knew that she and Henry were less linked by the flesh than by the spirit.

Because she had refused to live with him and to follow him from battlefield to battlefield, immediate witnesses even doubted their liaison. She had not tried to subjugate him by the senses, and by refusing to attach herself to his footsteps, she had literally introduced him to infidelity. He could not refuse a vulgar romp. Still, success or failure, far or near, she was assured her Pétiot considered her his wisest and surest counselor. She had always offered him a lucidity and an indomitable energy to discover a path leading to the throne.

As she read the sonnets of Ronsard, she wept with grief and recognition:

> Les villes et les bourgs me sont si odieux,
> Que je meurs si je vois quelque tracette humaine,
> Seulet dedans les bois pensif je me promène,
> Et rien ne m'est plaisant que les sauvages lieux.
>
> Il n'y a dans ces bois sangliers si furieux,
> Ni roc si endurci, ni ruisseau, ni fontaine,
> Ni arbre tant soit sourd, qui ne sache ma peine,
> Et qui ne soit marri de mon mal ennuyeux.
>
> Un penser qui renaist d'un autre, m'accompaigne
> Avec un pleur amer qui tout le sein me baigne,
> Travaillé de souspirs qui compaignons me sont :
>
> Si bien que si quelcun me trouvoit au bocage,
> Voyant mon poil rebours et l'horreur de mon front,
> Ne me diroit pas homme, mais un monstre sauvage.

Cities and towns are so odious to me
That I die seeing any human touches,
Alone in the woods pensively I wander
And nothing pleases me but wild places.

There are in this forest no boars so wild,
Nor rock so hard, nor stream, nor spring,
Nor tree, be it so deaf, which knows not my pain,
And which is not grieved by my sad desires.

One thought reborn from another accompanies me
With bitter tears which bathe my whole breast.
Tormented by sighs which are my companions;

So much so, that if anyone found me in the woods,
Seeing my hair standing on end and the horror
in my face,
They would say I was not a man, but a wild beast.

She continued to receive several avowals from Henry of his fidelity throughout the spring. Yet he still failed to risk ambush and bands of marauding soldiers to come south to her château on the hill of Bidache. As the winter snows cleared, she lost hope. Sobs rose in her throat as she wrote, her pride at his feet:

> After tomorrow your arbor will be finished and every day your walks grow more beautiful. I can easily relate to you all the news here for that is all I have to do. For a long time now, I have come to loathe this house and the whole place. It no longer speaks of nightingales. As a matter of fact, I have forgotten what their song was like, although I shall be happy to hear the first one for its sad music will bring to birth some lovely thoughts in my heart; as for that, everything has that power, even the kestrels which fly before my window. Goodbye. It is so late that I do not know what I am doing.

FROM BATTLEFIELD TO BATTLEFIELD

IF HENRY'S PASSION HAD cooled toward his mistress, at least he continued to respect and admire her. The poisoning of his cousin had sobered him, and Corisande's serious warnings had finally impressed him. In any case, he enjoyed corresponding with this woman whose devotion and intelligence were precious to him. Continuing to play the role of the faithful paragon, it didn't dawn on him to worry about trifling with her emotions. He enjoyed keeping their relationship open. To end it would be as irreversible as marriage; to end it would be a small death. In October he wrote:

> God knows with what joy I have received your letter. At this hour do you confess that you desire to afflict me? I have always loved you with all perfection; my love was founded on you and your virtues, these two pillars are indestructible. Let us leave this discourse, the die is cast. There ought not to be any more doubt between us.

Two days later he wrote to her again, words he hoped would sustain any illusions that remained. After describing the difficult but successful siege of Beauvoir-sur-Mer, he continued:

> My heart, I am a luckier man than you think. Your last dispatch reminds me of the diligence of writing that I had lost. I read your letter every night. If I love it, ought I not to love the sender? Never have I had such desire to see you as I have now. If the enemies

do not press us, after this assembly, I wish to steal away for a month . . . I pray to you, that you forget all the hate you bear toward those who belong to me. This is one of the first changes I wish to see in you. Do not fear or believe anything could ever shake my love. I love you more than ever. Good night, my heart. I am going to sleep, my soul lighter than it has been for 20 days. I kiss your eyes millions of times.

As he was finishing the letter, Agrippa d'Aubigné came in. When he saw to whom Henry was writing, he could not conceal his anger.

"To continue this affair with Corisande is fatal, Sire. In a word, she is Catholic. If you marry your mistress in these present circumstances, you will forever bar the road that could one day lead to the throne of the French monarchy, a Protestant monarchy."

"Aubigné, if you believe I am fighting for a Protestant takeover of the country, then you are supporting the wrong man. I could never change this country to a Protestant monarchy." He had never stated these words out loud or so clearly before, but continued lucidly. "In fact, I would not want to. I only want Catholics and Protestants to learn to live side by side and to accept and respect one another's beliefs."

"That is not what many who are following you want." Aubigné's glower intimated he spoke for himself as well.

"That is probably true, but they do not understand that the country will be divided by constant civil war unless the two religions learn to live together. The clergy can argue all they like, but they will only be officiating at burials unless they advocate more. Think back on your history, my man. Our ally Elizabeth I sent her Catholic cousin, Mary Stuart, Queen of Scots, to the executioner's block, another bloody story of Catholics against Protestants — in 1587. How long can this go on? It seems to me that religion is often an excuse to usurp power. Why can't the two live and let live?"

"Most people are not so broad thinking, Sire. But in any case, it is dangerous even to be seen with Corisande these days."

Henry threw down his quill and ink splattered on his letter. "*Sacrebleu!* Stop badgering me, and I will promise not to see my mistress again for two years."

His passion had waned to the point that it was easy to make this offer. Hadn't he just written of his desire to change her? Recalling how he had found her features fatigued and unappealing after Coutras, how she had aged and grown plump, he had felt ashamed when he had jumped from her bed to seek the company of sporting men during the day. He preferred to remember the downy cheek, the white throat, and supple arms of Esther rather than to lie where he was no longer aroused. Unexpectedly, he experienced a flicker of conscience as he remembered condemning Margot's adulterous behavior. But most men wouldn't dream of condemning his philandering, and he had discovered that the adoration of a beautiful, youthful woman rejuvenated his energy. In fact, he was afraid he would be unable to continue his rigorous activity without this feminine revitalization.

Still, he wanted to correspond with Corisande. It would do no harm, he thought, and probably make her happy. She was his staunchest advocate, and it seemed this noble woman had been his lucky star. Shortly before Christmas, he wrote to her again:

> I am well, thanks to His Grace, having nothing in my heart but a wild desire to see you. I do not know when I will have that happiness . . . I beg you to love me. There are three things of which I have no doubt — you, your love, and your fidelity . . . Truly, I would pay dearly for a chance for three hours with you. Good night, my love. I would like to be in the corner of your hearth to heat your soup.

In order to affirm his leadership, Henry agreed to preside over a Huguenot assembly at La Rochelle. Reviewing his situation with an objective eye, he found it deplorable. He had followed Coutras by a failure at Vimory and by another loss to the League at Auneau. His German mercenaries were undisciplined and their leaders unwilling to take risks. Guise, now in control of Paris, had made the most of Henry's slumps. King Henri III was licking his wounds in the city of Chartres, and the Queen Mother, old and tired, sat alone in the Louvre, mourning her son's weakness. There could not be three Kings, one in Paris, one in Chartres, and another in the Southwest. The lines were drawn. The Paris preachers were singing of the League's triumph, saying, "Saul killed his thousands, but David his ten thousands." Henry believed that his return to La Rochelle might rekindle the Huguenot flame.

Ten years had passed since the siege of La Rochelle, but when he stood to face the assembly, the audience before him still appeared pale and thin. How could he expect these brave men to consider philosophy when their stomachs rumbled above his voice? France, the State, was as unhealthy as the group before him — malnourished and sick to death of war. But he must convince them; a country was at stake. He addressed the assembly:

> As for myself, I have spared neither property nor life in this holy cause. If the difficulties increase, I feel that God will redouble my courage in the resolution we have taken to expend, in the defense of the churches, the last drop of my blood and the last item of my possessions ... I regret there are some who have failed to recognize my labors and by whom my actions have been misrepresented. I pray daily that God will grant me His Grace to lead His people through so many horrors and frightful deserts to a place of safety and rest.

He suppressed a momentary urge to laugh at himself. He was beginning to sound like Moses! But with these valiant words, Henry tried to hide his discouragement. "Safety and rest" were becoming his credo, and the country was as war weary as he. The people still failed or refused to see what was so very clear to him, as clear as the eyes of an innocent child, that religious tolerance was the only hope for peace. Even while he was speaking, the League passed a resolution in Paris, stripping him of all his rights as First Prince of the Blood and consequently of his claim to succeed to the throne. His fellow-Huguenots were angry with him too, accusing him of being too willing to bargain with the Catholics. They refused to understand that negotiations were necessary to achieve his goal to end the religious wars. They were unwilling to compromise their religious beliefs for the sake of peace.

In his despair, he wrote again to the only person he felt would understand. But even with Corisande, he pretended more optimism than he truly felt:

The assembly has gone well but if there were to be another, I would go stark mad. My speeches were minimally conciliatory yet I was still criticized. I argued for a strong opposition to the enemy whose aim is directed not only against the Protestants but, against the King and the state.

I hate interminable theological discussions, orations of high moralism. My instincts are for action. When, in addition I am lectured for the immorality of my conduct, the levity of my life, my favoritism to Catholics, I find it harder to sustain than a battle.

BLOIS AND PLESSIS-LEZ-TOURS

1588-1589

EVENTS WERE CULMINATING precipitously into a decisive moment for Henry. Having received the good news in July that the Spanish Armada had been wrecked off the Irish coast, he realized he need not worry about Philip of Spain for the moment, but the situation in France was increasingly ominous. Guise's power was growing and King Henri III's declining, and so he must consider his options. But he didn't guess — could not have guessed — what was brewing in the king's sick mind.

Having sought refuge in Blois, Henri III whipped up his hatred for Guise. Failing to understand that he was trapped, he became more and more angry — how dare the duc de Guise forbid him, the king, to enter Paris? He believed Guise cared only for himself and not for France and resolved it would be better for the country if Navarre were to be his successor. Conveniently ignoring the resolution just passed that barred Henry's access to the throne, he decided the only answer was to assassinate Guise. The king's special bodyguard, the "45," as the *mignons* were called, were adventurers with few qualms about killing, and they readily answered his call for help. The plotters chose the days just before Christmas for the execution of their murderous plan, and with suitable ritual, Henri III presented each assassin with a jeweled dagger. Then he calmly and piously ordered Mass to be said for their intentions and their success.

With his usual arrogance and confident of his powerful position, Guise arrived at Blois on Friday, December 23, 1588, for negotiations with the king, carelessly dismissing the sinister rumors and secret warnings that had begun to circulate. When the king failed to appear for his Council, which had been called for 7:00 a.m., Guise began to grow nervous about the delay. But finally, when he was summoned to the royal bedchamber he strode in without reservation.

There, in the candlelight of the cold dawn hours, ten of the "45" struck him down. Pouring blood and dragging his murderers with him, he staggered the entire length of the huge room before falling at the foot of the king's bed. As Henri gazed with horror at the duke's mangled corpse, he whimpered, "My God, how big he is! He seems bigger dead than alive!"

Henri III expected the League to collapse now that its champion was dead, and he was astonished when it gained strength from the martyrdom. Apparently the Valoises had learned nothing from the St. Bartholomew Massacre. From Christmas day onward, vast processions marched through Paris at night, plunging torches in tubs of water as they cried, "So may God quench the Valois race." Meanwhile, a fanatic Catholic junta known as the Seize, ruled Paris more firmly than ever, continuing to repudiate the king and sending for Guise's brother, the formidable duc de Mayenne.

Amid the chaos, Catherine de Medici lay on her deathbed within the Louvre Palace, as she listened to the mob in the streets, their chant becoming her dirge. How could the king have been so stupid as to kill his wily opponent? He was surely doomed, as all her children had been. She had willed her arthritic body from the bed more times than she could count, but now she gave way to despair. Her last, pitiful king had forfeited all hope of making peace between Huguenots and Papists, and even worse, had alienated the greater part of his subjects.

For thirty years she had struggled to support her children on the thrones of Europe, but they had proved themselves physically or mentally incompetent to fill such great roles. Their failures were her failure. She thought of Marguerite, isolated and lonely at Usson, and of Navarre's growing power. Though she had pretended all her life that the *Grand Chyren* of the oracle was her Henri III, the Oracle of Nostradamus* echoed in her ears. Her magic had been to no avail against the disruptive forces of the religious wars and the charismatic personality of Henry of Navarre. On January 5, 1589, at age 69, Catherine turned her head to the wall, murmuring, "I have been crushed in the ruins of the House of Valois."

In anguish she closed her eyes for the last time. None of her children was there to witness her passing.

* See page xvii

Henry received the news of the death of his old enemies with mixed feelings. He thought of Margot, surely mourning her mother and her former lover. Ironically, he had just written to Corisande to say, "I await only the hour when I shall hear that Margot has been strangled. That, with the death of her mother, would make me sing the cantique de Simeon!"

The timing seemed mysterious. Even if Catherine de Medici had irritated him more as a splinter than a thorn lately, he remembered his years at the Louvre with bitterness. As a political realist, he understood Henri III would be weaker for the loss of his mother. Indeed, the king soon indicated he had no illusions as to whom was his heir, despite the recent Paris resolution declaring Navarre's illegitimacy to the throne. Henri III's firm rule now extended little farther than a few towns in the Loire valley, so inevitably, to pacify Henry, he summoned him and presented him with the gift of Saumur, one of the prettiest Loire towns. Both understood the king was buying time. Henry carefully made it clear to Henri III that they had a common cause in defending the monarchy, while simultaneously making sure that his foreign allies understood he had not abandoned the Protestant cause.

As much as Henry would have liked to rest at the elegant château of Saumur, an imposing edifice with four corner towers, each crowned with a spire, he resisted the temptation to dally. Elongated windows looked out on a green valley and bright banners waved from numerous pinnacles. But no woman held him here, and clearly this was a turning point in his life. The throne of France seemed so near that he might reach out and place the crown upon his graying head. The people despised the weak Henri III and Guise was dead. But the Catholic League survived, now led by the duc de Mayenne. The greatest difficulty, Henry deduced, remained the French law, which recognized only a Catholic king. Surely he could discredit the League in the eyes of the French people, and the law . . . he would just have to deal with that prickly problem later.

On April 13, 1589, Henry of Navarre, wearing parade armor weighing seventy-seven pounds, rode into the town of La Riche with a small group of horsemen and stopped at the château of Plessis-lez-Tours to throw himself at his king's feet. This was not meant to be a flattering gesture or even an act of formal homage to Henri III, but a calculated piece of political showmanship to demonstrate his reverence for the French monarchy. Henri III, however, did not allow Henry to kneel before him but embraced his cousin instead as the people cheered.

"*Mon frère*," Henri III began, "I thank God you came. You are my indisputable successor, as I have indicated by the way I have just addressed you. This must be proclaimed throughout the city and the land. We must stand together to defeat our common enemy, the League."

So, Henry rejoiced, the king would ignore the earlier Paris resolution stripping Henry of his claim to the throne. When the two armies formally joined forces, the struggle now became one of the Royalists (Henri III and Henry of Navarre) against the Catholic League, as well as between the crown and the people of France who refused to recognize a Protestant king. This is exactly what Montaigne had been urging them to do for many months, Henry realized. When the king summoned the Parliament of Paris to the city of Tours to underline the legality of his cause, Henry of Navarre began a furious military campaign, storming town after town. He did not waste a moment, for he now felt sure that the crown could be his. When not leading a battle, he was planning the next one. His military instincts were always superb, and his forces soon controlled the entire area between the Loire and the Seine. And nightly he thanked the Goddess Athena for his victories.

Corisande passed from despair to a stoic attitude of resignation. Henry still wrote to her, keeping up the pretense, for what reason she could not understand. On March 29 he said, "I am very well, thank God, loving nothing in the world like you. I received your letter yesterday; there was scarcely time to read it." Perhaps she was his touchstone, his good luck charm, she thought.

He didn't even take the time to scribble his formula: "I kiss your hands a million times," but as always he informed her of his health, for in these times it was more difficult to stay alive than to succumb to disease or an enemy's sword. It seemed to Corisande he was constantly surprised to still be alive.

When she received his next letter, she wrote in its margin her own sharp cryptic remarks. Her grief would be hidden from him, but she would permit herself this private sarcasm. Henry began:

> My soul, I am writing to you from Blois, where five months ago they condemned me as a heretic, unworthy of succeeding to the crown, and here I am, the principal pillar of it. Notice the ways of God to those who always trust in Him! Because was there anything which had so much appearance of force than a seizure of the Estates? However, I called the One who can do all . . .

Corisande wrote beside his words: As do many others!

> Henry: I am very well, thank God; swearing to you truly that I neither love nor honor anyone in the world as much as you.

Corisande: There is nothing which appears that way!

> Henry: And I will remain faithful to you . . .

Corisande stabbed at the paper with her pen: Unfaithful!

> Henry: Til the tomb. I am going to Beaugency, where I believe you will soon hear talk of me.

Corisande: I do not doubt it – in one way or another!

> Henry: My heart, love me always as yours, as I love you as mine.

Corisande scribbled their epitaph: You are not mine, nor am I yours.

The Countess would see her king one day. But Pétiot had left her forever.

FROM PARIS BACK TO THE BATTLEFIELD

1589

AFTER GUISE'S DEATH, HENRY slowly and surely cemented his power, seizing one town after another. He believed his main goal was to save the monarchy. On April 30, at Plessis-lez-Tours, the King of France and the King of Navarre met to sign a truce to shore up the royal institution, Henry wearing the white plume which had become symbolic of his victories in the field. The people on hand for the occasion dutifully shouted, "Long Live the Kings." Events were moving quickly as he and Mayenne, who was seeking vengeance for his brother's death and power for himself, jockeyed for military control. As Henry secured victories at the Oise, the Seine and the Marne, his reputation expanded, and people began attributing magical powers to him. It seemed that Henri III might remain king after all, with Navarre as his military might.

However, this hope quickly disintegrated when Mayenne reached Paris ahead of Henry and prepared to defend his position. On July 30, Henri III's Royalist force, which included forty thousand foreign troops, invaded the city. Only a miracle could save the panic-stricken capital from falling at this first assault. The streets hummed with fanatic schemes and frantic action, women scurried about storing up against a siege, and overwrought fathers barricaded the streets.

Amidst the hysteria, one young Dominican friar of wild and divine imaginings decided to take matters into his own hands. He resolved to save his Catholic city from its ungodly foes, in particular, from Henri III, whose haughty, disdainful manner had angered so many. The next day, knowing no one would suspect a good monk of dastardly intent, he begged access to the king. He explained he had an important letter, which must be handed personally to the monarch. Allowed to draw close to Henri III, he quickly struck with a knife which he had concealed in his sleeve, stabbing the king below the navel.

"This wicked monk has killed me," Henri III howled. "Kill him! Kill him!"

Pulling the knife out, Henri used it to slash the friar in the face before falling. The king's bodyguards immediately fell upon the assassin and bludgeoned him to death. Later, his body was burned and his ashes cast into the Seine, the friar not living long enough to tell his story.

Despite Henri's shrieking and tears, for some unexplained reason, no one believed the king was seriously wounded. During the night violent pains and fever set in, causing people to whisper that perhaps the knife had been poisoned. Henri sent for his successor. However lamentable his reign, Henri III seemed determined to die well. Ordering his courtiers to take an oath of allegiance to his cousin, he instructed them, "If my wound proves mortal, I leave my crown to Henry of Navarre, my legitimate successor. If my will can have any effect, the crown will remain as firmly upon his brow as it was upon that of Charlemagne."

When he heard the news of the king's decline, Henry was residing at St. Cloud near Paris trying to figure out a strategy against Mayenne. He did not think it odd that his first reaction was to write to Corisande:

> The news I have of the King's condition since writing the above makes me change my tune, for the surgeons are now in great doubt of his recovery. If things take a turn for the worst (which God forbid!) I beg you, my friend, to wish me to show myself the man I have always promised myself to be. I repeat to myself that a decent heart will never favor the League, which has committed so dastardly an act.

Henry threw down his pen and announced to Rosny that he was leaving for Paris.

"I cannot help but wonder what will happen to you if the king dies now," Rosny said. "How will you be able to destroy this League which has been so powerful and so widely supported that it has made a crowned king tremble on his throne and almost caused him to abandon it?"

"But he was a weak king, Rosny," Henry scornfully replied.

"Yet this situation, already so difficult, seems almost insurmountable when one considers that the king's death will separate you, the King of Navarre, from the largest and most important party of your supporters. No longer will you be able to count either on the Princes of the Blood, who appear determined to exterminate one another, or on the upper nobility. Your position is such that, although you need the help of everyone, there is no one in whom you can place confidence. I shudder when I think of the possibility that such surprising and unexpected news might lead to a revolution, which would leave you with only a handful of faithful followers and at the mercy of your former enemies. In addition, you will be in a part of the country where every resource is lacking to you."

"And I'll wager that, as usual with these sinister affairs, the Guise family, or what is left of it, is responsible," Henry answered.

"You're probably right," Rosny agreed. "I've just heard there is evidence indicating that the sister of the duc de Guise won the love of this fanatic monk and poisoned his mind to take this action in retribution for the death of Guise."

"And as usual, it's a stinking perversion," Henry observed. "But please, keep the rest of your worries to yourself for now, Rosny. I would never get out of bed if I believed half of your gloomy ideas. I must leave immediately and hurry to the king's side."

But Henry of Navarre arrived too late. He learned of the king's death when the welcoming Scots Guard flung themselves at his feet, crying, "Sire, you are our King and master!"

For a moment Henry gaped at them. Of course he had dreamed of this happening some day but when it actually happened, he found himself too shocked to appreciate the thrill the news should have given him. However it only took a few minutes for him to realize there would be neither time nor reason to sit back and rejoice.

For his entire thirty-six years the country had been convulsed by warring factions; now it seemed that almost universal depravity had banished all respect for law and morality as well. The League's army of twenty thousand strong crowded the capital, noisily berating all Catholic Europe to rally around the pretender, Charles, Cardinal de Bourbon.* Henry of Navarre was now Henri IV of France by the decree of Henri III, but most Frenchmen would not recognize him as such as long as he remained a Huguenot. Nostradamus's Oracle whirled giddily around in his head. Magic or not, he was the heir to the future of France; Athena, the Goddess of Just Warfare, must guide the way.

Escorted to the chamber where the king lay, Henry beheld the body, with candles at the head and feet and Henri's loyal bodyguard shuffling around in confusion. A few knelt by the bier. All made way for Henry and watched as he bowed his head. He felt mostly pity for this strange man who had been driven successively by sexuality and religion, but who had been weak at the core. Henry had fought for this moment, and now he planned to do first what he did best, to ride from battlefield to battlefield to secure his throne. But how could he gain the people's support?

First, Henry issued an edict promising every security and support to the Catholic religion as the established religion of France. Still, since he did not mention converting to Romanism, nor promise to devote his energies to the extermination of the heresy of Protestantism, most Catholics remained suspicious and dissatisfied. So extensive was the discontent, that in one day Henry found himself deserted by all of his personal army except six thousand men, most of whom were Protestants. Nearly thirty thousand soldiers, who had been willing to serve him when he was an ally of King Henri III, now abandoned him, some to retire to their homes, some to join the enemy. Rosny's prophesies were proving dismally correct.

It appeared that neither Catholic nor Huguenot was willing to pledge allegiance to the new king. To a delegation from the Catholic nobles, Henry answered, "From whom can you expect such a change of faith except from a man who has none at all?" However he did agree to be instructed in the Roman faith before the end of six months — thereby making his Huguenot followers nervous he would desert them but also, by not promising to convert to Catholicism, angering all who held to the Salic Law.

Into the fray rose the specter of Spain as King Philip II, who was married to Elizabeth de Valois, suggesting that the people of France

---

*Charles de Bourbon (1523-1590), Cardinal de Bourbon, and Archbishop of Rouen. Also proclaimed as Charles X by the League.

put themselves under his protection. Above all, he would protect those of the Catholic religion. Henry understood this meant that Philip would most likely be working against his conversion.

The army of the League, led by Mayenne, prepared for a rush upon Henry's scattered and broken ranks. What was left of the royal army inherited from Henri III was in a shambles, and Henry IV could muster barely 20,000 men to conquer a rebellious country. After dividing the forces among several generals throughout France, on August 6, 1589, Henry set up camp with 8,000 loyal men at the port of Dieppe in Normandy, about a hundred miles northwest of Paris. Knowing that an attack against Mayenne's army of 35,000 men would be pointless, and that staying in the city of Dieppe would be suicidal, he decided to proceed inland to the city of Arques, where he would restore old military defenses.

Firmly he ordered a hasty retreat from Dieppe and appealed to Protestant Europe to hurry to his aid. Elizabeth I of England responded promptly to his appeal, promising to send a fleet and troops to the harbor of Dieppe. Henry then headed with his little army of Protestants toward the Seine with 20,000 Leaguers eagerly pursuing them, all the while watching for a chance to strike a deadly blow. Neither eating nor sleeping nor resting, night and day, Henry appeared everywhere, guiding, encouraging, and protecting his tiny band. His rear guard held the enemy in check at the western banks of the Seine until his Royalist army had retired beyond the Oise river. Upon the farther banks of this stream, Henry again reared his defenses, miraculously managing to thwart every endeavor of his enemies while he awaited aid from Elizabeth I. He had inherited the throne of France and he intended to keep it.

Again he slowly moved back toward the sea, hoping for a rendezvous with the English. Suddenly and unexpectedly all the Protestants of the region through which he passed began to flock to his standard. Then, from remote villages many of the moderate Catholics, who were in favor of the Royalist cause and hostile to Mayenne and the house of Guise, began to join him. In one short week he collected 7,000 very determined, committed men, whom he posted behind the ramparts of Dieppe. His vows of affection, compliments, and promises overwhelmed his followers, and they soon found it difficult to refuse anything from this delightful companion who demonstrated such infectious energy. The new king's willingness to share every danger quickly endeared him to all and became the necessary catalyst to unite his ill-paid force. He had an aptitude for carrying people along with him, and his troops, of remarkable heterogeneity, became energized by his vitality. For even in these hard times, his eyes glittered with excitement.

But the duc de Mayenne, the military leader of the League since Guise's death, had maintained large support. The spears and banners of his proud army, still numbering 35,000, gleamed from all the hills and valleys that surrounded the fortified city. For nearly a month an incessant conflict battered both armies, and every morning Henry anxiously scanned the watery horizon, hoping to find the fleet of England coming to his aid. Cheering his men with this hope, he successfully beat back his assailants again and again.

Suffering from gravel and stomach pains, a chronic bane to his existence, Henry's efforts seemed beyond human expectation. His bubbling, boiling belly threatened to get the best of him. Yet with exalted military genius he guided every moment, and at the same time shared the burden of the humblest soldier. He continued to write to his friend and lucky star, Corisande, "It is a marvel how I live with the labor I undergo. God have pity upon me and show me mercy."

Some of Henry's friends, appalled by the strength of the army pursuing them, urged him to embark and seek refuge in England. Henry shook his head and replied, "Here we are in France, and here let us be buried. If we fly now, all our hopes will vanish with the wind which bears us."

In a skirmish one day the comte de Bélin, one of the Catholic chieftains, was taken captive and led to the headquarters of the king. Henry greeted him cordially and noticing the astonishment of the count upon seeing but a few scattered soldiers where he had expected to see a numerous army, he said playfully, "You do not perceive all that I have with me, M. de Bélin, for you do not reckon God and the right on my side."

Yet he knew these words were brave bluff, for he and his troops were exhausted. He had not dared to admit even to himself how close he was to caving in. At that moment shouts from all over the camp erupted, interrupting them. Henry squinted and beheld the distant ocean whitened with the sails of the approaching English fleet. Cries of exaltation rolled along his fatigued lines, carrying dismay into the camp of the Leaguers. Tears streamed down Henry's face, finding easy passage through the furrows deepened with strain and worry.

"These are tears of joy, Count. France may yet be saved."

Henry's rescue came from the sea on September 22 — 6,000 English soldiers sent by Queen Elizabeth. A favorable wind pressed the fleet rapidly forward and resounding salutes echoed and re-echoed from English ships and French batteries. In a few short hours, with streaming banners and marching music, the fleet of Elizabeth I, loaded to its utmost capacity with money, military supplies, and men, cast anchor in the little harbor of Dieppe. The bulging war ship carrying Scots and English speedily disembarked. Not knowing his army still doubled that of Henri IV, Mayenne dared not engage his powerfully reinforced foe. Hastily breaking up his encampment, Mayenne retreated to Paris.

Henri IV, with money and men furnished by Elizabeth I, now was able to pay his soldiers their arrears. After the battle of Arques, as the Dieppe conflict came to be called, Henri IV snatched a short rest in a neighboring château, and before riding away he scratched with his diamond ring his profound hope on one of the windows: *Dieu garde de mal ma vie. Ce 22 de Septembre 1589. HENRI.**

His army began to grow steadily, and he soon marched with twenty-three thousand soldiers and fourteen pieces of artillery to lay siege to Paris. He had attained a psychological victory as well as a military one at Arques, and he grimaced inwardly, remembering how he had failed to capitalize on that after the battle of Coutras. But only one sanguinary assault convinced him he did not have sufficient force to carry the city. Raising the siege, he took Etampes instead, forty miles to the south.

Weary of the miseries of civil war, many of the citizens of Paris now felt inclined to rally around their lawful monarch as the only way to avert the horrible calamity overwhelming France. The duc de Mayenne rigorously arrested all who were suspected of such designs, even condemning to death four of the most prominent citizens. Henry quickly sent a message to the Duke that he would retaliate by putting to death some of the Catholic nobles who had been taken prisoner if the sentence were carried out. Mayenne defiantly executed two Royalists. Henry immediately suspended upon a gibbet two unfortunate Leaguers who were his captives. This decisive reprisal accomplished its purpose and compelled Mayenne henceforth to be more merciful.

Sweeping all opposition before him, Henry advanced to Tours. Few towns had the desire or energy any longer to defy Henry's claim

---

*God keeps me from harm. September, 22, 1589.

to the throne. Ignoring his own exhaustion, Henry capitalized on the country's battle fatigue. Seldom sleeping more than three hours at a stretch, he seized his meals where he could, but he knew his body could not tolerate this brutality much longer.

"It takes Mayenne more time to put on his boots," Henry bragged, "than it does me to win a battle."

"And everyone is quoting Pope Sixtus V," Rosny interjected. "saying that you will surely, in the end, gain the day, because you spend fewer hours in bed than Mayenne spends at the table."

"Ha! For once the Pope is right," Henry guffawed.

"It is now manifest to all, Sire, that if you would proclaim yourself a Catholic, the war would almost instantly end. The people would support you. You are now seen as the lawful monarch endeavoring to put down an insurrection." Rosny warmed to his theme, flinging his arms out wide as though to encompass all of France. "Your banner waves over fifteen fortified cities and over many minor towns. The forces of the League have been entirely swept from three of the provinces of France."

Henry only shook his head. "I think you are forgetting, Rosny, that Paris is still in the hands of the fat Duke."

He found time the next day to joke with Aubigné and described himself as a king without a kingdom, a warrior without money, and a husband without a wife.

Aubigné commented in his usual acerbic manner, "Yes, Sire, I must say, you are half-seated on a wobbling throne."

IVRY AND THE OUTSKIRTS OF PARIS

1590-1591

HENRY SPENT THE MORNING OF his thirty-seventh birth-day, December 13, 1590, in Tours.   It was a bitter and melancholy winter. He knew his army must be as tired and cold as he, and all must be longing for their families. Yet he could see no end in sight. Did his subjects not understand that he was a particularly humane man? Did they not see that he cherished kind feelings for all of his people? They must know by now that peace was his primary goal and that he was perfectly willing for the Catholic religion to retain its unquestioned supremacy in the country. He chafed at the difficulty of disseminating this message amidst the chaos of war. One message from Elizabeth across the Channel warmed his spirits greatly when she wrote, "There is nothing in the world that could make me happier than to hear my troops have in some way assisted a prince whom I would like to see completely served." How odd, he mused, that he had never met this grand lady in person.

No, he must not let despair overcome him. So far he had managed to resist the growing pressure to convert to Catholicism. His pride revolted from yielding to compulsory conversion, and he also refused to become the persecutor of his former friends. Consequently, he did everything in his power to mitigate the merciless strife and to win his Catholic subjects by overt clemency. But no efforts of his could restrain his Huguenot partisans, when provoked, from severe retaliation. Almost every part of France was scathed and cursed by war. Every province, city, and village had its partisans for the Catholic League or for Henry.

Through the long months of the dreary winter of 1590-91, the terrible carnage persisted, with success so equally balanced there was no prospect of any termination to this national calamity. Early in

March, the armies of Henri IV and the duc de Mayenne began to congregate for a decisive battle only fifty miles east of Paris near the Seine.

Night darkened the bleak plains, already soaked with spring rain. Numerous battalions of armed men with spears, banners, and heavy pieces of artillery, dragged axle-deep through the mire, hesitantly took their positions for an approaching battle. As the blackness of midnight enveloped them, the storm increased its fury, rendering the waiting men all the more fearful. The gale swept the plain, drowning all human sound with its loud wailing and its roar. All the night long, rain poured down in torrents, making it impossible to see even the nearest tent through the heavy curtains of water. Without even a watch fire to cheer the gloom, the contending armies anxiously waited for morning.

The soldiers, hunched under soggy blankets, looked up at the skies in terror as lightning danced from cloud to cloud with dazzling brilliance. They saw in the heavens the conflicting armies surge and fall back, hurling upon each other the thunderbolts of the skies. Both armies, exhausted and nearly frozen by the chilling storm, watched the sun rise on the damp dawn of March 14. Mounted upon his powerful bay charger, Henry rode slowly along his lines, addressing every soldier with words of encouragement and hope. He gave them no lofty speech, no false notes of enthusiasm; but mildly, gently, with a trembling voice, implored them to be true to God, to France, and to themselves. When he spoke, his eyes shone: "Your future fame and your personal safety depend upon your heroism this day. The crown of France awaits the decision of your swords. If we are defeated today, we are defeated hopelessly, for we have no reserves upon which we can fall back."

His men crowded closer to him, as though to draw warmth from his sincerity. Climbing upon an eminence where he could be seen by all his men, and where nearly all could hear him (in total, they numbered only six or seven thousand men on foot and two thousand five hundred on horseback), Henry clasped his hands and raised his eyes to Heaven, feeling overwhelmed with humility but with the will to succeed, and offered this prayer:

> O God, I pray thee, who alone knowest the intentions
> of man's heart, to do thy will upon me as thou shalt judge
> necessary for the weal of Christendom. And wilt thou
> preserve me as long as thou seeest it to be needful for the

happiness and the repose of France, and no longer. If thou dost see that I should be one of those kings on whom thou dost lay thy wrath, take my life with my crown, and let my blood be the last poured out in this quarrel.

Then turning to his troops, he said:

Companions, God is with us. You are to meet His enemies and ours. If in the turmoil of battle, you lose sight of your banner, follow the white plume upon my casque. You will find it on the road to victory and honor.

Henry donned the casque with the white plume, now the symbol of the Huguenot cause. Immediately, rushing squadrons swept the field in a deafening battle. The dying and the dead were crushed beneath iron hooves. Henry plunged into the thickest of the fight, everywhere exposing himself to peril like the lowest soldier. Counting on Henry's acute senses of hearing and sight, his men relied on his judgment of the quantity and quality of troops from afar.

The Leaguers began to waver. Suddenly they broke and fled in confusion. Henry headed the cavalry in pursuit so the battle might be more decisive. When he heard his men shout, "Remember St. Bartholomew," he realized they would strike the defeated with vengeance.

"They are our brethren!" he shouted. "Spare the French!"

Though covered with blood himself, he was greeted from his triumphant ranks with the shout, *Vive le Roi!*

"Let us praise God," Henry answered. "This victory is His." God is always on the side of reason, he told anyone who would listen. Then he turned to hurry to Rosny, who had been severely wounded in the battle. But he would live, the doctors assured him. "Already he is complaining," Henry laughed, with relief. He tried to look after other noblemen who had fallen for his cause and directed that the pensions of the dead go to their widows.

Even with Henry's merciful instructions, more than one-half of the army of the Leaguers was either slain or taken prisoner. Though the duc de Mayenne escaped, many of his best generals perished upon the field of Ivry or were captured. This decisive clash, by all rights, Henry thought, should establish him securely on the throne. Henry claimed he had won a nation on the battlefield of Ivry — but Mayenne still held Paris.

As always Henry thought first of his men and made sure they could rest before his next assault. Meanwhile, he and his captains discussed their next strategy.

"You will not be king until you have taken Paris. To conquer the city, you must cut her veins, her rivers of supply, in every direction," Aubigné advised.

For once Henry agreed and on May 14, exactly two months after his stupendous victory at Ivry, he presented himself under the walls of Paris, his visor lowered, his sword in his hand by his side. He smiled at the sight of the majestic city before him. He loved Paris like a creature of the flesh. Its presence excited him like a beautiful woman, and he hoped that, like a woman, she would deliver herself to him freely and quickly.

He wrote to Corisande, knowing she still loved him and wished to know of his every move:

> I am before Paris, where God will aid me. Taking her, I will be able to begin to feel the effects of wearing the crown. I have taken the bridges of Charenton and Saint-Maur by fire and have hung all who were within. Yesterday, I took the faubourg of Paris by force. The enemies lost a great deal there and we little . . . I had all their mills burned as I have done everywhere else. Their need is great and it is necessary that they be helped in 12 days or they must surrender. I have sent for your son to come because I believe he will do something fine out here at the front. I am very well, thank God, and love you more than you me. God owes me a little peace; how I would enjoy several years of rest! To be sure, I am aging greatly . . . I am most faithfully served and assure you the enemy will cause me more harm than fear . . .

Falling into his easy bragging style, Henry failed to mention he had once more made the mistake of delay, thereby allowing the Parisians time to fortify and supply themselves. He gave them twelve days to surrender, but it was soon clear the city would try to hold out until

Mayenne arrived with aid. Henry took possession of the river above and below the city to cut off provisions, and rearing batteries upon the heights of Montmartre and Montfaucon, he rained cannonballs upon the thronged streets of the metropolis. In the midst of this woeful storm, Henry's uncle, the Cardinal de Bourbon, died. His death went virtually unnoticed as the people simply had all they could cope with. The problem of succession had become incidental to the problem of survival.

A siege was not Henry's natural way of fighting; he was more a warrior of surprise and quick movements. But day after day the bloody siege continued, with bombardments, conflagrations, sallies, midnight assaults, and all the tumult, carnage, and horror of war. Three hundred thousand men, women, and children suffered in the beleaguered city. Henry cut off their supplies and famine commenced its ravages. When the wheat was exhausted, they ate bran. When all the bran was consumed, the haggard citizens devoured the dogs and cats. Starvation invaded like an enemy. On parlor floors and on the hard pavement, emaciated forms stretched in the convulsions of death.

No longer could Henry bear the agonizing sounds of the dying. He was more tortured than he had been outside the walls of La Rochelle when he had been a hostage of the Valoises, for now he controlled the outcome. Calling Aubigné to him, he said, "Let the order go from me to carry provisions into the city."

"Your heart is too tender, Henry. Too often you unbalance your strategies with impetuous decisions!"

"I am hoping this gesture of humane feeling will prove to my foes that I do not seek revenge and that I would be a generous and merciful king."

The duc de Nemours, a half-brother of the duc de Mayenne, had been left in charge of Paris. Encouraged by this unmilitary and charitable clemency, he drove several thousands out of the city, and Henry allowed three thousand to pass.

"Your mercy is extraordinary and perhaps unwise," Aubigné warned.

"I cannot bear to think of their sufferings. I had rather conquer my enemy with kindness than by arms."

"I fear this is rarely successful," Aubigné sniped, shaking his head.

The Parisians' resistance persisted and the siege ground on. The theoreticians at the Sorbonne continued to argue their academic question: "Could the people, constrained by famine, incur excommunication by giving in to a heretical king?" Famine bred pestilence; misery and death were rampant. On July 16 Henry begged the citizens to give in: "The necessity to which you are now reduced, and the frustration of waiting in vain for the help they have promised you, ought to open your eyes."

The department of St. Denis was already in royal hands and even the leaders of the League understood that Paris was coming to the end of her tether. On the night of July 24 Henry took all the remaining suburbs, rendering the condition of the besieged more hopeless and miserable. When Henry learned that the flesh of the dead was being eaten and the dry bones of the cemetery were being ground up for bread, he could not believe the rulers of Paris still refused to capitulate. But again his compassion triumphed over military firmness. He allowed the women and children to leave the city on August 20, then the ecclesiastics, then the starving poor, then the starving rich, each of these acts of generosity adding to the strength of his enemy. Trying to rationalize the situation to Corisande, he wrote:

> Paris is cornered in such a way that this week, there will necessarily be a battle or a deputation. The Spanish will join the fat Duke next Tuesday. We will see if he will have blood on his hands. I lead your son every day to the attack and make him stay very close to me . . . I saw yesterday some women who came from Paris who told me their miseries. I am well, thank God, loving nothing in the world like you. This is something that I assure myself you will never doubt. With this truth, I kiss you, my soul, a million times, your beautiful eyes that I will hold all my life more dear than anything else in the world.

When he finished writing his letter, he hurried over to the cloister in Montmartre, a suburb of the city. War always seemed to whet his carnal appetite. Sister Claude opened the gate and he followed her to a small building the nuns used as a greenhouse and potting shed. Because of the critical situation in Paris, it had fallen into disuse. The nuns were too busy with the wounded and dying to think of spring planting, and the eager couple opened the door upon an empty room. Sister Claude's outer black robes, which engulfed her tiny figure like a tent, fell from her shoulders.

Henry put his hands on her waist and lifted her to a potting shelf. Leaning close to her, he began to kiss her gently, behind the ears, on the eyes, and finally more hungrily on the lips. "Mmmmm, what a lucky day for me when I came with my men to bring food to your Sisters. Now I am the starving one and you will give me something to eat."

Sister Claude moaned slightly and helped him with the million buttons which closed an inner garment. She had refused before to remove it but today she seemed eager to reveal her young body. When he tried to take off her cap, however, she stopped his hands.

"No, you would embarrass me," she said simply.

He knew it was only curiosity prompting him. Would he still want her if he saw her shaven head? The face and body, so full and feminine might become grotesque when crowned with a bald pate. His lips moved to her breasts, down to her belly and to her thighs.

"Oh, Sire, no," she whimpered, grabbing his grizzled hair, pulling it with her fingers. He lifted her from the table and pulled her down to the floor with him.

"I will teach you about terrestrial ecstasy, my little sister," he cooed. "Today and every day that this insane siege continues."

He took her again as though to convince himself that domination and control were his.

"Fortunately, or unfortunately, you are more willing than Paris. I will return tomorrow and perhaps then you will remove your hat."

He left her buttoning her voluminous robes.

Rosny complained, "Henry, your men are becoming weary with this siege. Everyone's patience is wearing thin. I urge you — you must take the city by storm. NOW!"

"I could easily do so, Rosny, but slaughter would be the inevitable result."

"Many think you are in no hurry because of your female friends in Montmartre."

"Let them think what they like, but I will not attack for the reason I have given you. Your prim ethics tire me! You and all the nosy bitches! I am the King and father of the Parisians, and I cannot bear the recital of their woes without the deepest sympathy. I would gladly relieve them. I cannot prevent those who are possessed with the fury of the League from perishing, but to those who seek my clemency I must open my arms."

He expressed himself with even more emotion in a letter to his friend at Hagetmau:

> I love the city of Paris. She is my elder daughter; I am jealous of her. I wish to do her more good, more grace, and more mercy than she asks of me . . . I am the true father of my people. I resemble the true mother in the story about Solomon. I would almost prefer to lose Paris than to have her all ruined and dissipated after the death of so many poor people.

And that is what he did. More than thirty thousand perished by famine within the walls of the city. Mayenne finally marched to their relief with Spanish soldiers. Forced to raise the siege, Henry advanced to meet him, hoping to compel him to a decisive battle. Mayenne skillfully avoided an encounter and still more adroitly threw abundant supplies into the city. Two years had already passed since the Scots Guard had announced to Henry that he was King, yet Paris lay still out of reach. Once again, France was one large, wasted battlefield. Henry crashed his fist into the nearest wall.

"*Mère de Dieu!*" Would he ever be more than a theoretical king?

BOOK FOUR

GABRIELLE D'ESTREES
(1573-1599)

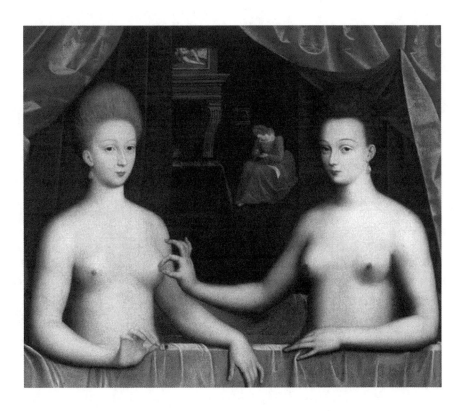

The models have been identified as Gabrielle d'Estrées (1573-99) and one of her sisters, the duchesse de Villars or Madame de Balagny. The manner in which the sister is pinching Gabrielle d'Estrées's left breast has been suggested as a symbol of Gabrielle's pregnancy with the illegitimate child of Henry IV. This interpretation would seem to be confirmed by the scene of the young woman sewing in the background — perhaps preparing a layette for the coming child. The painting was acquired by the Louvre in 1937. Artist unknown, ca.1594.

PICARDY

1590-1591

THE UNSUCCESSFUL SIEGE of Paris brought Henry a mixture of shame and outrage. How could he have failed again? If he couldn't take Paris, he would capture Chartres. But again, he was too slow and the city, warned of his planned assault, was ready when his forces arrived, led by one of his favorite captains, Maréchal Armand Biron. Another long siege ensued, and all the while, he knew that without Paris, he could not truly call himself King of France.

He charged into the tent of Maréchal Biron with Aubigné, who seemed to dog his footsteps these days and be never far behind. Meagerly furnished, the tent enclosed only a single cot, several campstools and a folding desk with brass hardware to protect the corners when the camp moved. The neatly swept dirt floor attested to the rigor of Henry's command. He might dress in a disorderly fashion when out of uniform, but in military matters, only the highest standard would do.

"I have no money and not enough men. How can I be expected to wage war successfully?" he griped to his captains.

Taking his time shaving his chin, Biron seemed in no hurry to answer. "It is not without its difficulties," Biron replied with a touch of sarcasm in his voice. "And you are still a Huguenot in Catholic France."

"That is another issue," Henry barked. "I did not come here to talk about that."

"But Sire, I fear that is the primary problem. Your Protestant leaders, who are politicians, not theologians, advise you to become a Catholic. They believe your adoption of the Catholic faith would reconcile the Catholics, and the Protestants would prefer you for their sovereign above any other realistic option they have. They would surely trust in the freedom of faith and worship which your just judgment would secure for them. And I agree with them. We must put an end to this cruel civil war."

"I don't need to be told that!" Henry snapped. "The intense violence I witness of brother against brother makes me puke. *Ventre-St.-Gris!* Farmhouses, cities, and villages are being mercilessly burned. Old men, women, and children are tortured and slain. It is beyond bearing."

"Our country has been ravaged by war for so many years now, it is a miracle there is anyone left to fight," interjected Aubigné, who had taken a seat on one of the stools despite his king's failure to sit down.

"Yet in spite of the olive branch I offered the Parisians, they remain hostile and unsympathetic," Henry complained. "This beautiful and sophisticated city behaves like a naughty child!"

"You sound like a hurt parent. Perhaps they will only believe you love them if you convert." Biron was persistent and persuasive.

"Perhaps," Henry replied. "But I'm not beaten yet," he muttered to himself and left his two captains.

He would get no comfort from them, that was clear. How unjust it seemed for Biron to chastise him about the war going on for so long, when he wished for its end more than anyone. He felt each dead soldier to be his responsibility. Proud of the way he had put the kingdom of Navarre back on its feet, he wondered if everyone had already forgotten how he had provided strong and sensible stewardship of his lands, how he had started road building and restored vineyards demolished by warring neighbors. But he knew those things really didn't matter when your friends and family were dying around you.

But he mustn't feel sorry for himself. Men followed him easily, believing in his energy and the symbolic white plume of victory atop his helmet. He wasn't sure why they trusted him; perhaps because he believed in himself, and he must continue to do so. He knew he could restore the economy and spiritual health of the whole country, if only he could reach the throne. He knew it! But in the meantime, how it hurt to see the countryside being neglected and destroyed. He remembered once seeing a woodchopper accidentally cut off his own finger. Henry had watched with horror as the man's blood spouted from the mutilated stump. So it seemed his country was hemorrhaging and everyone blamed him for swinging the axe.

Tired and discouraged, Henry again began to seek female company. He listened with interest one day to his master of the horse Roger de Bellegarde* proudly describe his mistress in glowing terms. "She is the most beautiful lady in all of France, Sire. I am certain of it. Her hair is as pale and smooth as narcissus and her skin as white and delicate as plum blossoms."

Although poor nobility from Armagnac, Bellegarde had become one of Henri III's "45" primarily because of his tall good looks. Having been present at the assassination of King Henri III, with characteristic opportunism, he had immediately pledged allegiance to Henri IV. Now he couldn't resist bragging to the new king of the marvel of womanhood he had conquered.

"Your poetry has captivated me," Henry said. "I should like to meet this angel, Bellegarde. You must introduce me soon."

Immediately Bellegarde regretted his loose tongue; the King's tactics were famous. Perhaps Henry would forget it if he didn't broach the subject again.

But Henry's interest had been aroused. He must meet the "most beautiful woman in all of France." The following week while they were camped near Chartres, he reminded his master of the horse that he expected an introduction at the Château de Coeuvres, where Gabrielle d'Estrées, this now renowned beauty, resided. Having no choice, Bellegarde conducted the king to the family seat of the d'Estréeses the next afternoon. The ride through the gently rolling valleys of Picardy soothed Henry, for despite his natural resilience, he felt drained by failure and anxiety. The unremitting search for arms, men, and money and the constant scheming to win allies and outwit his enemies, added to the weeks on horseback, broken only by rough sleep on a camp pallet, had taken their toll. When he experienced the stinging of the urological problem that intermittently plagued him, he cursed under his breath. Searching in his pocket, he found a clove of garlic to chew; this always seemed to calm his stomach and nerves. He had been in arms for so long that the luxury of ordinary living was almost beyond his imagining. So the sight of a Renaissance structure of gray sculptured stone, raised on vaulted arches and surrounded by a water-filled moat, announced long-awaited pleasure.

Despite the gloomy November afternoon, meandering garden paths, a pool with careful landscaping, and the long branches of shade trees, though now bare, conveyed a sense of tranquility. The

*Roger II de Saint-Lary de Bellegarde (1562-1646)

d'Estréeses' fortune had plunged during the recent period of war, but the family continued to enjoy a prestigious reputation. Henri II had treated Jean d'Estrées as a man of honor, and his son, Antoine, had acted as governor of La Fère until he was overthrown by the League. The king was dutifully impressed as he and Bellegarde rode along the avenue into the lower court where they vividly perceived the military interest of Captain d'Estrées evidenced by the cannon and cannon ball ornamentation. The mansion's wide façade with high dormer windows implied dominance and gracious living.

Henry tried to recall what he had heard about Gabrielle's mother. Hadn't there been a scandal? Ah, yes. Now he remembered. Françoise Babou de la Bourdaisière and her six sisters were jokingly called "the Seven Deadly Sins," and Ronsard had once christened her "Astrée" because of the rumored astronomical number of her lovers. The illustrious lady had finally run away to Auvergne with one of her lovers, the Marquis d'Alègre, and had lived with him at Issoire. There, the passion and turmoil of her life had caught up with her when she and her lover were brutally murdered in their bed, supposedly on the order of her jealous husband. Now Henry was to meet the deserted but vindicated husband and children.

He met M. d'Estrées first and decided he did not look like someone who could order an avenging murder. In fact, as they exchanged greetings and pleasantries, Henry found the man's countenance remarkably bland and inexpressive. They chatted inanely until M. d'Estrées said, "But I know you are not here to see me. I shall call my daughters."

"Excellent. M. de Bellegarde has told me so much about the beauty of your daughter Gabrielle that I can scarcely await the pleasure of seeing her."

"Ah, then I shall alert only Gabrielle," her father replied.

Henry was taken aback when Gabrielle appeared. He felt his heart take a dive to his gut in a way he had not experienced in a long while. A true work of art stood before him. Bellegarde had not overstated the case one iota. Only seventeen years old, her apparent innocence and careless inexperience glowed in her charming smooth face. Golden waves of thick lustrous hair were gathered at her neck, then allowed to cascade down her back. Her lips curved in an exquisite shape and her nose, a trifle large, was believed by his class to be a sure sign of good breeding.

"You are a refreshing sight to a tired soldier, Gabrielle," Henry offered. "Your presence illuminates this entire salon."

Indeed, her radiance awakened his senses, and he undressed her with his eyes. Gabrielle seemed not to notice — in fact, she hardly moved her eyes from Bellegarde and barely treated His Majesty with the respect and formality he expected.

"You are more than kind, Sire," she finally responded with a slight curtsy, learning firsthand that the rumor that His Majesty smelled more like a shepherd than a king was true. When she blushed slightly, the appearance of virtue titillated Henry all the more.

"Do you reside at Coeuvres all year round?" the King inquired.

"For the most part, Your Majesty," Gabrielle answered. "My father also has a house in Paris in the rue des Bons-Enfants, but of course Paris has been too dangerous for several years. I am often sad we cannot visit."

Henry could not help but recall Corisande for a moment. This girl certainly lacked her mystery, her flash of spirit. In truth, Gabrielle's face, on reflection, appeared somewhat vacuous like her father's, but her beauty had captivated him instantaneously. As usual, his passion was immediate and imperious, and he knew he would return soon — without Bellegarde. He listened to her chatter, "I love this château. I was born here and enjoy the company of my brothers and sisters, who live here with me and my father."

"Yes, I'm sure you do, my pretty one," Henry said. He thought of the girl's infamous mother whose unfaithfulness had become a legend. He did not regard this as a deplorable example for Gabrielle, but rather speculated with relish upon instincts she might have inherited.

As the gentlemen took their leave, Henry squeezed Gabrielle's hand meaningfully. Did she return his pressure? He was almost sure she had.

For a while Henry's battles removed him from the vicinity of Coeuvres, but as soon as he was near again, he hastened to visit the beauty who had occupied his mind since their meeting. First, he called Bellegarde to him.

"You realize, Feuillemorte," Henry warned, calling him by his nickname which described the brown tone of his skin, "that you shall lose my patronage if you continue visiting the charming Gabrielle."

"That doesn't seem fair, Sire," Bellegarde grumbled, hating his "dead leaf" name-tag.

"You know her beauty is more worthy of a king. And don't let me hear of your cheating either!"

Bellegarde turned and left. What could be said to this tyrant where women and love were concerned? He also knew he would not get many to sympathize with his cause, because Henry was too well loved by those around him. Feuillemorte would only be a laughing-stock.

The League occupied the seven kilometers between Henry and Coeuvres, reminding him of his dashes across enemy lines to find Corisande. Planning to take only his closest servants and to dress as peasants do, he cheerfully embarked on the sort of escapade that always excited him.

He spied Gabrielle walking in the garden as he and his companions rode up to the château. She was so young! He dared draw near in his dirty shirt and muddy wooden shoes, and she instinctively shied away from the filthy creature before her.

"You are more lovely than I even remembered," he whispered to her.

"How dare you!" But as she spat these words, she recognized the voice of the king. "But what are you doing in those ridiculous clothes?" she gasped.

"Why, I had to wear them to sneak through the lines, of course. And I was eager to see you again."

"But you look absurd. Those clothes only demonstrate what you really are."

"You are a daring one," he laughed. "And you are right, too. I have always envied the life of the mountain peasants."

Gabrielle stamped her foot like a spoiled child. "But you must leave! I shall not receive you like this."

"You mean you will not ask me in after I risked so much to come to see you?" he asked unbelievingly. He was no longer so amused.

"Of course not," she huffed, walking quickly and indignantly away toward the château.

Gabrielle's sister Diane had been watching the odd scene from the French doors leading into the garden. Who could that strange man be who dared speak to Gabrielle? She intercepted her agitated sister. "Gabrielle, who is that fellow?"

"Diane, that 'fellow' is the KING. He dressed in that ridiculous way to deceive the League soldiers. Aagh! He looked so repulsive."

"But Gabrielle, you didn't turn him away?"

"I certainly did!"

"You little idiot. He is the KING! You do not ever think! You may be a very lucky girl. I will go and get him and make up some excuse for your rude behavior. And be ready to receive him in a more friendly manner," she commanded. Rushing into the garden in pursuit of her sister's suitor, Diane didn't have far to run, for she found him seated on a rock in the garden, a somewhat perplexed expression on his face.

"Sire," she said, curtsying low before him. "I am Diane, Gabrielle's sister. I am sorry I did not have the pleasure of meeting you upon your first visit to our home. Please excuse Gabrielle's rather brusque manner. The silly girl behaved so coldly because she fears our father so. She was afraid he would scold her for receiving a strange gentleman in the garden without his permission. She is a well brought up girl, you know."

Henry smiled, suspecting a polite cover-up, but grasped at this slight hope. "Then she will see me?"

"Certainly. But she is rather embarrassed today. Perhaps it would be wiser for you to return in several days, and we shall plan a dinner party."

Diane perceived that Gabrielle's stalling had enticed Henry more than a generous reception would have. She would have to coach her sister in the manipulation of men, but she had been lucky this time.

"I shall look forward to it," he replied. He strode out of the garden gates with more of a king's stride than a peasant's. She looked after him with some wonder. What kind of man was this to leave his battlefields and risk death for a glimpse of a girl to whom he had taken a fancy? Whatever the story, the d'Estréeses would make the most of this opportunity!

Gabrielle's aunt, Isabelle Babou, was an ambitious woman. A dowdy dresser, who considered herself the ultimate in the latest Parisian mode, she covered her short fingers with rings, and a large cameo brooch always accented her ample bosom. Ringlets of brown hair framed a pudgy face that was not without friendliness. She often wore puce, considering that color to be the most becoming to her powder white complexion. Mme Babou perceived immediately that the entire family could rise with Gabrielle's success and launched a ruthless crusade toward that end.

"Silly girl, I am very vexed with your reticence and romantic reasons for refusing the king."

"They may seem romantic to you, Aunt Isabelle, because you are old. But Roger de Bellegarde and I are very much in love."

"Humph. What do you know of love? You are nothing but a ninny. Don't you realize, my dear, that there is no limit to what you might achieve as the king's mistress? It is well known there is no love lost between Henry and Queen Margot, and you might very well become queen one day. You will be the first lady in France, only in pretense at first."

"Oh, Auntie, you are crazy to think such a thing!"

"We shall see who is crazy, young lady. Do not mumble on about loving Bellegarde. Go ahead. Love him. But do not let the king know, and make yourself indispensable to him."

"You just want a position at court for yourself," Gabrielle accused.

"I am hurt to the quick, Gabrielle." She wiped ready tears from her lashes, thick with lampblack. "You know I have cared for you since your mother left, and I am only interested in your welfare. How could you say such an evil thing when I was only dreaming of the grand station you might achieve."

"You are very sweet and clever, Aunt Isabelle, I am sure, but I suspect the whole family of urging me for their own gain."

"Well, you are very spoiled and ungrateful. I know how you love luxury, and you would have everything you ever desired with the king. I foresee an illustrious future for you, dearie, if you play your cards right."

"Everything you ever desired." These words stuck with Gabrielle like a haunting refrain for the next few days, though she had scolded her aunt. She knew the family fortune was dwindling but she hadn't given it much thought. "Everything you ever desired." Recalling the desire in the king's eyes pleased her immensely. Yet she compared the two men who wanted her. Bellegarde stood straight as a bayonet and looked oh-so-elegant in his military uniform. Henry, on the other hand, appeared much older than his 37 years, with his beard sprinkled with white, his cheeks sunken, and his eyelids drooping with fatigue. She also recoiled from his thin body and bad teeth. It was hard to remember that the man who wore scuffed and cracked boots, a worn and dusty doublet, and baggy pantaloons was the king. She would just have to ignore the graying hair; perhaps her aunt was right. She did love all money could buy, and perhaps the power royalty offered too. The older lady saw her niece's negative attitude begin to wane as the week wore on. Indeed, Gabrielle even said to her aunt, "I am beginning to look forward to the king's visit with some curiosity."

Seated before the mirror regarding her china-smooth face and clear blue eyes, Gabrielle pulled her gown a trifle lower to expose more of her full breasts and alabaster shoulders. Then she quickly pulled it up, frightened by the thought that Henry probably would not need any tantalizing.

For this occasion Henry only wore a peasant's cape over aristocratic finery for his dash through enemy territory and when he arrived, his appearance relieved her somewhat. However, she soon grew nervous as she observed how the lavish dinner of many courses and obsequious service seemed to bore him. Even irritate him. Aunt Isabelle pressed every dish on him twice and waved away his excuses of a small appetite. Isabelle's motherly instinct prompted her to say,

"But you are too thin, Sire. A hearty meal is just what you need."

"You are very kind, Mme Babou," he replied, "But I usually do not have much time to eat nor in such good company." He turned to Gabrielle with these last words. He was as gallant in some ways as she had heard. Young she might be, but she was also clever enough to cover her thoughts and play the gracious hostess. He's interested in only one goal, she shivered. Watching him suddenly gobble his food, she guessed he was planning how to get rid of all this family as quickly as possible.

After coffee and liqueur and much ostentatious bowing and curtsying, Gabrielle and Henry were finally left alone in the petit salon. Under an unusually high forehead and perfectly arched brow, she noticed the king's eyes were a light hazel, more gold than green. His upper lip was folded in an expression of permanent irony and the fleshier lower lip lent a sensuous flair. She had heard what an energetic lover he was and wondered if she were making too much of her feelings of revulsion. He could be amusing and he certainly seemed smitten with her. Could Aunt Isabelle be right? Was this a chance too good to miss? Not daring to look at him again, she uneasily picked at the floral embroidery on the settee.

"Don't be anxious, *chérie*. A king is no different from any other man," he quipped.

"Nevertheless, you have quite a reputation."

"Ah, but no woman I have ever seen compares in beauty and grace to you, *ma belle*."

She raised her eyes; he sounded so sincere. Oh well, her family would be happy to know she had succumbed to the royal desire. An image of the handsome Roger floated before her. No! She couldn't stand this man. She pushed Henry rudely away from her.

"Please go away," she cried. "You are only making me unhappy."

"But how can my loving you make you unhappy, belle Gabrielle?"

Henry's calm command of the moment confused her, and her tears changed to stormy anger. "I'll never love you!" Henry was reminded of a petulant adolescent. "You are ruining my life and my chances to wed Roger."

"Don't be foolish. You will soon forget him, and I have much more to offer you."

"Please go away," she whimpered.

"All right, my love. Since you are upset tonight. But I shall stay at Coeuvres and see you tomorrow — when you have regained your senses."

But the next morning military matters called him away before the young girl awoke.

Henry was completely ensnared again. Even though his beard had become white, he loved with the freshness and exuberance of a young man. For him, love always seemed to spring forth with the inevitability and energy of a new season. This was his charm, his force, his weakness, and his excuse. Forgetful and unfaithful? Of course, but when in the arms of a woman, his profound distrust and his Gascon guile abandoned him. Like the legendary Don Juan, he knew how to make himself loved and to love again and again and again. The Béarnais was drawn to love as a fish to the lure. And the d'Estréeses would do more than entice him with their prettiest specimen. Craving Gabrielle as a drunkard does his wine, he became light-headed when he thought of her. Tonight she would visit her aunt at Chartres, and he would meet her there.

Upon Henry's arrival, he was ushered into the salon and was surprised to find Gabrielle without a chaperone.

"Where is Aunt Isabelle?" he inquired.

"She had to remain with one of my younger sisters who is ill."

"I am sorry to hear it. Nothing serious, I hope."

"I presume not. You are looking well."

Perhaps Isabelle was purposely giving him the chance he wanted. He suspected she was his ally.

"That is because I am happy to be in your presence. Ah, Gabrielle, the sight of you lights a fire in my heart that can only be contained by holding you."

Gabrielle walked toward the fireplace. "But why should I want to tame the fire?"

"Because if not, it will consume me. Tamed, it will burn eternally."

"You are a very persuasive man!"

"Yet you are proving more difficult to win over than Chartres. But I will continue my siege until you relent."

"You have a reputation for being persistent but not always successful," she said with a little smile.

Henry laughed. "And you're saucy, too. What a delight! But I promise you, you will not put me off the way Paris did. I learned my lesson there and know ways to make you succumb," he bantered.

"I can see I haven't a chance," she answered, while giving him an enticing smile. "Perhaps I had better surrender now."

Henry rushed to her. His fingers trembled with excitement as he unlaced her bodice, uncovering her breasts. She gasped, partly from fear and partly from embarrassment. Bellegarde had been her first and only lover, and she was not as experienced as the king perhaps suspected.

"Oh, you beautiful creature," he murmured as he deliriously pressed his rough, burning lips to her body. Her youth! He could not bear being without her. He found his voice amidst his ecstasy, "At least you will not forget my fervor. I want you to remember this glorious moment too."

He failed to notice she did not answer.

CHARTRES

1591

AUBIGNÉ WARNED HENRY, "We must strike Rouen! It is the rich capital of Normandy and the key to the entire province."

"I know that. You need not lecture me."

"Then why don't you do something? Rouen is vulnerable now, and the English would come to our aid if we attack. You must not evade the problem again."

"What, in your opinion, pray tell, is the problem?" Henry inquired with resonant irony in his tone.

"You know as well as I — the brigands roving and ravaging the countryside, soldiers setting fire to crops — honest people overwhelmed by taxation are often short of bread. They can no longer travel about safely to do their business. Everyone has been crippled by this incessant war."

"You are very eloquent today, Aubigné, but I think it is better to wait."

He didn't want to leave Gabrielle so soon. She felt so wonderful in his arms.

Maréchal Biron advised him too. "We must hurry to Rouen, Sire. This city will surely fall now."

But Henry preferred to listen to the d'Estréeses who urged, "Stay on at Chartres. This medieval gem will be more difficult to take than Rouen but most important to your cause because it is the granary of Paris."

He felt so vigorous when he was near his beloved Gabrielle. He was afraid he would begin to feel like an old man if he left her. He might be lonely and sick; this youthful exuberance he felt must promise well for the battlefield.

"We will take Chartres first," he informed Aubigné.

He could not admit even to himself that sensuality governed his decision or that he had traded victory for love once again. Rather, he thought, this new passion would make him stronger when he must fight again.

Aubigné had time on his hands at Chartres and sought out Rosny. He needed to talk about the king. These two usually argued, but this time they discovered they agreed more than they expected.

"What are we to do with our leader, Rosny?" Aubigné asked the king's financial counselor. "Nearly half of France is now enrolled under Henry's banner, and if we can, with God's help, defeat Mayenne in the months to come, surely we will see a ceremony of consecration with Holy Oil at Reims. But the king is sick with love." Aubigné rolled his eyes toward the ceiling in disgust.

"Yes, but that is only half the problem. Are you not forgetting the law of France which requires that its king be Catholic and Catholic only?" Rosny demanded. "I believe your optimism is premature."

"You are right to caution me," Aubigné admitted. "But we can never trust the Catholics! The Huguenots will be persecuted as long as there is a Catholic king!"

"Not if that king is Henry," Rosny rejoined, his plump cheeks glowing red with his intensity.

Aubigné nodded. "There is some truth in that. But I truly believe France must have a Protestant king to be independent of Rome."

"Listen, Aubigné, Henry has to be empowered in France before we need worry about the Vatican."

"And that moment is nearer than you think," Aubigné declared. "I think the people want him because they love him more and more. They see how he remains his old self. There is hardly a change in him, so that we who have lived with him for a long time might think ourselves still in Navarre. He travels like a modest gentleman of small means, scorns an honor guard, and protests when Biron, who must secure the safety of his person, disposes a company of arquebusiers to watch over him. Surely he is the only monarch in the world who sleeps without complaint, often I think gladly, on a mean pallet of straw or feather ticking, thrown upon the floor of a house that knows no permanent occupants."

Rosny displayed some of his vexation. "I would prefer the king ride in a style fitting his station so that his subjects will know him for what he is. But I must admit, the people seem to know and love him all the more because he is one of them. In fact, on second thought, I am not truly sad that we travel like gypsy mountebanks, because then I can save the gold my tax collectors gather in such small harvest." He offered Aubigné one of his rare smiles.

Spurred to defend his leader, Aubigné said, "Only in private is he careless with gold, spewing it in nightly showers on the sluts who warm the royal pallet. He uses new trollops more often than he changes his hose. One sleeps with him for a fortnight, another for a month, and all are amiable merry harlots. She who was most recently in favor is an English woman, who lived a long time at the court of Elizabeth I, and the king suspects she was sent by her who is his friend and ally to spy on him. But he pays her less gold than he does the others, and with each bag of money he saves, he sends still another knight into the tournament against the battalions of the pope."

"That is true, Aubigné. But I fear this new d'Estrées girl will hold him as the harlots do not. No man knows what seethes in the King's mind and he confides in no woman except Corisande, so at least we need not worry about English trickery winning Calais."

"I hope not," Aubigné said with discouragement. "But I fear that just when we have our chance to secure the throne, he will throw it away for his latest love."

Neither man had managed to reassure the other, and the days at Chartres crept slowly by.

Maréchal Biron surprised the enemy by bringing additional forces to Henry at Chartres on February 9, 1591. Still, the Gothic citadel held and Henry, with his traditional scorn for peril, was almost hit by a bullet outside the town. Never mind the danger, he would present Gabrielle with the keys to the city, just as he had presented Corisande with the standards of Coutras. And perhaps she would be pleased if he installed her uncle, M. de Sourdis, as governor of the city. He scarcely heard when Aubigné grumbled, "Sire, twelve hundred men have been lost because of your desire for this woman. Rouen would have been so much easier to take. Perhaps there is still time if we move quickly. We could intercept Mayenne and capture Rouen."

Finally, after two more long and bloody months, Henry could boast of a victory, but in his delay, he had greatly angered his precious ally, Elizabeth I. Still, he dallied, attacking Noyon because it would make a nice governorship for M. d'Estrées. He procrastinated even longer, installing Gabrielle and her father there, feeling young again with his mistress's caresses. Finally, he could resist pressures no longer. Queen Elizabeth insisted he take Rouen or forfeit English support. Since her favorite, Robert Devereux, Earl of Essex, was a general in the Rouen vicinity, she was particularly concerned. Henry remembered Elizabeth's help at Dieppe and knew he must not displease her. At last, in December, 1591, the siege of Rouen began.

Most of the English aiding Henry liked him, and Sir Henry Upton wrote in his diary a month earlier:

> He is a most noble, brave Kinge, of greate patience and magnanymitie; not ceremonious, affable, famillier and only followed for this trewe valor but very much hated for his religion and threattened by the Catholiques to forsake him if he converte not.

Yet the Queen worried about her Essex and complained:

> We hear, besides, to our no small wonder, how little the King regards the hazard of our men and how you, our General, at all times refuse not to run with them, to all service of greatest peril, but even like the forlorn hope of a battle to bring them to the slaughter.

When Henry finally did arrive, he pretended that Essex, whom he personally considered a young, spoiled, and incapable exhibitionist, could do no wrong in his eyes. He had too much Gallic shrewdness in matters of sex not to pamper a doting woman's darling boy. He needed to make sure the Queen would gratifyingly continue her support when Essex returned home.

But the king had waited too long to capture the League stronghold of Rouen. The people had taken the opportunity to fortify and provide for themselves. Leaving Biron to carry on the siege on November 11, Henry withdrew to intercept Spanish aid to the Leaguers, led by the duc de Parme, Mayenne's ally. After several months of cat-and-mouse games, unexpectedly, on February 5, 1592, Henry made contact with the Duke's forces of twenty-four thousand foot soldiers and seven thousand cavalry, near the town of Aumale. Parma swore he was fighting in France in order to protect the French Catholics, but Henry, among others, saw through this flimsy veil.

First in every charge, Henry teased his best soldiers to keep up with him. Several men close to him warned him to be more careful, for he seemed to want to be everywhere at once. Then, early in the battle an arrow struck him in the loin. His small force fled in panic with Henry staying in the saddle only with difficulty. His men finally managed to carry him off the battlefield. Not knowing how seriously the king was wounded as they hurried Henry to safety and the camp doctors, Aubigné felt a terror akin to that on St. Bartholomew's Eve.

The loss of blood accounted for his pallor, the doctors assured those crowded around him on his cot. Henry was more shaken than he revealed, having come to believe somewhat in a magical aura that was protecting him. He felt he was primarily responsible for his own fate but he also shamefully recognized he had been beguiled by the hint of Nostradamus's Oracle. Fortunately, the wound proved not to be serious, and after being carried in a litter for several days, he began to recover. Warmed by his men's concern, Henry thrived on their constant approval.

Luckily, Parma, not realizing how few men Henry had, did not press his attack and Henry escaped greater harm. But to Henry's chagrin, Biron had failed to gain the upper hand in Rouen. Mayenne and Parma took control of the city on April 21, 1592, and followed the straight road to Paris.

PICARDY AND TOURS

1592

GABRIELLE NEEDED FEW LESSONS IN the fine art of how to fool a man; it seemed to be an instinctive talent. Having settled down for a short stay with her aunt and uncle at the Governor's Palace in Chartres, she received word Henry had been wounded. She sat down at once and wrote to him, an anxious letter in a round, childish hand:

> My King and my beloved, I die of fear; reassure me, I beseech you, by telling me how fares the bravest of the brave. I fear his illness must be great since nothing else would rob me of his company. Give me news, my lord, for you know how the least ill of yours is fatal to me. Although I have heard twice of your condition today, I could not sleep without sending you a thousand good nights, for I am dowered with no feeble constancy. I am the Princess of constancy and sensible of all that concerns you, and insensible of all else in the world, be it good or bad.

> Ever your Gabrielle

She soon heard how enchanted Henry had been by her sweet words. She had revived his flagging optimism, which prompted him to turn his skill to his personal problems. He dashed off a quick note to her, telling her of his brilliant idea.

> My little bird, you must congratulate me. I have
> decided to find a husband for you, for then it will be
> more appropriate and easier for you to be my mis-
> tress.

Gabrielle was flabbergasted, and to make it worse, it didn't take long for Henry to find Nicolas d'Amerval, Seigneur de Liancourt — just the man he needed. One of the wealthiest members of the minor nobility in Picardy, Amerval was eager for the material gains the deal provided — about eight thousand *écus*. And of course, he wouldn't dream of offending the king.

Gabrielle didn't know where to turn for help. Perhaps her sister Diane would understand her reservations. Things were moving much faster than she had ever imagined and none of it made sense. Just when she was becoming accustomed to Henry's attentions and to being without Bellegarde, fate demanded more of her.

"Amerval is so small and ugly!" she complained to Diane. "No wonder Henry feels he will be the perfect insurance against any attraction between me and my 'husband.' "

"I imagine Henry still suspects a liaison between you and Roger de Bellegarde, and he thinks the rules of marriage will assure him of your fidelity," her sister replied.

"But, Diane, this is insane. I am to be unfaithful to my new husband, but only with one man — the man who arranged the marriage. And I love a third man." She began to cry. "If I must marry an old man, I will marry the king! Why should I marry just anyone he suggests? Is it so easy to make and break marriages?"

"I expect so, if you are the king. You can be sure it will be in name only, because the king is too jealous to allow anyone else to touch you."

"I know, I know. But it feels like he is adding bars to my jail."

"You are making a lot of a little thing, I think. After all, the king is in love with you, and he can't marry you himself for the time being."

Aunt Isabelle walked in just in time to hear Gabrielle's reply, "You wouldn't think it was such a little thing if it were you who must marry that old geezer! And how long is this phantom marriage supposed to last?" she whined.

"I know you are not starry-eyed over the monarch," Isabelle intercepted, "but you will enjoy power and money with him and only adequate food and drink with your precious Bellegarde."

Gabrielle glared at the two women who professed love for her and who were so zealously arranging her life. But maybe they were right. The proposed marriage began to look more tolerable to her when, in the spring of 1592, Henry signed an ordinance granting her a large dowry. A sham marriage need not necessarily be so bad, she told herself. She would have all the clothes and jewels she desired as the king's mistress. And surely she would still be able to see Belle-garde from time to time. She accepted Henry's plan, signed the marriage agreement, and the wedding took place in June in a small chapel of the cathedral of Noyon.

Misgivings flooded over her as she allowed Diane and Aunt Isabelle to arrange her veil. Why had she permitted them to talk her into this fiasco? And why wasn't Henry here? It was his charade. He had promised to take her away on her wedding night. In fact, she had been the one to insist that he do so in order that Liancourt would not touch her. At the thought of the warty man who would be waiting at the altar, she shivered with revulsion. What had happened to her life?

After the service she was handed a message — Henry, detained amongst his troops because one of his generals had been killed by a cannon ball on the walls of Epernay, extended his felicitations and regrets at not being present. Gabrielle was first dumbfounded, then furious.

"I will have vengeance!" she shouted for all to hear.

When Henry arrived three days later, he was greeted by a very spiteful young woman. "But why are you so angry?" he asked, appearing genuinely confused.

"Because I didn't want to be unfaithful," she cannily replied.

"You couldn't have been unfaithful with Liancourt, my turtle-dove. That old fart would not have dared!"

Quickly deflated by his truthful insight, she replied, "Maybe not, Henry. But you should have been here."

"I had no choice, charmante Gabrielle. But I shall take you with me whenever and wherever I can," he promised.

She calmed down quickly, remembering the extravagant dowry. For a while Henry ceased sleeping with the English whores Rosny had condemned so harshly as Gabrielle obediently adapted her life to his nomadic existence for a few months. However, when he had to take up rigorous military operations again, his mistress asked to be left behind. Gabrielle had submitted to his caresses, but he felt she seemed cooler than a woman in love. He began to imagine Bellegarde stroking her smooth skin, Gabrielle kissing Bellegarde, and instantly regretted leaving her alone. He wrote to her, pleading:

> My all, Love me completely . . . You will know every day my news; let me know yours, particularly regarding your health. I never left you leaving sadder and more constant. Be faithful, since my love cannot be altered whatever may happen, outside of a rival. Let me know how you were welcomed at Mantes. I am and will be until the tomb, your faithful slave. I kiss your hands a million times. I do not know what charm you have used, but I did not experience so much impatience with the other absences as this one. It seems that a century has passed since I left you. You have only to solicit my return. I have neither artery nor muscle which at each moment does not remind me of the hour of seeing you, and which does not make me feel the displeasure of your absence. Believe, my dear sovereign, that love never was so violent for me before.

Once again M. de Rosny and Aubigné worried about their king. The marriage of Gabrielle and Liancourt had not solved anything, for Henry still raged with jealousy.

"He is impossible when he has these amorous obsessions," Rosny complained. "All he does is sit in his tent and write letters to her. We shall never see Paris again at this pace."

"If only we could engage his interests elsewhere," Aubigné plotted. "And this one seems so mediocre compared to Corisande. At least he could think with her. I don't trust this chit at all!"

"He doesn't either; that's the trouble. He only seems to know how to be a man with men. He has become a jellyfish. I am finding this waiting interminable, and the men are beginning to grouse also."

Indeed, Henry was writing to his mistress again.

> My beautiful angel, if at every hour it was permitted to me to think of you, I believe the end of each letter would be the beginning of another. Thus, incessantly, I would converse with you, since absence deprives me of doing it otherwise. But business, or more exactly, importunities are in greater number than they were at Chartres.

He expected Gabrielle to join him at Tours. But she failed to come. What was she doing? Why did she treat him so badly? Because he always put France first and his women second? But he had no choice and she must know that. He heard she had gone to Mantes but lost her for a few days after that. Beginning to resent her independence, he grumbled to Rosny, "When I do ask her to join me, she only does so with as much bad grace and as much delay as possible. She seizes on every pretext not to come."

It wasn't just Gabrielle who had turned his mood so sour, for he had been feeling bleak since hearing of his dear friend Montaigne's passing in mid-September. What a loss to the country was this great thinker's death! Henry wondered who would keep him company in his old age — if he ever should reach such a time. He knew Corisande would miss Montaigne greatly. His own birthday next December, he swore, would be celebrated in Paris! And Gabrielle would be there to celebrate with him.

As Henry rightly suspected, even as he was writing to her, she was abandoning herself again to his archrival, Roger de Bellegarde.

Instead of Gabrielle, Henry was surprised to see his sister Catherine, turn up, distraught and miserable, in Tours where he was temporarily lodged. She hadn't anticipated Henry's ill humor, and he rudely put off receiving her for days. She longed for someone to talk to. Corisande was far away in the Pyrénées, Henry was disagreeable, and she doubted if she could expect any friendliness from Gabrielle, who wasn't even there. Catherine was secretly glad because, although curious, she dreaded meeting her brother's new mistress and Corisande's present competition.

One day, out of lonely desperation, she found herself telling her story to Guise's widow, Marguerite de Lorraine, who had attached herself to Henry's moving court for the moment. Mme de Lorraine, well into middle age, was still an attractive woman, skilled in the ways of love, and not an unwilling listener.

"After my brother called off my marriage to the comte de Soissons," Catherine related, "the Count and I exchanged letters secretly.

Corisande always helped us, and when Henry found out, he was furious. He never gave up his suspicions about Soissons's loyalty after that anonymous letter condemning him. He even wrote to Corisande saying, 'I would not have thought this of you, and I am only going to say one word. I will never forgive the people who are stirring up trouble between my sister and me.' "

"But the king usually forgets his anger very quickly," Mme de Lorraine observed.

"I can see you know him well. But I am afraid that is only true as long as he is obeyed," Catherine declared. "But Corisande continued to help us and a year later, in March, 1592, we arranged to marry secretly in Pau. Soissons told his men he was going to visit his sick mother. Henry, who is always suspicious, found out our plan and sent M. de Rosny to M. de Ravignan, President of the Council in Béarn, with the message, 'I am ill-pleased by the journey my cousin, the Comte de Soissons, has undertaken. I have only this one thing to say to you, that if anything occurs to which you agree or give your help against my wishes, your head will answer.' "

"He didn't mince words, did he!" Mme de Lorraine exclaimed.

"No, and we didn't have a chance. Rosny discovered us in the palace courtyard. He was accompanied by Ravignan's soldiers, who would have taken Soissons by force if necessary."

"Oh, Catherine, what a disappointing wedding day!"

Easy tears welled up in Catherine's eyes. "It was so humiliating too. Rosny demanded we hand over the promise to marry that we had written, and he destroyed it before our eyes. I felt Rosny was ashamed and pained at what he had to do, but Henry has a marvelous power over his men."

"Still, it is not like Rosny to do something he considers unfair," Marguerite de Lorraine commented.

"I know," Catherine murmured, "but he did that day."

A page knocked on Catherine's door. "The king is ready to see you," he announced.

Rising, Catherine followed the boy immediately. Henry embraced his sister.

"Forgive me, Catherine, for not seeing you earlier. This has been a devil of a campaign, the damn gout is bothering me, and I'm afraid I know why you are here."

"You do, Henry." Nervously, she wandered about the room, then suddenly and purposefully took his hand. "I beg of you, as my brother, allow me to marry Soissons. We both wish it, and he will pledge his faith to you. You have made and broken several engagements for me for reasons of political convenience. Now you have broken your word again, when you know I am very much in love with Charles."

"Impossible, Catherine! Soissons cannot be trusted. He is both shallow and treacherous. I am certain he expects me to destroy myself eventually, and he knows you would inherit Béarn and all the lands of the d'Albrets. Instead, I have arranged for you to marry the duc de Montpensier. I shall expect you to meet him shortly."

Catherine's eyes registered her shock. "Oh, Henry, how could you be so callous? Now it is my turn to say 'impossible.' I must tell you I am determined to remain true to Soissons. You cannot really believe the lies about his betrayal. He has continued to serve you well — despite what you have done to us!"

Henry's face became purple with rage. He was too angry to speak, and Catherine watched him with growing anxiety and disappointment.

"Do not contradict me, Catherine. As a daughter of royal lineage, you understand that political expediency is more important than your feelings, which, I might add, are only transitory."

"My feelings are permanent, which I doubt you can understand." Keeping her wits about her, she decided to change her tack. "Think how much you miss Gabrielle. I want Soissons in the same way. It cannot matter that much whom I marry, for I am not a direct heir to the throne. Surely you will have children who will follow you. You have such compassion for your subjects. Why can't you be sympathetic to those closest to you?"

"I cannot believe you are being so blind and idiotic. I do not want to discuss it further!"

Catherine started to mention that at the time he had ordered Soissons arrested, he was involved in arranging a marriage for Gabrielle to secure her for himself. It was grossly unfair. But she had always obeyed her brother. She kept her silence and left the room.

MANTES

1593

HENRY QUICKLY TURNED HIS energies to his own problems. Gabrielle's indifference and immoral behavior had finally destroyed his patience, and Catherine's attitude only increased his vexation. Writing to his mistress, he vented his anguish and anger:

To the Dame Gabrielle d'Estrées:

There is nothing that confirms me more in my suspicions or serves more to increase them, than the way in which you conduct yourself toward me. Since it pleases you to command me to banish all suspicion, I will; but you will not take it ill, if, in the openness of my heart, I tell you the grounds on which I suspect you, inasmuch as you appear not to have understood certain things that I have laid to your charge . . . It was for this reason yesterday, I began my letter with the words: "There are none so deaf as those who will not hear."

You are well aware that I was offended at the journey taken by my rival. Your eyes have such power over me that they save you half my complaints; you have satisfied me by the mouth, not from the heart. Had I known then what I have learned since, at Saint Denis, of that journey, I should not have seen you . . . I should have broken with you altogether . . . Yet I would rather burn my hand than write this to you, and cut out my tongue than that such words should be spoken . . . Have you banished the cause of our disagreement, as I hoped you would?

Which of your promises have you fulfilled? By what faith can you swear to me, you who have broken faith a second time? . . . You send me word you will keep the promises that you made me previously . . . ONE SHOULD SPEAK OF DOING, NOT OF GOING TO DO.

So much do I long to set eyes on you that I would cut off four years of my life to see you as soon as this letter, which now I bring to an end, kissing your hand a thousand times. And so, alas, you think me unworthy of your picture?

He was so agitated, he forgot to sign the letter.

Four months later, in early spring, Henry lay with his mistress in his arms, content after a sensual night. He was the most credulous of lovers, and a little pretended sweetness and complaisance cured his jealousy momentarily. Delighting in gazing at the golden waves of her hair over her white, silky shoulders, he felt extremely tender after their hours of pleasure.

"I have been tormented with doubts about you, *chérie*. Why have you teased me so?"

"I apologize for having been too coquettish, perhaps even unwise," she answered stroking his rough sunburned cheek.

"But why did you act so cool, when I see now that you love me?"

"Oh, Henry, it was a little bit your fault. You must admit, even the most loving woman gives way sometime to the temptation of juggling with a heart of which she is absolutely sure."

"You beautiful vixen! Still, I think it was a bit childish of you — and mean," he replied.

Always prompt in love to believe what he wished, the king listened with eagerness to the lying words. He allowed himself to be charmed by their musical perfidy and departed the next day, stopping to write her after traveling only a few miles:

How afflicted I am this evening, when I no longer find the subject who made yesterday evening so sweet! A thousand kinds of delight haunt me, so many singular rarities. In brief, I was more enchanted by you than by the magician who made your case be found. Certainly my beautiful love, you are admirable; but why do I praise you?

He wrote again the next day:

Do not fail my love, to come on the day you promised. The further I go, the less I am able to support your absence. You have me, I confess, more charmed than ever before. Bonjour, my mistress, I kiss your feet a million times.

Henry came to Mantes and counted the hours and the stages of the voyage his mistress would be making to come to him. Rosny came to him with the news that Gabrielle had set out only on the 20th of the month. Henry kicked over a washstand near him and stomped around his tent in a rage.

"If Bellegarde is with her, I will kill him. He has no right to touch her!"

"Why don't you punish him?" Rosny asked. "You are the king. You could have him banished, imprisoned, or even murdered."

"Shut up your filthy mouth, Rosny. I despise assassination — and you know that. That is the style of the Valoises. Moreover, I have been challenged and so am compelled on my honor to win her affections fairly."

"I think that is both fantastic and commendable, Sire."

"Sire! Why do you call me that today?"

"Because you are playing king today, Sire."

"I don't enjoy your humor, Rosny. Please leave me," Henry replied coldly. He disliked the way he felt when his passion clouded his judgment and particularly when it was obvious to his counselors. But damn them! Didn't they have blood in their veins too? His anger finally cooled and he wrote again to his mistress:

You assure me by one of my lackeys, who returned quite late, that you will not fail to come as you promised. I waited for you in vain today, and was saddened when you failed to join me in time for dinner.

The news he brings me consoles me much . . . but the bearer of your letter tells me later by word of mouth that you do not plan to leave until tomorrow morning. The dispatch from La Varenne* should have made you hurry in my opinion. Jesus! I will see you the day after tomorrow. What joy!

He had gone from despair to ecstasy in one paragraph. Consumed with passion, he didn't see that he was groveling before a lazy, indifferent, young woman, his royal dignity lost to the blaze of his desire. He wrote to her again on the same day, seeming more to sing than to write:

My beautiful love, it will be tomorrow that I will kiss your pretty hands a million times. The hour of meeting draws near, and I hold it dearer than my life. But if you are late by only one day, I will die. Send La Varenne tonight, instructed with your commands. I have found a heart of diamonds which will make you die of envy. I kiss your feet a million times.

But the evening ended without his courier La Varenne reappearing. And the next morning the hours crawled by with tedious waiting, also in vain. Noon. Not only did Gabrielle not arrive, but the king still had not received the least note from her explaining or excusing her delay. No one has treated me this way before, he thought. How can I go on in this way? She is disturbing my work! Why do I allow her to act in such an offhand manner with me? She's shaming me in front of my men. Disappointed to the point of exasperation, but withdrawing his claws as best he could, he sent a courier to Gabrielle with another billet:

I had no news from you yesterday. I do not know for what reason. If you linger out of respect for Easter Day, I must tell you I hold the day in no such respect. If it is laziness, you should be ashamed. It is noon, and I still have not heard from you. This is very far from the assurance your words gave me of seeing you tonight. When will you learn to be true to your word? I do not make so little of promises!

---

* Guillaume Fouquet de La Varenne (1560–1616) was a French chef who became a friend and statesman in the service of Henry IV.

At last, Gabrielle arrived. The mere sight of her appeased his anxiety. He embraced her ferociously, saying only, "You are mine now." With her presence he was able to push away the visions of his mistress in Bellegarde's arms. For several months he made Mantes, in the north central part of the country, his capital and kept her with him. His men, including two thousand English soldiers, camped outside the walls.

Catherine and Gabrielle met with all the conformities of court etiquette, even within the travelling tent cities occupied by Henry's army, each polite to the other and careful to reveal no open conflict before Henry. It did not take long for everyone to know they detested one another, their mutual antipathy springing as much from character as from circumstances. Both forced stiff smiles, masking considerable ill will and scorn, but never did declared war actually erupt.

Catherine had every right to be jealous, for tuberculosis had made her look older than her thirty-five years. Pretending she didn't know that Gabrielle made fun of her long nose and provincial dress, she told herself that her assailant was shallow and callous. Her amiable and sensitive nature made her particularly vulnerable to Gabrielle's bitter tongue. Having suffered greatly because of her brother's whims, she relied upon a supple intelligence, extensive knowledge, and Huguenot piety to sustain her.

Catherine was unhappy, not only because of her own situation but for her friend Corisande, whom she had left in the Pyrénées. She shuddered to think how much it would hurt Corisande to see Henry so wild about this nymph. How demeaning it was to attend Gabrielle's triumph, to see her feted and adulated when she had looked forward to one day seeing her friend marry her brother. Now she must witness instead the fickle monarch playing with this flippant creature, and she was appalled as well by rumors that Gabrielle wished to draw Henry to Papism.

One day, however, despite her dislike, Catherine was driven to friendliness, simply by the extreme kindness that was her nature. She couldn't help noticing that Gabrielle looked as forlorn as she and lonely as well. Returning to her tent, she looked for her copy

of poems by Ronsard and La Boétie, retrieved the little book, and
went out again to find Henry's mistress. Shortly, she interrupted her,
taking a walk, scuffing up the camp's dust.

"Perhaps you would like to look at these poems which I love so
much," Catherine offered with a tentative smile.

"You are very kind, I am sure," Gabrielle said, "but I don't really
enjoy poetry."

"I see," Catherine answered. Not waiting for a reply, she turned
and scurried quickly back to her tent with her book.

Longing to leave Mantes, Gabrielle spent many hours pacing,
feeling frustrated and confused. She missed Bellegarde but was afraid
to write or receive letters from him. She didn't want to lose either
Henry or her first lover. Catherine's high station, her generosity and
tenderness, and Henry's obvious affection for her made her even more
resentful. Might Catherine turn Henry against her? When the king
took up arms again to attack Dreux on the supply route to Paris, she
was much relieved. She thought this would at least allow her some
freedom again.

However, she was beginning to understand the monarch would
not tolerate her affair much longer. Aunt Isabelle echoed this thought,
warning her daily that her lover would not endure Bellegarde's hovering forever. Gabrielle appreciated that Aunt Isabelle was greatly
enjoying her position as the new mistress of Philippe de Cheverny,
Henry's legal advisor, and naturally feared her niece might jeopardize her own situation. But being fairer than was her wont, Gabrielle
thought her aunt might be right this time about the limit to Henry's
patience.

When Bellegarde's absence grew more protracted, much to her
surprise, Gabrielle discovered she missed Henry instead. He was so
good to her and put up with so much. On May 12, she received a letter from him written from Dreux:

> These verses will give you a better idea of my condi-
> tion, and more agreeably, than any prose. I dictated
> them, though I didn't arrange them:

Charmante Gabrielle,	Charming Gabrielle,
Percé de mille dards,	Pierced by a thousand arrows
Quand la gloire m'appelle	When glory calls me
Sous les drapeaux de mars,	Under the flags of Mars
Cruelle départie,	Cruel departure
Malheureux jour!	Unhappy day!
Que ne suis-je sans vie	How lifeless I am
Ou sans amour.	Without love.
Partagez ma couronne,	Share my crown
Le prix de ma valeur;	The prize of my valor;
Je la tiens de Bellone,	I hold it from Bellone
Tenez-la de mon Coeur.	Hold it with/from my Heart.
Cruelle départie,	Cruel departure,
Malheureux jour!	Unhappy day!
Que ne suis-je sans vie	How lifeless I am
Ou sans amour!	Without love!

On June 15 after the battle he wrote to her again:

It is Tuesday. It is more than eight days since I have the honor of seeing you. I have never desired it so much, having never experienced my love so violently as I do now. I swear to you, my dear love, that if you could see what is in my soul for you, you would leave Saturday. I am going to sleep, not having closed my eyes for 48 hours. I close, kissing your hands a million times.

Gabrielle gradually became aware that although Henry was angry when she didn't write, he was afraid to anger her. His hesitant style seemed touching to her in a way it never had before. She read on:

I have been patient today after having no news from you. The only reason I can see is the laziness of my lackey or that the enemy has captured him, because I refuse to attribute the blame to you, my beautiful angel. You make me use this refrain in all my letters:

> Come, come, my dear love, honor with your pres-
> ence the one who if he were free, would go 1000 miles
> to throw himself at your feet never to budge.

Why did she always treat him so cruelly? She began to believe in his love and fear losing it.

Henry's campaign proved successful. When Gabrielle arrived at Dreux, Henry, in a lavish mood, commanded that a victory dinner be arranged. Offering the wine of the country to all his men, he toasted them for their brave and loyal service.

Marguerite de Lorraine had also journeyed to Dreux for this festive occasion. Looking more beautiful than ever this evening, she began to flirt with Bellegarde. Who had invited him? Gabrielle saw Henry watching with interest as Mme de Lorraine cleverly took Bellegarde's attention away from her, and Bellegarde appeared to become more and more infatuated with his lovely new friend.

Seizing her chance to calm Henry, Gabrielle leaned over and kissed his ear, giving it a sensual bite.

"You see, my lover, your *bête noir* has no time for me."

"Until later tonight perhaps."

"But Henry, don't be silly! You know I will be very busy elsewhere. Don't you have special plans for me?" As she continued to stroke his thigh under the table, Henry laughed and pulled her hand up toward his groin. He saw Catherine turn her eyes away in disgust and said, loud enough for his sister to hear, "I have plans for you now!" His eyes gleamed.

Gabrielle regarded him with new affection. Perhaps she truly was beginning to love this tenacious and persistent man. He showered her with so much love, it was hard to resist.

In his joy, Henry shortly saw to it that his loyal and beautiful mistress acquired the title of Marquise de Montceaux. With the title went lands and money, and Gabrielle found it more and more convenient to be in love.

ST. DENIS TO CHARTRES

1593-1594

ALL OF HENRY'S COUNSELORS who were not blinded by Huguenot fanaticism advised him to return to the traditional faith of the majority of the French people in order to secure possession of the throne. Four years of sterile negotiations and a costly war had made it clear that the Catholics would never recognize a heretical sovereign, even if convinced — and they were not — he would respect their religious liberty. In addition, the ancient tradition of the land, which forbade anyone other than a member of the "true religion" to rule, was still firmly in place. The threat of Spanish domination was less acute as Parma had died from complications of a battle wound in December 1592. However, Henry understood Philip II's ambitions and so deduced that only his conversion could assure salvation from that fate.

Rosny, although a Huguenot and a man of deep religious convictions, exhibited a strong political instinct. Unlike Aubigné, who continued to hold the dream of a Huguenot king of France, he decided the time had come to lend his influence to persuade the king to accept the Catholic faith. Respected for his ability, courage and integrity, others believed him the right man for the job. Moreover, he wouldn't lose his temper as Aubigné would.

Finding Henry still abed one morning, Rosny took a seat at the foot. He suspected the king must be suffering from either his chronic urological problem or stomach complaint to be supine at this hour. When he expressed his concern, Henry grumbled, "Too much is made about my health; I don't like being treated like an old man."

Somewhat reassured, Rosny decided to broach the subject on everyone's mind.

"Henry, that you should wait for me, a Protestant, to counsel you to go to Mass, is a thing you should not do. Although I will boldly declare what you know as well as I — it is the prompt and easy way of destroying all malign projects against you. In one stroke, you would abolish most enemies, sorrows, and difficulties in this country. As to the other world," he continued, smiling, "I cannot answer for that."

"Ah, Rosny, my friend, I wondered when you would begin badgering me. I have not turned Papist for fear of alienating the Huguenots, as my heart could not bear to harm all those men who for so long have spent their goods and their lives in my defense. It is beyond my power to keep myself from loving them, whether nobles or townsmen. All those years when I was a prisoner of the Valoises, I disappointed them, and I do not want to betray them again."

Moved by the sincerity and emotion in Henry's voice his advisor answered, "I can understand, Henry, but I believe you should be converted for the sake of France. I am sure you are aware that, in the main, it is the French peasant who has remained loyal to Catholicism. Protestantism is, to a certain extent, the religion of a liberal, semi-aristocratic elite."

"Yes, I know this to be true. For it was the followers of the intellectual Calvin who started the religion. Yet somehow the ideas spread among my fellow rough Gascons as well. Protestants hold that there is no other requirement for salvation than faith alone, and perhaps that is convincing and attractive to the uneducated. Yet how do you know it is easier to change a peasant's than an aristocrat's faith?"

"A good point! I don't know," his friend pondered, "but I do know that many ministers argue that one can be saved in the Catholic as well as in the Protestant faith."

"But why cannot these people be tolerant of one another?" Henry mused. "In Catholicism, only the Roman Catholic Church has authority to interpret the Bible. Protestants hold that each individual has authority to interpret the Holy Book. But I am not fighting to settle particular points of theology! I only want people learn to abide one another's religion."

"They are afraid of what they do not understand and what they cannot know," Rosny replied. "Your extreme tolerance is actually more surprising than their intransigence. Each has been raised in his own faith and taught that all others are heretical."

Henry sighed. "Perhaps it is easier to be broadminded when one is at the top of the heap. If I could banish their fears, maybe my credo of mutual acceptance would stand more of a chance. It is because of religion that so many have followed me, and because of religion that so many have found a 'moral' reason for war. If I convert, I am afraid more will abandon me than the few who will follow me because of my ideas about tolerance."

Rosny left without knowing whether he had impressed Henry with his arguments or not. He was encouraged to hear that the King continued to sound out Huguenot reactions to his possible conversion. Indeed, the next day Henry related one story to him, laughing: "I asked a tactful Huguenot minister, 'Would you agree one can be saved in the religion of the Catholics?' When he answered me in the affirmative, I told him, 'Then prudence requires I should be of their creed, not yours, because being of theirs, I can be saved according to both of them and you, while being of yours, I can be saved well enough according to you but not according to them.' Prudence dictates I should follow the most guaranteed road, don't you think?"

But Henry still was not ready, despite hints by the Third Estate, as the commoners were politically dubbed, that they might desert him, or despite pointed jokes that of all the cannons, the canon of Mass was the most likely to win over the towns of his kingdom. Pure reason and political logic were on the side of those who were pushing him to abjure his Protestant faith. Also, the time seemed ripe because Mayenne came up with a brilliant maneuver. He wrote to Philip II of Spain, "If it would be agreeable to your Catholic Majesty, a choice could be made of one of the princes for king, and if you would do us the honor, the Infanta your daughter might be given to him in marriage . . . thus we would hope by this means to put an end to all our miseries and to conserve both religion and the state." Of course he had himself or his son in mind to be the groom that Philip would choose.

Villeroi,* a former cabinet minister of Henri III, pushed Henry harder, letting him know that the princes and lords with him were disposed to recognize the King of Navarre and negotiate with him if he would become Catholic, with guarantees for the Huguenot religion and the party, and to do so in good faith, without dissimulation. But Villeroi refused to write this publicly for fear the Spaniards, under this pretext, might at once seize several important cities. Still, Henry procrastinated.

---

*Nicolas IV de Neufville de Villeroi, (1543-1617) Secretary of State under four kings, Charles IX, Henri III, Henri IV and Louis XIII.

Chancellor Cheverny tried to work through his best auxiliary, Gabrielle, and spoke to Rosny on the subject. "The Marquise de Montceaux could do more than anyone, I think."

"The Marquise de Montceaux? Ah, you mean *la charmante Gabrielle*," Rosny jibed.

"Of course," Cheverny replied with a sniff. "She prefers to be called la Marquise."

"*Bien sûr*," Rosny smiled.

"There is no doubt she is the key," Cheverny continued. "Since the hope of coming to royalty by marriage has grown in her mind, and since she has realized no minister will be able to dissolve his first marriage, that only the Pope is capable of this with one blow, she is powerfully persuaded the king should endear himself to the Vatican. As often is the case with converts, she brags at having been the first to plunge. And Henry is interested, most interested."

"Ah," Rosny said, "and so you think she will employ her great beauty and the convenient hours of the day or night to bring about the conversion?"

"*Exactement!*" Cheverny beamed.

In spite of the flightiness she had shown, Gabrielle was endowed with the shrewdness of the women of her family and the intellect of her brilliant grandfather. Having heard many members of the court declare that if Henry became Catholic, every city in France, including Paris and Rouen, would open its gates to him, she wondered why he hesitated. What could he possibly gain by remaining a Huguenot?

Joining the king again at Mantes, she spoke to him at dinner. These campsite meals were not much to her liking, but she knew better than to complain tonight.

"Henry, you cannot defend against all these pressures much longer. Besides, if this silly war would stop, you would have more time for me."

"That's the best reason anyone has given me so far!" Admiring her creamy bosom tightly cupped in lavender satin trimmed with velvet, he did not see as she did the luxurious folds of her train trailing in the mud beneath their feet. "You know, *chérie*, Aubigné thinks I should not convert, and I have always trusted his opinion. Besides, Gabrielle, you have agreed with him until now. Has anyone been coercing you?"

"Cheverny believes you should abjure your faith, and soon. He asked me to talk to you," she admitted. "But that should be no surprise.

He also mentioned that the League would finally be exposed as an instrument of foreign aggressors, and that made good sense to me."

"The surprise is not that Cheverny asked you to talk to me but that you truly seem to desire that I become a Catholic. Why should you care?"

"Oh, Henry, don't you see? Then the Pope would be on your side. He might even be willing to annul your marriage to Margot. Obviously Pope Clement will take no action to help a heretic!"

"How refreshing to see you as the jealous one, my turtledove. I didn't really think you were concerned about the state of my soul."

"But of course I am, Henry."

Henry didn't answer her, for he was busy wondering if she could care enough about him to want to spend more time with him or to be jealous of his tie with Margot. Or was it only self-interest motivating this new concern? Was she only dreaming of becoming queen one day? She certainly had never shown any evidence of great faith — in any religion. But it did seem that her dependence on him and her loyalty to him were increasing daily. And when night fell, Gabrielle made sure he was reminded of her many charms.

Gabrielle also decided it would help her cause to write to Catherine. She imagined Henry's sister would see it as effrontery on her part, but she tried to explain:

> Dear and Respected Madame: Those who call upon His Majesty to accept conversion become more clamorous daily and press upon him the argument that the war will not end if he will not renounce the Huguenot faith. I do not ask that you add your voice to theirs, but the withdrawal of your opposition to such a move would clear His Majesty's mind and heart. Do you but reflect that he who is your close friend is a son of the Catholic Church, and you will surely know that all such are not devils with cloven hooves. It is my honor, Madame, to be your respected servant, Gabrielle d'Estrées

Upon receipt of this missive, Catherine's hand shook with anger. She was so tired of the struggle. Perhaps she would drop her opposition to his conversion because she must admit it was the only possible way to end the terrible violence that had torn France for as long as she could remember. Also, she knew Gabrielle to be more influential with her brother than she. Never, never would she agree to his marriage to this clever, corrupt woman. But what was she thinking? Henry would never heed, much less, ask her opinion.

Henry felt like a dam being pushed by a rising flood. He saw the cracks appearing in his façade — he had given in a bit to Gabrielle and a bit more to Rosny. But the greatest fissure in his confidence was the continuing war. How could he refuse to convert if it truly would stop the flow of blood? And he would, at last, truly be King of France. Aubigné and others continued to hope he would be the first Protestant king of the country, and that had always been his dream too, but more and more clearly, he saw it as an impossible dream. And he must not let Mayenne and the Spanish outwit him at this critical juncture!

When he had made the flippant remark to Gabrielle about the state of his soul, he realized he had honestly not given it enough thought. He was so much a man of action and often leaped before looking carefully. His religion relied on the traditions he had learned as a child, and he had not spent much time studying the subtle difference between Calvinism and Catholicism. It was so much easier slipping into the rituals he knew but he believed that the end of the war, peace, and tolerance were more important to him than the rigorous dissection of theology. For him, tolerance seemed as important a belief in and of itself to hold up to all the other religious doctrines. But he knew he wouldn't win that argument with either side.

Very soon after his mistress joined him at Mantes, he resolved to cross the Rubicon. On May 17 Henry called a conference at Suresnes, where he instructed the Archbishop of Bourges to solemnly announce the decision taken by His Majesty to embrace the Catholic faith. With exceptional attention to detail, Henry first had the Archbishop gain assurance from the Leaguers that the only obstacle to their submission to the king was that of religion. He did not want this to be an empty gesture.

Then on June 28, to the surprise of everyone, the Parlement de Paris removed the Spanish threat by a decree stating:

> The court . . . having now and always no inten-
> tion other than to maintain the Catholic, Apostolic,
> and Roman religion, the state and crown of France
> under the protection of a Christian, Catholic, and
> French king, has ordained and does ordain that there
> be no agreement to transfer the crown into the hands
> of a foreign prince or princes; that the fundamental
> laws of this kingdom must be kept, and the decisions
> given by this court for the declaration of a king who is
> both Catholic and French be executed . . .

On July 22 the Assembly of Paris declared invalid the bulls which Sixtus V had published against the king, also naming them contrary not only to the rights of French kings but to canon law itself, which maintained that no one could be excommunicated without previous warning. The Archbishop of Bourges, they determined, as patriarch of France, had the right to absolve the king "since it was more expedient to proceed without delay in a work so pleasing to God and so salutary to France." Religion and politics, it seemed, could work together when it was so advantageous to both parties.

The next day the assembled clergy invited the king to St. Denis in order to ascertain if he were ready for the necessary formalities. The night before he was to appear in the assembly, he wrote to Gabrielle:

> Tomorrow I begin my talk with the bishops. My
> hope of seeing you keeps me from writing a long letter.
> Sunday I will take the perilous leap. As I write to you,
> a hundred boors surround me who will make me hate
> St. Denis as you do Mantes. Goodbye, my sweetheart;
> come early tomorrow for it seems like a year since I
> have seen you.

No matter who persuaded him or the pressures of political expedience, this conversion remained a frightening step for Henry. Earlier in his life he had accepted a marriage, not of his choice but because of his royal duty. Now his religion, which he believed should be a man's most private choice, would also be dictated by the needs of his country. He chose not to look too closely at his increasing desire to be king, preferring to interpret his behavior as being for the benefit of France.

On the 24th, the bishops commanded he attend a five-hour discussion of Catholic dogmas — Purgatory, the Real Presence, Confession, Papal Power. He was required to affirm each one.

"Must one pray to all the saints?" Henry inquired. The bishop replied in the affirmative.

"Is auricular confession obligatory?" It is.

"And what about the authority of the Pope?" They replied, "He has absolute authority in all matters spiritual, and in regard to temporal matters, can interfere, to the prejudice of kings and kingdoms."

"What could happen if I and the Pope should disagree on a temporal matter concerning the welfare of the people of France?"

The bishops answered, "We cannot imagine the possibility that such a situation would arise."

On the Eucharist and the Real Presence, Henry promptly declared, "Here I have no doubts, for I have always believed the bread and the wine to be the true body and blood of our Lord."

Henry lay down upon his bed, exhausted from the grueling session with the clerics. All these small questions of dogma couldn't matter that much. Yet blood had been spilled throughout France for generations supposedly over just these points. When would men learn to get along and be kind to one another? Or at least agree to live and let live? Rosny knocked at his door.

"Sire, there is a lady to see you. She says it is most important. Her name is Mme d'Imbert."

"*Ventre-St.-Gris!* Why has she turned up on my doorstep? And at this moment? Tell her I am too busy to see her." He thought of their bastard, Gédéon, and his other illegitimate children. Life had moved too fast for him to concern himself with them. Perhaps one day he could make amends.

"Sire, she looks at the end of her strength. She seems to have lost all her pride and told me she was once your mistress. I'm sure she has come to ask for help and from the looks of her, she badly needs it."

"Rosny, I am too tired. I don't want to see her again. Please tell her to go away and not to bother me again."

Rosny started to dissuade Henry from this course but turned and left. He always obeyed this king who relied on familiar charm rather than majesty, and who gave orders as one asking for favors rather than as a sovereign who commanded.

I can't be responsible for every woman I bedded, Henry said to himself, though feeling vaguely uncomfortable. He had seen disapproval in Rosny's eyes. Damn him anyway! He's just jealous because the women prefer me to him.

On July 25, 1593, the streets were strewn with flowers, huge tapestries hung from balconies, and the crowd was so dense Henry and his coterie had trouble pushing their way through. Again and again the procession halted, and a grinning Henry removed his hat and greeted his subjects. The Parisians responded with the fervent cry *Vive le Roi!*

A wide square, lined with narrow town houses, extended in front of the cathedral, whose façade presented a rather cockeyed appearance due to the asymmetry of its crowning towers, one pinnacled and one with a mansard roof. Henry decided he liked this cathedral of St. Denis better than Notre Dame. Built in the twelfth century by Abbot Suger with the theme "God is Light," the lofty enormous windows in the choir and the soaring ribbed vaults always sent his spirit heavenward. Notre Dame was darker, and he still harbored bad memories from his visits there before and during his wedding. He would find inspiration for this conversion in the bright light of St. Denis, he thought. All the kings of France were buried here, including Henri II, Catherine de Medici's husband, Charles IX, and Henri III. Was he truly the only one still alive and therefore the next in succession? It was difficult to keep his mind on the religious duties at hand and not dwell on the political implications of his actions.

The day was bright, perhaps a blessing from above for what he was about to do, Henry hoped. The Archbishop of Bourges, who stood at the entrance of St. Denis, silenced the crowd and asked ceremoniously, "Who are you?"

Henry replied in a loud voice, "I am the King."

"What would you?"

"I would be received into the pale of the Roman Catholic Apostolic Church."

Clad in white satin from head to foot save for a black hat and mantel, Henry dropped to his knees and took the oath of abjuration. Then he handed the archbishop a written copy of the same words. The doors opened and he entered the church, again to kneel before the archbishop and seven bishops. He recanted his heresy, swearing to live and die in the true faith, and as his pledge, he kissed the archbishop's ring.

What a long way he had come since he had stood at the altar with Margot in front of Notre Dame. He thought he should write to Corisande to rationalize his decision. He had explained to his friends using the words he had first heard spoken from Rosny, his treasurer of the kingdom, "Paris is worth a Mass." This coinage suited his Gascon flippancy, buffoonery and self-mockery. But he knew it was more than that. France was worthy of peace, France deserved the best king, and he was that man. And the people would only recognize him as king if he converted.

He didn't think often about the state of his soul, but surely God would forgive his numerous transgressions if he could restore peace and prosperity throughout his country. He admitted to himself that he did not know the true state of his religious beliefs, and certainly his decision was largely driven by the tragic necessity of ending the religious wars.

The cheers of the crowd assembled inside were so loud that the voices of the choir could not be heard and order was restored with difficulty. The oath of abjuration was repeated. Then the Bishop Elect of Evreux heard the king's confession in a booth behind the altar, and the Bishop of Nantes celebrated High Mass. France had a true Prince of the Blood and a Catholic for its king.

Only one woman was present in the cathedral: Gabrielle. Dressed in a gown of white satin cut from the same bolt of cloth as the King's doublet, she sat alone in a corner, protected from view by brocaded screens. When she left the cathedral, the women of Paris began to shout, "Long live Gabrielle!"

A political earthquake ensued. Henry sent letters to the parliaments of every province in the country, announcing his conversion and asking support. Desirous of an official conciliation with Pope Clement, he sent a mission to Rome before the end of July. Mayenne, perceiving the tide of support for Henry, and understanding that his ties with Spain had become a burden, ignored the protests of the Spaniards and the Papal Legate and signed a three-month truce with the king. Less than three weeks later, Mayenne decided he needed more latitude and proposed that the armistice should be extended until the end of the year.

Henry, with everything to gain and little to lose, graciously agreed. For all practical purposes, the Estates General, declaring itself incompetent to regulate the succession, was no more, and to the man, the Third Estate rallied to him. All over France, towns and lords began to declare for Henri IV — even the Huguenots. He was nervous, however, about how Elizabeth I would receive the news of his conversion, for he still was dependent on her as an ally against Spain. Therefore he lost little time in assuring her of his constancy to her and to England.

In a quiet moment he gave in to his need to write to Corisande:

> My religion was one of feeling. Though I was once a convinced Calvinist, I have long been veering towards Rome, possibly under your influence. No doubt, the Roman Church's authority, its disciplining of society and its traditional role as a prop of monarchy appeals strongly to the autocrat in me. Yet, in the last analysis, my conversion was probably a matter of temperament. A faith with such delightful saints as François de Sales with his dictum "always condemn the sin, but show mercy to the sinner" was far more attuned to my earthy nature than the pure icy grandeur of the reform. My sister and your friend has a more Calvinist personality than I.

As usual, he could not remain long indoors, and tossing away his pen, he strolled outside for the view of Paris from the hill of Montmartre, where he and Gabrielle had been residing. It was quieter up here than at the Louvre, but even so, Henry felt he could not stand the closeness of the city any longer. Impulsively, he decided to move his mistress to Fontainebleau, where he always enjoyed hunting in the château's forests, thick with oak, birch, and chestnut trees. The foxes and even the small deer could hide among the high ferns and blackberry bushes and provide the sport that enabled him to forget the knotty problems besetting him.

Racing back indoors, he shouted orders to all within hearing, "Hurry, hurry! We must leave Paris at once!" Fearing a military emergency, everyone obeyed, and only when Gabrielle was settled in the carriage did she ask him what had happened. Although his conversion had disarmed the fanatics, he still felt it necessary to travel with a Swiss Guard of two thousand men, and so she had no reason to suspect his answer. "I just realized," he said, "that the forest of Fontainebleau is the only place in the north where I feel at home."

Gabrielle started to protest but then burst out laughing. "I cannot say I don't like surprises, but next time, please give me a little warning when I am to move house!"

They found the place in shameful disrepair and the gardens sadly neglected. The caretakers, mice, and squirrels inhabiting the place were shocked out of their lazy habits as Henry set to work immediately rebuilding the palace and planning a sylvan labyrinth. After ordering exotic trees and ornamental shrubs, he astounded the gardeners by putting his foot to the spade whenever he had the time.

"There must be something of the frustrated farmer in me," he told his mistress.

Some type of royal château had existed on these grounds since the twelfth century and in 1528, François I had begun an extensive renovation and assembled an art collection there. Among its treasures Henry found the *Virgin of the Rocks*, by Leonardo da Vinci, and directed that the masterpiece be hung in an oval chamber that served as his cabinet meeting room. He also commissioned an equestrian bas-relief of himself to be carved by Mathieu Jacquet. Henry's figure on horseback, impressively brandishing a sword, thereafter looked down from the fireplace upon the fine chimney wing, which in turn commanded Henry's favorite vista of Fontainebleau's shimmering lake.

Henry had major structural additions in mind as well and immediately ordered that a brick and stone building be constructed perpendicular to the main château. He called upon Ambroise Dubois to supervise the interior decoration, which he wanted dedicated to his military victories and to the myth of Diana, the Goddess of the Hunt. A long, book-lined gallery leading to the aviary opened onto the Garden of Diana, where he placed an antique statue of the beautiful goddess. In this area he included a parterre with deer and an exotic plane tree. Sharing his love of greenery, Gabrielle strolled there every afternoon when the weather allowed. But she had many indoor duties to occupy her, overseeing all of Henry's projects for the renaissance of the palace.

Henry's rapport with Gabrielle proceeded more smoothly in this autumn of 1593, for Gabrielle announced she was pregnant with Henry's child, probably conceived at Fontainebleau. Henry was ecstatic. He had sired a number of bastards, but this child would be special, a royal child even. For wouldn't he be born after the coronation? And might not Gabrielle one day be his wife? He had no children by Margot — perhaps this would be his first heir.

Gabrielle's news made it easier for Henry to shrug off what he heard about Esther d'Imbert — that she had taken to her bed and died of sorrow after he had refused to help her. It was difficult to imagine anyone else miserable when he was so satisfied.

Gabrielle, relieved to see Henry so cheerful, basked in his worshipful eyes. This child surely would be another link in securing the throne for her. And she realized, still with some surprise, that she cared quite a lot for Henry now. He had been so good to her. She felt as content and happy as she had ever been.

The Béarnais, as his enemies still condescendingly called him, decided, with his unerring political instinct, to be crowned immediately, even though Reims, the traditional crowning place of French kings, remained theoretically in League hands. Moreover, Pope Clement VII had not as yet confirmed his abjuration, refusing to grant an audience to his ambassadors. But, instead of waiting until his right to the kingdom was beyond dispute, he decided to use the coronation as an instrument, not as a consummation; he simply would choose another site and ignore the Pope. He chuckled to himself — he had learned a few things from the Valoises after all.

As in most important moments in his career, Henry wanted to write to Corisande. It was as though she had become his conscience. He knew she had come to Paris upon hearing of his crowning and was staying near his sister at the Louvre. Odd that they had not yet crossed paths, for Corisande's son had risen in his service at an admirable clip. They would always be connected, he thought, as he wrote to her:

> I see I am still a true man of the South, for I am not only a natural politician but I am fully aware of the law's strength and of the vital interdependence between the parliaments and the monarchy.

> I consider the legality of all my public actions, and
> I don't believe I have ever acted illegally. The im-
> pact of my coronation would be legal as well as
> psychological — to put on the crown will be both
> a sacramental confirmation and a seal of legality.

The ceremony took place at Chartres on February 27, 1594. Henry determined that this cathedral with its soaring spire, jeweled windows, and mysterious carvings provided exactly the sublime setting
he wished for, and in addition, was situated within Bourbon ances-
tral country. Surrounded by six spiritual and six lay peers of France,
Henry kissed the sword of Charlemagne, then lay prostrate before the
altar, naked save for a satin shirt, while the Bishop of Chartres prayed
over him. The bishop then anointed him on the head, on the chest,
between the shoulders, on the elbows and in the elbow joints, saying
each time "ungo te in Regem." Then Henry stood to be vested in the
dalmatic and the tunic, both of blue velvet sewn with golden lilies, followed by a golden chasuble, damascened with pomegranates — after
which he knelt again to be anointed in the palms of the hands. The
gloves, the violet velvet boots, the ring, and the scepter were presented
to him by the great lords, and finally the bishop took the crown from
the altar and placed it on his head, whereupon this glittering being
was enthroned, while the vast congregation shouted "*Vive le Roy, Vive
le Roy! Vive eternellement le Roy!*" "*Bibe lou Rey!*" would have sounded
sweeter to his ears, but he admitted the crown of France and not the
crown of Navarre had been his ultimate goal.

Hautboys, bugles, trumpets, fifes, and drums sounded throughout the nave while outside, cannons roared salutes to the new king,
musketeers fired volley after volley, and heralds threw fistfuls of gold
and silver coins among the crowd. Then the *Te Deum* was sung, the
human voices resonating in the vast vaulted ceiling of the gothic cathedral. A Pontifical High Mass followed at which the king communicated, and a coronation banquet culminated the joyous and triumphant day.

Henri IV, the monarch, was finally invested with all the attributes
of kingship — the scepter, the crown, the ivory hand of justice, and
the sword — symbolizing political, legislative, judicial and military
power. This splendid and awe-inspiring sacrament had consecrated
Henry's divine election to be king just as it had done for St. Louis,
Charlemagne, and Clovis. His destiny was made holy. He had be-

come France herself. This idea could overwhelm him. No, he would rise to the challenge!

Henry's body felt older and weary, but the toughness of his spirit responded to the joyful cries. He would serve France well. To achieve this end, he had destroyed the House of Valois — more truly the seeds of destruction had been within Charles IX, Alençon, and Henri III, he thought — and he had virtually defeated the League, so astutely led by Guise and Mayenne and backed by Catholic Europe. He lifted his hands and acknowledged his people, his exhilaration beyond all previous experience. More than any other person present that day, he understood the French people's veneration for their ancient monarch, the charismatic rock upon which depended all law and all society, almost as Catholicism depended upon the Pope. Within a week, the League was collapsing.

Throughout the year of 1594, in districts governed by the League, the aristocracy flocked to the king in order to assure their status. The most fanatic Leaguer sensed that something extraordinary had happened at Chartres. And they were right. Monarchy, which had been desecrated in France for over thirty years, had returned, cloaked in its original mystical attire. Henry hoped he could use the institution to protect the rights of the Huguenots and instill the idea of religious open-mindedness in his people. For now, he knew both Protestants and Catholics only warily trusted the peace his coronation promised.

PARIS

1594-1595

THE KING FOUND HIS SUBJECTS ready and eager with devotion, but uncertain about formally capitulating. This meant it would be necessary to complete the pacification of France by buying submissions, and he watched the royal treasury slide dangerously low as he paid for each territory holding out. Toulouse received 1,470,000 pounds for its oath of loyalty; Cambrai cost over 1,000,000 pounds, while for Amiens, Péronne, and Abbeville, he paid 1,261,000 pounds. Yet he dared not refuse compensation, for a peaceful France was worth every *écu*.

Paris, however, remained recalcitrant, and at Easter Henry chose to utilize the season to convince the citizens of his sincerity. He believed he knew how to please them and began by attending Holy Week services with ostentatious devotion. On Maundy Thursday he brought the poor to the Louvre and washed their feet himself, according to the ancient custom; that evening he visited the sick in the Hôtel-Dieu, distributing alms with a lavish hand. By torchlight he visited the prisons, pardoning those who merited it and freeing those who had been imprisoned by the League. The people's good opinion seemed to grow with each gesture of piety as bitter tea grows more palatable with each grain of sugar. But Henry would be content only with their total allegiance.

On March 22, 1594, just at dusk, the king rode toward the Porte St.-Jacques, the portal by which he had entered as a young bridegroom. With this entrance he would symbolically proclaim Paris as his own. He proceeded down the Grande rue St.-Jacques and passed the rue de Cluny, noticing the Sorbonne on his left. The massive buildings with their wrought iron gates still fascinated him, the life of the intellectual holding a constant mystery. The streets remained nervously silent, just as they had been sixteen years before. But as he arrived at the Pont Notre Dame, the crowd began to cheer and cry *"Vive le Roi!"* No intellectual would ever experience this adulation!

"I can see these poor people have been tyrannized!" Henry exclaimed with emotion. "I must see what can be done for them," he said to no one in particular. He had no desire for vengeance, for they were his people now, and he was already thinking what would be best for their welfare. He began by pardoning everyone, even the infamous Seize, the junta which had controlled Paris for the League.

The prolonged religious and civil wars had left destruction everywhere. In some towns the population had decreased by two-thirds. Textile looms, once threaded with bright colors, resembled drab leafless trees, and immobile plows loomed like scarecrows in barren and dusty fields. Paris had not succumbed by military means, but finally by his conversion. Henry planned to rebuild France just as he had reorganized his own province and reconstructed Fontainebleau. He always could motivate men to work for him, not by terror but by example, his own zest and exuberance inspiring them to his projects.

He relied above all on his friend and companion, the Baron de Rosny,* a man he recognized as having both good sense and a vast capacity for work. When Rosny came to office he found a debt of 300,000 pounds and 23,000,000 in annual income. After the deduction of local charges, this amount only supplied seven million as the king's net revenue, all of which went into warfare, pensions and gifts. Rosny set to work not only to restore equilibrium but to lay away a reserve as well.

While Henry was enjoying his first successful months as king, Gabrielle, noticeably pregnant at his coronation, gave birth to a son. On June 7, in the valley town of Chauny, near the border of Picardy, Henry heard the good news.

"Pass kegs of spirits to the troops!" the happy father ordered. "Military activities are suspended for the day, and I command a salute of 101 salvos be fired in the child's honor."

"Henry is creating the pretense that the baby is legitimate and heir to the throne," muttered the crowds around Fontainebleau, where the new mother lay.

Gabrielle rested within, propped up on pillows in Henry's own bedchamber. From the large bed she viewed a massive candled chandelier suspended from a white and gold ceiling. Across the long room, tall multi-paned windows framed the garden and Trinity Chapel, erected on the site of an old abbey. Except for her servant busily

---

* Henry would make Rosny duc de Sully in 1606.

heating water in the fireplace, the scene was tranquil and serene when Henry returned.

"You look more beautiful than ever," Henry remarked, stroking her cheek.

"Have you seen our boy?"

"Yes, *chérie*. And what a husky fellow he is! What would you like to call him?"

"What do you think of César?" she asked with a timidity unusual for her, revealing her apprehension at going too far.

Henry smiled. "Fine. You must have a grand future in mind for him."

"Of course I do," she answered, now with a proud smile.

"I'll leave you now so you can rest."

Gabrielle's reputation was far from untarnished, and the attending physician believed he was only repeating common gossip when he suggested to the king there might be some question of the child's paternity.

"Do you think I am some idiotic blind lover?" Henry shouted. "It is only vile gossip her detractors have stirred up against her."

Yet it galled him. Gabrielle was young and beautiful, and he knew his rugged life added years to his appearance. It would only be natural for her to seek a younger lover. And he could not forget that in her veins ran the questionable blood of the Baboux, a dangerous heritage from a spouse's point of view. Henry recalled the many times he had confronted her with her indiscretions, but Gabrielle, tearful and aghast had always managed to sway his doubts. Besides, he had been so sure of her fidelity of late.

The doctor, of course, shrugged his shoulders in acquiescence. If the king's desire to father a child in Gabrielle's womb was so great as to deafen him to the rumors of the child's paternity, why should he care? Little did he dream that what concerned Henry was not simply the question of César's paternity, but also how to legitimize this child born of adultery.

In July 1594, the King summoned Cheverny, his chief legal advisor and Aunt Isabelle's lover. It was most convenient to have a member of the family help him in this delicate matter.

"Is it possible to eradicate the stigma of illegitimacy for César?" he asked.

Cheverny would have liked to sit. He was carrying more weight around since he had begun participating at the royal table. But Henry's habit of pacing precluded anyone finding a chance to rest, which was only acceptable after the king had settled down. Instead, Cheverny leaned heavily upon the back of a chair and said, "I have anticipated such an interview with Your Majesty and have made some inquiries. I have found you need not marry the mother of César in order that the baby prince be recognized as the legitimate offspring of royalty. There is a precedent which would enable you, under letters patent in the form of a decree, to declare this child your lawful issue."

"Do you mean that with the stroke of the pen, I can declare César legitimate?" Henry asked incredulously.

"That is correct, Your Majesty. Provided that Nicolas d'Amerval, better known as Seigneur de Liancourt, is no longer in a position to make a claim."

"Then we must initiate immediate proceedings and begin preparing Gabrielle's divorce suit," Henry commanded.

"Yes, Sire," Cheverny replied.

Church prelates in Amiens, previously supporters of the League, were now anxious to win Henry's favor, and the king decided to give them their chance. On August 27, Gabrielle addressed a formal supplication to the bishop of that diocese. Having taken care to look her most ravishing, she was the first witness at the mock trial. Her eyes demurely lowered, she told the prelates, "Despite my protests against a marriage to M. d'Amerval, my father adamantly insisted and threatened me with the punishment of filial disobedience if I did not acquiesce." She went on to assure the court, "No, I knew nothing of Amerval's impotency before our marriage; yes, I lived with him for almost one year."

Low conversation rippled through the courtroom for it was common knowledge they had not shared the same roof for more than a few days. Amerval, looking even more shriveled and aged than Gabrielle remembered, took his oath to tell the truth and give his testimony. Given his appearance, it was not difficult for the court to accept the words of the witnesses and pile sham upon sham.

"It is true," he avowed, "Our marriage was never consummated; we never lived together as man and wife. This was because of my impotency. Yes, it is true I had four children by my first wife, but since then, I suffered a serious accident. No, I did not tell my wife this. No, there is no one who is inciting me to procure an annulment."

The same questions elicited the same answers from Gabrielle. No, she did not wish to continue the marriage; no, there was no one

who was influencing her to ask for this annulment. Additional inter-
rogations brought to light no further evidence. The case obviously
had been settled before it ever came to court, and on December 23
the official verdict was rendered: the marriage between Amerval and
Gabrielle d'Estrées was null and void. Not long after the successful
conclusion of the case, the judge was awarded a very profitable Episcopal See, and young César was on his way to being the legitimate
son of the man who had just been declared the lawful King of France.

After the divorce, a significant change took place in the living
arrangements of the king and his mistress. For the first time since
Henry had occupied his capital, Gabrielle moved into the Louvre. A
suite of rooms on the second floor, which stood near the king's own
private chambers, was prepared for her.

Decorating the rooms to suit her aerie personality, Gabrielle installed écru curtains as light as gauze, which fluttered at the windows
in the summer breeze. She detested the heavy velvet drapery hanging
throughout most of the palace. Across the bed she tossed a pastel
counterpane and champagne satin pillows, embroidered with floral
designs and sewn with silk thread. She wanted to create a room both
fragile and lovely to echo what Henry felt about her. She was tougher
than he imagined, but she intended to be the king's diamond in a satin
box.

César and his nursemaids occupied another suite directly across
the corridor. Within a few months Catholic Paris began to enjoy the
spectacle of the man they had heralded as a heretic monster disport-
ing himself with his mistress. Subtly and slowly the tide turned as the
gawking mob relished the visibility of its king, his mistress and the
new babe. They were charmed by his stream of jests, invariably illuminated by a sometimes rueful, but always captivating, grin. The enemy of so long quickly became a Parisian hero, idolized for his great
lusts and hearty laughter.

On the evening of September 15, with a cool breeze announcing the change of season, Gabrielle and the king triumphantly rode
through Paris by torchlight to be welcomed with shouts of applause.
Gabrielle, dressed in a gown of pale green velvet and gleaming with

jewels, was carried on a litter. The king, on a great white stallion, wore black velvet slashed with gold, and his usual plumed hat. He seemed to want to call attention to his mistress rather than to himself. Preceded by marching troops and accompanied by a splendid escort of cavalry and mounted nobles, they rode to hear yet another *Te Deum* at Notre Dame, where the members of Parliament were present in their long red robes.

In this first public appearance of Gabrielle as a member of the royal entourage, Henry turned to her and commented, "The people, and especially Parisians, are an animal which lets itself be led by the nose."

"Don't be so cynical about your loving subjects, darling."

"Sometimes they appear so blind as to still believe that Pope Clement is my real enemy. I am determined to show them and the world that Philip of Spain is France's true opponent. In a short time I will declare war on Spain. I refuse to tolerate their threat any longer or their machinations against me in Rome. For all I know, their spies could be in the crowd today."

"But will the people fight for you?" she asked.

"I didn't know you had such a practical mind, *chérie*. Yes, I think they will. The Huguenots should be reassured by Parliament's recent reenactment of the Edict of 1577." His tone was instructive.

"Oh, Henry, don't be angry, but I've forgotten the terms of that one," his mistress admitted.

"This law grants Huguenots the maximum freedom of worship allowed until now. For that alone, they will be willing to fight for their Catholic king."

Henry was right; he found it easier to raise an army than ever before. He was the legitimate king, and the French people had long resented foreign interference. The duty of nobility was to always be ready for service when the king needed them, and this was the rationale behind their not being allowed to hold a job or engage in commerce. Tradition demanded they be remunerated to serve the country when called. As all these men had to be paid, the financial drain of the military became overwhelming all too quickly, and Henry had no idea where to turn for funds — except to Gabrielle. When he asked her for aid, he received the answer he wanted. The d'Estrées family was proving to be an important piece of his treasury.

"I love you, and I love France. Of course I will help. These are difficult and important days."

"You are too generous, my sweet one." He embraced her with tears in his eyes.

Indeed, the siege of La Fère was brought to successful conclusion only because of Gabrielle's diamonds, which she gave as security for a further loan from the Grand Duke of Tuscany. Court gossip concerning the striking fondness between Henry and Gabrielle grew, but Aubigné, always sarcastic, said to Rosny,

"This lady knows how to keep the affections of our great prince so that he will be as faithful to her as she is to him."

François Annibal, Gabrielle's brother, was not so cynical. When he saw his sister, he was amazed by her change in behavior and wrote to his father:

> Gabrielle was a strange young woman. I do not believe a serious thought passed through her head from the day of her birth until some mystical moment long after she became the mistress of King Henry. What happened to her at that time, I cannot explain. I can only add my observation to that of so many others, that she became a new woman, as it were, in the course of a single day. When one reflects upon the influence she exerted on King Henry, it would not be impertinent to reflect that the change in her character took place in the course of a night rather than a day. Henry aroused a quality in her that had been asleep. I remember the first occasion upon which I became aware of the transformation. I had been given command of a regiment of dragoons, and called on King Henry to take leave of him before joining my troops. The King asked me to wait for a few moments, as he said Gabrielle wished to bid me farewell too. I remonstrated with him that my men were awaiting me in the village of Montmartre, and that I could ill afford to be tardy on this, my introduction to them.
>
> Fear not, he told me, Gabrielle will join us at 4 o'clock. I dared not reply that Gabrielle was never

punctual. But King Henry was right and I was mistaken, for as the old clock presented to Charles IX by the clock makers' guild began to chime the fourth hour, Gabrielle presented herself to the King's apartment. From that time forward, I never knew her to be tardy in anything, and she came to resemble Henry, who usually appeared at a given place before the appointed time of his arrival, much to the consternation of those who had assembled to greet him.

It is to Henry that credit must be given for the remarkable alteration in the character of Gabrielle. A soldier is taught discipline in the field, a cleric learns the same behind the walls of a cloister, but a beautiful woman can respond only to the instruction of a man she loves.

Believing his open personality and calculated tactics had successfully won over the Catholics, Henry began to relax, calling Rosny an old woman when his counselor warned him that Paris remained dangerous. Why would anyone still be against him when he loved his people so?

Henry granted audiences to citizens several times a week, willing to listen no matter what the supplication, and a string of squally days seemed to have encouraged everyone with a gripe to try their luck for some benefaction from their notoriously generous king. It was about a year after his coronation, in December 1594, when a young scholar named Jean Châtel obtained an interview with the king at the Louvre. No one was paying much attention to the trivial queue of petitioners that rainy afternoon, including Gabrielle, who enjoyed being near Henry of late and was half-heartedly doing needlework at his side. Suddenly, in the candlelight, Châtel struck wildly at the king with a knife. Henry's reflexes were fast, and he recoiled quickly. Nonetheless, the blow rendered a cleft lip and a broken tooth. Screaming, Gabrielle jumped up, overturning the frame holding her crewel. Châtel was seized before he could strike again. Gabrielle began to cry and tried to wipe Henry's face with her skirt. Henry, though pouring blood, immediately said, "Let us be merciful to this man. He must be mad."

His plea of clemency fell on deaf ears, which only heard the roar of fear of a larger revolt, and his ministers and lawyers ruled, "no pity." The public executioner burned off the lunatic's hand with the knife in it, tore him with red hot pincers, then tied him to four horses which pulled him to pieces. Finally, his mangled quarters were burned, their ashes scattered in the wind. The Paris mob, Henry's new admirers, screamed their intense approval as they watched these excruciating tortures.

Henry learned Châtel had been a Jesuit pupil. Knowing the Jesuits were dedicated to the service of the Papacy and had been among the most genuine of the hardline Leaguers, he foresaw the danger of a mass punishment in the hysteria following the assassination attempt. He watched with mixed emotions as the people celebrated his escape, chanting *Te Deums* in the churches of Paris and lighting fires of joy and gratitude. He increased his cautions, but in the end, realized he was unable to prevent all Jesuits from being blamed and their consequent mass expulsion from France. They were now in the position the Huguenots had been in during the Valois years. Would the country never learn?

He had so often faced death in a cavalier manner, but this time, despite his supporters' adulation, he could not throw off an unaccustomed melancholy. Seeing himself as the father of his people, he called the crime "patricide." The following week, attending a procession in Paris, he dressed entirely in black with a small bandage over his wound still evident on his grieving face. One of the lords near the king said,

"Sire, see how your people rejoice to see you!"

But Henry shook his head. "These are a people all right. If my worst enemy were now standing where I stand, they would shout even louder."

This brush with death frightened others as well as the king. His court officers cringed at the prospect of what would happen to France should the king die without an heir. The babble in the marketplace in every village throughout France concerned the fate of the country if Henry had been killed or should be killed, and everyone believed he had a solution. It was not long before Henry's long-time Huguenot minister and friend, Philippe Duplessis-Mornay, received the news of the personal attack. Duplessis-Mornay wrote to Henry:

As I see it, we have been close to shipwreck. I maintain that if we wish to assure the life of Your Majesty, it is necessary to urge your marriage. Immediately! When one sees the State will not die with your person, things will not have to be quite so vigilant. All other precautions are too weak against the devilish schemes of this world.

To Mornay, a brush with death such as the king had experienced should be the means of drawing him back to his Christian duties, and in this tone he continued:

God wishes to be heard when He speaks; he wishes us to feel it when He strikes us . . . I am sure that Your Majesty will profit from this affliction . . . thus converting yourself entirely to Him in turning from all that provokes His wrath. Sire, it is not as a censor that I speak, for I would not be so presumptuous, but with the zeal of a servant.

"Mornay is an old maid," Henry barked. "He reminds me of my mother with his tight morality. I'll bet he gobbles senna leaves for constipation like she did! He and Rosny will drive me mad." Yet Henry felt a twinge of guilt, criticizing his friend in this manner. After all, they had been childhood friends — for at least thirty years now — and he was sure of his minister's loyalty.

"Henry, you must not be disrespectful," Gabrielle warned.

"You, of all people, should not defend him. Mornay's strong moral sense cannot tolerate my relationship with you. Most likely he sees you as a siren with golden hair, riding at my side. He is just jealous of your lying beside me in my bed when I receive my ministers."

"I'm afraid many feel as he does."

"Damn them all!" he cursed but could not stop the thought that perhaps it was unseemly to treat his mistress as though she were his queen. The simplest solution to the whole problem would be to marry her and make her the queen. But he was afraid the time was not ripe for such a measure. At least the first step had been taken — Gabrielle had been released from her marriage vows. The next step was to ensure the legitimacy of their child, César.

"Sit down," he directed Gabrielle. "I want to read to you the act which I will send to Parliament."

When she had made herself quite comfortable, he began, ". . . since God has still not ordained that we should have children through our legitimate marriage, for the Queen our spouse has been separated from us for ten years, we have wished while awaiting children who can legitimately succeed to this crown, to have others who in their own place will be both worthy and honorable . . . for this reason, recognizing those graces and perfections of both body and soul which we have found in the person of our well-beloved Gabrielle d'Estrées, since we have sought for some years as someone whom we judged worthy of our friendship, and since this woman after long pursuit on our part and in recognition of our authority has condescended to obey us and to please us by giving us a son who presently bears the name of César Monsieur . . . we have resolved in affirming and recognizing him as our natural son to accord these letters of legitimization. We accord to him these letters, inasmuch as the stigma that it attached to the birth of our son excludes him from all hopes of succeeding to this our Crown, and all depending thereon, and also to our Kingdom of Navarre and all our other property . . . His state would be but a poor one, were it not for this, his legitimization . . ."

Gabrielle clapped her hands. "Oh, Henry, do you think they will agree?"

"Of course they will. France is beginning to love you as I do."

The implications of the document went far beyond the legitimacy of César to the more dangerous question of the king's marriage. It was obvious the children whom he said he was "awaiting" would not come from Marguerite. There was then, without doubt, the question of another marriage; this juxtaposed with his high praise of Gabrielle who "merits" his friendship, put his ministers in a state of grave uneasiness. The thought of Henry without an heir was unthinkable, but for many, the thought of Gabrielle as queen was even more unthinkable.

The issue of Spain refused to die. Mayenne continued to hold hands with them in the hope of changing the status quo in France, and Henry's allies, England and the Netherlands, had their own reasons for wanting war with Philip. Finally, against the counsel of many of his officers, on January 16, 1595, Henry declared war on Spain. He hoped not only to vanquish the Spanish from France for good, but also to rally his countrymen against a common enemy. He felt this would strengthen the identity of the nation. The beginning of the war was a disaster, as his soldiers, still battle weary, failed to rally to his cry.

One defeat followed another until, at Fontaine-Française he realized he was again fighting for his life and not just his solvency. The challenge and risk of battle spurred his cocky Gascon spirit and he carried off a victory where all odds had been against him. The unnatural melancholy which had dominated his personality since Châtel's blow disappeared with the smoke of battle. After Fontaine-Française, where he claimed the enemy "made an elephant out of a fly," he again sustained several discouraging stalemates. However, in early September, when he journeyed to Lyon, the people, who had grown weary of the demands of the League, received him with loud enthusiasm. Here he was greeted by a festive city at peace, and here Gabrielle awaited him. In the splendor and comfort of the archbishop's palace in the old medieval part of the city, on the west bank of the Saône river, he relaxed awhile with the feeling that the war was almost at an end.

PARIS and LYON

1595-1596

HENRY FELT HIS PERSONAL LIFE resembled the messy tangled twine which always resulted when, as a child, he attempted to weave Jacob's ladder with fumbling fingers. There seemed to be knots and snags at every step up the ladder. He knew his goals and thought he should be able to attain them. But some unexpected problem always seemed to impede him. He couldn't help but be reminded of Nostradamus's Oracle when these reverses occurred; could he really be "le grand Chyren?" For it seemed nothing was ever assured. He had hoped to gain official recognition from the sanctified body of the Vatican, but now negotiations seemed irreversibly stalled. Then surprisingly, he received an unexpected boost with the arrival of a letter from François Cardinal de Joyeuse* in Rome. Formerly, Joyeuse had represented the League at the Vatican, but like many, the Cardinal wrote, he now believed Henry to be the leader of the times. Joyeuse petitioned the king, promising his service and devoted attentions. Probably laying odds it would be more profitable to follow me, Henry thought, and so he is suddenly willing to change his colors.

Replying to Joyeuse on October 16, 1595, and assuring him of his gratitude, Henry told Joyeuse he could not render any more valuable service than to help in winning the pope over to the idea of his conversion. He reasoned it would be in the best interest of all Europe for the pope to acknowledge that Henry was a member of the Roman Catholic Church.

But at the very moment Henry was protesting his sincerity to Joyeuse, his actions on a second front seemed blatantly contradictory. He was simultaneously engaged in drawing up a petition to the Bishop

---

* François de Joyeuse (1562-1615) was a French churchman and politician. Anne de Joyeuse, killed at the battle of Coutras, was his elder brother.

of Paris, requesting the dissolution of his marriage with Marguerite de Valois. The Bishop was appalled, guessing that if word of this reached the pope, it might well end all other negotiations with the Vatican. The king's sudden and urgent interest in annulling his marriage could not have been more poorly timed. When Aubigné heard of the travesty, he hurried to speak to Henry, feeling for the moment as though he was dealing with a child. "Henry, you do not want France to go the way of the kingdom across the channel. If you fail now with the pope, your conversion will have been in vain."

"The pope! He expects us to think he is God!"

"So do you," Aubigné replied, laughing. "Surely you can postpone the question of your marriage until the primary issue with the church is settled. Besides, everyone is saying you are peopling France from the wrong side of the blanket, and that is bad enough. PLEASE, leave the marriage question alone for the moment."

"Very well, you nosy, meddling bastard, but get out of here!"

At least he gives in when he knows he is wrong, his minister reflected.

For Henry these were bitter days when, contrary to his own spontaneous spirit, he cautiously weighed and measured every act, only to find that whatever decision he came to, some faction would find a way of turning it against him. The Spanish continued their wily schemes, heaping calumny upon him and begging the pope to send troops against France. Yet the pope remained aloof to their pressures, though admitting reconciliation with France was in the interests of the Holy See. Joyeuse brought this to the attention of the Vatican daily, expecting his petitions would ingratiate him with the new king.

Henry mused about how he remained the man in the middle even though he had become a Catholic. The Vatican didn't trust him and neither did the Huguenots. Also, as he had expected, Queen Elizabeth I, being politically astute, was shocked and severely disappointed by his rejection of Protestantism. His conversion hadn't simplified things as he had expected, and the multiplicity of political factions failed to diminish in number and noise.

Finally, when Henry felt he could wait no longer, Joyeuse sent him some good news — the pope had agreed to recognize France and its king. Henry whirled Gabrielle around the room, giddy with his success. As they danced he sang a song of the troubadour Bernart de Ventadorn, finding the voice of the southwestern mountains remained the best expression of joy for him.

Gabrielle laughed as they turned. "Dancing never has been your favorite pastime, *chéri*. You must be delirious to behave like this."

"I am, I am, my darling. Now old Mayenne will cave in, I am sure. The League will not dare oppose me now that the pope accepts me." He even hopped on the dance floor.

"I don't like to add vinegar to your sauce, Henry, but your Huguenots won't be so happy about the papal absolution, will they?" Gabrielle asked with a frown.

"Don't worry, my pretty one. We can handle them," he cheerfully replied. "The important thing is that the League's fire is finally extinguished."

When Dijon fell to the king in the summer of 1595, Mayenne had his back to the wall. His army was in disarray and he had nowhere to turn for support. So, when news of the king's reconciliation with Rome reached France, Henry's assessment was justified; Mayenne had no choice now but to bow to the king. In late January of 1596 his old enemy arrived at Gabrielle's castle of Montceaux on the Marne for a personal reconciliation. Mayenne ceremoniously condemned the arrogance of the Spaniards and the papal cat-and-mouse games, and then signed a preliminary peace treaty with Henri IV. Henry's counselors chafed at the amount Mayenne was paid to swear his peace, but for the king, it meant good riddance. With these two antagonists finally tamed, Henry felt he could breathe more easily. However, it was only to be a short idyll. Word soon reached him that the city of Cambrai was besieged by the redoubtable Spanish general, Count de Fuentes. Despite his seventy years, the Spaniard had never lost his military flair, and Henry had great respect for his reputation. But as he had once written to Gabrielle, "There is no man so deaf as he who does not wish to hear," and in the soft September air of Lyon, the king put aside the persistent vigilance of his mortal enemy in Madrid, the pleas for help from his beleaguered towns, the strident demands of the Paris bourgeoisie, and narrowed his world to Gabrielle and the pleasures of love.

Cambrai begged for help; messengers arrived at the arch Episcopal palace with their reports of imminent disaster, but the king, though assuring them of his help, dallied, the cloud of passion once more fogging his judgment. Henry finally had to face the extent of his difficulty when his treasurer made the state of his finances clear to him. At first glance, Gabrielle was the only one who could and would remedy the king's poverty. But her sacrifices were not enough. In April 1596, Henry wrote to Rosny:

> I would like to tell you of the state in which I find myself, which is such that I am facing the enemy but do not have a horse on which I can fight nor a full suit of armor to put on my back; my shirts are all torn, my doublets out-at-elbow; my saucepan is often empty, and for days I have been eating where I may, my butlers saying they have nothing to serve at my table, all this because I have had no money for six months. So ponder well if I deserve to be treated in such a way; whether I must longer allow the financiers and treasurers to make me die of hunger while they keep their own tables dainty and well served; whether my house should be in such need while theirs are in wealth and plenty, and whether you are not surely obliged to help my loyalty as I pray you.

On September 24 Henry finally left Lyon for Paris, knowing he had neither men nor money to buy men. He must first go to Parliament and present his need for the funds with which to continue the war. A week later, with the amorous days of Lyon far behind him, he presented himself in the hall of the Paris Parliament, again the leader and a man of decisive action, the man who could assess facts and face them.

> I have come to speak to you not in royal robes or with a sword and cape like my predecessors, but dressed like a father of a family, in a doublet. My predecessors gave you words; I, with my gray jacket, will give you deeds. I am gray outside, but you will find me gold within.

Sensing he had captivated his audience with his colorful language, Henry continued in a brusquer manner:

> I have come in haste on the advice of my counselors who tell me my presence is needed here. So far I have done well in this war, God has given me strength over our enemies, but now there is grave danger in the north.

Volunteer soldiers will never be enough; I must have mercenaries and for that I must have money. The Swiss are waiting at the Marne, but they will not cross without being paid. Everything is going well. I came at a walk and will return at a gallop. The only thing lacking is money. I have lost my best horses and must get others for the journey.

But Henry had waited too long in Lyon, enjoying the luxury of his mistress's caresses. He left Paris on October 8 with his gold, but when he reached Cambrai, it had fallen. Elizabeth I may have been angry with Henry over his conversion, but she had the sense to know that not to help him now with the Spanish incursion on French soil would also endanger England. Loyal to the Protestant cause and not wanting to halt the spread of Catholic Spanish power, she sent Essex to the continent to effect the fall of La Fère for the French in November.

CHATEAU DE FOLEMBRAY,
PARIS, and AMIENS

1596-1597

EVERYTHING GABRIELLE TOUCHED prospered. Her father, her brothers, and her sisters were living in greater luxury than they had ever known; and she indulged as never before in dreaming of marriage to the King of France. She basked in Henry's favor even more when she gave birth to a second child, Catherine Henriette, on November 11, 1596. Her fertility matched her beauty and Henry was enchanted.

In December Henri IV traveled to the château de Folembray, originally built by François I, that had been abandoned during the long years of civil war. Bats and owls haunted the chimneys and turrets, and it seemed an odd place to choose for his forty-second birthday celebration. Even stranger was the company assembled there. But for Henry it prompted recollections of his youthful days playing among the stone circular walls at Pau as he now watched his son, César, happily exploring the dark nooks of the old castle. Gabrielle flitted around him solicitously, like a doting wife of many years, and he relaxed as he had not done in years.

Catherine de Bourbon also arrived for the festivities, having persuaded Corisande to take part as well. She brought her friend eight large pearls she had recently purchased in Bordeaux, and Corisande warmly embraced her for such a thoughtful gift. For more than three weeks this strange ménage continued. The king spent most of his days in the forest of Coucy hunting deer, while Catherine and Corisande tiptoed awkwardly and suspiciously around Gabrielle or sat tensely before the fireplace in the dark, barren great hall of the château. Corisande attempted to lessen her frustration by talking to Catherine.

"It doesn't seem fair," she mourned. "Gabrielle is too much of a child to offer him anything beyond her body. And he is too complicated a man to be satisfied by such a shallow passion as she can give."

"It is her self assurance and youth which attracts him," Catherine observed. "His optimism constantly needs to be fed by the exuberance and hope of the young. You know, Corisande, it is not that Henry runs from pain, but I think he seeks renewal and affirmation in the eyes of a younger woman."

"You are always generous and sweet, Catherine. But I cannot be so passive. I could have given him the love he needed to ease whatever pain he met; I could have loved him through whatever dangers he encountered. He wanted me to love him, but he was unwilling to give himself." She halted and tears trickled silently down her cheeks. She recalled the suffering she had known, widowed young by the violent death of her husband, living through war, fleeing from a besieged city, waiting for her lover who didn't come. She gathered herself and continued, "I have wanted to see Henry for many years now and finally accepted the fact that if I saw him, it must be with his new mistress at his side. I thought if I saw them together, my affair with Henry would finally end for me. As if that isn't bad enough, my old enemy, Aubigné, is here as well and rarely leaves his master's side. He has taken up his old game of baiting me; even accusing me of playing the part of Circe. It is Gabrielle who is Circe!"

"For him, any mistress is a scandal," Catherine commented. "Just ignore his barbs."

Corisande blinked back her tears with stoic fortitude. She compared her graying hair and heavier body with the fresh, fecund body of the lovely Gabrielle. How she resented the way his mistress always linked her fingers in Henry's rough hand in front of everyone. At these difficult moments she turned her thoughts to her son Antonin and her daughter Catherine. Both were a comfort to her. She followed Antonin's successful military career with pride — indeed, he appeared to be consistently recognized with favor by the monarch — and rejoiced in the brilliant marriage she had secured for her daughter Catherine. She could enjoy love's strong emotions in another guise.

Catherine understood Corisande's grief from personal experience. She too had fallen deeply in love but it had been snatched from her embrace. When she smiled at her friend, it looked more like a grimace. "It seems, dear Corisande, our love is to be wasted like all the blood on the battlefields of France. I must marry wherever my brother's interests dictate — the King of Scotland, who would have given Henry soldiers and money for my hand, the duc de Savoy, the duc de Lorraine — at various diplomatic junctures they have all been mentioned."

"I once thought love was eternal," Corisande said, "but Folembray's crumbling structure and barren halls demonstrate all too poignantly the harsh impact of time."

"Windows and gables will crumble, but true feelings will not," Catherine said with authority, squaring her shoulders against the melancholy echo of their conversation.

Corisande shrugged. "I am not sure we are not the stupid ones by keeping faith with lovers who do not merit such constancy and fortitude — for lovers who are not willing to make the sacrifices marriage demands."

Corisande was to have only one moment alone with Henry. The next afternoon she heard a confident knock on her door.

"Come in, please," she called.

Henry strode in and took her in his arms, giving her a fond kiss on the cheek.

"You are looking well, Corisande. It is good of you to join my birthday celebration. I believe you have fared time's erosion better than I."

Shaken by his touch but pleased to have him with her, she smiled. "You look good to me, Henry."

Her eye caressed his worn cheek and she would have liked to touch his hair. She barely heard him as he reminisced about their days at Hagetmau, so lost was she in his physical presence. " . . . so pretty," he was saying, "compared to this stark castle." But his next words seized her attention.

"I loved you too early, Corisande, when I had too many battles yet to be fought. Gabrielle hasn't loved me as you did, I don't think. You perhaps believe me imperceptive, but I understand that you loved Henry the man and she loves Henry the King."

"It is a comfort, Henry, that you realize that. But she is perhaps braver than I; she has defied all conventions to be with you."

"That is true. You were too proud to follow me across France, from battle to battle. Why couldn't you do that, Corisande?"

"Call it pride if you must but I don't regret it. I couldn't do otherwise. I would never have been happy as the king's mistress. You may think I am not happy now, but at least I am not ashamed of my behavior. And I am pleased to see you King at last. Perhaps France is your true mistress."

"Perhaps, *chérie*. I always listen carefully to your wise words. I still have much to do for France. The country is like an apothecary shop, full of sweet things and pleasant odors but also full of poisons and foul smells."

"And you are the only one who can administer the proper restorative tonic to the country," she observed. "I have always believed that."

"I hope you are right. You were always an angel to me, and I am glad you are here to celebrate with us."

Suddenly it seemed they had nothing more to say to one another. He kissed her again and left.

The royal party returned to Paris not to do business, it appeared, but to amuse themselves. Henry clasped Gabrielle's waist and whirled her around the ballroom floor. With an incessant round of parties and balls, it was often daybreak when the merry couple returned to the Louvre. Henry had no time to listen when his counselors brought him the pasquinades appearing daily in the Paris streets. Rosny tapped Henry's shoulder and interrupted the dance, handing him a scurrilous pamphlet entitled, "The Life and Morals of Henri IV."

"They are calling you a libertine, Sire."

Henry laughed. "Let them. They should be able to say what they like, don't you think, Rosny?"

Too distressed by what he saw happening to his king, Rosny didn't answer. Henry had forgotten France again and his only desire was to please his mistress. Why did he have to be so easily manipulated by women?

On March 13 the king was dancing once more when a courier, his boots and cloak covered with a heavy coating of dust, rudely shattered the party with his arrival. The man dropped to one knee before Henry. Sensing a crisis, the musicians stopped the pavanne mid-beat. Henry broke the seal and ripped open the message.

"Spain," he announced to the entire company, "has launched a surprise attack on Amiens."

Gabrielle immediately broke into tears. Only the sound of her sobs broke the silence until Henry interrupted her wailing. "I have played the king long enough! It is time I returned to the King of Navarre!"

He had failed. That he knew in a flash. It was not enough to be called king. How could he ever have thought so? Comparing his own recent behavior to that of Henri III, he was mortified. But perhaps he could save the situation. No one moved. No one dared speak. Henry turned to his weeping mistress and said, "Gabrielle, we must put off our finery!"

Henry spent the rest of the night rallying his troops and shortly before dawn, rode north toward Amiens. Witnesses reported there had been no battle, scarcely any bloodshed. The Spaniards had walked in and taken all they could have hoped for. It was a significant victory for the Spanish, and French morale plummeted to its lowest level since the siege of Paris. Silently watching Henry's departure, the citizens wondered if their king had engaged in more battles and fewer balls, this tragedy might have been averted. He had to face the brutal truth of an empty royal treasury, and again begged Gabrielle to open her strongboxes. She gave him every penny of ready cash she possessed, a total of fifty thousand *écus*.

Henry reached Picquigny between Amiens and Abbeville a week later. An aide wrote to Paris, "The King has enough courage for everyone, but unless we are helped by men and money and munitions, things will go very badly."

Indeed, conditions were far worse than he had expected — no food, no money, and no help for the sick and wounded, and there was already the threat of mass desertions. Having always taken personal responsibility, now, without apology, he expended his anger and frustration on those whom he had always considered his friends, "Sancy,* you and the Maréchal de Bouillon** advised this war, and your ill-starred advice is likely to be the ruin of France."

Even Biron,*** who had once saved the King's life, did not go unscathed, as Henry remarked caustically in front of him, "It is strange that whenever I am not present in person, things proceed either with little fortune or much negligence."

The king perceived immediately that his cause was hopeless with the provisions at hand. Without a rest, he turned right around and headed back to Paris where he would blame the Parlement for his lack of funds, struggling to hold himself upright in the saddle and cursing his body for becoming weak during his recent days of revelry. Aubigné watched this sorry sight, but he knew it would be hopeless to try and stop the monarch once he was on his chosen course.

On April 12, when the King arrived in the capital, he wrote to the Venetian ambassador:

> I am in such a state that I am on the road to ruin and cannot see the remedy, and if my dearest friends and confederates do not help me, who will?. . . My dear people are so absolutely ruined that I can look for no help from them. Everything is in such decay that the whole world sees it only too well.

Next he called upon the wealthy men of France to hear his plea:

> Gentlemen, it is not care of my health alone that has recalled me from the frontier, but that I may also call upon each one of you to think of the straits we are in, knowing that no one could better, or more forcibly put the evil before you and obtain the remedy. You, in your goodness, last year succored the poor, the infirm, and the suffering of your towns. I come to ask

*Nicolas Harlay, seigneur de Sancy (1546–1629) was a French soldier and diplomat.
**Henri de la Tour d'Auvergne (1555-1623) was Maréchal de France and became the duc de Bouillon by marriage.
***Charles de Gontaut, duc de Biron, was made Maréchal de France in 1592, but was executed in 1602 for plotting with the Spanish to assassinate Henri IV.

for alms for those whom I have left at the frontier. You have helped those who were in the streets, or in houses seated by the fireside. I ask for alms for those who are in active service, and who are serving day and night risking their lives so that you may live in peace.

That night he collapsed. The royal physicians announced his condition was not serious, but the people of Paris were alarmed. Gabrielle refused to leave his side, and a small bed was carried for her into the king's bedchamber and placed at the foot of the canopied four-poster.

Henry's appeal had been touching, yet the magistrates met with indifference when they tried to raise money. The king remained at the royal château at St.-Germain until the end of May, his enforced rest giving him an opportunity to reflect on the ills of the nation. Amiens was in the hands of the Spanish, and he was penniless. He had been too late at Rouen and Cambrai. But he would not give up; he would win back Amiens to prove to his people that their faith in him was merited or he would die trying. But how?

He called upon Rosny, who had an uncanny ability to turn centimes into francs. Rosny suggested a tax on the land of all the nobles who owned property, a revolutionary idea because there had never been a property tax before. The nobility balked as could be expected, but Rosny proved to be a tough enforcer of his clever law. Money began to trickle into the treasury.

Although chafing to be on the battlefield, Henry appreciated the time with Gabrielle. Afternoons in the garden with the children became a mutual habit.

"My love for you is greater than ever," he told her. "You have demonstrated a devotion for me that no one else could equal. You have sacrificed your fortune, placed your jewels in jeopardy, collected money for me, and nursed me when I was ill. How can I ever thank you?"

"That is easy, *chéri*. You must let me return with you to Amiens. I can see you truly need me now."

"Perhaps I do, my love. But I cannot allow you to share the danger of this siege. I would never forgive myself if you were harmed. And you have César and Henriette here."

"I insist," the woman beside him replied.

Reflecting on the remarkable change in Gabrielle's character, Henry was amazed. She who had loved luxury and who had refused to travel when the sun was not shining, now, deliberately and of her own free will, was begging to be lodged in a draughty tent. When Henry returned to Amiens, Gabrielle accompanied him. A heavy spring snow fell daily and the roof of the tent sagged, but his mistress made no complaint.

Throughout the summer Henry carried on the siege of Amiens, winning back the loyalty of his soldiers and reviving the hopes of his people by his determination and vigor. Determined to expel Spain from French land, he often led the attack and admitted to Aubigné, "I would rather lose my crown than be branded a coward."

"You are just a daredevil at heart," his minister replied.

By the end of August it was apparent the Spanish would not hold out much longer. On September 15 they acknowledged their defeat and ten days later formally withdrew from Amiens. Elated, Henry, bearing little resemblance to the dark taciturn figure who had ridden out of Paris in June, watched and applauded the retreat.

Success, as always, was the magic formula which drew people to their leader, and from all sides congratulations poured in. Even Margot wrote from Usson and praised God "For the happy victory it has pleased Him to give Your Majesty. I must express the great joy with which I received the welcome news."

From Rome, d'Ossat* assured the king that "Victory will help French affairs in Rome."

But it was to Corisande that Henry wrote on the day after retaking Amiens: "Madame, I well recognize that you have served me greatly. Also, I well know that your presence was most necessary." He went on, thanking her for the continuing gallant service of her son. She would be glad to read that, he knew.

Henry entered Paris once again triumphantly. A few months earlier L'Estoile, the royal historian, had written, "All Europe hangs on the outcome of this siege." He had not exaggerated, for the question of peace depended in large measure on whether Henry could make good his promise that he would rout the Spaniards from Amiens. Now his enthusiastic people made the streets almost impassable, and Henry found it difficult to contain his joy. Mounted on his elaborately bridled charger, Henry once more was the master of men and events. He had saved his state and in celebration wore parade armor of a lustrous blue and gold surface with a red silk lining and gilt rivet heads of heraldic design. He had learned that pageantry helped engage his

* French diplomat in Rome.

people. He could no longer wear the garb of a peasant from Navarre.

With the glorious sound of the cheering crowd drumming in his ears, he reflected upon his achievements. He had won a crown despite the fierce opposition, he had founded a Bourbon dynasty, ended religious war, expelled a foreign invader, thereby securing his country's boundaries; he had made at least a temporary peace between Catholic and Protestant, and in addition, he had taken the first step toward establishing the frontiers of France. For nearly half a century, war had meant only humiliation for France; she had grown accustomed to being beaten in the field, invaded and occupied, or rent by sordid struggles within herself. Now she had faced her foes abroad as an equal and overcome them.

Henri IV had given his country a taste of glory. This heady tonic brought new self-confidence and renewed energy, and he now wanted to prove he was a ruler who could bring prosperity as well as victory. He had so many plans to improve his people's welfare — plans for roads, agriculture, and artisanry. His eagerness to put these projects in place mirrored his passion elsewhere. And perhaps once his people accepted him, the ever-elusive spirit of tolerance he sought for his people would be disseminated as well. He had rid the country of the foreign invader; now could he eradicate religious bigotry and hatred?

NANTES

1597-1598

WITH PITIFUL OBSTINACY CATHERINE held to her love for Soissons. Yet she still genuinely loved her brother, whom she addressed as "my good and worthy King." Now an eccentric old maid over forty, she also clung stubbornly to her Protestant faith and when she was in Paris, she enabled Huguenot courtiers to hold services in the Louvre. Considered an odd, frustrated person as well as a tiresome, sickly, bluestocking by most people at court, she was tolerated because she was the king's sister. Indeed, her position held great respect in Béarn and Navarre. Salic Law barred her from the French crown, but she was permitted to succeed Henri as sovereign in her home provinces.

In March 1597, Henry asked her to come and see him in order to discuss her marriage plans once again. When she appeared, he noticed how ill dressed and strangely bejeweled she was.

"Catherine, we can not continue this foolishness any longer," he said, trying to project a moderate tone. "You are my only sister, the sister of the King of France. You must marry where it is important to the kingdom."

"I would rather remain unmarried than marry someone I don't love."

She is the most obstinate woman, I know, Henry thought. "Catherine, you must realize that is impossible for you. I have chosen the duc de Bar to be your husband. He is heir to Charles III of Lorraine and a most eligible prince politically. Your love for Soissons cannot be more important than this."

For once Catherine's anger flared, conquering her natural instinct for sweetness and amiability. "Henry, I do not doubt your brilliant intellectual qualities, but your heart is tyrannized by your senses and hardened by immense egotism. Why can you not think of my feelings in this matter?"

Henry was astounded. She had never spoken to him so harshly, and more painful still, she had struck a kernel of truth in her words. "I will tolerate no more disagreement, Catherine," he replied. "I will inform you later of the date of the marriage contract."

Catherine turned and left, too miserable to reply. Whatever he ordered, she knew she must obey.

Determined to insure stability at home, Henry decided the most certain way to secure peace would be to give the Huguenots more confidence in their right to worship. Rosny was fast becoming his most trusted counselor despite his old maid tendencies, and he decided to test his newest idea on him.

"I would like to appoint trusted Protestant followers to positions of responsibility. Do you approve?"

"Will you make an announcement of this new policy?"

"No, why should I?" Henry asked, somewhat irritated.

"You know both the Huguenots and the Catholics are going to remain dissatisfied. The bigots on one side are as greedy for power as their counterparts on the other, and neither will be content until their religious foes are driven out of France."

"They will soon realize I will not stand for that attitude. I am determined to never allow a repetition of the St. Bartholomew's Day Massacre. You know as well as I, Rosny, that every ruler makes religion an excuse for extending their power. Ever since the Treaty of Augsburg in 1555, when I was only two years old, every authorized ruler had the right to impose his chosen religion on his subjects. That is part of the problem today."

"I hope your role of mediator will convince them," Rosny responded, "but I fear it will only cause apprehension in both groups."

Henry began his usual pacing. "You are probably right that neither faction will be satisfied. That is the nature of all of us, is it not?

But there must be some compromise we can all live with and I must do something now. My old Gascon philosopher friend Michel de Montaigne was the first to make me aware of the idea of tolerance, and my experience has taught me how right he was. I respect everyone's right to opinions arrived at by honest reflection based on his individual experience."

"That's all very interesting, Sire, but how do you plan to proceed?" Rosny inquired, truly curious. "Your boyhood Huguenot friends are furious with you for not placing more of them in positions of power."

"I will enlist the help of Gabrielle and Catherine," Henry declared with enthusiasm. Warming to his theme, he waved his hands in generous gestures. "Gabrielle will attempt to convince the Catholic lords to accept the inevitable with good grace and Catherine will urge the Huguenots to demand less for the time being."

"And I wish you, and all of us, luck," Rosny grumbled.

Gabrielle remained close by, receiving visitors with Henry as though she were queen. Sir Robert Cecil, Queen Elizabeth's Secretary of State, a grave hunchback who was a coldly accurate judge of humanity, was favorably impressed when he saw her in March. He wrote to his sovereign, "She is great with child, and truly a fair and delicate woman. I stayed little with her; and yet she was very well spoken and very courteous." In mid-April 1598 she gave birth to their third child and second son, whom they named Alexandre.

For a short while Henry was encouraged, since not one prominent Huguenot deserted him. Through the autumn of 1597 and the winter of 1598, he worked, reasoned, and wrote, resulting in the promulgation of the Edict of Nantes. Because hatreds remained intense, it was the best compromise he and his advisers could work out. Careful to grant rights to the Huguenots while still deferring to the Catholics, he hoped to present the rules in such minute detail that there would be little or no room for argument. Feeling tremendous pride and an incredible sense of accomplishment, he wrote into law that every Huguenot, in every bailiwick, was granted the right to perform acts of worship, without hindrance.

Having come to Nantes for the birth of the child, Henry signed the edict there. How Henry wished Michel de Montaigne were alive to share his joy when he heard the news. Unlike his philosopher friend, who believed tolerance to be a fundamental principle of good and right behavior, Henry viewed it primarily as a necessary maneuver to preserve France. For him it was as much a matter of political expediency and a means to end the crushing religious wars. Tolerance was becoming his religion, the pragmatic and sensible idea he was willing to proselytize about, for only with the end of hostilities would he be able to rebuild France from within and protect her from outside aggression.

Henry's desire was to rule over a country at peace. Reading aloud to the Town Council the details of the agreement, Henry hoped the tenets would become the true legal and theological end of forty years of civil war:

> The royal treasury is authorized to pay the wages of Protestant clergymen, as it does those of Catholic clerics; the King specifically authorizes Huguenot ministers to receive donations and bequests. On the other hand, Calvinist worship is forbidden in those ancient towns of the League that had stipulated for its exclusion in the treaties of peace and submission they had formerly signed with the King.

Freedom of worship was also forbidden in such towns where there were no Protestants. For all practical purposes the last clause was meaningless as Henry had granted Huguenots the right to hold worship services wherever they wished, provided they applied to him. One of the most important clauses of the edict, Henry explained, ordered that the Parliaments of all cities and towns be reorganized on a new basis, in which Protestants would be granted equal representation and thus be assured of the administration of impartial justice.

The edict continued:

> Finally, members of the Reformed Church are declared capable of acting in every civil capacity and most military capacities. Only the posts of Constable, Grand Marshal of the Army, Grand Admiral of the Navy and a handful of lesser key positions are reserved for the Catholics.

The Catholics promptly objected to the edict in full, and Henry feared his kingdom would be torn apart once again. Then, in a surprise move, Catholic leaders asked for an audience with Gabrielle, who seemed to have gained new confidence with her new babe in her arms. She explained to them, "I know full well what is the King's wish with regard to the Edict of Nantes, and he will not do otherwise. He will accept no compromise, and defeat is unknown to him. Nor do I myself see any good reason for wishing to prevent those of the Reformed religion, who have been good servants to the king, from entering into the States and other Parliaments, seeing as he allowed this right to other Leaguers, who had taken arms against His Majesty."

For once, Rosny and Aubigné kept their peace.

Thereafter, the king heard no more opposition from the Catholics, and when the document was presented to the Parlement de Paris, it was registered by unanimous vote. Henry felt the exhilaration of major achievement; here was the testament to the religious peace he had been fighting for. Perhaps his belief in tolerance and his example of tolerance had been necessary to end the civil wars and make it possible for the country to start anew.

PARIS

1598-1599

SPRING ARRIVED ON SCHEDULE and the king chafed to marry his mistress. He wanted no other for his queen. And how could his subjects object? Gabrielle had helped him at Amiens and had been indispensable in assuring the success of the Edict of Nantes. In addition, her womb had proven fruitful. The first vital step toward achieving this goal would be to obtain a divorce from Margot, who hung on in his life like a rotten tooth. Royal messengers began making frequent journeys to Usson.

Two years earlier Marguerite had written to Gabrielle, proffering her friendship and her devotion. Henry remembered the letter and his hope kindled. She had said:

> Please accept my assurance — and be so good as to convey it to the King — that my desires are completely conformed to his will and to yours . . . I hope you will accept what I have spoken so freely to one whom I hope to have as my sister and whom I honor and esteem second only to the King himself.

When they had received this missive, it had been somewhat of a mystery as to what she was up to. Most likely, she aspired to remain in his good graces, he decided. Now Henry learned his wife would not be adverse to a divorce if he would satisfy her creditors and increase her allowance. Most important to her, however, was the freedom to return to Paris. For this and this only, it seemed, would she swallow her pride. Not wanting to be mean, he readily agreed, but required in return that the queen also make certain concessions. Margot, appearing to keep the momentum alive, in early November announced that she, Queen Marguerite de Valois, had given a magnificent gift to Gabrielle: the duchy of Etampes.

Etampes was poor and its revenues small, but it was, nevertheless, a duchy and Gabrielle would be entitled to add the name duchesse d'Etampes to her string of titles. Henry stayed on in Nantes for a while longer, even heating the linen for his baby by the fire with his own hands while Gabrielle looked on.

"Part of your power over me must come from your ability to bring me the joys of home and family," he said.

She laughed. "You look like a good bourgeois father. I remember when I first saw you. You stank more than the peasants and I thought you must be crazy. Now you have made me love you! Who would guess, seeing you now, that you had just issued an edict which will affect an entire country?"

"Sometimes I think I prefer doing this. I never have to doubt my children's love as I do that of the adults in whom I place my trust," he grumbled.

"I hope you do not include me in such a dubious group."

"I wish I did not, but in truth, I don't know if I can trust anyone anymore. But I have been melancholy lately and so have taken the tonics the doctors prescribed. They don't understand that nothing does me more good than the sight of you, the one remedy for all my sadness."

Henry continued to be overjoyed with this third addition to their family and sent her a spate of letters in his graceful hand with an exuberant flourish. He wrote, "What a joyful afternoon I spent with my children. You have given me so much happiness."

This mood only urged Henry to further his campaign to make Gabrielle his queen. She had been given increasingly greater rank, becoming first marquise de Montceaux, then duchesse de Beaufort, then duchesse d'Etampes, and finally *pairesse* de France, in preparation for the ultimate honor. César's birth had been greeted by a *Te Deum*, as though he were of royal descent; though just a boy, he had been affianced to a noble's daughter and created a duke with a title.

With each orchestrated coup Henry became more and more certain of his decision. Gabrielle would make a beautiful queen, a fertile queen, and César, whom everyone said resembled him, would make the perfect dauphin. Rosny continuously warned him that César's legal position as heir to the throne was just as doubtful as that of his younger brother. Indeed, César had been born of a double adultery since at Cesar's birth, Gabrielle had still been Liancourt's wife. This irritated Henry beyond belief, and he simply chose to ignore his ministers.

Encouraged, Gabrielle began to flaunt her conviction that she would become Queen of France in a short time, and the court treated her as though she had already mounted the throne. When Henry encouraged this behavior by assigning a permanent detail of royal household troops to guard her, she was delighted, and she carefully appeared in public only with a full escort. In November 1598, Gabrielle took the only step short of the marriage remaining — she moved into the official bedchamber at the Louvre reserved for the queen.

Gabrielle had been around court long enough to learn the customs decreed appropriate for the Queen of France. In fact, she made it a point to know the proper etiquette and ordered it to be observed. At first it was just a family affair; her sisters were in attendance on her, and when she arose in the morning they curtsied and dressed her in her underclothes. It seemed like they were in a play. But soon, great ladies vied with one another for the privilege of fastening her gowns, combing her hair, and applying rouge to her cheeks.

The king's ménage with Gabrielle was now on a permanent basis, yet she knew he still dallied with other women occasionally. However, she dared not be angry or complain. Had not Henry given her everything? And only this morning she had heard Aubigné refer to the court as "the court of the beautiful Gabrielle." He had been joking, but it was true. Her family, however, frustrated her complete enjoyment of her circumstances.

Diane told her, "I heard a bystander ask your name and a royal archer loudly answered, 'That's no one, only the king's whore.' "

"You are just making up a spiteful story because you are jealous!" Gabrielle spat back at her sister.

"And you are fast becoming insufferable with your airs!"

Gabrielle was seen everywhere with the king, who strode through Paris with his mistress at his side. He took her along for the hunt, and caressed her before all the world. They rode together hand in hand, she resplendent in her favorite green, her golden hair studded with diamonds. And of course, it was she who presided over every ball and court function.

The people loved this king who disliked pomp and finery, who occasionally was careless to the point of leaving his doublet half unbuttoned, his breeches hanging down, his aiguillette unfastened, and his stockings framed around his heels. However, it soon became all too obvious that this personal neglect did not extend to his mistress, whom he dressed like a queen. Her exquisite gowns were often decorated with floral motifs. One of the great embroiderers of the time, Robin, drew and colored his models in the king's garden under the guidance of a horticulturist. Ironically, on occasion she was waited on at dinner by the young duchesse de Guise, who might have been queen herself, had the League triumphed.

A reaction to the extravagant fashions of Henri III, as well as Henri IV's rougher style, had created a marked return to simplicity. Charitable societies that raised money to help the destitute and the sick were organized by religious bodies. Some of Henry's contemporaries took the view that the luxury trade was an important factor of industrial prosperity, but the country as a whole supported the royal proclamations against sartorial excess. Henry seemed to support both sides; while ratifying laws obstructing the import of gold and silver fabrics from abroad, he appeared blind to the contradiction in his generous behavior where Gabrielle was concerned. When the baptism of their second son, Alexandre de Vendôme, was due, Gabrielle insisted that it be performed with honors reserved for a Son of France. Rosny flatly refused to pay for the festivities on the grounds that he was NOT a "Son of France." Gabrielle respected Rosny despite her dislike for him, but now she felt threatened.

"He is nothing but a lackey and a bureaucrat," she wailed to Henry. "What right has he to refuse you money?"

"His advice has always been blunt but excellent, Gabrielle. Would you please stop your weeping. It is getting on my nerves."

"Oh, Henry, he is a quarrelsome man with a coxcomb's pride! His vile manners have won him a host of foes to whom he is malicious and vindictive."

"That may be true," Henry replied, "but where my interests are involved, he has always been indefatigably and unshakably loyal. During the war with Spain he was able to wring desperately needed funds out of the treasury in the teeth of corrupt officials."

"Well, I think he is ludicrous and eccentric and he won't spend a *sou* on happiness."

There was some truth in her accusation, Henry knew. He understood that Rosny was singularly unappealing in his private life, even avaricious to the extent that he jilted his fiancée, whom he loved, to marry a richer girl. He had been able to amass a considerable fortune in the wars by small economies and systematic plunder, supplemented by shrewd dealings. He hid his baldness by sporting extraordinary headgear, and all the court joked about his follies, one of which was dancing. Each evening a man named Le Roche, valet of the chamber to the king, played the dances of the day while M. de Rosny danced them by himself, wearing hats, each more extravagant than the other, in front of a few privileged spectators. Henry had no difficulty ignoring this bizarre behavior when he received such valuable service.

Henry's extended silence caused Gabrielle to foresee a glimmer of hope. She dared to persevere. "But Henry, Alexandre is your son."

"Hush, Gabrielle. I would prefer to lose ten mistresses than one servant like Rosny."

Gabrielle blanched and said no more.

Henry immediately regretted his harsh words. Feeling he had perhaps gone too far, he chose this moment to cheer her up. He would always choose to placate rather than enjoin battle.

"I have asked the pope for an annulment of my marriage with Marguerite," he announced.

Gabrielle gasped with pleasure and threw her arms around his neck. "And? What has happened?"

"Margot is still residing at the château d'Usson in the Auvergne," Henry continued, "in disreputable retirement after many picaresque and lecherous adventures. I'm sure you have heard the stories of how she has wandered the roads with strange lovers and been captured by bandits. She has turned fat, I'm told, having added the vices of the table to those of the bed. In fact, I must say, she is the worst of wives!" Henry chuckled.

"I've heard some say that in the first terrible months of her exile she fell prey to a despair so black, she lost the desire to live," Gabrielle commented. "It makes me shiver to think of her. Of course I want you to divorce her, but I feel sorry for her now."

"I suppose the stories of her gloom might be true. But ultimately she chose life rather than death — even life under duress, which meant taking lovers from amongst her servants." He laughed harshly. "Despite the hardships, she has outlived both her mother and her brothers."

"It is hard to believe she is your wife — forgotten by the court which once proclaimed her 'a goddess from heaven rather than a creature of earth,' " Gabrielle mused. "Before I ever knew anything of royal life, she seemed to live in a fairy tale."

"Courts are fickle places, my pet."

Henry found delight in comforting his mistress. Her petal-smooth skin never failed to arouse him, and he crushed her under him like a flower under foot.

Gabrielle had lost her battle with Rosny, but normally her power over the king was complete. When he resisted her wishes she would weep and faint. When he objected to making her father master-general of the ordnance, she threatened to leave him and enter a convent. Her father became master-general. But despite Rosny's plainspoken threats, the King was determined to marry her.

Rosny's beard bobbled when he warned him, "Most certainly marriage to Gabrielle will be sufficient to cause an uprising among your nobility, Sire."

At that moment Aubigné burst in unannounced. "Henry, Gabrielle's coach has been involved in an accident."

Henry trembled and turned pale, something he never did in battle. "Where? We must go at once. Hurry!"

"I believe she is being brought on a litter to the Hôtel-Dieu."

"*Oh, mon Dieu*, is she so gravely injured as that?"

"I do not know. But do not worry yet. All may be well." But his words were lost on the panicked king. Rosny, watching them, understood he was fighting a losing battle regarding the proposed marriage.

When Henry reached the Hôtel-Dieu on the Ile de la Cité, he found Gabrielle propped up in bed drinking tea. The hospital, founded in the seventh century, was built of stone which kept the rooms cool even in the summer's heat. The musty smell of age, however, seeped from the stone's pores.

"Thank God, my love. You are not badly hurt?"

"No, but terribly frightened." He noticed the teacup began to rattle in its saucer. "The carriage overturned when a dog frightened the horses. Most providentially, a low wall prevented us from turning over completely."

"Oh, then all is well," Henry sighed. Sitting on her bed, he stroked her hand while the nurses tittered in the corner. To see the king and the beautiful Gabrielle in their ward would provide them with a story for a lifetime.

Toward the end of June, the pope's representative summed up the marriage conundrum graphically, writing:

> His Most Christian Majesty is more determined than ever to procure the dissolution of his marriage by the Holy See, and all his actions are directed toward this end. I have been warned that he will speak to me about this . . . No one dares speak or give him contrary advice. Monsieur de Sancy, who has frequently and courageously expressed himself, for he wished to reconcile the King with his present wife, the Queen, has lost much and is presently in disgrace.

Henry made it clear to his ministers that they could talk ad infinitum of eligible European princesses, but his resolve was set upon a marriage to Gabrielle. Although the Edict of Nantes had won him the severe disapproval of the Holy See, he wrote personally to the pope on January 20, 1599, begging for permission to marry his mistress. Margot, true to her promise and in return for another generous sum to pay her exorbitant debts, sent her signed statement agreeing to an annulment. Still, the wheels turned slowly. That spring Henry wrote to Cardinal de Joyeuse in Rome, exhorting him to do everything in his power to hasten the decision.

Even while Henry wrote supplications to the pope, at home he began preparations for his marriage with Gabrielle. Those who found little to admire in the king's mistress had an ardent spokesman in Rosny who relentlessly badgered Henry.

"Your Majesty, this marriage is madness. As your mistress she is at best unfortunate; as the Queen of France she would be intolerable."

"Rosny, that is absurd. She is beauty and grace itself. My people love her."

"You are fooling yourself, Sire. They condemn her for her parentage, her ambitious relatives, her love of luxury, and her talent for intrigue. They do not see the gentleness, the devotion, and the affection you boast about."

Rosny's choice of hat for the day particularly irritated Henry, but the man's plump cheeks and usually friendly face generally pleased him. It was always difficult to argue with this particularly rational minister, no matter how much he disagreed. "Well, they will have to learn they are wrong."

"But Henry, they blame her for the loss of Calais, even for the capture of Amiens. They forget the money she gave to retrieve that precious city. I know the people have a short memory, but they will not forgive her that. Indeed, they should not!"

Yet Henry refused to listen. As always, everything dissolved in his overflowing love. He saw no contradiction in being frugal himself and then letting money rain over Gabrielle. He decided she must have a house when he wasn't in residence at the Louvre and found one a short distance away. She was able to access the royal apartments quite secretly by going through the gardens of the Tuileries, then through a small wicket gate, leading to a staircase up to the king's chamber. The house was as elaborate as it was convenient. A fifteen-foot table, handsomely carved, furnished her dining room hung with Turkish tapestries on the high walls, and a silver service and enamel dishes were purchased for her use. Flemish green silk, the color she preferentially chose, covered the walls of the bedroom. She was the flower in Henry's garden.

Her chests and armoires bulged with the clothes Henry decreed she must have. Henri thought she looked most ravishing in green or black satin, but there were also dresses of crimson velvet trimmed with gray fur, a white satin embroidered with gold, and a smooth yellow silk with full white sleeves from which to choose. Parliament wondered why he needed money for his army when he could buy a house and the Duchy of Beaufort for Gabrielle, elevating her to the rank of duchesse.

Henry expected more trouble from the nobility than from Margot. Therefore, he was surprised to receive a note from his wife in which suddenly she refused to agree to the annulment if he were to marry such a strumpet as Gabrielle.

"Why has her offer of friendship, which was so generous before, now cooled?" Henry demanded of Rosny.

"You should understand her better than I, but probably because her vanity is wounded," his shrewd minister replied. "She is loath to have in her place a woman of such inferior birth and infamous life, about whom she now hears all kinds of rumors flying."

"Hah! She is the Queen of Infamous! You probably bribed her to do this to me," Henry stormed. "You have been conspiring against me, Rosny."

"You know that is not true!"

"May you both roast in Hell!"

The king's heart continued to rule his head, and he sent another emissary to Rome to help Joyeuse. In token of their betrothal, he gave to Gabrielle his coronation ring, a great square-cut diamond.

On January 31, 1599, Henry planned to give his sister away to the duc de Bar at services conducted in Paris with the grace due to a king's sibling. There would not be many people present but of course, Catherine de Bourbon's lifetime friend sacrificed her pride and came to the celebration of the nuptial benediction. Corisande dreaded seeing Gabrielle again, but even more, she could not bear to hurt Catherine. The colorless winter skies added to the pall and a silent snow muffled sound and joy.

"I chose neither the groom nor the season to marry," Catherine laughed ruefully with her friend on the eve of the ceremony. "If I had been a Catholic, I believe I might have preferred a nunnery to this fate."

"And I might have joined you!" Corisande replied.

"Corisande, my dear, I, who once longed so strongly to be married, am now apprehensive about the union which will take place tomorrow."

Privately, Corisande sympathized completely with her friend, but replied, "Catherine, it is natural to be nervous. But the duc de Bar is known for his amiable character."

"You are right. I should look on the bright side. But I should never have allowed my brother to manipulate my life to such a degree. Have you seen the pamphlet my loyal friend, the formidable Vicomtesse de Rohan,* has secretly published? It is a sharp attack on Henry's heartless treatment of me in refusing to allow my marriage to Soissons. The Vicomtesse wrote, (I've memorized the words) 'And still this diamond of firmness, this Béarnais marble opposed it without the least sign of changing, of sorrow, or pity.' She is absolutely right."

*Catherine de Parthenay-Larchevêque, vicomtesse de Rohan 1554-1631. Unusually gifted in mathematics and literature, she wrote privately and occasionally performed in dramas.

"Yes, she has a clever tongue. I hear she once told Henry she was too poor to be his wife and too well born to be his mistress. She must be one of the few to refuse him!" The two women laughed somewhat bitterly.

"It is also upsetting because my husband-to-be is a Catholic, and the pope insists upon my conversion. Although I can understand the reasons, it is still almost impossible for me to accept my brother's conversion."

"But has Henry not promised you that you may keep your faith?"

"Yes, that he has done. He had to browbeat his bastard half-brother, Charles de Bourbon* — you remember, the somewhat disreputable Archbishop of Rouen? — into marrying us in his private chamber. Henry knew this would anger the pope, but it seems my brother is more sympathetic to my religious convictions than to my amorous ties. Perhaps he sees this union as an opportunity to symbolize the union of Catholics and Huguenots in France — like his own arranged marriage to Margot."

Ritual and manners cloaked private emotions when, the next morning, the marriage words were pronounced. Henry dutifully kissed Corisande's hand before immediately returning to the Louvre, and Catherine repaired to Bar with her new husband. A solitary carriage bore Corisande back to Hagetmau.

---

*Charles de Bourbon (1554-1610) Archbishop of Rouen. He was the bastard son of Henry's father Antoine de Bourbon and his mistress Louise de La Béraudière de l'Isle Rouhet. Therefore, he was Henry's half-brother.

FONTAINEBLEAU

1599

CONVINCING HIMSELF THAT THE news from Rome would be favorable, on Shrove Tuesday, about one month after his emissary's most recent departure, Henry publicly announced his wedding to the Marquise de Montceaux would take place on Easter Sunday. The citizens of Paris seized the occasion for a celebration in the streets, and members of the nobility strove to outdo each other giving banquets and other entertainments for their future queen.

"Are you happy, *chérie*?" Henry asked his mistress. "You seem most serene."

"Of course I am." She paused, remembering Aunt Isabelle's dire predictions. But they had all worked hard to make this happen. She continued, "I made a secret deal with Sillery* prior to his departure, promising him the council post of keeper of the seals if he succeeded. Therefore, I feel certain he will exert every effort on my behalf."

"But my love, Cheverny already holds the position of keeper of the seals," Henry argued.

"But Cheverny won't care because he is Aunt Isabelle's lover."

"You are a conniving one!" Henry laughed. "But are you finding time each day between schemes to stand for your dressmakers?" He asked because the seamstresses had been forced to set aside the extensive new wardrobe they had been making for the future queen because of the not unwelcome change in Gabrielle's figure. She was expecting for the fourth time. Apparently, neither Henry nor his mistress was disturbed by the prospect of the bride walking down the aisle of Notre Dame carrying a child.

*Nicolas Brulart de Sillery, French diplomat

"Yes, but it is tiring. I amuse myself with fantasies of what it will be like to be your queen. But, more important, you truly make me happy, *mon amour*."

"My beautiful, foolish pet. I want you to walk with me outside today. I have planned a special canal at Fontainebleau, which will be constructed in record time, to be built through the trees for our wedding flotilla. The engineers are busy night and day. You will be a beautiful bride and a perfect queen."

But Rome remained unyielding. Becoming increasingly impatient, Henry twice summoned the Cardinal de Gondi* to the Louvre.

"Is the Vatican delaying purposely?" Henry inquired.

"To the best of my knowledge, there is no deliberate procrastination on the part of the pope," Gondi replied.

"Then I must request that you dissolve my marriage to Margot — and now!"

"I could not take such an action on my own authority," the Cardinal answered.

"No power in heaven or on earth will prevent my marriage to the duchesse de Beaufort," Henry proclaimed loudly, his anger so great that many in the Louvre heard him swearing for an hour after the cardinal's departure. How maddening were these deliberations over his personal life. He should be able to just do what he wanted at this point, he thought. His victory at Amiens had ushered in three remarkable years of peace. He had managed to end Spanish meddling in France's affairs, end Catholic opposition to his accession to the throne, and end the religious civil war in the country.

The king's fury cooled as he paced. It really is rather simple, he decided. He would allow neither the silence of Pope Clement nor the obstinacy of Cardinal de Gondi to sway him. Across the channel the daughter of fat Henry VIII still held onto the throne shaken by royal divorces. He had announced he intended to marry Gabrielle, and plans for the wedding would go forward as smoothly as though the Vatican had already granted him his divorce. Just as his wedding with Margot had been arranged without the permission of the pope.

*Henri de Gondi, Bishop of Paris, d.1622.

Although it was already late morning, Gabrielle reclined in her boudoir at Fontainebleau. It was so difficult to rise after all the many sumptuous banquets. If only she could resist the petits fours trimmed with angelica and other candied fruits. Her sister Diane burst in upon her.

"Gabrielle, Gabrielle," Diane gasped. "I just consulted a Piedmontese astrologer named Bizacasser. You have probably heard of him; it is said he is seldom at fault in his predictions. He claims he is willing to stake his life that your marriage will never take place and that you will never again see Easter Day!"

"But all the world is talking of my marriage to the king," Gabrielle rejoined. "Only God or the king's death could put an end to my good luck." She paused and with ice in her voice, asked, "And why did you have to tell me such a frightful tale?"

But she knew why. Diane was jealous; even though all her family had risen with her and she had been more than generous, they all wanted to be in her place.

"I only thought you should know," Diane sniffed.

Gabrielle didn't know if it was all the rich food or her sister's portentous news, but she began to have nightmares. She dreamed of death by torture, death by poison, and Rosny's disapproving face floated forever nearby. She had been a witness when Châtel had struck Henry; now it was she who had been struck. In her dream, an angry mob cheered as her warm blood ran onto the cold marble floor. God surely was angered with her and her family for their greed, and now she would be made to suffer.

Busy days of dressmakers and celebrations would divert her until the isolation of nighttime would bring the recurring night terrors. One morning Henry came in to share coffee with her. She had not yet pushed away the final scrim of sleep when she heard Henry say, "My confessor has suggested we be parted for a short time before the marriage."

"But why on earth?" Gabrielle grew cold with dread.

"As the future queen, he says you owe a good example to the people of France." After clearing his throat, he grinned. "After setting so many bad ones, three to be exact, and one more on the way. He has advised me to send you to Paris, away from the palace at Fontainebleau."

"He is just a busybody and a troublemaker — like all my relatives. And you think it's funny!"

"No, not really. But I believe we should do as he says."

Gabrielle's gloom deepened. Her anxiety combined with the excitement of preparing for the ceremony that would make her queen were exhausting, and her physical condition was further complicated by her pregnancy. When the time for departure arrived, she completely lost her courage. Abandoning all self-control, she burst into tears and Henry could not comfort her.

"I'm afraid I will never see you again," she mourned. "I should have heeded my dreams and never taken your advice to separate, not even for a day."

Henry's eyes watered with sympathy. "Gabrielle, my love, you are simply suffering from irrational fears. I can see you are overexcited and overwrought about our marriage. You can surely relax now, for it is only a matter of days."

"But Henry, the astrologers! More than one has prophesied I will die an early death — unwed!" She choked hysterically.

"Gabrielle, you have already lost too much sleep over their foolish babbling. Obviously they are wrong, for we are to be wed. I promise you. Now calm yourself."

The pair stood at the river's edge, apparently unable to reach a final decision. Henry's convincing tone finally seemed to soothe her and they embraced. Gabrielle clung to him, giving him lengthy instructions for the children and for those servants who were not accompanying her.

"César should not ride without you or a groom, Henriette must have at least two hours in the garden, and . . ."

"Do not worry, *chérie*. You know I shall see they are well taken care of."

Gabrielle tried to settle herself in the boat. Henry was right. She was overwrought; she must try and calm herself. Once in Paris, she decided to go to the house of a friend, M. Zamet, for dinner. She wanted to escape from the fawning and the curious, and she doubted anyone would expect to find her there.

Sebastien Zamet was one of their more bizarre friends, a fabulously rich banker and a naturalized Italian from Lucca. Money, not heritage, was his claim to nobility, and he openly acclaimed himself lord of 1,700,000 crowns. He had begun his career as Catherine de Medici's shoemaker and had rapidly advanced to become a court moneylender.

M. Zamet busied himself over his unexpected guest. "Mme la duchesse, please let me make you more comfortable. You are as beautiful as ever, è vero, but the trip must have tired you."

"Yes, becoming a queen is proving more tiring than I'd expected." She gave a short little laugh. "But how many would like to be in my place!"

"I do not wonder that our good king has chosen you, for your presence will give the throne a grace which has been missing for a long time."

Gabrielle began to calm down with Zamet's soothing words; flattery was always good medicine for her. Shortly after dinner she began to feel unwell again and decided to return home. To insure privacy for the night, she thought again of going where she was not expected — to her aunt's house. Aunt Isabelle might restore her tranquility. Upon reaching her destination, complaining to the servants that she had eaten a lemon at supper and was suffering from indigestion, she retired immediately.

The following morning, a Wednesday, she rode in a litter to the church of Petit Saint-Antoine where a sacred concert was being held. In unusually warm weather, crowds lined the streets to greet their queen-to-be, who appeared sallow and drawn. She roused herself to respond to their cheers, smiling and waving. Twice Gabrielle complained of the heat to her companion, Louise de Vaudémont, but remained in her seat until the service ended. Then she informed Louise she intended to return at once to her bed at her aunt's house.

"I am afraid, Louise. Please come and stay with me," she begged her friend.

"Certainly, my dear. I would be anxious too if I were to marry the king. You are probably just overexcited. It's perfectly understandable."

How many times Gabrielle had heard those words. "You are just overexcited." But certainly that would not cause her to feel so wretched. When they arrived at the house, they found no one there, and Gabrielle barely contained her disappointment at not finding Aunt Isabelle at home. She felt like a child in need of a hand to hold. Complaining of a splitting headache, she suddenly swooned to the floor. Louise, terribly frightened, sent the lackeys who had driven their carriage from church to summon the doctors from the Louvre.

The physicians surrounded her bed and, unable to decide on a diagnosis, nervously watched their patient. By the next morning she seemed recovered.

"I should like to be dressed," she said. She soon regretted her decision, for she felt extraordinarily weary. She could not remember feeling this way with her previous pregnancies and wondered if she might lose the baby. At about two o'clock in the afternoon, she burned with fever and her throat seemed on fire. Sharp pains shot through her stomach. Was this just another one of her nightmares? Why couldn't she wake up? She felt feverish one moment and in a cold sweat the next.

"Let me write to the King," she requested during a moment of respite.

> Dearest, I am very ill and I beg you to come to me with all possible haste. The doctors seem unable to help me and I fear for my life Please hurry!

The doctors observed her throughout the night but were powerless to help. Frightening convulsions followed by rigidity and asphyxia distorted her face beyond recognition; her eyes rolled upwards and the pupils appeared protruded, fixed and staring. Her tongue hung from her mouth as though she were a wild bitch, terrifying the physicians. Her labor then began, and the agonized woman shrieked with pain and fear. After a stillborn child emerged from her racked body, she appeared to have lost the powers of speech, hearing, and sight. Cheverny, who finally had been called to her bedside, ran to Gabrielle's aunt, Isabelle de Babou, to relay the disastrous news, his mind racing with the implications of Gabrielle's demise.

"Her pain is so great that everyone just stands by helplessly. Her servants are unable to do anything."

"Why did you not call me earlier? Has she received the Last Sacraments?" her aunt asked, amazing Cheverny with her control.

"No, she is not capable of receiving them and so must be content with her Easter duty which she made only a short while before. Her face, once so beautiful, now in a moment, has become hideous and frightful to look upon."

"She must not die," Isabelle said firmly. "We would be ruined."

On Thursday evening Henry received Gabrielle's note begging him to return to her at once. He immediately imagined the worst.

"She has been poisoned," he cried to Rosny. "I'm sure she has been poisoned!"

La Varenne, whose duty it was to attend Gabrielle while she was in Paris, sent another message to the king confirming his mistress's perilous state. Henry left Fontainebleau before dawn Friday morning after receiving Varenne's word that Gabrielle's condition had worsened.

He decided to ride instead of taking a boat and began to be terribly afraid. Don't die, Gabrielle, don't die. Poor Gabrielle! He recalled her strange fears, her terror at their separation, her inability to leave him. Why had he not heeded her cries?

At Ville-Juif, he was handed another note from La Varenne:

> We are grieved to inform you there is no point in hastening to Paris, for Gabrielle is already dead. You had best save yourself the grief of seeing your disfigured mistress.

Stunned, Henry turned his horse around. Her warnings had fallen on deaf ears; how could he have been so callous and confident? He allowed his horse to take him back to Fontainebleau; La Varenne was right — it was better not to see Gabrielle in death. Bewildered by his grief, he sat alone through the dark hours of Good Friday night. Why had this happened? What should he do?

Yet Gabrielle lived on. La Varenne and others, fearful the king would marry his mistress on her deathbed, thereby establishing his bastard sons upon the throne of France, dared to lie to their king. Moreover, a strongly held etiquette disallowed a king of France to be present at a deathbed. His ministers stood wooden-faced by her bed, ignoring her screams for Henry. At 5:00 a.m., the morning of Holy Saturday and thirty-six hours before the moment she would have become Queen of France, Gabrielle d'Estrées took her last breath. Her stillborn child would accompany her to the grave.

That same morning Henry went straight to a pavilion set in a pine garden where César was playing. His sturdy prince looked so small and helpless to him. He burst into tears as he told the child the terrible news. César began to weep too and Henry tried to comfort him.

"But she will come back, won't she?" César asked, not fully comprehending.

"No, César. She is gone from this earth."

"But she told me she would be queen when she came back so I am sure she will return," the little boy replied, looking more concerned and frightened now.

"We have lost a mother and a wife, César, but we have each other," Henry said. Picking up the child, he held him on his lap for a long while, looking more like the boy's grandfather than his father.

"But I wanted my mama to be queen," the five-year-old snuffled.

Henry thought of how beautiful Gabrielle would have looked on her wedding day. "And I wanted you to be king," Henry said softly, "but that cannot be."

The two abject creatures sat a long while in the garden with their arms around each other, putting off entering the empty château.

Sinister rumors of poison began to circulate, and Henry sent for the doctors who had been at her bedside. They all insisted the cause of her death had been puerperal convulsions. In too much distress to press an inquiry, he never learned that statesmanship had dominated over compassion at Gabrielle's bedside. The doctors, those who felt any guilt at not calling the king to her side, told themselves they had saved him the horror of seeing her in such a grotesque state. The next day Henry wept copiously on receiving a letter from his sister:

> My dear King, I know well that to your bitter grief, words can bring no remedy. Therefore, I will only use them to assure you I feel your loss as deeply as I feel the great love I bear you, and as the loss of so perfect a friend itself compels me, I long to be by your side. That it may please God, my King, to lessen your grief with the years, I pray with all my heart; and on this, my dear, good King, I kiss you a thousand times.

Henry sat down immediately and replied:

> My dear sister, I received much consolation from your letter. I have great need of it, for my affliction is as much without equal as was she who is the cause of it; regrets and lamentations will go down with me to the grave. Yet since God has sent me into the world

for my country's sake and not for my own, all my powers and my energies will be employed solely to the advancement andpreservation of this, my realm.

He sobbed as he wrote:

The roots of my love are dead, and they will never spring up again; but those of my friendship for you will be ever green, my dear sister, whom I kiss a million times.

On the Tuesday following Gabrielle's death, Henry returned to Paris bringing his three motherless children with him. Isabelle de Babou received them and bustled about the children as though she were their mother.

"Ah, you have brought the poor, dear orphans. Shall I take custody of the children now, Your Majesty?" Now that Gabrielle was gone, she thought she had better be more formal.

"Of course not. They are not orphans — and I will raise them myself."

Aunt Isabelle gasped. "But Sire, that is impossible. They are bas —

"Shut up, you silly bitch!" he interrupted. "Now leave me alone!"

Not only did Henry proclaim he would raise Gabrielle's children, but he also directed that his mistress would receive honors befitting royalty. For once, Rosny dared not object.

For the next four days an effigy of Gabrielle made of stucco and wax was propped up in a sitting position on a huge bed in a chamber of the Hotel d'Estrées. Under a baldachino made of golden fabric, the image was eerily lifelike, dressed in white satin, with a golden cloak lined with ermine around its shoulders and a ducal crown was balanced upon the head. In order to maintain the pretense that Gabrielle was still alive, princesses and other great ladies presented four elaborate meals each day to the mannequin. Pretending to be angels, heralds hovered at the foot of the bed, offering holy water for those coming to offer condolences.

Although in life Gabrielle sometimes had been a subject of mockery and contempt, now Paris flocked for a glimpse of her effigy. A legend before her death, this sudden violent ending ensured she would live on in the public's mind. Curious Parisians crowded the streets, hoping for a view of the royal litter laden with the body of the ambitious lady who had seduced their king. Many whispered that indeed, here lay a woman who had been struck down by the hand of God Himself.

Gabrielle had held the king relatively faithful in his love for her over a period of nine years. As Henry rode from Fontainebleau to the rue Froidmanteau where funeral preparations were underway, Paris observed a man grown shockingly older. It was hard to believe their king was only forty-six years old, for thin and hagard, he looked closer to sixty. His hair and beard had turned completely gray and become frizzy. His face, always swarthy from outdoor activities, now appeared a muted gray, dry as arid soil, and deep furrows seemed to drag down the mobile mouth. How could this grizzled creature possibly give them an heir?

Giving Gabrielle the obsequies of a queen, Henry ordered the court to walk in procession behind her cortege to St. Denis, and he trudged beside the casket with his head bowed. The Parisians lining the streets wept for their king, who looked so distressed. He held the hand of a small boy who walked beside him. For a week Henry wore black and then changed to the violet of half-mourning, as was the royal custom. It seemed that a wife whom he loved would always remain just out of reach.

BOOK FIVE

HENRIETTE D'ENTRAGUES
(1579-1633)

**CATHERINE HENRIETTE DE BALZAC D'ENTRAGUES,
MARQUISE DE VERNEUIL**
Artist Unknown, 17th c., oil on canvas
Palace of Versailles, France

MALESHERBES

1599

GABRIELLE HAD NOT BEEN LONG buried when Aubigné, pressured by the king's other counselors, took up an old theme with Henry.

"You must marry, Sire, not only for the good of France but for your own good as well. I'm sorry to enlighten you, but if you don't already know it, you are looking much older than your years and you still have not provided an heir for the throne."

"Christ's blood, Aubigné, I lost half of myself when Gabrielle died. Haven't you the decency to leave me alone with my grief?"

"A king cannot afford that luxury. You must find yourself again, put aside this mourning and take up the reigns of government. It is worrisome to see you so affected by this death."

"What did you expect? To Hell with all of you!"

Henry continued to show no enthusiasm for the list of suitable princesses his ministers presented to him. Yet somewhat to their surprise, he seemed not totally against their suggestion of a niece of the Medici family of Italy. Marie de Medici, the twenty-six-year-old daughter of the late Francesco I, Grand Duke of Tuscany, was a sound choice. Her uncle, the present grand duke, was anti-Spanish, respected by the pope, fabulously rich, and able to exert invaluable pressure on the Florentine money market. Realizing her credentials impressed Henry, Rosny pushed the advantage.

"She is reputedly virtuous, Henry, of stable character, and with a queenly bearing, we are told. Moreover, there is no reason to believe she would not provide you with the healthy offspring you need."

Henry chuckled, the first such sound they had heard from him in quite a while. "And I'm sure you understand the practical consideration, Rosny — that if I were to engage in such a marriage, her uncle might cancel the enormous debt I owe to Florence."

"Exactly! And the idea must be a good one, for this is the first time you have laughed in many weeks."

"I presume Margot would agree to this marriage with a woman of such sound virtue and background?"

"Surely she would. She only refused an annulment which would have placed a woman of questionable virtue on the throne."

Henry growled audibly. "Get out of here. You all bother me like wasps! May torrents of urine rain down on your foolish heads!"

Besieged by a depression unlike any he had ever known, Henry paced the room. The loss of Gabrielle had driven him into a paralysis and melancholy that, in turn, catapulted him into a frenzy of whoring. He believed this helped him push away frightening thoughts crowding into his tormented mind. He wrote to his sister, admitting that his grief was "incomparable." "The root of my love is dead," he complained. "It will sprout no more." Catherine, in sympathy with her brother's sorrow, replied with a promise to be a second mother to the children.

Everyone talked of his charm and warmth, yet did he really know how to love? Had he been slow in showing his manhood last night? Perhaps he would lose his throne if he lost his potency? Had any woman really loved him? Perhaps Gabrielle had. Corisande probably had. But he had destroyed that. Hadn't he often been cuckolded by his mistresses — and his wife? That was the real and tragic truth of the matter. His passion demanded he constantly make love, be in love. But perhaps he was not a good lover. He shook himself. What kind of mystic thinking was this? Hadn't he always been a rational man? With shame he thought of Corisande, now plump, dowdy, and forgotten in her retirement. He remembered poor Esther d'Imbert, whom he had turned away when she needed him so desperately. Had he truly loved these women and then been so callous? And what of his sister? Had he treated her as badly as she claimed? But she knew the responsibilities of royalty. Corisande was right. France was the only mistress he would never betray, the only one he could not forget. He lay down, for once too tired to care.

Bassompierre* asked if he might enter.

"Hello, my good friend," said the king.

François de Bassompierre hailed from Lorraine but being twenty-five years younger than Henry, he had somehow escaped becoming a Guise man. Bassompierre reminded Henry of his own youth and consequently, he had befriended this impudent dueling adventurer who displayed an excessively bawdy humor as well. "Stick by me and you will be a Maréchal de France one day," he had advised the younger man.

Bassompierre was struck that Henry didn't jump up and clap him on the back as he generally did. "I'm sorry to find you still so morose, Sire. I'm certain you will find solace for your grief only by putting someone equally entertaining in her place."

"I am getting too old, François."

"Rubbish! You have always collected women like a boy does marbles. Once a collector, always a collector. Why don't we visit Malesherbes? It's not far — only halfway between Blois and Paris, and there is a beautiful woman with auburn hair I want you to meet. She has a most alluring bosom and a pair of flashing black eyes which are sure to charm you," he tempted.

Henry smiled, remembering how he had been tantalized by Bellegarde's description of Gabrielle. That had been a most successful meeting.

"All right. I will go," he agreed. "I'll do anything to escape myself!"

Bassompierre hoped he detected a note of eagerness in the king's voice.

Riding at a leisurely pace toward Malesherbes with his young friend a few days later, Henry thought the flat land around Paris seemed dismal. He longed for the ponderous mystery of the mountains at night and sighed. The excitement of waiting for his prey to dart from the brush as dawn broke over a rocky ridge would always be preferable to the dull silence of the plains.

Henriette d'Entragues was the eighteen-year-old daughter of François d'Entragues, Governor of Orléans and Marie Touchet, who, ironically, he had formerly known as the mistress of Charles IX. Henry

* François de Bassompierre (1579-1646), courtier loyal to Henri IV, who became maréchal de France under Louis XIII in 1622.

recognized M. d'Entragues as a renowned opportunist. Having declared himself for the League and holding his city against the Huguenots, he then changed his colors when the League leaders began to capitulate. After Henry became king, d'Entragues had offered Orléans to him for the exorbitant price of twenty thousand *écus*.

More than pleased to welcome the king to his château, M. d'Entragues was effusive in his greeting. Henry found himself sincerely happy to see Marie Touchet and asked about her Valois son, whom he had vowed to protect so long ago.

"How is little Charles, Marie? I am glad to see he doesn't need the help King Charles once made me promise."

"He is not 'little Charles' anymore, King Henry, and I am afraid he is acquiring a somewhat terrifying reputation. But I believe you will be more interested in his beautiful half-sister!" She smiled. Was she enticing him with herself? She had certainly changed since he had last seen her.

Marie was right. Henriette's sulky yet lively grace, provoking airs, and cruel amusing wit infatuated the king at once. He had no idea he had just met the archetypal adventuress who would know how to exploit his wild jealousies. If the court had been afraid of the conspiring of Gabrielle and her relatives, they would have trembled at the dangerous schemes of the d'Entragueses.

Determined that this visit by the king would be the first of many, Marie Touchet carefully tutored her daughter: "Henriette, if Henry was ready to marry Gabrielle d'Estrées, there is no reason why he should not make you his queen instead. And the country loves him so wholeheartedly, I think they would be willing to accept anything he does."

Henriette silently agreed and laid her plans carefully while M. d'Entragues also devised his plans. Flattered to have the king in his house, he invited him to return often to enjoy the excellent hunting and fishing. Henriette lured him like a feather-fly does trout, darting hither and thither, enchantingly elusive in the muddy waters of dishonest love affairs. Her father controlled the line, and it wasn't long before they had Henry firmly hooked. Soon he was staying in a château only a league from Malesherbes, his attraction for Henriette a matter of common knowledge. Within six months after Gabrielle's death, the king groveled at the feet of a girl less than half his age.

Henry became irritated as Henriette assumed the role of the virtuous daughter of virtuous parents and pretended wide-eyed innocence before his advances. "I am not permitted to see you unless chaperoned," she whispered.

But her refusals only provoked his passion all the more. On August 5, 1599, he brought her a special present. When Henriette opened the satin box, lying among the soft folds she found a magnificent pearl necklace. Quickly remembering the high stakes for which she was playing, she politely said, "I cannot accept such a gift," whereupon Henry carefully placed the necklace back in its satin case. He sensed she was playing with him, but it only drove him to want her more. He must have her, he must! Besides, he enjoyed nothing more than showering gifts on those he loved; it was an uncontrollable urge.

The next day he sent her a large box of crystallized apricots. Receiving them with gracious appreciation, she demurely covered her bosom with a soft shawl. He had a fleeting and uncomfortable idea that perhaps she was using him exactly as he had used others. Henriette also made sure he would learn she had already taken lovers, the prince de Joinville and his old rival, the duc de Bellegarde. In fact, Henry was the one to catch the prince and the duke fighting a duel over Henriette. Had she planned it? Probably. He ordered the two suitors away from Malesherbes for good, and then furiously turned to her, stating, "When the king is your lover, then you should know better than to see another man."

"But you are not my lover, Sire," she demurred, blushing prettily. "I will be!"

But Henry soon found he had no reason to have been so sure. Henriette was as alert and vibrant as he. The two were spun of the same cloth of scandalizing colors. She reminded him of the mountain lionesses of his home. Watching him with eyes a bit slanted, showing honey lights in the irises, she stalked him gracefully with lithe and calculated movements. Her mind was as quick as her body, and she was the first to pounce upon a slow conversation, turning it into spirited play.

Although charmed by her cleverness and vitality, Henry perceived that where he was spontaneous, she was calculating; her wit and gaiety were but the tools of her ambition, an ambition that would goad her to be Queen of France. The games she insisted on playing, at first distracting, were fast becoming tiresome.

"Will you not come to my house tonight?" he asked.

"You know my parents will not allow it," his diffident demoiselle replied. She paused. "Unless there were some promise which would ensure my good name, a written promise that would ultimately lead to marriage."

"But that is unthinkable, Henriette. You overreach to ask such a thing of your king."

"Then you have no right to expect me to stay in your house for the night," she huffed.

Henry was outraged, but it did not take long for his desire to obliterate his reason. He dreamed of her pink, sensuous mouth, longed to cup his hands around her white breasts, to have her. Damn! No woman had ever dared do this to him before.

At last the desperate king literally bought her from her greedy father, who asked for the title of maréchal although he had never seen a battle. He specified a large sum in cash to be paid down immediately, and a document promising that if Henriette should have a son by the king, he would marry her as soon as he was divorced and so legitimize the child.

Henry called Rosny into the gallery at Fontainebleau and showed him the text which he had just composed:

> We, Henri IV, by the grace of God, King of France and of Navarre, promise and swear on our faith and word as a king to Monsieur François de Balzac, Monsieur d'Entragues, knight of our orders, who gives us our companion Henriette-Catherine de Balzac, his daughter, that should the said Henriette-Catherine de Balzac, within six months, beginning from this day, become pregnant and should she bear a son, then at that time we shall solemnize the marriage publicly in church according to the required customary ritual.

"What do you think of it?" the king asked

Rosny could not believe his eyes and in answer ripped the paper to pieces.

"The lady is no novice, Henry. I have heard she is demanding — rather, her father is demanding — no less than 100,000 crowns for the price of her favors."

"She is worth it," the besotted king replied.

"Henry, Henry, you cannot do this!" Rosny exclaimed. "It is well known how you would not allow your sister to make an unwise marriage. Surely you would not do so yourself."

"Catherine has nothing to do with this."

"But we have spent months trying to clear your marriage to Gabrielle with the pope. You are obviously not oblivious to the fact that your marriage must be considered and approved by many people."

"I was clearly wasting my time in showing you this document," Henry snarled. "Now I shall have to write it anew."

The d'Entragueses were ecstatic when they received the king's promise. Their daughter had been sold like a common whore, but the exceptional buyer allowed them to exult in the promise of their future.

The news of the king's foolishness traveled fast. Aubigné conferred with Rosny. "This time he has gone too far — beyond even my wildest imaginings," Aubigné began. "Despite your frantic, and I must say, wise disapproval, Rosny, Henry has agreed to everything save the title of maréchal for the father. This document in which he swore to keep the bargain 'before God on our faith and word as a king' is dated October 1, 1599."

Rosny agreed. "This sordid transaction is surely the most disgraceful and irresponsible in Henry's entire career. To satisfy his lust the old buzzard has once more jeopardized the future of the French monarchy!"

"Henriette will now join the hordes who have felt the imperial prick," Aubigné sneered.

"What is his charm, do you think?"

"Well, he is the King."

"No, it is more than that," Rosny opined. "He is so alive, so vital. And his buoyant optimism is contagious. Perhaps the ladies believe a little of that will rub off. Hah!"

Henry knew everyone was talking behind his back. But neither did he care nor feel cheated when Henriette came to him at last. That slip of paper seemed little to pay for the young and lithe body, which brought new vigor to his body and a bounce to his step. He had been too weak to play tennis* lately and forced to find satisfaction with pall-mall. He could still hawk or hunt and often called M. Bassompierre to accompany him — until he decided the sight of Bassompierre's strong, muscular body only depressed him more. Now he felt like a young bull when he was with Henriette, aroused at merely the sight of her and his desire became unrestrained as soon as he touched her. How could he have doubted his virility? The fact that Henriette was no virgin might have bothered him, but he told himself he knew the d'Entragueses for what they were — blatant adventurers. He preferred to ignore the fact that his coy mistress was an outright liar. But never mind, he found her totally absorbing and entertaining.

Soon, however, Henry began to confuse the d'Entragueses by pursuing a course of action contrary to the promise he had given them. His council, having studied all the royal lineages of Europe, had settled on the Tuscan noblewoman Henry favored, primarily because her dowry promised to be large and the Medici line had also proven fertile historically. Finally acceding to their demands to marry a "virtuous princess" in order to give France an heir, Henry consented that negotiations with the Grand Duke of Tuscany be pursued. As a first step he wrote to his former advocate, Cardinal de Joyeuse, in Rome, exhorting him to push the investigation of his annulment. To M. Bellièvre, his newly appointed chancellor, he openly announced his intention of marrying, concluding, "Advance this affair as much as possible, so that I can be married shortly, which is what I want most in the world."

His next meeting with Henriette was expectedly stormy. "I hear you intend to marry 'a virtuous Italian princess,'" Henriette snarled. "How do you think you can do that when you have promised to marry me?"

"I have promised to marry you, my love, if you conceive a male heir six months from our agreement. I must be prepared for all contingencies, don't you think? And I must always put the country first and foremost."

---

* Most historians believe that tennis originated in the monastic cloisters in northern France in the 12th century, but the ball was then struck with the palm of the hand, hence the name the name *jeu de paume* (game of the palm). Rackets came into use in the 16th century, and the game began to be called "tennis." Pall-mall is a sort of croquet.

"How dare you make fun of me like that! I never, never should have believed you would protect my reputation, for obviously my name means nothing to you. You are treating me like a common trollop and I will not stand for it."

He could not bear for those around him to be unhappy and, as usual, attempted to restore his companion's composure.

"Please, Henriette, you know I must humor my counselors, who worry me morning, noon, and night about the succession. You and I know I will do what I please and it will not hurt to string these chattering ministers along a bit. And you should know better than to believe everything you hear."

"I hope you are telling the truth, for I believe I am about three months pregnant." She sat back, obviously ready to enjoy the effect her trump card would have.

"Why, that is wonderful news, my love," he said, immediately relishing the thought of his continued fertility. Embracing her heartily, he felt his optimism quickly rise to the surface like a hot spring.

For Henry, the night gave him all the joys he could have expected, as Henriette was momentarily appeased. He delighted in the sensual pleasure of her soft flesh, and not least in the sense of power as his body took hers. An unexpected memory of Corisande, speaking once long ago of the necessity and difficulty of living only for the moment, flashed through his passion. He had no time to do otherwise.

On December 17 the Holy See decreed that the marriage of Henry of Navarre and Marguerite de Valois was null and void, since the union had been the result of coercion of both parties. Having been indifferent to this marriage for most of its duration and finally free to take another spouse, he remembered Margot with surprising affection. He felt a desire to write her a note.

> My dearest Marguerite, I assure you that I still wish
> to love and cherish you as before. I hope you know I
> have more concern for you than ever before and hope
> to be your true brother in act as well as thought.

The marriage negotiations proceeded, and toward the end of April, at the Pitti Palace in Florence, a solemn contract of betrothal was signed between Marie de Medici and the proxies of His Most Christian Majesty. Marie had been born in 1573, and so he was 20 years her senior. Other European royal suitors had applied for her hand, but a fortune-teller's prophesy had made her believe that her destiny would be with France, making Henry the winning bidder.

At first Henriette was confused, then wild with anger. "Henry," she seethed, "I am seven months pregnant. What excuse do you have now?"

"I don't need an excuse, Henriette. I don't see why you are complaining. Have I not treated you generously? You are luxuriously installed in the Hôtel de Larchant — against the wishes of my ministers, I might add. I simply told them my bird needed a beautiful cage."

"I refuse to be put off by your clever speeches. Are you conveniently forgetting you signed a promise to marry me?"

"Henriette, you can easily understand that that was done in a moment of foolishness. Kings must heed public opinion and the advice of their ministers to some degree."

"That is not what you told me several months ago." She began to scream with rage and pound Henry with her fists. Henry's ability to remain sanguine throughout the predicament of being publicly betrothed to one woman and secretly bound to another enraged her all the more.

"If you do not cease this ridiculous behavior, Henriette, I shall no longer be in the mood to give you what I had planned. I think you would regret missing such a present as I have in mind."

Henriette ceased her temper tantrum as quickly as it had begun. "What?"

"I have secured for you, my love, the territory of Verneuil in Picardy and raised it to the status of a marquisate."

"Oh, Henry," she cried, throwing her arms around his neck, genuinely forgetting her fury in this moment of happy surprise.

"And you will hence be known as the Marquise de Verneuil. But Henriette, this is only on the condition you will stop plaguing me about that promise I gave you. I cannot abide by such an agreement and you know it. The council would never accept you as queen, and I should think that being a marquise would more than satisfy any ambitions you might have."

"Perhaps," Henriette smiled. Realizing she could push Henry no further at the moment, she accepted the bribe with apparent equanimity. For didn't she and her parents have in their possession a sworn and written promise in the king's hand?

Henry, with relief, believed he had freed himself from a most fraught situation. In order to be sure, he wrote to her from Fontainebleau on April 21:

> Mademoiselle, Love, and honor as well as all the favors you have received from me would have sufficed for the most frivolous maid in the world, unless she were gifted with a naturally evil character such as yours. I will not wound you anymore although I could and should do so, as you well know. I am asking you to return to me the promise in question and not to give me the trouble of recovering it by some other means. Please return also the ring which I gave you the other day. This is the subject of this letter to which I would like an immediate response.

He wrote to M. d'Entragues on the very same day, begging him to "return the promise which I gave to you at Malesherbes." He insisted his decision was based on "personal reasons, not reasons of state" and maintained every civility, and claimed to be his "good master."

Neither letter received an answer.

Henriette begged her mother to reside with her until the eagerly awaited birth of her child. "I cannot risk an overt refusal of the king's demand to forgive his vow, nor do I have any intention of acquiescing in it," she explained.

"You have only six more weeks until the birth and if we can guard his written promise for this short time, I have no doubt you will be Queen of France," her conspiring mother replied.

"Six long weeks! And you make it sound so easy. I am going insane with worry. I am terrified of giving birth — so many women die or the child dies. In either case, I am the one to suffer. What if it is a girl? I cannot stand the waiting, this helpless emotion, not being able to do anything to make it be a boy!"

"Henriette, calm yourself," Marie Touchet commanded, "or you will do harm to yourself or the baby."

Henriette tried to adhere to her mother's warning, and at least had the sense not to complain of the conditions she found so intolerable. Her mother, with profound relief, observed her taking precautions to bear a healthy child. Throughout the month of May Henriette also attempted to placate Henry by hiding her own ambition and employing her former wiley and seductive ways. But she didn't feel very desirable, carrying so much new weight ahead of her.

When her pregnancy neared term, the king brought her to Fontainebleau and installed her in beautiful apartments, exhibiting unexpected consideration by not choosing those previously inhabited by Gabrielle. Perhaps this was as much for himself as for her, Henriette realized.

"Do not leave me," she begged. "I need you to be with me when our child is delivered."

Although she had won him back to her side, he remained firm on this point. "Matters of state, too important to be postponed, demand my presence elsewhere," he reminded her. "You will be well taken care of here, Henriette."

While it was true he was needed elsewhere, it was equally true he recognized Henriette's pleas as but another element of her scheming. She hoped that if the king were present at her delivery, he would be moved to keep his promise to her, even if the child she bore were not a son. As quick to discover her ruses as Henriette was to employ them, Henry remained unmoved by her woeful entreaties.

In mid-June he departed for Lyon, and Henriette was significantly left alone for the delivery of the child. He couldn't help but recall his separation from Gabrielle when she had been about to give birth. But he felt very differently about this woman. Her beauty had stimulated him, bringing him back to life after Gabrielle's death, but she could not replace Gabrielle. He only wanted her for his mistress and truly didn't want another fight with the pope or his ministers. Some might believe being king meant having the power to do what you desired, but he knew only too well how it curtailed more freedom than it bestowed.

Not all of Henriette's tearful pleas were simulated. "Please, God, let it be a boy; please, God, let it be a boy." She murmured the words day and night until they assumed the rhythm of her breathing. She was genuinely frightened and distressed. Fearful of the suffering and

danger in bringing forth a child, her terrors increased when she recalled the fate of the king's last mistress.

"I can find peace nowhere," she moaned as she strolled in the
garden with her mother. "I am unnerved to the point of feeling ill."

"You must relax, Henriette. You are too accustomed to control-
ling your life as well as those of others. You cannot hasten or retard
the measured step of pregnancy."

"But why did Henry leave me now? I know all would be well if
he were here, but his absence makes me even more distraught."

The next day was particularly oppressive, until the sultry heat
broke with a violent thunderstorm over the castle. Feeling restless,
Henriette insisted on walking outside, allowing the wind to whip her
hair, pulling it back from her face like a dark mane. The gale lashed
the trees, threatening to tear them from their roots. She felt such a
force must be extraterrestrial, pulling the world into a whirling vortex
of the unknown. Her terror increased as the howl of the storm in
the bending trees roared around her, but she refused to go inside, the
wildness of nature akin to the restless energy within her. Why was
Henry not here? You must calm yourself, she thought, and yet she
felt like the only human being left on earth. The wind seemed to be
weeping for the passing of a life.

The crashes of thunder and lightening grew more terrible as
night fell. Henriette became hysterical and no one could quiet her.
Irrational, uncontrollable, she tore at the sheets, ripping them with
her sharp nails, while screaming that the tempest was tearing the
child from her womb. Before morning she gave birth somewhat pre-
maturely to a stillborn male child.

Marie Touchet looked at the white face of her daughter.

"Henriette, your baby is dead," she said.

She received no answer. Henriette's despair overwhelmed her,
and she withdrew into a shell like a hermit crab. Lying in bed for
weeks, she responded to no one. It would have been less frightening
if she had cried; rather she seemed dead. The depressed state that
made her so subdued and withdrawn was completely unlike the lively
person she had been. People said her wit and laughter had left her
body with her lifeless child. Inwardly, she railed against her fate, as
she understood that all her conniving and machinations had failed.
It didn't seem fair. So many hours spent planning her strategy with
her mother and father! The nerve-racking pregnancy! And all to no
avail! She blamed the king even more for he could have soothed her,

and then the child she had carried so attentively would have been brought into the world alive. In that case she could have held the king to his promise, she was sure, and she would have reigned as Queen of France. She would never be more than Madame la Marquise while in her imagination she had already pictured herself on the throne of France.

Henry arrived to console her, but she even refused to respond to him. He told her he loved her, but he did not promise to make her his wife. Nothing mattered anymore; she had failed to get what she wanted. She noticed the king's sympathy did not keep him with her long, for by the second week of July he returned to Lyon with the excuse of the territorial problem of Savoy,* a state still under contention.

Ambitious and confident, Charles Emmanuel, the Duke of Savoy, had followed a policy of expansion for his duchy. A decade earlier, in the autumn of 1588, taking advantage of the civil war sundering France during the reign of his first cousin Henry III, he occupied the Marquisate de Saluzzo, which was under French protection. When Henry became king, he demanded the restitution of that land, but Charles Emmanuel refused, and a war ensued. The conflict broadened, eventually involving France and Spain, and finally ended with the Peace of Vervins on May 2, 1598, but still left the current but separate question of Saluzzo unsolved. After the Duke began talks with Spain, Henry threatened to reopen the war.

* The problem of Savoy continued until January 17, 1601, when the Treaty of Lyon was signed between France, Spain, and Savoy. Based on the terms of the treaty, Henry IV of France relinquished Saluzzo to Savoy. In return, he acquired Bugey, Valromey, Gex and Bresse. Eventually, the territory of Bresse was attached to the French military government of Burgundy.

GRENOBLE

1600

HENRIETTE NEED NOT HAVE BEEN totally despondent, for thoughts of her continued to titillate Henry. Free of the promise he had so foolishly given, he could be free of her completely if he so desired. Yet he wrote to her daily. His short missives began to awaken her fantasies, and she begged him to let her come to him as soon as her health permitted.

Losing his willpower by the end of August, he wrote the words she had begun to hope for, "Hurry to me, my love. I can wait no longer to hold you again." Since she had failed to bear him a son, it could do no harm to see her, he told himself. No longer could he be trapped into marriage, and so he could well afford to resume his role as lover, without Rosny or anyone else complaining.

Henriette lay back against the coach cushions, enjoying the rocking motion. She would get even somehow; she was smart enough to turn the tables again, she told herself. The bitterness of her disappointment had sharpened her dangerous claws, and she had roused from her despair with her ambition glowing like the diamonds Henry had given her. If the paper promise she held from the king were not enough to win the queen's crown, it might at least be enough to seriously discomfort him.

She had just learned that Henry's marriage to Marie de Medici had been celebrated by proxy at Florence the week before, on October 5. The ceremony was performed by the pope's nephew, Cardinal

Aldobrandini, with Roger de Bellegarde, Gabrielle's old paramour, standing in as the king's proxy. The irony of Bellegarde's presence had caused more than one guest to smile. She heard the ceremony had been full of splendor and magnificence. The marriage supper that followed was an Italian spectacle with food shaped into the forms of birds and animals and rare plants. After dessert a cloud opened to reveal the goddess Diana and a eunuch singing the glory of the King of France and his new queen. Through it all, the affianced bride was seated alone, exhibiting a cold poise and aloof demeanor. One did not know whether to pity her or admire her.

Henriette's jealousy smoldered as she thought of the woman who had won the right to be Henry's queen. She would find some way to avenge the wrong Henry had done to her. Her lips curved in a grim smile as she remembered that on occasion, the king's mistress had held more power in France than the queen. She would make history repeat itself and take lessons from the renowned Diane de Poitiers! Indeed, the idea of being queen seemed to have gone to her head, when in the third week of October, Mme la Marquise traveled to Lyon in an uncovered litter. In the same queenly manner she continued south from Lyon to La-Côte-St.-André near Vienne. When Henry learned of her presence at Grenoble, he convinced Bassompierre to make the exhausting journey with him. However, the welcome he received scarcely repaid him for his pains. In place of a loving mistress, he found a volcano, sparks flying.

"Henriette, my love, at last we are together again. And I am glad to see you are looking so well!"

"You cannot expect me to be happy when I am only here as your whore, not as your wife."

"Come, come. I thought we had laid all that behind us. Now we can really enjoy ourselves."

"How can I forget that I have been in bed recuperating from giving birth to your stillborn bastard? And I shall never let you forget it, Henry! Now, where am I to stay?"

"In my tent, of course. Where else would I have you stay?"

"It's not important where you would have me stay. It is only where I would like to reside that counts, and I would insist upon something infinitely more comfortable."

"As you wish, Henriette. You are hardly the lover I expected to find while making the journey from Grenoble without stopping for rest or to change horses. Now I shall instruct Aubigné to find you more luxurious quarters."

"Please don't speak of quarters for me. I am not your wife, and neither am I part of your military establishment."

"I shall remember that, Henriette."

"According to our agreement, you would have married me if our child had lived. You must feel very proud of yourself to have escaped so neatly."

"You know my promise was foolishly given, that my ministers would never have agreed to our marriage, promise or no promise. I must marry royalty."

"But you gave me your promise in writing, king or not!"

"My dear, it is finished. Our child died, and I must marry where my duty lies."

"Yes, I hear your 'duty' lies with Marie de Medici. Is she beautiful, Henry?"

"Why should I answer you? I warned you this is a dead subject, Henriette."

"Dead. Like our child."

"Hush! I am leaving. Tonight," he threatened.

Suddenly she was frightened again. "How could you, Henry, when I have come so far to see you?"

"When you have come so far? And why, I might ask, did you come at all?"

"Oh, quiet. I don't really feel angry with you anymore. Why don't you come kiss me; it's been quite a long time, you know."

"You beautiful bitch! I believe you have me crazed. Now you shall really feel my fury! You are very attractive when you are so angry."

"And you have the ability to make me angrier than anyone."

"I don't know why I continue to write to you or to see you."

"Oh, yes, you do. And I do too. Ah, now you are smiling. Please tell Aubigné I will stay here in your tent. For the moment anyway."

Usually able to remain detached, now Henry could not control himself. He hated the way her fury aroused him as they raged at one another, and his men questioned why her temper seemed to entice rather than repel their leader. They witnessed her power to evoke a certain violence in him, and how she brought him down to fight with the weapons she had chosen. They were amazed on the following morning to see the reconciled lovers riding back to Grenoble together. An English agent, observing the king's relations with his mistress, wrote in his dispatch:

The King hath brought his mistress hither whom he doth embrace with more kindness than kings commonly do their wives, and doth honor with as much respect as if she were his queen. She doth dine ordinarily and publicly with him when he is attended by Princes of the Blood.

Henry's folly with Henriette amazed even those who knew him well. He had been driven wild by women before, insisting upon taking the standards of Coutras to Corisande, insisting upon a marriage with Gabrielle, a woman said to be lacking in virtue. But with Henriette, he allowed her to lead him by the nose like a peasant boy dazzled by a mistress of high birth. Perhaps he really had lost part of himself when Gabrielle died, and where his heart had been, there still lay a numb chunk of stone. His friends wondered why she attracted him so, why he allowed her to shame him. He seemed not to care whether she hurt him. But he had married Marie de Medici; and all hoped he would not allow Henriette to hurt France.

He threw himself gladly into the churning tumultuous waters of Henriette's lust and demands, perhaps hoping he would feel alive again as she dashed him again and again at the rocks, as she alternately received him into her arms or cruelly rejected him. At least she absorbed his energies and her fierce penchant distracted him from his present sense of failure and dissatisfaction.

They managed to coexist in relative accord until the beginning of November when Henry learned of the arrival of Aldobrandini, the papal legate. The timing could not have been worse. This was the man who would be the mediator in the Savoy affair. To add more reason to be careful and be embarrassed, it was Aldobrandini who had officiated at the marriage between Henri IV and Marie de Medici in Florence. Henry knew it would be folly to welcome the cardinal in Henriette's presense.

"You will have to leave Grenoble for a short while, my pet," Henry told Henriette. "You must realize it would be extremely awkward for you to be here when the cardinal arrives."

"I do not wish to go, Henry, and in fact, I refuse to go," she announced, making herself more comfortable among the pillows on the divan.

"Gabrielle, I will not allow you to reveal to the legate the promise I made to you. Moreover, no one would believe it would oblige me to marry you, nor would it possibly nullify my marriage in Florence. Your games are useless and irritating, to say the least."

"You are a cruel and wicked man, Henry," she replied.

"But not as scheming as you, my pretty one. You are an ambitious bitch under that beautiful mask. I should have left you long ago!"

"And I should not allow you to talk to me like that. But you cannot do without me, and you know it."

"Worse that that! You impel me to a course of action which I cannot justify."

He felt like slapping the snide smile off her face. "I will not argue with you any longer," he barked. "This behavior must stop now. You should feel lucky since I have arranged a boat to take you in luxurious style on the Lac du Bourget, then down the Rhône to Lyon. There, you will be given a royal reception. You might enjoy knowing that it will be similar to one given to Diane de Poitiers, another royal favorite."

The comparison seemed to please Henriette.

"You are very persuasive," she said. "I'll do you this favor this once, but do not expect such contrite behavior in the future."

Henry breathed a sight of relief. At last, she would be a safe distance away. Preoccupied with concluding the problems with Savoy, but even more concerned with the subsequent arrival of Marie de Medici herself, he knew he could not deal with his argumentative mistress at the same time. What might she have done? He cringed at the thought of Henriette revealing the incriminating contract that she held in which he promised a conditional marriage to her while making simultaneous plans to wed Marie. Surely its existence would abruptly end his marriage plans to the Italian princess. He knew Henriette could not be trusted and would pursue any means to entrap him.

Henriette might have stayed at Lyon to await Henry's return, but hearing of the imminent arrival of Marie de Medici, she surprised him by bolting for Paris. She appeared finally to sense the danger of continuing to rant. She knew her position to be precarious and saw that her complaining might drive him to Marie for good. She knew her absense usually made him long for her, and she decided she should wait awhile to draw him closer with flattery and feminine wiles.

❦

Marie de Medici was scheduled to arrive in France during the summer of 1600, but the Savoy campaign gave Henry the perfect alibi to postpone the arrival of his wife. Extremely practiced and versatile at writing words of love, and in order to palliate the delay, Henry wrote to her frequently. On May 24, a month after their solemn betrothal and without ever having seen her, he wrote one of his first letters to Marie:

> The virtues and perfections which shine forth in you and make you universally admired, have for a long time now incited in me a desire to honor and serve you as you deserve. What Hailincourt* has reported to me about you has increased my desire. Since it is not possible for me to express my affection in person, I have decided that while waiting for this happiness (which shall soon be mine if heaven listens to my prayers) to send my faithful servant Frontenac** to perform this office in my name . . . He will uncover my heart to you and you will find there an impassioned desire to cherish and love you all my life as the mistress of my affections, and henceforth to assume the witness to this in person and to conform the pledge of my fidelity.

Despite all his flowery language, he finally could procrastinate no longer and gave the word that Marie de Medici was to sail from Leghorn on October 17, 1600.

---

* Ambassador to Rome.
**Antoine de Buade. The de Buades were a family of distinction in the principality of Béarn. Antoine de Buade, seigneur de Frontenac, grandfather of the future governor of Canada, attained eminence as a councilor of state under Henri IV; and his children were brought up with the dauphin, who became Louis XIII.

BOOK SIX

MARIE DE MEDICI
(1573-1642)

HENRI IV WITH MARIE DE MEDICI
AND THEIR CHILDREN
Artist: Frans Pourbus the Younger, 1607; oil on canvas
Musée de l'Auditoire, Ste.-Suzanne, France

LYON

1600

TWENTY-SEVEN YEARS OLD AT the time of her marriage, Marie de Medici was as deliberate and humorless as Henriette was spontaneous and clever. She believed a display of passion to be crude, neither had she demonstrated any sign of being particularly bright. At the court of the Medici she had been taught that dignity and constraint were the highest virtues, and she had not the imagination to doubt it. Having learned her queenly role well from her father, Francis I de Medici, Grand Duke of Tuscany, and her mother, Joanna, Archduchess of Austria, she had no concept of how to deal with such a master of improvisation as her new husband.

A luxurious fleet of Tuscan, Papal, and Maltese galleys escorted Marie and seven thousand Italians of her court to her new life. Because of rough seas and dallying at various Italian ports, they didn't drop anchor in Marseilles until the third of November. More than one unlucky Frenchman was pushed into the freezing water as the excited people crowded the wharves to view their queen for the first time. They ogled at the bulwarks of her ship, glittering with precious stones, and a "hurrah" arose into the clear harbor morning when Marie disembarked in a golden gown. The people cheered her with enthusiasm, for her manner appeared noble and kind, unlike the last de Medici who had ruled on French soil.

A closer look, however, left them less fervent. Marie was no beauty, and her ponderous body matched her plodding mind. Dark skin was considered beautiful in Italy but not in France, and her large, slightly protuberant eyes were thought handsome in Milan but not in Paris. The people whispered that her hair, a not unattractive chestnut, but worn high and un-powdered, and her face without makeup looked sorely out of style. And they wondered whether the king would mind that his wife was taller than he.

The Chancellor of France, the constable, four cardinals, and a number of noble lords and ladies stood at the bottom of the gangplank to welcome her, but they could only offer Henry's regrets for his absence. Trying to make amends, he had sent a carriage with damask curtains at the windows, brown velvet upholstery and silver trimmings. But Marie was indifferent to his gift — and appalled. Could her husband really be so blasé about her arrival? The Marseillaises seemed to sense her discomfort and filled her days with receptions, balls, and processions. These diversions helped until November 16, when the Italian women who had accompanied her returned to Italy. Again she realized how alone and abandoned she felt. Two weeks had passed since she had disembarked at Marseilles, and still her husband had failed to arrive.

Little did she know that he was simultaneously corresponding with Henriette, who wrote to him sometime in November 1600:

> . . . in truth I am forced to confess my sorrow, not because you have any obligation to fulfill the vows of your subjects, but because your nuptials were the funeral of my life . . . In my wretched exile, I have nothing left but the single glory of having been loved by the greatest monarch in the world, by a king who had so wished to humble himself as to give the title of mistress to his servant and subject . . . Remember, Sire, a young lady who once was yours and with all that she can accomplish in your trust, which has as much power over her honor as Your Majesty has over the life of your very humble and obedient servant and subject.

Henry was impressed by the humble and loyal tone of her letter. Perhaps he had worried too much about the danger his mistress could inflict. But he had learned to distrust her when she acted docile. He remembered Margot before Agen! Not one to worry for long or about what might happen, he simply decided to enjoy the relative tranquility.

He wrote again to Marie, saying that nothing but the business of Savoy could keep him away. Disappointed once more, Marie decided two days later to travel north to Aix and then on to Avignon. She was having problems with the language and longed for her Italian ladies-in-waiting to help buffer the foreign tongue and curious country. The trip itself proved difficult, for winter had already set in when she left the coast. No one really seemed to know what to do with her or what to tell her, and so they mostly ignored her. She insisted on pressing onward, for the king had promised he would meet her at Lyon. His delay did not seem like a propitious way to begin a marriage, but she never could have dreamed her husband was dallying with his mistress instead of meeting her as promised.

Not until December 2 did they reach the outskirts of Lyon, and once more her husband disappointed her. Finally, at the end of the week she received a short note:

> My affairs with the duc de Savoie are settled at last; I shall leave my army in the care of Biron, and be with you by Saturday at the latest. I have had two bouts of fever, I am still not entirely well, but the sight of you will cure me.

Could she believe him this time?

She would see him finally, on December 9. As Henry neared Lyon, he recalled his approach to Paris when another bride had awaited him. He thought of Margot, her beauty, her deception, her wit. He remembered Corisande, Gabrielle, Henriette, and all the other fleeting affairs. Someone had accused him recently of having had forty-seven mistresses, and some called him "Le Vert Galant."* He chuckled to himself. He would celebrate his forty-seventh birthday in just a few days — one mistress for every year of his life.

But Corisande had always been right when she said France was his true mistress. He had fought for her, he had dedicated his life to her, and he relished continuing the endeavor. He hoped to continue the spirit of mutual acceptance between Catholics and Protestants, which he had worked so hard to engender. Now he must meet his bride-by-proxy to secure an heir to the throne of which he was so proud, and he prayed Marie would be worthy of the challenge.

---

* "Evergreen Gallant," and the title of a book about Henri IV by Jean Plaidy, (see Bibliography).

PARIS

1601

AFTER ANOTHER UNEXPLAINED delay at Fontainebleau, Marie finally entered Paris on February 9, two months after she had met Henry at Lyon. She had not been disappointed when she finally laid eyes on her husband. He kneeled before her and kissed her hand, which she found appropriate. He spoke politely to her and praised her beauty. Naturally reticent and shy, she was unable to return his smooth chatter but also being well educated and well versed in formal practice, she assumed that would change.

And it had. His warm eyes engaged her and she found the matters of state, about which he spoke in her presence, interesting. However, she thought some of his demands odd, if not insulting. For instance, now she was made to ride in a carriage with César at her side, and she could not help but stare at the child of her husband and his mistress, Gabrielle d'Estrées. The little boy appeared even less happy than she. Then to her surprise, the royal train did not turn toward the Palace of the Louvre, but stopped at the Hôtel de Gondi, where she was told she must reside until her apartments at the Louvre were properly prepared.

Further disappointments followed for when, three days hence, she was escorted to the palace, she found it in serious disrepair. It was clear that Henry had lavished all his energy on his country estate at Fontainebleau, where his mistress had been ensconced in splendor, and allowed the center of government to lapse from its former royal state. But this was the lesser shock compared to one that occurred only a few days after her arrival. Henry commanded that Henriette d'Entragues be presented to the Queen. Marie had understood enough of the gossip to know who this beautiful woman was. The king left no doubt, saying as Henriette curtsied before her, "This is my mistress who now wishes to be your servant." Paris feasted on the confrontation for months, talking of nothing but Henriette's arrogance and Marie's composure.

Marie had sensed her husband's heart was not committed, but she had begun to hope for a loving marriage when he spoke words of love to her at Lyon. Bewildered and angry, she did not know how to banter with double-edged barbs or conspire behind closed doors. Instead she bore the insults ponderously and quietly and turned to her fellow countrymen who had accompanied her from the court of Italy. Her maid, Leonora Dori, known as Galigai, and Leonora's husband, Concino Concini were clever and willing to enter fully into the intrigues necessary to exist at the court of France. And when Marie announced that she was pregnant, many realized she possessed the winner's weapon after all.

Henry demonstrated how important the moment was when he made himself available for the birth of the dauphin. On September 27, 1601, he overcame the reprimand of the midwife, who had told him he and others must leave the queen's bedchamber. "This child belongs to everyone," he crowed.

FONTAINEBLEAU

May, 1609

AS HENRY RODE OUT TO INSPECT the progress of his latest improvements on the estate at Fontainebleau, always his favorite residence, he decided he did his best musing on horseback. The rhythm of the horse matched the rambling, forward progress of his thoughts. His marriage to Marie de Medici could not be called successful, except that she had provided him with the necessary heirs, including the dauphin, the future Louis XIII. He chuckled remembering how Marie had complained early in their marriage over the considered necessity of "watchers" in their bedroom, whose duty it was to assure a royal heir. But their presence in the legitimate bedroom had not altered his philandering. And what had Marie thought, he wondered, during her lying-in for the birth of her children — in the same suite at Fontainebleau where Gabrielle had also given birth to his progeny? Moreover, to his queen's horrified indignation, he insisted upon his favorite bastards being brought up in the royal nursery. How she had screamed at him over his allowing César and Alexandre to cavort with Louis before their father's loving eye! He had given in to Marie on one thing, finally agreeing to allow Marguerite de Valois's return to court. The former queen often visited the royal nursery, taking genuine pleasure in watching Henry's children grow up. He had to admit he even enjoyed her company. After all, they shared a rich past.

Though Marie defended Margot, she despised his mistresses and feuded with them in rude language, shocking the French courtiers. She'd especially begged him to dismiss Henriette d'Entragues from court, but he never would. After all, Henriette had given him two children. Nevertheless, he had watched Marie's power as queen consort grow as she provided him with the heirs he'd wished for. Louis XIII had been born only 11 months after their wedding, Elisabeth followed in 1602, then Christine, Duchess of Savoy in 1606, Nicholas Henri in 1607, Gaston, Duke of Orleans in 1608, and now another daughter, Henrietta Maria, who had arrived just this year. Tears still sprang to his eyes when he remembered the death of little Nicholas Henri, the only son to bear his name, who had died at age 4.

All those long days on the battlefield now seemed so far in the past. How had he done it? Had fate always been in control — with the early death of his mother, the cruelty of St. Bartholomew's massacre, or the early and shocking defeats on the battlefield? Or had he actually affected the outcome of history, achieving his goal of bringing tolerance and peace to France? He sat up in his saddle. He believed he had done well — but there was still so much to be done. Spain was threatening his southern border again and Austria and the Hapsburg Empire were saber rattling as well. The Protestants in Germany had refused to fight so far, and he knew another war would be terribly unpopular. What should he do?

PARIS

May 14, 1610

THE AFTERNOON WAS BRIGHT AND warm, and the king traveled in a carriage open on both sides. He wished to visit his good friend and financial counselor, the duc de Sully,* to discuss the previous day's festivities for the coronation of Marie de Medici. Henry felt every one of his fifty-seven years, and it was hard to believe he had now reigned for twenty-one years. The coronation of his wife had been both splendid and exhausting, and because of fatigue, he paid no attention to an unusual commotion in the street. During the ritual ceremony at St. Denis, Marie had been anointed on the head and on the breast by the cardinal de Joyeuse, but not on the joints or on the hands as a king would be. His queen was happy now, he reflected, as was he. They both had their separate lives and understood each other to some degree.

The coach was forced to stop on the rue de la Ferronerie on account of crowds that had descended upon Paris for the coronation activities. Near an ironmonger's shop, a man with flaming red hair suddenly jumped onto the running board. Henry looked his murderer in the eye, and then a knife grazed a rib, a second blow pierced his lung, and a third severed his aorta. The wild man struck again, accidentally burying the blade in La Force's cloak. The duc d'Epernon,** La Force,*** and Roquelaure, who accompanied him in the carriage, watched in shock as the few bodyguards on horseback outside the wagon dismounted and rushed to his aid.

"It . . . is . . . nothing," Henry murmured.

Before they could reach the Louvre, the King of France was dead. Assassin François Ravaillac appeared to be insane and without

*Formerly the Baron de Rosny.
** Jean Louis de Nogaret de la Valette, duc d'Epernon (1554-1642)
*** Jacques-Nompar de Caumont, duc de La Force (1558-1662), served Henry IV as Maréchal de France.

accomplices, but it was rumored that several plots were seething. No doubt this was true, as Henry IV, always refusing to be a partisan, had been attacked by all parties. Having fought for a unified France, he intended to keep it that way.

Henry's predator was an intense Catholic who fanatically believed Henry should have compelled all his Huguenot subjects to abjure their faith or face divine retribution. Toleration of any religion other than Catholicism was heresy to Ravaillac, and he had dedicated himself to killing the king for months before finally performing the cruel deed.

Henry lay in state for six weeks before being laid to rest on July 1 at St. Denis. Within hours of his death the Parliament of Paris named his queen as the lawful regent for their son, Louis XIII. Despite her familial connections to the pope and her love of the Jesuits, Marie was encouraged by the Parliament to continue Henry's policy of tolerance, with the support of the political elite of France. His country had become accustomed to the peace that this respect for one another's religions afforded.

Corisande had not been to Paris for many years, and it was days before she would hear the painful news. She had made her life as mother and grandmother for over a decade now, but she could not reconcile the word "death" with the vigorous man whom she had loved so intensely. She associated Henry so closely with France, she could not imagine the country moving forward without him.

Marie de Medici and her eldest son, age nine, knelt beside Henry's bier, his other children kneeling directly behind them. She and her husband had not bothered to share ideas, she thought. Yet now she must direct the kingdom as he had wished. She had disagreed with him often, but admired his subtlety and political flair.

"Your father was an extraordinary man," she whispered to the dauphin, appearing so childish and vulnerable though dressed in royal regalia.

Marie restrained herself from looking back to the rear of the cathedral to see if her order to forbid Henriette's presence had succeeded. Probably not, since of course all of his bastards were attending the mourning ritual. How would she discover her way through the morass of Protestant and Catholic constant intrigues? she wondered. She bowed her head lower, suspecting that only Henry could control the combustible situation going forward.

EPILOGUE

HENRI IV WAS A MAGNIFICENT king by all criteria. With the help of his clever minister, the duc de Sully, he made successful war with very little means and succeeded in defining the boundaries of modern day France. He reestablished the finances of state, primarily with a new household levy called the *taille*, and developed the commercial and industrial capabilities of his nation. Henry and Sully gave France a ten-year truce, which the country remembers as a Golden Age, and instilled a spirit of religious tolerance in a divided nation.

The king restored Paris as a grand city, including building the Pont Neuf over the Seine in 1604 to connect the Right and Left Banks of the Seine. Henry IV also had the Place Royale built (known as the Place des Vosges since 1800) and added the Grande Galerie to the Louvre. The "grand plan" included rebuilding France's roads and lining them with elms, repairing and building bridges, laying out a network of canals, returning peace to the countryside, creating breeding studs, draining marshes, and reorganizing the administration of the forests. Henry's progressive strategy also called for the establishment of factories for the weaving of gold and silver cloth and creating workshops for rug making and for crystal ware, which exist to this day. Moreover, his tax reform was all encompassing and remarkably successful. By the end of the sixteenth century, the population in France had grown to approximately 400,000 souls as war no longer took its toll.

If Henry had lived a normal lifespan, he would have seen his progeny populate the thrones of Europe, both Catholic and Protestant. His first daughter, Elisabeth, married Philip IV, King of Spain, and Henrietta Maria wed Charles I, King of England. Moreover, he established the Bourbon dynasty upon the throne of France until the execution of Louis XVI during the French Revolution.

Marie de Medici's fears about the future stability of France were justified, for she would stupidly fall under the influence of her maid

Galigai's Italian husband, Concini, and dismiss the most able duc de Sully, resulting in her gradual wasting of the wealth amassed by Henry. She was also a weak bastion against Roman Catholic incursion and was eventually dominated by the powerful Cardinal Richelieu until Louis XIII reached his majority at age sixteen. There were even rumors that the duc d'Epernon had known the king's murderer and that he had conspired with Marie in the assassination, and that he had not warded off Ravaillac's blow in the coach on the fateful day. Indeed, it was known that Ravaillac stayed at the home of the duc's mistress Charlotte de Tillet prior to the murder. Since Epernon was Roman Catholic, had originally been a supporter of Henri III, and had objected to Henry's ascension to power, Epernon's involvement is entirely plausible.

Henry's love for his people in the abstract proved more successful than his love for those closest to him. His benevolent feelings for the people of France were expressed when he said, "Whoever finds fault with my people finds fault with me; let us care for the people, it is they who make us all live; I love my people like my children; I wish that each family could have a chicken in the pot on Sundays!"*

And the feeling was mutual. During the French revolution, the people scattered the remains of their kings at St. Denis to the dogs. But when Henry's tomb was opened, the people cheered their love for him.

---

* "Si Dieu me prête vie, je ferai qu'il n'y aura point de laboureur en mon royaume qui n'ait les moyens d'avoir le dimanche une poule dans son pot!"

CHRONOLOGY

December 13, 1553	Henry's Birth in Pau, southwestern France
March 13, 1569	Battle of Jarnac, Protestant Defeat; Henry's uncle Louis I, prince de Condé, killed
August 18, 1572	Henry of Navarre's marriage to Marguerite de Valois
August 24, 1572	St. Bartholomew's Massacre, Paris
January 1574	Battle of La Rochelle, Huguenot defeat
Spring 1574	Anjou becomes King of Poland
May 30, 1574	Death of Charles IX, Paris
December 1574	Anjou crowned Henri III, Reims
February 1576	Henry escapes from French court to Southwest
May 6, 1576	Treaty of Beaulieu ("Peace of Monsieur"), Nérac
March 1580	Marguerite returns to Paris
May 1582-87	Henry's affair with Corisande d'Andoins
July 1585	Catherine de Medici signs Edict of Nemours
October 19/20, 1587	Huguenot victory over Henri III at Coutras
December 23/24, 1588	Henri, duc de Guise, and his brother, Louis II, Cardinal de Guise, murdered by Henri III, Blois
January 5, 1589	Catherine de Medici dies at Blois
August 2, 1589	Death of Henri III in Paris; Henry of Navarre designated legitimate successor to the throne
September 23, 1589	Henry victorious over League at Arques, Normandy
March 14, 1590	Henry victorious over League at Ivry
November 1590	Henry meets Gabrielle d'Estrées, Coeuvres/ Chartres
February 1591	Henry defeats League forces at Chartres
July 25, 1593	Henry abjures Protestant faith at St. Denis

February 27, 1594	Henry crowned King of France, Chartres
March 22, 1594	Henry enters Paris, *Te Deum* at Notre Dame, Paris
December 1594	Jean Châtel attempts to kill Henry, Paris
March 1597	Spanish seize Amiens
April 13, 1598	Promulgation of Edict of Nantes, Nantes
April 1599	Death of Gabrielle d'Estrées, Paris
Late spring, 1599	Henry meets Henriette d'Entragues, Malesherbes
December 1599	Annulment of marriage to Marguerite de Valois, Château d'Usson
December 9, 1600	Henry marries Marie de Medici, Lyon
May 13, 1610	Marie de Medici's Coronation, Paris
May 14, 1610	Henry IV assassinated by François Ravaillac, Paris

HENRI IV'S KNOWN ILLEGITIMATE CHILDREN

(1) Fleurette, Pau, Jeanne (1572)*
(2) Esther d'Imbert, La Rochelle, Gédéon (1587-1588)
(3) By Gabrielle d'Estrées
    a. César, Duc de Vendôme (1594-1665)
    b. Catherine-Henriette (1596-1663)
    c. Alexandre, Grand Prior of the Knights of Malta (1598-1629)
    d. Stillborn child at Gabrielle's death, 1599
(4) By Henriette de Balzac d'Entragues
    a. Gaston-Henri, duc de Verneuil (1601-1682)
    b. Gabrielle-Angelique (1603-1627)
(5) Charlotte des Essarts, Paris
    a. Jeanne-Baptiste (1608-1670)
    b. Marie-Henriette (1609-1629)
(6) By Jacqueline de Bueil
    Antoine, Comte de Moret (1607-1632)

*Listed as a boy in some sources.

BIBLIOGRAPHY

Abbott, John S.C. *Henri IV, Makers of History,* Harper & Brothers, NY & London, 1884.

Bakhtin, M. *Rabelais and His World,* MIT Press, Cambridge, MA, 1968.

Blum, André, *Costume of the Western World, The Last Valois 1515-1590,* Geo. C. Harrap & Co. Ltd, London, 1951, and D.I. Wilton, *Costume of the Western World, Early Bourbon, 1590-1643,* Geo. C. Harrap and Co., Ltd., London, 1951.

Buisseret, David, *Sully and the Growth of Centralized Government in France 1598-1610,* Eyre and Spottiswoode, London, 1968.

Coudy, Julien, ed. *The Huguenot Wars,* Chilton Book Co., Philadelphia, PA, 1969.

Dumas, Alexandre, *The Complete Works of A. Dumas, Marguerite de Valois,* The Wheeler Publishing Co, NY

Garrison, Janine, *Marguerite de Valois,* Librairie Arthème Fayard, Paris, 1994.

L'Estoile, Pierre de, *Mémoires-Journaux,* ed. G. Brunet et al. (12 vols.), Librairie de bibliophiles; Paris, 1878-1896.

Guadet, Joseph, *Henri IV, Sa Vie, Son Oeuvre, Ses Ecrits,* Slatkine Reprints, Genève, 1970.

Guessard, M.F., ed., *Mémoires et Lettres de Marguerite de Valois,* Société de l'Histoire de France, Paris, 1842.

Haldane, Charlotte, *Queen of Hearts, Marguerite de Valois,* Constable & Co., London, 1968.

Higham, Roger, *Road to the Pyrenees,* J.M. Dent & Sons, Ltd., London, 1971.

Lévis-Mirepoix, duc Antoine de, *Henri IV, Roi de France et de Navarre,* Perrin, 1977.

Lewis, Paul, *Lady of France, A Biography of Gabrielle d'Estrées,* Funk and Wagnalls Co., Inc., NY, 1963.

Mann, Heinrich, *Young Henry of Navarre,* The Overlook Press, Woodstock, NY, 1984.

Mattingly, Garrett, *The Armada,* Houghton Mifflin Harcourt, Boston, MA, 1959.

Mahoney, Irene, *Madame Catherine,* Coward, McCann, & Geoghegan, Inc., NY, 1975, and *Royal Cousin, The Life of Henri IV of France,* Doubleday & Co., N.Y., 1970.

Pitts, Vincent J., *Henri IV of France, His Reign and Age,* The Johns Hopkins University Press, Balimore, 2009.

Plaidy, Jean, *Evergreen Gallant,* GP Putnam's Sons, NY, 1973.

Ritter, Raymond, *Cette Grande Corisande,* Albin Michel, Paris, 1936, *Charmante Gabrielle,* Albin Michel, Paris, 1947, *Henri Lui-Même,* Albin Michel, Paris, 1944.

Roelker, Nancy Lyman, *Queen of Navarre, Jeanne d'Albret, 1528-1572,* Harvard University Press, Cambridge, MA, 1968.

Ross-Williamson, Hugh, *The Last of the Valois,* Michael Joseph, London, 1971.

Lord Russell of Liverpool, *Henry of Navarre, Henri IV of France,* Robert Hale & Co., London 1969, NY 1970.

Seward, Desmond, *The First Bourbon, Henri IV, King of France and Navarre,* Constable & Co., London, 1971.

Sneath, Guy, *Your Guide to the Basque Country,* Alvin Redman, London, 1966.

Stern, Karl, *The Flight From Woman,* Farrar, Straus & Giroux, NY, 1965.

Stone, Donald, *France in the 16th Century, A Medieval Society Transformed,* Prentice Hall, Inc., NJ, 1969.

Taine, Hippolyte, *A Tour Through the Pyrenees,* Henry Holt & Co., NY, 1976.

Vaissière, Pierre de, *Henri IV,* Librairie Arthème Fayard et Cie, Paris, 1928.

De Valois, Marguerite, *The Memoirs of Marguerite de Valois.* First appeared in French in 1628.

Wilstach, Paul, *Along the Pyrenees,* Bobbs-Merrill Co., Indianapolis, IN, 1925.

Wolfe, Michael, *The Conversion of Henri IV, Politics, Power, and Religious Beliefs in Early Modern France,* Harvard University Press, Cambridge, 1993.

ACKNOWLEDGMENTS

I heartily thank my professional team at Green Rock Books:

Nick Pirog has designed yet another handsome book cover. He seems to understand what I have in mind and has a flair for coming up with a relevant and intriguing image. Andrea Nelkin's hairsplitting attention to detail makes her the perfect editor, and her knowledge of the French language and history proved to be a wonderful fit for *The Royal Huguenot*. It is a pleasure to work with her. And, Jeremy Wang-Iverson's job has only just begun in promoting this new book. His enthusiasm and ideas for public relations are inspiring to one who prefers the writing to the publicity, and his publishing background has prepared him to be a worthy guide through the process.

Again, many thanks to my patient husband, David, who sometimes hints that my devotion to research and writing is like living with a graduate student. But I don't believe he thinks that's all bad. This book took a very long time to come into being, as I actually began the research at Cambridge University Library in England. I came across letters of Henri IV to his mistresses and out of curiosity, translated some of them from old French into English. I thought they would make a wonderful historical novel. That was many years ago, and fortunately I finally had the time and inspiration to come back to the subject.

Our son Daniel fortuitously spent a college semester in Pau, France. One day while visiting him, we chose the gardens in back of Henri's castle to practice Daniel's lines in French for a Molière play. During that session I dreamed up the scene where Henri catches Marguerite with her lover by the river. The material just seemed to haunt me for a number of years. Also, thanks to Daniel for my author photos, as he is a skilled professional photographer, and to Aaron Hirsh for some editing, as he is by far the best writer in the family.

I also want to a thank a few friends — Lucy and Dan Stroock, Vera Volny and Maggie Gilboy — who all expressed interest when I talked about Henri and his mistresses. Their curiosity helped drive the project. When a great deal has already been written about a subject, it's daunting to think one can add much. But it seems that the American audience lacks exposure to this history, and so I greatly appreciated the enthusiasm of those who encouraged me to persist with a subject I found fascinating.

NELDA HIRSH is the author of *Julia Du Val* and *A Bohemian Life: M. Evelyn McCormick (1862-1948)*. Nelda is also the founder and publisher of Green Rock Books. She and her husband share their time between New York City and Boulder, Colorado. Her next book, *Catch the Beat: An Illustrated History of American Dance*, will be published in 2016. You can email her at neldahirsh@greenrockbooks.com.